SOMEWHERE IN BROOKLYN

Live Free!

SOMEWHERE IN BROOKLYN

A Novel

J.K. Savoy

Library of Congress Number: 2002094778

ISBN : Hardcover 1-4010-7595-9

Softcover 1-4010-7594-0

This is a work of fiction. Names, characters, places and incidents either are the product of the author's imagination or are used fictitiously, and any resemblance to any actual persons, living or dead, events, or locales is entirely coincidental.

This book was printed in the United States of America.

To order additional copies of this book, contact:
Xlibris Corporation
1-888-795-4274
www.Xlibris.com
Orders@Xlibris.com

16088-SAVO

Chapter One

First Light

"Joe, you motherfucker! You're gonna know what it is to be black, 'cause you're gonna burn!"

I sat paralyzed in my chair as Jamal lunged toward my throat, broken bottle in hand. The rage in his eyes was blinding. His vision of securing power through force had made him the voice for all of the one hundred or more floor waxers and porters that had taken over our office in Jersey City that November evening in 1973.

Avi and I were preparing to dispatch night work crews at Beria Building Maintenance, where we worked as managers when, suddenly, a group of militant workers led by Jamal crashed into the office. The odor of kerosene followed them through the door as it left its hinges. Until then, my commute from Brooklyn was the only war I had anticipated.

Having witnessed the Newark riots of 1967 firsthand, I knew that they must have awakened questions of equality long suppressed in the minds of New Jersey's black population. What I feared, as I sat helplessly, was that I was about to become Jamal's first answer to those years of subjugation.

I felt the glass pierce my skin. Jamal pressed the bottle shard even harder to my throat while screaming, "You call them motherfuckers and get their honkey asses down here or we're gonna torch this place and your white fuckin' asses in it!"

I winced as the saliva accompanying his words spattered my eyes. Jamal reached across my desk and grabbed my phone. He shoved the receiver into my face with a chorus of approval from the assembled multitude of militants and regular workers.

I replied, "I'm not sure where they are. I'll have to track them down."

I saw the slightest wink of support coming from Avi's otherwise detached appearance. With a stone-cold stare, he handed me a phone number and signaled with his index finger for me to dial the Skyview Tennis Club where the company's owners were waiting for their turn on the courts.

Meanwhile, Jamal stepped back slightly while shouting, "Well, get trackin' honkey! We ain't got all fuckin' night."

The Beria Corporation was located in a predominately black section of Jersey City. The buildings surrounding it were nothing but burned-out shells. My employers were the second- and third-generation owners of the company. The company's founder was a turn-of-the-century immigrant from Eastern Europe named Anton Beria.

Anton began a window cleaning business with nothing but a horse, a water pail and a squeegee. Over the years, he amassed a throng of loyal customers through hard work, dependability and fair treatment for all. He later extended this behavior to the employees who were needed to help perform the work as his reputation and enterprise grew. His descendants were a different story. What Anton created with nothing but his calloused hands, they would further while wearing nothing but the finest tailored suits.

Instead of nurturing business relationships as the legendary Anton did, they generated window cleaning and building maintenance contracts. It became a business of numbers for numbers' sake. In addition to the grandfather's original creation, they added banks, shopping centers and massive amounts of real estate to their power-portfolio.

The process of making tons of money was foremost. Little attention was paid to the people performing the labor behind the fortune. Just as the owners were developing their third generation of rule, a great deal of the workers had this as their first and only jobs, following their own fathers and uncles before them.

Roger, the late Anton's son, finally came to the phone and said, "Be brief!"

I tried to explain to Roger, as succinctly as possible, why his jobs were getting a delayed start. There was, of course, the riot and its need for resolution before we could get to the dispatch part of our workday. But the most pressing problem was the broken bottle shard at my neck, instead of at his.

I hoped to quickly convey to him that there was reluctance on the part of his maintenance laborers to work another day with no benefits, near-minimum wages and missing records for hours already worked and the corporation's history of firing people for no apparent reason.

Roger answered, "Just get them to work and we'll figure things out tomorrow! You gotta learn to handle these kinds of situations. You're a smart boy."

Then he told me that Kevin, his son, was paging him. Soon, I realized that I was being counseled by a dial tone. I told the men that Roger would try to settle their grievances with the Beria family the next day. I wouldn't dare repeat to the men the detail of the instructions that he gave me.

Roger not only put me off with his detached indifference, he totally put my life on the line with his knee-jerk answers. As much as he heard my panicked words coming from the phone, he chose to see our predicament through the bottom of his rising wine glass at the country club bar.

The reply from the men, voiced by Jamal, was all too predictable, "He says tomorrow, like he's sure there's gonna be one? Fuck him! Fuck you! Motherfuck you!"

The escalation of rage in the men reached its boiling point. They began to throw objects. My skin tightened in direct proportion to their increasing hostility. Hands and faces of those outside of my small office were pressed against the windows. Jamal and his lieutenants were inside. A desk crashed as it was turned over. My phone was thrown against the wall. There were cheers and chants from the militants, "Burn, baby, burn!"

From somewhere in the crowd, a camouflage-dressed hulk pushed his way through and landed between Jamal and me. The other militants moved back. Jamal turned and sought refuge within his cohort.

The hulk's name was Zach. At first he just stood there silently looking at everyone, one by one. Derek, who was always at Jamal's side, quickly reached into his coat pocket. Jamal just as quickly shook his head, no. Slowly, Derek's hand retreated.

With a single swipe of his massive right hand, Zach took the bottle from Jamal. Derek's coat immediately became a straight jacket as Zach pulled the collar down to lock his hands behind him. Everybody's eyes were on Zach. Silence became their only statement. For every step that Zach took toward the mob, they yielded three.

With nothing but the power of his presence holding the mob at bay, Zach said, in a soft yet deliberate tone, "Joe ain't done nothin' to you. Him and Avi don't deserve this. They ain't shit around here." My head lurched forward as Zach grabbed my tie.

He pulled me away from the crowd and continued with his statement, "This tie around this fool's neck ain't nothin' but a leash. Now let his sorry ass alone. Get the fuck to work now and we'll talk tomorrow with the man, not his dogs. This is bullshit."

I hoped that it wasn't wishful thinking on my part, but most of the men seemed to welcome Zach's intervention. The entire episode may have gone too far for the regular workers. Until that day, as far as most were concerned, a paycheck was still a paycheck even if it was a little short. Still, the young militants together with Jamal wanted to go for blood, any blood, as long as it was white. If you weren't with them then you were a Tom or a boy or worst of all, in my case, a white boy.

The silence from the mob was broken by a thunderous voice working its way into my office saying, "Hey! Give it a shot! We waited this long. What's another day?"

David, an old-time floor waxer, sauntered through the militants while eyeballing them up and down. He paused and then said straight to Jamal's face, "Hey chump!"

Derek restrained his comrade as David continued his stroll. David was the leader of the non-militant workers. In all of the time that I knew him his broad grin never broke his face, even when he might be throwing someone across the room by the scruff of his neck. When he spoke, all present listened. It was only a week before that David nearly emptied a spray bottle of toilet bowl acid into the face of Jamal's brother.

Zach and David stood like lightning rods. Old-time workers slowly moved toward them. The militants gathered in a small circle around Jamal and Derek, their backs to one another. Every person on either side must have wondered what was in the pocket where each other's hand rested. The men's attention shifted to old issues that had long divided the two groups. I sensed a reprieve for myself, albeit temporary.

"Give me my paperwork, Joe. Where's my crew?" David bellowed as his floor waxing crew gathered supplies, "Come on, git your lazy asses in that truck an' git to work, you motherfuckers!"

Those were sounds that I thought would never fill my ears again. Both groups broke ranks, melded into their customary work crews, and then piled into vans together. Icy glances for one another seemed to have replaced heated words. The silence of their walk to their vans was interrupted only by a bottle shattering in a garbage can.

Zach remained in my office and instructed some men to right my desk. He placed the remains of my phone on it and quickly scanned the shape-up area to be sure that all of the workers had left. Then, just as unexpectedly as he arrived, he was gone. As quickly as the storm of rage came upon us, it left with the last work van leaving the driveway.

Avi straightened his tie and remarked, "I knew this was coming, if not tonight then tomorrow, if not down here, then maybe in the alley. Good thing that new guy spoke up. By the way Joe, is that the Jamaican boy that you hired last week?"

Avi was a Jewish Partisan who fought the Nazis in the forests of Europe during WWII. Most of his family died in the concentration camps. He came to America after the war and had been a manager at Beria ever since. How many people could endure a Gestapo officer's interrogation while a machine gun barrel is held to their eye? Avi did. Considering Avi's past, that night of rage must have seemed like a minor scuffle.

I turned to Avi and answered, "Yeah, Zach just finished up his second hitch in 'Nam a few months ago. Thank God he's still a warrior at heart."

Avi shook his head and smiled at me dismissively. Then he looked away, took a deep breath and began singing something from an opera while sorting through time sheets. At the pinnacle of his crescendo the singing stopped, as did the smile.

In an instant, he spun around and grabbed me by my shoulders. Coldly, he looked me in the eye while saying, "You tell me that he's a warrior at heart, as if he has always been a warrior. How do you know this? I don't think anyone knows he's a warrior until he has to become one. You're just a kid, Joe. What do you know?"

Avi began walking away. Then he turned, regripped my shoulders and said, "Maybe that boy was in school or was a farmer before someone put a gun in his hand. Maybe he couldn't shoot it so good until someone else shot theirs at him. So maybe, then, he learns to shoot his pretty good, too."

His grip tightened on my shoulders as he paused for a moment. Then he shouted, "When someone says it's time to stop shooting, he has to walk away and leave the lives that he took behind him! He's not so lucky with being able to walk away from the memories." Avi's eyes seemed to redden. Maintaining his grip, he looked away from me. His hands trembled as his eyes rolled back.

For a moment we stood perfectly still until he held his index finger up and said softly, "So maybe this makes him behave a little different from then on. You talk about seeing a warrior's heart? Maybe what you see is the armor he wears to protect his heart. But it doesn't change anything. It doesn't change anything at all, Joe."

Finally, he released me and said, "Joe, do you know that if an experience doesn't finish you, it becomes you? What happened here tonight has become part of who you and I are. This is true for every word you ever hear and for every voice that speaks it."

Speechless, I remained pressed to the wall as again he paused, this time to stare at the last piece of broken glass hanging in the door. His eyes closed and he said, "So, maybe like anyone else, all that we see in him are the results of the experiences that life had him travel, including tonight's. He traveled through a war, so we think we see a warrior. But what we may never see is his heart. He gave back the gun, but he probably kept the armor. Remember Joe, the warrior in us doesn't always need a shooting war in order to surface. Sometimes a just cause will do just as well."

With eyes wide open he added, "Sorry Joe. I got a little carried away, didn't I?"

I shrugged as Avi's hand patted my shoulder then stretched outward to join his song in progress. When he returned to the height of the same note he had left, the loose glass on the door submitted to his voice and shattered on the floor.

The following day, Kevin, Roger's oldest son, talked to me about the incident. His approach to settling the problem was, "Joe, we'll give them all a token raise. You'll never hear a dog barking if he's chewing on a bone. Then, down the road, we put Jamal and his lieutenants at permanent job sites, separate from one another of course. It's easier to get rid of the instigators one at a time if they only have strangers around them for support. All you have to do for now is to tell them that they are getting more money. We'll take care of the rest. Trust us, Joe; we know how to deal with matters like this."

I stood there incredulous as the vision of myself as a dead messenger flashed before me. Was this fool so naïve that he didn't consider that if these men were separated, they might use telephones to keep one another updated? Did he fail to realize that they might gather together in automobiles and return to this building to torch it if they smell a rat?

I snapped back and said, "When I tell the men that they are all getting a raise, Jamal or Derek is going to say to them, 'This is the kiss we get before the fucking!'

"Who knows? They might throw the money back in my face. Think about it. If those two are smart enough and forceful enough to have convinced the men to do what they did yesterday, they can do the same thing or worse any time they choose."

Kevin nodded to me and then looked at his watch. I added, "Kevin, a couple of bucks is not going to win support for us with the rest of the men. The issues are deeper than money. They go to respect. If I throw them a bone to chew today, then next week or next month or next year, I'll have the same argument with them that I had yesterday. The slight difference being, I might be choking on the end of the barbeque spear that's been stuck up my ass. When that time comes, are you and Roger ready to go eyeball to eyeball with the men and take your shots like you expect Avi and me to do?"

The moment I saw the color leave his face, I realized that the only blood to ever spill on Kevin's clothing, up until that day, might have been from the silver spoon he was born with piercing his cheek. When he lowered his glasses and looked at me eye to eye, I knew that I had his full attention.

Then I told him, "That's not the way to plan for the future, never mind being able to actually live in it. Kevin, you're treating these people like they're working on a Southern plantation two hundred years ago. The only difference is that slave owners called it like it was and at least fed and housed them.

"Every day that I go down to the dispatch office, I feel like Master Jeff, the strong boss, riding on a horse and holding a whip. Big fucking deal, your floor machines may have replaced the cotton 'gin, but it doesn't look like the iron collars fell from anybody's neck. Hey, look Kevin, to me this is just a fucking job! Any minute I can walk away. Are you and your daddy ready to sit in my chair if I do?"

Kevin's eyes moved toward the bolted door to his and his father's office. I pointed to it and added, "Don't you and your father hear the message? You've been putting them off for too goddamn long. The chickens have come home to roost. If you don't recognize your workers as people, you're going to lose your business, your life or both. It's just as easy for them to storm your bolted fortress next. The courage to go up the stairs, break down the door to your office and land in your face is now in them." His Adam's apple took a fast rise above his collar then settled back as he smiled sheepishly.

Kevin's formal education was in law. Prior to joining the business, his father placed him in his friend's prestigious firm where he worked for one year. This would solidify valuable business contacts for a lifetime. Kevin then ascended to the seat beneath his father's boot heel. His brother, Justin, would follow the same recipe two years later.

Roger arranged Kevin's marriage to his friend's daughter, Barbara, with the same manipulative manner that he had arranged Kevin's eventual climb to the throne. Roger's sights were surely set on Kevin's two children to someday perpetuate these traditions.

All of the workers at the company looked up to Kevin as the boy who had it all. Kevin seemed to be able to make all the right moves. His very first move was to land in the right cradle. In spite of having the world at his fingertips, Kevin spent Monday mornings in the room above the shape-up area, eavesdropping on the worker's conversations, hoping to hear the sordid details of their wild weekends.

He would park his Cadillac in his reserved space while admiring my old Triumph TR-3 sports car parked under the air conditioner drain. His father wouldn't allow him to have a car beneath his station.

I learned much about him, his life and his secured future while serving as his flight instructor. That's how we met. I witnessed him grow stronger as an individual, confronting his fears while attempting to adapt to my world in the sky. Kevin was extremely competitive and looked forward to every challenge that I presented him. He learned very quickly and respected me as his teacher.

He gave me a job after I had had it working for bare minimum wage at a profession that called for so much extraordinary skill. Usually, a commercial pilot-flight instructor is the sad face on the bottom of the general aviation totem pole. Job openings with the major airlines were quickly closing as Vietnam veteran pilots with high jet hours became available to the industry. In aviation, in the early 'seventies, you were considered to be an old man at twenty-five if you weren't already hired by a major carrier.

I had felt a sense of gratitude toward Kevin for hiring me. However, his approach to this problem with his workers filled me with a sense of doubt about him as a person. Just as I had challenged his skills as a pilot in my world, I was challenging his integrity in his world. I thought, "Where once I relied upon my own skills in defying gravity to survive, I am now reliant on his word."

What kind of answer would we give those men? They would soon fill my office seeking his words, spoken from my lips. My engine was in flames and the grim reaper was laughing from my wing.

"Kevin!" I exclaimed, overwhelmed with an epiphany, "Every time that you need a supervisor or manager, you hire an outsider much like the way you hired me. The one thing that all of the other bosses and I have in common is that we're all white.

"Don't you get it? Why not give supervisor jobs and other opportunities that arise to the porters or waxers that show some leadership potential?"

Kevin stared at me over his glasses, paused in thought, and then he said, "My dad and I never gave much thought to upgrading any of them beyond doing anything other than the janitor work that they were hired to do. Joe, where are you going with this?"

I needed to figure out where I was going with my question and perhaps find an acceptable option for all concerned. I sensed that he also was looking to me to find one since he didn't look disinterested. I sought to involve Kevin in the decision process.

I asked, "In all these years, didn't Beria, Inc. ever have any person, who worked in the back, prove to be successful as a leader in any way, even in an interim situation?"

As if to pass the question on, Kevin looked to Avi who knew every one of the thousand or so people working from our office or on the various job sites.

After a moment of reflection, Avi said, "We have colored site-supervisors at some of the small office buildings. But they're only in charge of their own families that work with them as their helpers. We're not talking about the kind of guys we dispatch from here."

Knowing that Kevin might be reluctant to present a revolutionary approach to quell the coming revolution, the thought that site-supervisors existed at all seemed like a solid bridge for my forming idea. I saw uncertainty in the eyes of both Avi and Kevin.

I upgraded it to receptiveness by saying, "Still, it's a precedent! You have success at the job-site level, so why not try it at the home office? We can begin by having one of the men help in daily dispatch. Avi and I can train him and monitor everything as it progresses. Then, with someone else dispatching, I can have more time to sell contracts and help to build the business. But I'll make myself available if either of them needs me."

"Okay Joe, exactly who might you have in mind?" asked Kevin. He must have thought that I actually had a person in mind that would fit this job description.

Quickly, I thought and answered, "Why not Zach, that huge Jamaican? He saved our asses yesterday by jumping between us and the militants. Since he was recently hired, he is enough of an outsider that no one can accuse you of playing favorites."

Avi looked toward me with his eyebrows raised and a glimmer in his eye and said directly to Kevin, "This might work. If Zach accepts the offer, we will tell the others that he was hired with this in mind. That might make it seem like the riot wasn't what caused the changes and the credit won't go to that prick, Jamal, and his militants."

After Kevin and Roger discussed the idea, they agreed to try it. Of course I knew if it failed the blame would fall on me. If it succeeded the credit would be theirs.

Zach hoped to leave his memories of 'Nam behind him and create a future for himself. He had shown a disdain for conflict while not having a fear of it. He was highly principled and, as we would find over time, totally honest. Above all, he was a complete outsider as far as the men were concerned. He would show no favorites since he hardly knew anyone under him. If his decisions were challenged, he had his two hundred and sixty pounds of muscle to aid in their enforcement.

The men both resented and respected Zach. His position would prove to be a tough one to defend; I guess he knew this as well as Avi and I did. Soon, a term that I had never heard before was buzzing around the company. The militants had tagged him White man's nigger. In spite of the resentment and suspicion, business as usual would be the theme. Soon, everybody waited to see who would be the next man to move up.

The long-anticipated raises that the men received were respectable. A larger paycheck helped to keep the noise level down. The recording of hours was to be kept better. The time-books had become open at all times to the men for their inspection.

Even with these advances, Jamal and his group of militants were patiently waiting for our first slip-up. Peace was being given its chance, but the odor of kerosene lingered as it had permeated the office walls and our memories. In the meantime, they gave Zach half a chance. This was twice as much as I had hoped for.

Two openings for supervisors came up at large shopping malls that we serviced. Naturally, I asked if we could promote from staff to these positions. Roger and Kevin went along with the idea as progress was made. Two men that showed the most initiative were selected. They knew that the worker's futures depended on them and that they must not fail. They excelled.

As the months went by, more of the old-time employees became supervisors. In addition to their new positions, they were to get benefits and sometimes use company vehicles. I had little reason to be in the dispatch room those days, although I preferred to conduct my sales-related calls from there rather than from upstairs. Zach knew his job rather well. I simply felt more comfortable being able to see the changes firsthand.

One day as I walked through the alley, separating the office from the back, a hand landed on my shoulder. I turned and asked, "Jamal! What's happening?"

To my surprise he answered, "Joe, maybe you ain't as prejudiced as I thought. You did some good things here for the Brothers."

This was an incredible compliment, especially from a guy who almost carved his initials in my throat. From the first day that I had started work there, Jamal had accused me of being prejudiced. When I asked him why, he told me that it was because all of the white people that he ever met were.

"You been hangin' out in Brooklyn, I hear. Is that right?" he asked.

"I'm actually living there. I have a short-term sublet in Brooklyn Heights."

Jamal gave me a facetious grin and gently punched my shoulder as he said, "Man, right there with them rich-ass honkeys. Joe, you a young dude. You oughta party in Crown Heights. I'd take you there myself, but no one ever gonna talk to me no more."

Jamal looked left, then right and then quickly dropped a nickel bag in my shirt pocket while I looked away.

He patted my pocket and said, "Maybe a little soul food for your head will loosen your uptight honkey ass. You need to get yourself a soul woman, Joe. Ain't nothin' like some brown sugar to sweeten up your sheets. One more thing, you better not trust them motherfuckers upstairs. You may be a cracker, too. But you ain't never goin' to be family to the Berias, no matter how much of their dirty work y'all do. Just remember, white boy; they'll fuck you in the ass while they look you in the eye. I ain't finished with them motherfuckers by no means. I got no plans for your white ass, as long as you keep on keepin' on doin' what you been doin'!"

For some reason, unknown to me at the time, I figured that the least said was the best said. I answered only, "Thanks Jamal, word to the wise."

Prior to the changes at Beria, there would be times that I would have to go next door to the bar to find a lost worker. When I seemed like I wanted to go in to look for him, there would be four or five people blocking my way.

I knew things had really changed when I heard a voice from inside the bar say, "Hey Joe! C'mon in, let me buy you a drink."

I never drank while at work; I made no exception in that case as I sat with my Coke in hand with David. After twenty years with the company, he was finally promoted to run maintenance operations at a large department store. He was still celebrating.

"David, take it easy on the drinks. I don't want to tell Zach to replace you in the first week of your gig." David peered over the foam in his beer mug, smiled, and looked me dead in the eye.

Through his never-ending grin he answered, "Joe, you ain't nobody no more to tell anyone to fire my black ass. Don't be gettin' me wrong now, I owe this new gig to you and I won't forget that. Zach ain't no one to do it neither. He still be learnin' his own shit. Mister Roger told me that I report only to Kevin or his self. When I asked if I reports to Mister Joe, he told me that you're only doing sales and they said somethin' about other management stuff."

I sat motionless and thought, "Why is it, the last one to know about a job change is the person doing the job?"

I asked David, "When did they tell you this?"

He ordered another round for us and answered, "The first day that they sent me to the run the store, you know, last week sometime. They tell me if I have any problem or questions, I should call them. Then they tells me the other stuff 'bout you and Zach."

David slapped me across the back and said, "Man, I'm gettin' to know more than the white folks around here. 'Bout time!"

I laughed with David about how I had either fallen off the grapevine or had risen above it. In either case, I didn't hear a thud nor see the big picture beneath me. David sensed that I had a deeper concern as I pushed aside my Coke, and my rules, and ordered a Black Russian. After the last of the work crews went out, I pulled the steel gates down and headed home to Brooklyn.

I felt toward Zach as proud as a brother might feel about a sibling. He had the job of dispatcher down to a system that proved to be both effective and fair to all of the men. Avi and I would bring all of the work orders to him. It was then his job to have them carried out. He coordinated the people to the projects as he saw fit. The men had a spirit in them that wasn't seen at Beria Building Maintenance since anyone could remember.

I was glad in a way that I would be able to focus more on sales, but confused as to why I was cut off from the leadership positions that I had both envisioned and fostered. I would have the weekend to wonder what was meant by other management stuff.

"Who the hell is this?" I shouted, while closing my apartment door.

Marcie from Canarsie, my crash-in lover, was sitting in the kitchen of my sublet, drinking chamomile tea with a guy that I had never met. It would be cliché if I said that they looked like deer caught in the headlights, but they did. I came home earlier than usual that night.

"Ritchie is a realtor. He was showing me an apartment. I told you that I was looking for my own place," said a startled Marcie, while stirring an empty teacup.

There was dampness in the air near the bathroom and a faint odor of after-shower talc. I stood there looking at the two of them and said nothing. Ritchie began making small talk about world events.

I ignored his attempts to distract me and said to Marcie, "He was showing you an apartment while the two of you were in my apartment? This Ritchie's quite a realtor."

Ritchie stood up and backed away from me. I held my hand up to him and waved the international no-problem sign, then pointed to the door. He took the hint and his briefcase and said goodnight.

Marcie opened the door for the realtor and said to him as he left, "Well, thanks, Ritchie. Call me if there are any more listings."

Marcie liked to deposit some of her clothing in my only dresser every time she came over. We were at the point that I had one drawer left to myself. The tiny, Henry Street studio fifth-floor walk-up reeked with her Chinese Flower fragrant oil. Over time, it must have corrupted her olfactory senses because every day she would apply more, thinking that it was never enough. It was beyond enough for me. This was too much.

Marcie started cooking and talking about imaginary apartments. My mind couldn't handle any more bullshit. She wasn't that important to me. If it weren't for the fact that her ass was a dead ringer for my ex-girlfriend's, we may have never met.

I recalled how months before, Nina, whom I had been living with, and I had gone to a party. We declared a truce and promised that neither of us would wander off to a bedroom with anyone else. As I left the bathroom at the party, I heard the all-too-familiar groaning from the bedroom. I looked in and saw an even more familiar pair of naked buttocks dancing in the wind. The other end of her was trying to suck the life out of some guy through his pecker as he lay across the bed among other bare bodies.

I was infuriated. What truce? I had passed up many opportunities that night myself, but I thought a deal was a deal. After I slapped her across the ass and reminded her about our promise, I was shocked to see not Nina's face, but instead Marcie's.

She broke free of the penis, smiled, then looked me up and down and said, "Wow, what a way to introduce yourself! I could really get into some pain right now, but I promised my dyke that I'm all hers after this."

I immediately apologized, telling her that I thought she was someone else. I also apologized to the owner of the penis whose moment had not come due to my own arrival. I apologized to the dyke who was sitting next to the two of them on a plain yet sturdy wooden chair. She scowled at me as she removed her hand from her own crotch and replaced it with Marcie's.

Marcie giggled and said to her lady, "C'mon, let's go upstairs."

I thought during that moment, "At least it seems like she keeps her promises."

Marcie threw her halter-top and shorts back on. As the dyke headed for the door, Marcie reached for her bag and then scratched out her phone number on a match cover. She handed it to me and said, "If you ever manage to break free of your else, or if you want to bring her along with you, call me."

What a pattern, she has her hand on one crotch while she reaches out for the next.

"I'm not a crook!" said President Nixon from the television. He was trying to pull the wool over the country's eyes.

Marcie was trying the same thing on me from my kitchen. I turned off the television then turned to Marcie.

I shouted, "Don't mistake kindness with stupidity, especially my kindness!"

I grabbed her dresser drawers and threw the contents out of the window on to the yard, five floors down. I picked up the phone, called her father and told him to pick up his daughter. I told his daughter, "Get the fuck out, now!"

I had made no promises of fidelity to Marcie and had no expectations of the same from her. The entire relationship was based upon a case of mistaken identity and had gone too far. Although it may have been the 'seventies, when boundaries of any kind were being erased or at least ignored, somehow I felt there was a territorial imperative issue going on, even if it was only in a sublet.

I would have the weekend to sort out my thoughts about sex, love and career. She would have the weekend to sort out her wardrobe and to hook up with someone else.

I was appalled by the thought of going to another bar to meet another someone who would discreetly interview me through the conversational résumé. My income and career potential always got me directly to the sex suit competition. But I would be long gone when it became time to walk down the aisle to claim the flowers and the crown. Until that night, Marcie was a step above the solitude that had become my preferred choice from all of the above.

All I could do was laugh when I found the tear-off end of a condom wrapper on the floor. At least theirs was a real estate venture with certain safeguards built in. Knowing Marcie, I was sure that the agency was protecting itself against the client.

The wrapper sunk beneath a clump of toilet paper in submission to the force of my yellow stream. The flush water circled, as the wrapper, my love life and my career all seemed to be following the same course.

The weekend was mine. My schedule was all clear. Jamal's soul food lay ready in the bowl of my water pipe, welcoming the candle's flame. The wings of a lone pigeon fluttered outside my window. He settled into the drain gutter. I settled into the pillow-couch and placed the headphones over my ears. A full Moon provided light. "Dark Side of the Moon" provided enlightened verse.

Smoke-filled bubbles left the pipe. The lunatic left the hall. Someone in my head that might be me gazed into the glow of the burning embers and inhaled a dream.

Found in September's Child's guest sketch book

Chapter Two

Acquiescence

"Joe, Kevin wants to see you upstairs, right away," said Zach with a look of uncertainty on his face. Then he gave me a tentative glance and quickly looked away. He was always hanging around the front office with his ears to the door. As I ran up the stairs to the office, I wondered what Zach might have heard besides those instructions.

"What's up, Kevin? Zach told me that you needed me, pronto."

"We have a big problem. Sit down, my father will be in shortly." Kevin smiled uneasily as he tapped his fingers on his desk while staring toward the door.

Anxiously, I asked Kevin, "Is there something wrong with the new system? Nobody tried to kill anyone or anything, did they?"

I wanted to come right out and ask what was happening, but management shouldn't listen to rumors, such as my conversation with David, let alone dignify them.

Roger entered the room like a raging locomotive with a trail of cigar smoke rings in his wake. In a single jumping motion, he landed his small round body on his swivel captain's chair. Placing his hands behind his head, he resembled a two-handled teapot on a black burner engulfed in a cloud of smoke from his little cigar-spout. The power of his announcement would soon overshadow his comical appearance.

With his finger pointing at my face, he said, "Joe, we have to make some changes around here. There's nothing wrong with all that you did or how things are going in the back. We need you to put your attention in other directions. You're a boy with ideas. We need that at Beria. Don't worry, we have all of that stuff with the laborers under control."

Immediately, I pictured the back as being mine with a knife sticking out of it.

His cheeks puffed and puffed. From where I envisioned smoke to burst, words poured forth saying, "Joey, we're going to make things better for you. From now on, Kevin will take care of elevating the porters to supervisors. Zach will take care of helping Avi with dispatch and controlling the waxers and porters. Avi will take care of payroll and be Zach's direct superior with the dispatching."

His face drew closer and closer to mine through his cloud of smoke. Then his extended finger reached toward my shoulder. Did he expect that I should kneel before him? I stood astonished as he dubbed me Assistant Director of Operations.

"That will be your new title, Joey," he said as Kevin grinned with approval, "You're going to concentrate on getting new business for Beria Building Maintenance and dealing with special issues as they arise."

Three more puffs and the little engine that could make me or break me forever became the little teapot as he landed back into his chair. There's always been something about the word special that made me suspicious. Whenever a sitcom had a very special episode, you knew that someone was going to die. With that in mind, I anxiously anticipated their meaning of the other word, issues.

Roger's eyes were incongruous with his smile. Were these people propping me up so all might salute, or were they just spreading the sticks below the stake to which I was about to be tied? Roger re-lit his already burning cigar. I wondered what form the other combat boot might take before it dropped. I sat back and waited.

With a Cheshire smile on his face, and while pouring everyone a round of Chivas Regal, Roger said, "Here's the pressing problem, Joey. Too many of our workers are receiving unemployment benefits. Our experience rating with the State is ridiculous! We have to bring it down. We are paying an absolute fortune to the government."

His voice lowered slightly, then he asked, "Joey, do you truly believe in justice?"

As a true believer of justice, I gulped my scotch while nodding to the affirmative.

He shook his head negatively and said, "How unjust it all is! It's as if the laid-off porters still get paid almost in full, as if they're still working here. Meanwhile, they're sitting on their black asses and laughing their heads off at us while they collect benefits."

He pounded his fist on his desk. Again, he pointed to my face while saying, "I'm sure that the money that they are ripping us off for could go toward better things. Better things! I believe that you know what I mean, Joey?"

With total disorientation as my guide, I felt my inner self rising from the mud after falling from the sky, only to meet me at the pit of my stomach. I blurted out, "Let me guess. There is a special issue here that's already been decided, right? My question at this point is, how do I fit into your picture that I don't even see? And no, I don't really know what you mean."

If I could have held a magnifying glass to a bull's-eye on a target, surely the fine detail within the red dot would spell middle management. Roger studied my reactions as he leaned toward the wall behind his high-backed chair.

Then he blew a long stream of cigar smoke toward the ceiling and straight up my ass saying, "You're going to earn your raise. By the way Joey, you got a raise! How about that? Good going changing things in the back. We see some big things ahead with the idea of upgrading the porters. That's part of why we're all sitting here today. You see, we want to put more resources in that direction. Now that's justice, isn't it? And Joey, there's an immediate way that you can fit into the plans for our company's future. By the way, you should start thinking of it as your company's future, Joey. Am I right, Kevin?"

Like a stuffed doggie in a toy store window, Kevin's head bobbed up and down on cue. Roger placed his feet upon his desk. He looked straight through the crack between his shiny new Italian shoes and right into the core of my being as he began outlining my future. My future, in what I should begin thinking of as my company.

With his eyes locked on mine, he said, "When we fire someone, they go right over to the unemployment office. The State immediately sends us a form. The moment we get it, we will return it, telling them that the porter quit. Then the ex-employee will naturally call for a hearing.

"Here's where you come in, Joey. You go to the hearing and say that you represent the company. Damn it Joey, just remember, it's your company too! You know, you really look good in a suit. Go to my guy on Broad Street and get a new suit on me, Joey. People trust and believe a guy who looks good in a nice new suit, right, Kevin?"

Suddenly, my body felt as if had been released from a mold and fallen to Earth, re-sculpted in Roger's design. As if to toast its arrival, I knocked back the remaining Chivas and looked toward Kevin. As expected, he was nodding affirmatively to his father.

Through the Beria family smile, he said to me, "Like my dad said, Joe, all you've got to do is tell them the truth, he quit."

With my long-sought-after rank and title glowing atop my resume, I left Roger and Kevin's office as the still-smiling Kevin leaned back on his captain's chair. While crossing his leg, imitating his father's teapot pose, he kicked the phone from his desk.

Walking to the dispatch office, I recalled a conversation that Kevin and I had as we left a meeting where he turned a customer's mind completely inside out. After hearing Kevin work the guy over, I almost believed him myself. Following that meeting I said to Kevin, as we got into his car, "I guess that a lie can one day be justified by the truth it created." Though I had meant it sarcastically, Kevin liked it. He must have seen it as my sanction of his policies and basic approach toward business, as our shared view.

But after hearing Roger's view of the world, and my place within it, I didn't know what to believe. I did see my talents as being recognized, but somehow I felt that the bosses were lying to me. On the other hand, I was being bullshitted by the workers too.

I remembered that just a week before, Louie, one of the floor waxers, approached me with his hat in hand and said, "Mister Joe, I can't work tonight 'cause my Momma done passed." Immediately, Crow, his partner, yelled out, "Again?" The two of them slapped five, laughed and went off to work.

For all concerned, I had to look at the big picture. So I glanced at my reflection in the window and thought, "Everyone is bullshitting everyone else who is bullshitting them. That's how it is in business and this is just business. Hey, look at me. I have a big raise and a title. Wow! And to think, just a short time ago, I felt that this was just a job."

On one hand, I thought about the trust that the man upstairs and his son had in me. On the other hand, I saw the step up that the promotion would place on my résumé.

"Ha! Who needs a résumé? I can think of this title as my future in my company."

If I only had another hand, I might have asked myself, "Or should I?"

Soon, the flakes of shattered euphoria settled and then simmered in my mind like yesterday's oatmeal, without the substance. I felt the scepter of power in my grip. But then came the tough part, using it. Sitting on the steps outside of the main office overlooking the dispatch area, I lit up a cigarette and blew the smoke at my reflection in my shiny new shoes.

"You look like you must have got yourself a soul sister over the weekend like I told you, Joe. Man, you look beat, but not in a bad way," said Jamal as he sat alongside of me. He lit his cigarette with mine.

I mumbled to him, "Don't I wish it was that simple, Jamal? Don't I wish?"

He got up whistling and walked over to the dispatch area to pick up his work. As he walked away, I thought, "What he did to me in my office that night was pure bullshit. But it was kind of direct and in a way, truthful."

I realized that the truth was, that my new job would be to get the soul brothers from the blind side. Like my own reflection in my shiny shoes, his fiery words that once inspired me were obscured by the smoke of confusion.

I shook my head and thought, "What if the people that they fire are pricks and truly deserve it? With the pricks out of the way, maybe it will clear the way for the other workers to advance."

Like Roger said, "The resources would go toward better things." I had to look beyond all of this. I did, and saw myself one day with these problems behind me, speeding away to my airplane in a brand-new Jaguar.

The hearing room was painted in typical State of New Jersey gas chamber green, with office furniture probably older than the trees from which it grew. An old Roman-numeral clock on the wall had a tick that was in synch with the pounding of the lump in my throat. I entered the room and took a chair.

I was greeted with, "What are you doing here, Joe? Don't tell me that they upped an' fired your ass, too," said Eddie, the dismissed worker, as he laughed and held his hand up to slap me five.

He was sitting with his wife and baby across the table from me. His clean, pressed Beria Building Maintenance uniform said he was every bit ready, willing and able to work. The baby turned to me and smiled, then looked away, then back to me as if to bait me into a game of peek-a-boo. I looked down and consulted my shiny shoes, as if seeking words of justification for my presence.

I thought, "Every career has its share of the eye sockets of others that must be used as rungs on success's ladder. This will be over soon enough, and we'll all go on."

"So why are you here, Joe?" Eddie's question didn't go away.

I managed to raise my head and look past his eyes. I simply said to him, "Kevin sent me, Eddie." I couldn't say another word. I felt my stomach acid burning at my throat and mouth while the sweat dripping from my armpits spilled into my shirt.

Eddie was kind of a decent person and a good worker. He did have a thing going on with a barmaid on the side. Sometimes it diverted him from showing up for work on time, but he never missed a day. Except for his being as stubborn as a mule, I couldn't imagine why he was fired. But I wasn't there to be imaginative.

The hearing officer sat down and opened Eddie's folder. She read some of it quickly and then looked up at me. She read some more, and then looked up at Eddie and his family. She asked Eddie some routine questions.

She stared at me for about thirty seconds then asked,

"Why is this applicant for unemployment benefits no longer on the Beria Building Maintenance's payroll?"

I straightened my tie and nervously buttoned my new suit jacket as I prepared to speak. A thought occurred to me, "Maybe Eddie deserved promotion and Roger wanted an Uncle Tom in position instead." I thought further, "Not my concern!"

Knowing that I was about to lie, it was as though my leg rose to seek the big picture and the first rung of power from my new title. I looked into the eye of the officer while my words took aim at Eddie like projectiles awaiting a gently squeezed trigger.

I said softly, "Because he quit."

As soon as the words left my mouth, I wanted to call them back. But it was too late. They had landed on Eddie's ears.

Eddie exploded to his feet, leaned over the table and said to my face, "Joe, you're a lying motherfucker! You know damn well that them motherfuckers fired my ass! Man, I need this fuckin' money. I got a baby, damn it! Ain't you got no conscience? They bought your ass, Joe! You ass-kissing son of a bitch!"

His wife grabbed hold of him as he reached for my tie and said, "Ain't worth it, Baby! We gonna live past his lie. He gotta live with it."

I couldn't look at them. The hearing officer closed the folder and said, "Application denied. Next case."

The elevator door closed. But it failed to remove me from what I had done.

"If an experience doesn't end you, it becomes you. This is also true for every word you hear, and for every voice that speaks it," echoed throughout the halls as I ran from the building. I could hear my heart pounding the word liar-liar-liar with every beat. Was the blood trail behind me from the hatchet in my hand?

Kevin told me to report to him by phone as soon as the hearing ended. Again, I followed orders. I told him, "Everything went okay. Eddie was denied." Those words escaped through my throat somehow, even as I choked on them.

Like Caligula's personal cheerleader, Kevin raved, "That's fabulous! Come to the office right away. There's another hearing next week. I want to hear all the details of this one. Wait until I tell Roger. He'll be very proud of us, Joe."

"Wow, proud of us," I said to myself. I felt like I was being initiated into a death squad. I hung up the phone. If there had been any food in my stomach, it would have been on my shiny new shoes. Within the sanctuary of my company car, I drove through the streets of Jersey City for hours trying to sort out what had happened.

All that my eyes could see before me was Eddie's face. All that my mind could hear was his voice saying to me, "They bought your ass!" His means of living was denied by my word. But Eddie had the final word, and it had defined me.

Suddenly, I began to feel hot and itchy. I pulled to the side of the road and tore off my suit jacket and shirt. As they fell to the seat beside me, I imagined them as the uniform of an S.S. officer who had just gassed a family. My tie lay beside them, missing only a license and rabies tag.

When everyday actions at the job affect buildings or companies or business people like ourselves, it can be called just doing business. How was what I had just done business? What had I just done in just doing my lousy fucking job? How did I, so recently a liberator of men, become an executioner of men? A criminal had replaced the commuter who simply drove in to his job that morning. A raise and a title had replaced his soul. The reflection of my eyes in the rear-view mirror wondered what they saw.

My sales job was to sell other businesses cheap contract labor as replacements for their long-time employees with costly benefits packages. In order to participate in this noble task, I had signed a restrictive covenant as part of my employment agreement. It said that "I would not divulge to anyone the business practices that I may witness while in their employment." I only wish that it could erase what I had witnessed myself do that day. There can never be any justification for lying in order to help create anyone's truth.

My bewilderment was furthered when I walked into Roger's office to hear him on the phone saying that he was the accounts payable officer of an office building that Kevin was soliciting for a cleaning contract. A competitor had the account. Roger called the competitor's receivables clerk, pretending to be "Mr. Smith" from the payables office at the account. Then he asked the other cleaning company what the breakdown was on the last check that the account sent. His excuse was that a temp wrote only a total and he was trying to adjust the books. He had a keen sense of how people would thoughtlessly throw figures out over the phone.

"And how much was the regular monthly service? You say two thousand? Okay, thanks a lot. You really helped me." After hanging up, he turned to Kevin and said, "Go in at eighteen for the monthly, throw in a free window cleaning."

Kevin clapped like a seal with a fresh fish landing on his nose. The Berias got themselves another contract. There was a father passing on to his own son a legacy of routine lying, deceit and taking unfair advantage as part of the normal workday. I began realizing what my position in this company, our company, was and it was not upright.

"Joey, you really did a great job today. There's a future in the Beria Company for people like you with real guts!" said Roger while patting me on the back, with Kevin proudly cheering us on at his side.

He added, "Kevin must have told you that we need you to do it again next week. Keep up the good work." Roger lit up a cigar and smiled, his stream of smoke engulfing us all.

I answered, "I don't think I can do this again. Send someone else."

They met my words with silence looking only to one another while I hung my head down, unable to look into the eye of anyone.

"Well Joe, maybe this new opportunity isn't for you?" Kevin said, knowing that his father was about to try to twist me around to his way. He must have sensed the emotion building within me as my eyes swelled and my breathing became labored.

He said to his father, "Let Joe stay with the sales and let him help Zach set up the work in the back. There are enough other things to keep him busy. I'll show my face in dispatch next week and pitch in if needed."

They signaled me out of the room. I thought that the next thing was to tie me to the radiator and fill my water bowl. The door stayed closed for over an hour. Word of my betrayal spread throughout the ranks like wildfire.

"What could those motherfuckers possibly give you to make you to do that?" Zach asked while looking at me as if to read my thoughts. He knew damn well what I had done, but he wanted to hear straight from me why I did it.

"I don't think I feel too good, Zach," I said as I dropped my head to the desk.

Zach waved his hand at me in disgust while saying, "I already told the men that them bastards made you do it!" Then he grabbed my arm and asked, "They did make you do it, right?" I knew Zach must have really gone out on a limb for me with the men.

I mumbled to him from within the pile of papers on my desk, "Yeah they held me down and made my mouth move. The words were printed on a big poster that they had me hold up to myself as I spoke them.

"Zach, I did exactly what they told me to do. I should have walked out but all I could think of was my fucking raise and the toys I can buy with it. Nobody twisted my balls but me. The Berias just gave me permission!"

Zach pinned me to the wall as he said with the rage of concern, "Joe, you dumb-ass fool! You better not ever, I mean ever do that shit again! You won't make it to that goddamn car of yours if you do. The word's out, you go down hard with the next one."

As Zach's hands left my arms I answered, "I already told them upstairs that I won't go to any more hearings." Then I looked up at Zach and asked sarcastically, "Who are they sending the next time, you? I'm sorry Zach, it'll be probably be little Kevin Beria cutting out the hearts of mankind, personally."

Zach met my sarcasm with a look of disbelief. Then he shook his head and mumbled, "Motherfuckin' fool!"

My walk to my car was like moving through a sea of icebergs with only stares from the men and not one word. Jamal acted like I didn't exist as he looked away from me. I could only hope that Zach was right, that I would make it to the car that time. When I turned the radio on in my car I expected to hear "Nowhere Man". Instead there was the usual bulletin; Nixon was being investigated by another prosecutor. It seemed that both the president and I had survived the day, but would either of us survive his career?

A month went by without incident. One night, I was preparing to close the building when I heard a voice behind me say, "Hey, how does the White man's nigger like his new job? Hey, motherfucker, I'm talking to you!"

I knew it was Jamal's voice. I turned around to answer with only the hope of finding a convincing reason for my actions at Eddie's hearing. To my immediate delight and astonishment Jamal was calling out to his nemesis, David, the supervisor.

David replied, "I'm doing a hell of a lot better than you'll ever do, Mr. 'By Any Means Possible.' Ain't never going to be anything possible with you. Know what I mean?" David then laughed tauntingly as he gathered supplies for his job site.

Jamal stepped between David and the supply cabinets. He placed his fingers over David's mouth then brought his fingers back to his own nose and said to him, "First off, it's, "by any means necessary," chump! Second, maybe you can't quote the brother 'cause your black lips got the smell of white shit all over them, motherfucker."

David's knife proved to be faster than Jamal's steel-toed boots could find holes in the cyclone fence. He stuck Jamal in the ass repeatedly while asking playfully, "Who's the chump? Who's the chump?"

Jamal fell from the fence. David then kicked him as Jamal ran away screaming, "It ain't over, motherfucker."

David answered, "Only a runnin' nigger gets an ass wound! And I oughta wash your dumb-ass mouth out with toilet bowl acid like I did your dumb-ass brother!"

David finished gathering his supplies, laughed and said to me, "Them dumb-ass young pups ain't never going to get it right. They just going to get more and more stupid every day. Joe, where's the case of wax I ordered?"

With his supplies in his van, David went out to his job site. Zach went upstairs to meet with Kevin. When the last man left, I walked down the dark alley to pull the steel door down. The worst minute of my workday was when I was the last to leave and I had to lock up the alley. I would lower the steel, corrugated gate to the ground and lock it. My face was then a foot from the ground while my ass was up to the hands of Fate.

I was wrong. Walking toward that door through the dark alley and into a .45 automatic in Jamal's shaking hand was the worst minute in my life. He pressed the gun to my stomach. I looked down at the .45. The breech was pulled all the way back. His hand trembled even more. He pushed me with the gun back toward the dispatch office.

All I could say was, "Jamal, that sure is a big gun!" Boy, did I feel stupid.

Once in the shape-up area he pushed me and said, "Get the fuck out of my way Joe! I'm going to kill that motherfucker! I should kill you for what you did to Eddie on the way to me gettin' him. David got no excuse for what he did. You, you're a cracker. You're made for fuckin' people over."

"Jamal, I feel terrible about Eddie. Honest to God, I'm not like that."

His brow lowered. The gun didn't. He turned his head slightly and spit. Then he said, "Don't bullshit me, Boy! Just look at how you used the Brothers to move your white ass up. Now move your ass the fuck outta my way while you can. Where's that Nigger?"

He turned the gun away from me while looking around the back room for his tormentor and said, "I'm going to put four bullets in his ass! One for every time he stabbed mine." Then he put his foot through Zach's office door while looking for David.

"Damn! Where'd he go? He disrespected me, man! I got good reason to kill him. Where's that motherfucker's black ass?"

I wanted to keep him talking. His trembling subsided as the gun pointed downward. My entire life had become reduced to the confines of the present situation.

I said desperately, "Jamal, there's no reason big enough for your kid to lose his daddy. The same bullet that puts David's ass in the ground puts your ass behind bars."

Again, the gun looked straight at me as Jamal said, "Fuck you, Joe! And don't you be trying that psychology shit on me. I know what I got to do and I know who I got to do. You keep talkin' that shit to me and maybe I'll shoot the other side of your mouth that all your bullshit be comin' from."

Jamal groaned, then he looked up, and then he looked back to me saying, "Man, you give a white boy a half-ass education and you still got yourself a half-ass white boy!" Jamal felt that I needed another look down the barrel to complete my day so he pointed the gun into my face.

Then he lowered it and simply said, "Shit, man! Fuck all you motherfuckers! Y'all ain't worth shit! Nothin' ain't worth shit, nothin'!"

He raised the gun upward. I thought that he was going to place it to his head. Instead he reached out with his other hand and squeezed the handle. There can be no better feeling than seeing a clip of bullets leaving a gun when it's not through the barrel. Jamal put the gun back into his belt. Taking the clip out must have been an act of self-control welcomed equally by me and his sense of survival.

"Jamal, I didn't see any of this. Why don't you just go to the job now? I guess I must have let you in so you could get some floor pads. Kevin and Zach are still upstairs." He put Zach's door back on the hinges, grabbed some floor pads and left.

A year before, this man may have shot me. He must have really believed Zach about my turning down the next hearing job. I knew I would never again let the men who once trusted me, down. My career may have stalled when I refused to step into the unemployment office to lie again, but standing firm in my decision had allowed me to see who I was, or at least who I was not.

When Muhammad Ali was summoned to be sworn in as a soldier, he said, "*Ain't no Vietnamese ever called me Nigger, now why would I want to go where they live and kill them?*" He was famous enough that the press was present to watch when the Army asked him to take the step forward at the swearing-in process, thus agreeing to the oath. He stood still. The media was his witness to that fact. Ultimately, he remained free.

Managers and workers alike took their step each day as players in Roger and Kevin's sick drama. We were not unlike our own soldiers were to the North Vietnamese soldiers. We fought and sold out one another while the puppeteers cashed in on any way things happened to go. Just business as usual, different name but the same game. A soldier might see a flash and then feel the bullet before it kills him. In business we might only see a smile and feel a handshake.

"I couldn't reach you at work. They told me that you left already," Nina said. She was waiting in her car in front of my apartment as I pulled up.

I stuck my head into her car while the rain fell upon the rest of me. I thought about the incident, snickered and then told her, "I was working in the back. I guess a gun would have to go off before you would know anyone's there. What brings you here?"

Quickly, she went into her breathy seductive mode and said, "Well, Arlene is having a party tonight. None of the crowd knows that we broke up, Joe. So maybe if you're not busy tonight . . . "

She paused and formed her pleading pout. A year before, I would have responded to it and served her whim. Let me guess, she needs me as her ticket to a couples-only party. I answered, "Nina, lose the fucking pout and get to the point."

She got right to the point of her finger, using it to massage my arm while her words tried the same on my libido, "Maybe you and I could go there together. I mean, after we say hello to everyone, you can do whatever you want."

Before it could go any further, I took hold of her finger and said, "And you can do whoever you want, right? Nina, don't insult my intelligence! You didn't drive all the way to Brooklyn Heights to sell me on going somewhere, so I can do what I want. I can do what I want by walking up that stoop and let the door shut behind me. If you're just itching to go swap body crabs with your friends, don't beat around the bush. Just say it."

With impending rejection looming, she went into automatic eyebrow flutter. I recalled how when we were living together, we would often go to Arlene's parties. Before we got to the door, Nina would drop two Quaaludes, then whatever happened, just happened. Eventually, I would find her naked ass passed out on a bed with a half-dozen others who just happened by.

True, I also had opportunities but jumping into the body beds would only serve to make me feel confused, not aroused. Usually I would meet someone else who felt like I did and go off to another place where it was private and more intimate.

My back was getting soaked from the rain. I jumped inside the car and sat behind the wheel while Nina slid over and immediately lowered the vanity mirror. Between her attempts at every expression that ever worked on me before, her eyes darted back and forth to the mirror, summoning her hands to adjust each and every minor flaw in her hair and make-up, real or imagined. I lit up a smoke, a bad habit that I had no control over, and watched the habit that I had walked away from put on her show.

Nina was a woman who would pay any price for beauty. I discovered this at her sister's house when an old school photo revealed a nose that had gone the way of the surgeon's floor. Reinforcing the world's perception of her carefully crafted facade was her life's obsession.

Her game plan was simple. Focus, plan and then create herself each day with her imaginary audience's approval as her reward. The make-up was bound to thicken as surely as the illusory crowd would thin, as the seasons moved behind her.

If one were to search for her soul, he must first descend through the vortex of her intrigues, to the depths of her persona. There before him would be the veneer of her reflection. Underlying that would be the engine of vanity that propelled her very existence. Nina's vision of herself was to look like the centerfold photo that every adolescent boy might keep beneath his bed and fantasize about. The longer I remained between her sheets and beside her, the more isolated I became in my indifference.

While living with her, it became increasingly difficult to define our relationship. I could never introduce her as my girlfriend, since she didn't behave like a friend. I couldn't truly say that she was my lover either. That might imply that she was capable of love beyond that for herself. There was one word that truly described her and it was an anatomical one. I would introduce her only as Nina. Her signature would reveal itself soon enough.

I met Nina and her friend Arlene a couple of years before while I lived in Jersey. I was stoned out of my mind at the community pool, lying on a lounge chair. I had gathered enough control to raise my head from the chair when I saw two redheads in tiny bikinis entering the water. One had a huge flaming Afro, the other ordinary, straight red hair. If only I could get up I would have introduced myself to the Afro, but not that day.

The next day at the pool, the straight-haired one placed herself next to me as I lay on my lounge. After dragging her body across my face to take a drag from my cigarette, she said, "Hi, I'm Nina." Again, she leaned over me to flick the ash.

I looked around for the Afro-haired one. Nina blocked my view with her body while taking full charge of the cigarette. I asked her, "Where's your friend?"

"Oh, Arlene lives in Brooklyn. She just visited me with her kids yesterday. What's your name?"

That was where I should have gone back to sleep. Instead, I thought, "Why the fuck not, any port in a storm."

A year later, Nina's back in Brooklyn and I'm living with her. I stayed with Nina two months longer than I should have, only because of the kids and they weren't even mine. Then we split up, but I fell in love with the neighborhood. The storm left my life; I remained in port and got the sublet.

With fifty feet of downpour between her car's door and my building I thought, "Hey, what the hell! I've got shit for plans tonight, may as well see where her life leads me." Our relationship was truly defined; at least it was in my mind.

The elevator door opened on Arlene's floor. The music grew louder from her apartment as we drew closer. The instant that we walked in, we were hit with a blasting, never-ending, driving bass highlighted with the constant falsetto refrain of, "*I like what I like, 'cause I like what I like, 'cause I like it,*" from the stereo. Arlene's favorite marching song to the bedroom played to synchronized, flashing red lights. We were just in time. There had to be twenty-five couples already there.

The floor was shaking from the tribal-like dancing. The coffee table had a mirror with lines forming, Happy Birthday_ _ _. The name of the guest of honor had already been snorted. Teacups were stuffed with joints, but you only had to breathe the air. There were candy dishes filled with nothing that you could buy over the drugstore counter, 'Ludes, Tuinals and Nembutals. The 'Ludes went the fastest.

The players were like moths drawn to the red glow from the bedroom. Clothes fell to the floor. Couples fell to the beds, and the games began. Quaaludes were both a hypnotic and a muscle relaxer. Some husbands became too relaxed to play. They could only be spellbound observers as their marriage vows and their egos broke before them.

Lisa was the most aggressive of the group. She had to try everything that she saw in the movies. When asked why she could never successfully re-enact the infamous scene in Behind the Green Door, she would say, "It's good to find a hard man. But forget about finding five at one time that are stoned on 'Ludes." Two years before, she was a devoted mother and housewife, baking cakes and cleaning compulsively.

Her husband, Hal, had wanted to be free to openly continue his affair with his secretary, Susan. The solution was to have Lisa put some skeletons in her own closet. He turned

Lisa on to pot and Quaaludes and started bringing her to parties. After a short time she was doing all the drugs and bad boys that she could get her hands on. When Lisa finally figured out why Hal chose the name Susan for their baby daughter, she sought to truly realize her own potential.

I wondered, "If you're going to play at being single then just be single."

Even the cannabis-filled air couldn't dull my cynicism. When my ex-wife, Deanna, and I felt that we should see others, we divorced. Nina's friends believed they could remain married, partake of the free love generation, and feel no remorse.

It's one thing to take a pill and become someone else. It's another thing to stay that way. No restaurant has ever titled its menu, It'll Be Shit in the Morning. It is the obvious outcome, but who would want to think of that while trying to satisfy his hunger? Another thing about orgies, people truly smell bad!

"Hey, man, 'scuse me, I didn't see you," said a lumbering figure with his eyes nearly shut that crashed into me while he was staggering sideways to the bathroom that I was about to use.

His attempt to open his eyes was in vain. He asked me, "Man, you got any heroin, man? Like I think I dropped too many downers. I gotta try 'an level out, man."

He unsuccessfully grabbed on to the shower bar after slipping on the rug, and then he fell to the floor, becoming tangled in the curtain. He moaned, and then he made a choking sound. I went over to him and raised his head slightly.

Suddenly his eyes opened wide and he shouted, "Oh wow! There's a joint under the tub!" His head fell out of my hand and landed on the tiles with a thud.

A woman entered the room and yelled, "Jack, you stupid bastard! How many pills did you do, you fuckin' junkie?" It was his girlfriend. She began shaking him as she screamed, "Jack, wake the fuck up!"

His eyelids were starting to flutter to the incessant music. All we could see were his eye's bloodshot whites as she pried them open while trying to keep him awake. As gravity lowered his jaw, he groaned his answer to her, "I don't know how many I took, man! Man, like how many are left in the jar?"

By then, I had guessed that her name was also, Man. She looked in their stash bottle. After seeing only three Tuinals left, she shouted, "Oh my God!"

Someone turned on the shower. We threw Jack in clothes and all. He screamed from the cold water. We screamed, trying to keep him awake. People were screaming in the bedroom. Joe Cocker was screaming, "With a Little Help From My Friends," on the stereo. Jack threw up. I took a leak. I left Nina to her performance-screaming in the next room and headed for the train home.

"Hold the elevator! I can't stand going anywhere with that junkie bastard anymore," Jack's girlfriend mumbled while she ran to the elevator, drying her hair with a borrowed-then-discarded towel.

She punched the lobby button then turned to me, smiled, and said "Hi! I guess since we kind of showered together, we should at least know one another's names. I'm Barbie. What's yours?"

We headed for the subway. I had been trying to reintroduce myself to the world as Ken for the past year but that would have to wait, at least until the next day.

I woke up to the sight of a string of laundry hanging from one end of her bedroom to the other. The ceiling fan created an odd symphony of flowing sheets and shadows. I found my clothes on the floor, after separating them from Barbie's. She was sleeping like a stone, which accounted for the absence of the three Tuinals that had been left in the jar. Quietly, I let myself out and headed down the hall.

Before I could press the elevator button, the doors opened. A somewhat familiar face appeared from behind a hat as he removed it to wipe the vomit from his shirt. Then he said, "'Scuse me, man. Hey, is this the fifth floor?"

I answered, "I don't know, I don't live around here. Yeah it's the fifth." After seeing the number five sign on the wall, I assured Jack that he was home. He put his hat back on his head and walked past me while deliberating each step, sporadically moaning and holding his stomach. He dry heaved and then held his arm out to open his apartment door, fifty feet away.

Turning away from him I asked myself, "Has the world ever been any different? Everybody's just fucking everybody else every way they can."

Found in September's Child's guest sketch book

Chapter Three

Pegasus

When your inner workings begin to change your outer appearance, people may notice the results before you do. Suddenly you hear things like, "Hey Joe! Is that an earring?" followed by, "Yo, check it out! Joe got an earring. You gotta hold back his hippie-hair to see it, but it's an earring alright! Man, first the beard and now this. Joe, you turnin' freak on us or what?" David had found out my secret. I had a brand-new gold ear stud.

Just that weekend, I was riding my new Harley down the Jersey Turnpike, playing eye tag with a girl driving a Ford Pinto. When I signaled her over to smoke, she shook her head no and pointed to her watch. I pointed to my heart, and then to the shoulder of the road. She smiled and gave me the okay one-minute sign. We both pulled over.

I lit one up. We shared it and some tender moments, thanks to a fold-down rear seat. Before we parted she said, "I have to be in Albany in three hours. Should this be good-bye, let me give you something to remember me with."

She reached into her bag and took out a small gun, then

put it to my head. My heart was either between beats or at a stop when I heard a loud click. A hand mirror appeared before my face, and then I saw it. She had shot an earring post into my lobe.

She smiled and said, “I sell these earring guns. Aren't they cute?” She was right; we never saw one another again. I couldn't help but remember her, whenever I looked in the mirror or when my comb would grab the stud.

I guess that I was starting to look like a character in the old werewolf movies when the hair started bulging out of his formal wear. Kevin had been complaining about my making business calls on the motorcycle rather than in the company-provided car. I figured as long as I wasn't taking the client to lunch, then what the hell. I knew that my position in the hierarchy was being compromised by my actions but somehow I didn't care. My self-respect was mending and the workers were talking to me again.

My appearance wasn't all that had changed, the Beria Company, my company, moved into newer, fancier, offices although directly across the street from the old building. Big deal, the spirit of the corporation possessed a new corpse. The king and his prince of a son spared no expense in giving themselves the plushest offices that money could buy. My office was beneath theirs, next to Zach's, next to the garages.

Eighth Street in Greenwich Village would be filled from one end of the block to the next with motorcycles from thirteen states every Friday night. But unless your bike was a Harley or an antique Indian, it was best to park your Jap somewhere out of sight. Not wanting to become victim to any unwritten anti-U.S.A. protocols, my Harley Sportster sat safe and happy, nestled between two all-American Hogs.

The window of Bing's Bongs was filled with roach clips from around the world, rolling papers from all over the country, hash pipes made from every material imaginable.

But there in the corner of the window, there it sat, a lovely Sterling Silver lady. Her arms reached high above her. Her hands clasped the silver chain that she hung from. Her tiny face had a look of longing. Her legs pointed down and then crossed as her feet flared and formed a one-snort cup.

"Mister Bing, I want that hope spoon. The one shaped like a silver woman."

"Don't you mean the coke spoon, Son?" he answered.

To which I replied, "I have only hope."

While he was making change, a large poster of a giant landmass grabbed my attention. I looked closer and saw that the entire body of land was comprised of fornicating couples and groups in every position known to Humankind. They were so numerous that they were falling off into the sea. But that didn't stop them.

"You sure you didn't pose for that one, Son?" Bing asked.

I looked over to the shopkeeper, then quickly back to the poster. He laughed and said, "No, not that one, anyone can pose for that."

He pointed to another poster by the very same artist. I said "Holy shit!" as I saw my face, beard and all. I was standing among the rubble of what had been New York, wearing only a loincloth, a scowl and wielding a lead plumbing pipe as my weapon.

Another of this artist's posters was of the Israeli athletes who were slain at Munich in 1972. They were competing eternally in Olympic Games among the clouds. The coloring and detail of those drawings was so spectacular that I couldn't stop looking at his works.

Then my eyes became drawn to and remained fixated on the same artist's greatest poster of all. It was of an ancient warrior mounted on a Pegasus-like creature. The winged horse's hooves and the warrior's legs were becoming increasingly snared by barbed vines growing from the Earth beneath them.

The warrior had a look of desperation. He seemed to be both pointing and pleading to me no matter where I stood. The vines had attached themselves to every part of both him and his stallion. His struggle to look skyward was in vain as were his pleas.

He was holding his other arm up toward his mounted comrades who were flying free upon their winged steeds. They could only look back to him as they flew off toward the setting Sun, beyond the horizon. Their hands held no weapons but their eyes looked as though they were armed with the dream of better things.

I hung the Pegasus poster on my office wall for those times when I needed to close off to the reality of my vines and have only thoughts of better things.

Was my company car somehow becoming jealous of my motorcycle? While keeping bugs out of my teeth, it was somehow putting them in my mind. While driving to a business call, my eyes might have been on the road toward my appointment, but the car would always find yet another junkyard. Not the kind of junkyard where a Chevy might find its ancestral Chevys, but places for plain old household and business trash.

I would drive up and ask the guards if I could go in and just walk around. Who could say no to a starry-eyed werewolf in a nice suit driving a Chevy with a mind of its own? Once inside, I usually rolled up my pants and took off my shoes, just to get a true feel for the place as I wandered among the rubble.

There was a peaceful stillness in the junkyards, much like that of a cemetery. There was no hierarchy, no climbing to the top nor pushing others to the bottom. Everything settled indiscriminately into its own chaotic order. Nothing pretended to be anything except what it had become – junk.

I would imagine the value the refuse may have once had to its owners, before it became irrelevant. That which was yesterday's treasure to its beholder was decomposing equally with what long before had been thought of as rubbish.

Creaking cranes opened their jaws and deposited the newly discarded to the ever-growing fold. Between the clatter of the recently departed, falling to their resting places, there was an almost surreal ambiance of music. Seagulls sounding like endless sonar echoes circled above the piles like a white tornado as if weaving an avenue to eternity. A gentle rain fell with a random rhythm on old tin panels. Jets departing Newark Airport provided a rolling roar as they faded into the clouds. I would stand quietly, as did the debris, and see no difference between us, while sharing in the final dignity of the trash before me and beneath my feet.

My sublet had expired. I felt that I shouldn't make a long-term commitment to an apartment. There was an opening at a commune in Park Slope. The Slope was a brownstone community near Brooklyn Heights. It had the basic look of the Heights except the ancient mansions had become rooming houses and of late, communes. I left my suit at the sublet and attended a member's meeting to interview for the vacant room.

The members were all right, I guess. Two of them, Sally and Jim, were part-time poets and singer-musicians. In addition to sharing the master bedroom, they shared a love of heroin and Sally's baby girl, Tammany. Sally's kid was half-Polish and half of whoever was holding the other end of the needle, one forgotten night.

Two of the others were also musician-songwriters named Sean and Billy. They each had one of the smaller rooms and a shared love for Sally's voice.

The fifth was a law student named Howie; he had half of the parlor floor. Howie decorated the halls of the brownstone with posters of Abbey Hoffman and Jerry Rubin. He seemed to have a sincere desire to make real changes in the world. When he spoke during the meeting, he projected pure leadership and appeared to be the driving force for the group.

When they asked me what I did, I told them that I was a flight instructor, but I might be looking to set up some kind of shop in the neighborhood. I just didn't know what kind yet. I thought if I told them that I was a corporate goon serving capitalistic war mongering pigs, it might make me fail the interview. I passed. The spare room at the end of the hall, next to the bathroom, would be mine.

There must be a magic element encased in the bedrock of the Boro of Brooklyn. If you're exposed to it long enough it brings something out in you. For lack of a specific term I called it Brooklynite. When I first landed in that place, I heard its whisper in the distance calling me to do things that I never imagined that I would do. The whisper had become a voice that I heard growing louder every night that I got closer to Brooklyn.

If I wandered the world around me in search of home, I would eventually find it seven miles east of Jersey City, New Jersey where I was born. A warm sense of belonging would radiate from the brownstones and replace the feeling of emptiness from the still wet sheetrock of my sterile office.

I often thought of walking away from being the corporate hack that I had become. Then I realized that I actually had been walking away ever since I lied at Eddie's hearing. Was I in search of the mind that I lost?

"Maybe I should jump back into the world of flying?" I thought. I recalled how, when I was a child, I would look to the sky and wonder about all of the places beyond the place I stood. Then I recalled all of the times that as a pilot, I would fly to different places and look at the world below, wondering if I might ever find my place upon it.

I wondered, "Perhaps my horizon isn't so distant. Maybe it is just eleven miles east, at least for now. Maybe if I shut off the noise in my head I might hear true adventure declare itself to me. If what I have is conventional security at its best, then I'll gladly accept pure adventure at its worst."

Speaking of adventure, there was a big business meeting at the commune. Since I had been a member for nearly a month, it was about time that I participated in this Socialistic experience firsthand. I sat through the whole thing. The carrot cake was nice as was the herbal tea. Everybody was civil and agreeable until an issue came up that was so explosive, it seemed like it was about to tear the very fabric of the commune apart.

Howie looked at the group very seriously, and then he said, "The odd penny of the phone bill was paid last month by Sally and Jim. Since they reside here as a couple with a baby, it cannot be considered to be a single payment. Therefore it is fitting that one of them should pay it this month, since the bill shows an odd cent again. Must we review the bylaws, or can we just consider this in the payment rotation?"

The quarter spun like a silvery orb when I threw it on to the table. To the surprise of everyone I said, "You know, I was really digging the carrot cake and Sean and Billy's guitar licks. This should settle these arguments for at least a couple of years. But tell me; don't you people have anything more important to do than to slice one another up into penny fragments?"

Howie looked at the quarter as it whirled around the table. As he moved toward it, he glanced at Sally and Jim, to let them know that this was far from over.

The plywood sheet that served as the entry door to the commune slammed behind me. I left the ringing sound of a spinning coin, to pass under the chaos of dueling wind chimes, to the refuge of the darkened street. I sat on the lowest step of the stoop only to see another silvery orb show its face from behind the evening clouds.

The Moon rules the night like a silent stoic sentinel, ever vigilant as it looks off beyond its host. An eternal beacon whose radiance contrasts the overwhelming darkness. A true friend whose phases are always predictable and whose dark side remains ever so discretely hidden. In awe of its brilliance, with color removed from sight, I followed its glow in hope of deciding what was right or might be illusion.

I wandered through a hedgerow maze of wall after wall of brownstones, following my feet as they followed the glow. There was no destination in my mind; there was only the Moon. The city's noises around me blended into a single clamor of all that was ever called to it. Sounds within the sound seemed to be speaking out while in search of one another, or perhaps saying, “Get out of my way!”

How anticlimactic for a walk upon a moonbeam to end in front of a little abandoned store on First Street, right off the main drag, Seventh Avenue, next to the Stack O' Barley Tavern.

I asked myself, “Why would I be drawn to this little store?” I was confused and at the same time I felt sure of something, I just didn't know what.

I wondered, “Could this be the source of my, until now, imaginary Brooklynite?” “No. That's just a convenient answer to what shouldn't even be a question,” I answered.

There was a stoop next door. I sat down and looked around. In spite of my inner turmoil, I didn't feel the urge to go anywhere else except right there. I couldn't determine what type of business could have gone on inside of that place. It had boarded-up windows and a horrible, imitation white brick façade. There was a graffitied black door that was unlike that of a business; it was more like that for a house and not a very secure one at that. Besides the flimsy lock, there was only an old peephole and no name or anything to say who or what may have been there. What the Hell, I had nothing but time to kill. I adjusted my position on the stoop a little more upwind of the tavern's dumpster and lit up a bone.

I looked around and found myself within a walled canyon of the tenements of First Street and the stores and apartments of Seventh Avenue. An alley was nowhere to be found in the matrix of asphalt and stone. I felt alien and yet strangely familiar to that spot in the Universe. I looked skyward to watch my evening's companion disappear behind my puff of reefer smoke blending with the passing nighttime cumulous clouds, my body and mind absorbing the mood of the summer's night.

The muffled shrill of distant sirens and the faint roar of humanity were abruptly eclipsed by the sounds of banging, crashing and an intermittent thud. I jumped to my feet to hear the warlike screams of two young boys as they raced one another, high above the street, atop the block-long line of parked cars, locked bumper to bumper. The hoods, trunks and roofs were their track. Dents and cracked glass lay in the wake of their charging footsteps.

"Yo, you lazy ass, you ain't got shit for speed! I can beat you twelve out of ten times you fat fuck!" taunted one young boy to another as they jumped from the hood of the last car parked at the curb in front of the store. A window screen fell to the sidewalk from the building next door as a woman's head emerged.

Her piercing voice rang out, "You shut both your mouths, Willie, and 'specially you, Demetrius! And don't be runnin' up and down the tops of them cars cursin' at one another. Ain't no way for brothers to be actin' in public. Now get in the house, the two of you!"

She stuck her head further out of the window and said to me, "I'm sorry the way my boys was behavin' here tonight, Mister. Please don't think poorly of us."

The boys nodded politely to me while smiling from ear to ear. Then as fast as a shot they ran into the hallway next door. I said to their Mama, "Ma'am, don't worry. I was enjoying the show. You have a good night."

I had never seen a footrace along a line of parked cars before. There's always a first time for everything, I guess. The other kids playing on the block were plain loud, not in a bad way, but just loud. Something about these kids though was unusual. There was no single dominant race.

Within the anarchic childhood spontaneity, there was this incredible mosaic of random pigmentation. For the hour that I was sitting on the stoop, not one kid made a racial crack to the other. They insulted one another very creatively, however, but with no mention of the obvious.

Then, from down the block, a man ran toward us chased by another waving a steel garbage can, yelling, "You motherfuckin' shit! I'm gonna fuck you up!"

The kids fled to the safety of the stoops or jumped up on the hoods of parked cars as the men dashed between them. At the top of the block, the garbage can met the intended head. The target fell to the ground covering himself with his arms.

The small muscular West Indian said to his victim, "You keep your fuckin' pop-eyes off my woman, motherfucker! Next time, mon, it be your ass in the garbage can rollin' down the fuckin' hill!"

They went their separate ways. I had determined two things about that block. The kids were most definitely athletic, and old-fashioned monogamy seemed to be alive and well, at least the idea of it was.

The block stayed alive with a mix of kids, their parents and passersby until well after midnight. A few people joined me on the stoop. One was a dog walker in combat fatigues who hung out with me long enough to help me finish my reefer. Two others were musicians playing guitar and recorder. They amused themselves by trying to guess the riffs that the other was playing. The guy playing the recorder was particularly good, especially since most of the riffs he played were meant for guitar.

"Hey, it's "Aqua Lung"!" yelled the guitar player to his friend.

"No it ain't, man, you ought to know "Stairway To Heaven" by now. It's all you ever fuckin' play on that rat's-ass guitar of yours, dude!" said the hippie with the recorder, stopping his playing for the moment it took to answer.

"No! Not the shit you're playing. I mean the guy on the Jethro Tull album cover, man! Get a load of the dude comin' up the street. It's "Aqua Lung" come alive."

The musicians began to provide Jethro Tull's melody to the rhythmic chirping of the broken wheel of a supermarket shopping cart as it was pushed up the hill toward us. As it got closer, the symphony grew with addition of the shuffling sound of one dragging leg as the cart that supported the weight of 'Lung approached. The labored breathing of the old man further complemented the music in progress as the shopping cart turned toward us and then stopped.

His clothes, beard and skin had become one and the same color from years of exposure to the elements. The cart contained old suitcases and shopping bags bearing stomach acid stains accented by old, dried food particles. Projecting from the cart was a large board. Stoned as I was, I couldn't stop thinking that if he had a room to go with it, his search might be complete.

Although he stopped directly in front of us, it was as if he was looking beyond us. He couldn't keep his eyes from the door of the old storefront. He stared at it for about two full minutes, his quivering lip ever lowering from the weight of the drool amassing beneath it. He pointed momentarily toward a trap door that must have led to a cellar.

His head slowly turned away from the store. His upper body bent sideways in compensation for his immobile neck as he strained to glance upward at the Moon, revealing itself from behind the passing clouds. Then with great effort, his body righted itself while his head, again, lowered. He sighed as the drool flowed back from his cheek to his waiting lip.

His full attention was directed toward me. He seemed as if he had to ask me something very important. He groaned slightly. Then upon the wings of muscatel-tale breath came his message, "Gimme a buck!"

The old man's trembling hand reached toward me. We all backed away. The guitar player pointed to 'Lung's once-green-and-yellow-plaid pants as they began to darken with piss. I complied with his request for a buck almost immediately, as did the others. The essence about him revealed this to be his modus operandi. 'Lung took the money and shuffled up toward Seventh Avenue, disappearing around the corner.

"We're going over to Saint Mark's Place and jam with some people. Why don't you come along?" the recorder player asked me.

The guitarist said, "Just don't anyone call the rhythm section back to join us."

I walked with them to Saint Mark's. Since I lived on that street it was an obvious choice. What a coincidence, their destination was the same house as mine. All this music and I live there too! Sean and Billy joined the two musicians in playing Joni Mitchell's "Michael of Mountain" while a recently Jim-less Sally added her guitar and voice. Feeling a party coming on, I went upstairs for the rest of my stash.

"What the fuck are you doing here? This is my room!" I hollered to the two naked hippies that were trying to bounce the stuffing out of my mattress. Another guy was hanging out in the hall.

The hall guy answered me, probably because his friend couldn't, and said, "Hey man, she's whacked on 'Ludes and she's been doing everyone all night. I had her already. Do you want some before she goes, like unconscious?"

I guessed that she was getting into the commune spirit, what with everyone sharing her like they shared the toilet. I should have thrown a pail of cold water on them, instead I said, "Tell your friend not to forget to flush when he's finished. And by the way, keep the fuckin' mattress!"

Somehow I felt that I lied during my interview at the commune. I told them that I was looking for a store. Not wanting to believe myself to be a liar, the next day I spoke to the realtor whose sign was in the window of the tiny store on First Street. I rented it. Only one hundred bucks a month . . . One door, no windows . . . Just don't park in front . . . Plenty of room inside the store for my Harley . . . No shower, just a crapper and a sink.

Benny, the landlord-realtor, would serve as my tour guide of the fifteen-by-fifteen-foot store. Benny tried to act like the building belonged to someone else, but as he spoke he kept mixing up the words theirs and mine while referring to the owner. It didn't matter to me but it did to him.

As I walked around with my head bobbing up and down, absorbing the surroundings, he said, "It used to be an after-hours joint back in the 'fifties. There's a double sink under the bar. The basement has some junk down there. A while back we had a squatter that used to commute between here and Prospect Park.

"He kept filling the place with rocks and old books and other shit. He left some bags with the rocks and the other crap behind after we bolted the joint. He disappeared, thank God. The only problem here is that you're gonna have to watch out for bums crawling in through the hatch. If you want me to clear out the cellar I will."

No sooner than I inhaled the store's energy I said, "Don't bother Benny, I like junk. Maybe I'll find something interesting there, who knows? By the way, I'll take it."

There was absolutely nothing about that store that anyone would want. All that I knew is that for some mysterious reason, it wanted me. My judgment became overpowered by my curiosity. Benny handed me the keys and wished me good luck. Who could ask for anything more? All this and a junkyard in the cellar, wow! I had absolutely no idea what I was going to do there, but it was a place to hang out and get my head together. I parked my sleeping bag on the floor and gave a last look at the strange, wondrous street before I tried the place out that night.

When I closed the door, I felt enveloped by an unusual, comforting, calm feeling, as if being held by a force surrounding me. When I shut the light, the feeling became more intense. Imagine that, intense calmness.

I took a large candle from one of my boxes and lit it. The shadows gave form to the energy that I felt, as if they were massaging my mind with their movement as they appeared to dance on the walls. Neither words nor pictures came to mind as I watched. I felt as though a higher definition of peacefulness than I'd ever known was articulating itself to a part of me that I never knew.

A tiny glimmer of morning light came through a slit in the boarded window. Before I could orient myself to my surroundings, I heard someone pounding on the door shouting, "Open up, Dude! It's cool, I live next door."

Through the peephole I saw a kid looking up and down the block. He didn't seem menacing, so I opened the door. He said, "Yo, I'm Steven, what's your name, Mister?"

Instead of saying Joe, out came, "My name is Kenny. I just took over the store."

Before I could say another word, this sixteen-year-old took the floor. With the knowledge and conviction of a tour guide, he said, "They'll come right in through where that window was. You see that cellar hatch outside? Two minutes with a hacksaw, and they'll be in and cutting up through the floor. You see where the air conditioner was? Pop that board out in two seconds and they're all over your ass. Whatcha got in the boxes, Kenny?" He lit up a smoke, walking around like he owned the place.

I gave him a real stern, threatening look while saying, "What if I told you I had perimeter alarms and security weapons in there?"

He replied, "What if I told you that you're full of shit? Who the fuck do you think you are, James Bond?"

The kid had balls, but I had to keep him at a distance and with half an eye on him, too. I looked at him and said nothing. I waited for him to blink and when he did I asked, "How do I know that you're not the one who might be coming in through the places that you told me about?"

All of a sudden Steven turned back into a kid. I got the feeling that he didn't want to be thought of as a thief. It was that or he didn't want to be found out to be one.

He flicked his cigarette through the open door and said, "Hey Kenny, my Moms is the super of the building next door and kinda watches this one, too. I'm here to say hello for her and give you our phone number if the heat goes out at night."

"Your idea of hello is to try to scare the shit out of me?" I asked as he looked at me and laughed. I had a feeling that he could be trusted.

"Kenny, what are you going to do with this place? You don't look like a shop owner or nuthin' like that. You gonna open up a club like they had here years ago?"

He had a good question there. Maybe I should make some kind of shop so I won't have been lying in my commune interview.

"When I figure it out Steven, you'll be the second one to know."

I was on my way to investigate a scandalous crime. A piece of paper had been under a chair at one of our accounts for one week. My job was to drive sixty miles just to witness the paper, prepare a written report and set forth a plan for its removal. I was to then tell Zach to drive sixty miles to also witness the paper, effect its removal then take appropriate steps against the negligent porter. His report would then be added to the file.

"Good Morning, Mr. Todd. You might remember me, I'm Joe from Beria Building Maintenance," I said to Buford Todd who was waiting for me in the lobby.

Todd was the typical, petty purchasing agent who did nothing all day but send memorandums everywhere he could in order to appear productive as he awaited five o'clock or thirty years, whichever came first.

Todd answered, "Yes, I remember you, Joe. I believe you investigated the un-emptied wastebaskets last year. That problem has not re-occurred. By the way, good job on that one."

I thought, "For that I should receive the Navy Cross, at the very least."

Like a battle-weary admiral pacing the bridge with his hands clenched behind him, Buford Todd told me to follow him as we marched down the hall. He turned to me and asked somberly, "Were you briefed on the present situation by your superiors?"

My mind heard the sounds of distant guns. My heart fluttered from the sense of impending doom. I was led to an office where a piece of paper was lying under a chair. The hands of the admiralty unclenched long enough for him to point and say, "I have been watching this paper for over a week now. Not one of the cleaning staff from your company has made an attempt to remove it. We pay good money for your porter service. Apparently it is nonexistent in this office."

His words seemed to go right through me. All I could think was, "He's got to be thirty years older than I am!" A vision of myself appeared in a mirror that hung on the wall behind him. In my reflection, I was wearing a yellowing white shirt with a coffee-stained tie just like his. I was thirty years older and didn't look one day wiser.

I shook off the hallucination and said, "I'll be back with some sandwiches and water, Mr. Todd."

I had no idea why I said that. I froze in my tracks because the world felt like it moved. It was as if a volcano was growing beneath me. I held on to a chair while Buford Todd just stood there, perplexed. I wondered, "If nothing else in the room was moving, could the tremors be coming from within me?"

As surely as flakes of skin would fall from Buford Todd's face, my inertia was being hard pressed to survive from the surge of energy that I felt as if it grew from the pit of my stomach and burst through my every pore. I was suddenly filled with righteous rage! I had read that righteous rage always preceded the true self's emergence. I looked back in the mirror, winking at my reflection as it held its fist high in the air.

Buford Todd had no idea of my suddenly transforming inner self. He looked at me with befuddlement all over his "Elmer Fudd" face and asked, "Why? What do you mean by bringing me sandwiches and water?"

I tried to suppress my feelings, but they kept getting stronger. Then I heard a voice coming from the mirror say, "I can't stand beady-eyed little moles with facial dandruff acting like they actually have a purpose in this or any reality. This particular garden slug has only one function, to annoy the shit out of any living thing around him."

I looked away, and then hearing another voice, I looked back at the mirror. "Just do your job Joe, and then get out of here!" said the reflection of my suit and tie.

Suddenly, an arm held itself high after breaking through the sleeves of both suit and shirt. The face in the mirror was winking back at me mouthing, "Fuck this shit!"

The more I tried to rally some civility from within, the more my surging feelings kept pouring out. I felt almost possessed. Fuck almost! I heard a voice from within say, "Whatever this is that I'm feeling, I like it! I want more! I am actually having fun at work!"

With the sinister power of the Cheshire cat smile, I held my prey by his little corporate tail and said, "Buford, you must be famished after watching that paper for over a week. The least I can do is bring you something to eat and drink. Imagine the incredible powers of concentration that you possess to be able to stand here and look at one piece of paper for a whole week. I'm sure impressed. Thank God I came here to rescue you."

He tried to speak but I cut him off and added, "To think, a big-ass company actually pays you to jerk people off like this, Buford. You know, couldn't you like just call me and I would have just spoken to the porter? Like, spare the fucking world the melodrama, man!"

Old Buford Todd just stood there as I circled him, waiting for the next thing to say. I could have caught my tongue before the words flew out, but I didn't because I didn't want to. I asked myself, "Could it be because of all the pot that I had been smoking lately? Why am I finding it increasingly difficult to censor my words? It was once commonplace for me to smile, say, "Yes Sir," and then tell them what they wanted to hear. Maybe I'm smoking all that pot so I won't give a flying fuck. Who knows?"

Was righteous rage a precursor for intuition to choose the words that would set a new course for my life? I wondered, "If this is the new course, it's a hell of a lot more fun than the toilet flush that preceded it!"

I thought about how much Roger, Kevin and my position in the corporate world meant to me. Then I saw the little waste of flesh, bone and dandruff scales before me. So I said to Buford Todd, "Let me ask you a question, Buford. If you were in the position to say that you didn't care about something, would you say you don't give a flying fuck or would you say you don't give a rat's ass? I think rat's ass is a bit pedestrian, don't you?"

I looked down the long hall and envisioned an endless line of hands holding tin cups from the bars of their office doors, hoping for water or pensions. I shook the image from my mind, leaving only Buford in his off-the-rack corporate uniform before me.

I asked, "Hey Buford, cat's got your tongue? You don't have to answer me. Buford, this shit is really fucked up. Maybe you should take all your pages of documentation of this stupid little matter and wipe up the bullshit from your lips with them! And maybe you can pick up that little piece of paper under the fucking chair while you're at it."

He seemed lost for words and his pits were really sweating. His little brow wrinkled as more flakes fell from it to the floor. I lit a cigarette and threw the match into the wastebasket across the room.

Finally he spoke, "Roger Beria is going to hear about this! We don't pay good money for sarcasm." He closed the office door behind us as he began seeing me out.

I stopped and turned, then looked him dead in the eye and said, "If the sarcasm is that good, you should pay for it. You know, some people even pay for spankings, man."

I pointed to the door handle that he was holding and added, "By the way, that's the only office with a locking door. Did you know that?"

Somehow I hit a hot spot. He began to act defensively. He looked down as if to desperately seek other violations and mumbled, "I had to put that lock on because of the new word processing machine we got last week."

His face became blank as he exclaimed, "Oh no! I didn't give your people a key. Well then they should have asked for one when they found the office locked."

He was beginning to smell like an onion cooking in his little beads of sweat. Nothing more had to be said except, "Buford, with all due respect, you're an asshole! By the way, do you mind if I take some of those old cable reels around back with me?"

At that point he would say anything just to get me out of there. I had seen the cable reels on the way in. I felt they would look great in the store. I put as many reels into the Chevy Nova hatchback as I could. Instead of driving to my next meeting in Newark, I headed straight for Brooklyn.

Upon unloading the cable reels into the store, I had every intention of going back to finish my appointments.

But over in the corner I saw a small sledgehammer. I picked up the hammer and looked at the ugly gray walls. I began screaming while I smashed the wall with the hammer. Chunks of plaster flew all about me, and then settled to the floor.

Beneath the ugliness of ancient plaster was incredibly beautiful natural brick. After smashing it about a hundred times a whole section was exposed. It looked great and I loved the exercise that I was getting from hammering and screaming. I thought less and less about going back to work with every strike and every scream. I began to hear other voices between the sounds of the hammer impacting upon the wall. I looked to the door to see two forms appearing through the dust cloud.

"Hey Mister, need some help?" It was the kids who raced up and down the cars the night I met the store. They even brought their own hammers.

"Sure I can use help. Just knock off the plaster and try not to damage the brick. Yeah, and I promise not to scream."

Like "The Anvil Chorus" at full volume, we smashed at the wall, sending broken plaster all over one another. I had no idea how long we were at it. It didn't seem like it should be getting dark outside, but it was.

From beyond the dust abyss we heard, "Willie! Demetrius! You get yourselves in here for supper and I mean right now!"

They looked up from their work. Their jaws dropped upon hearing their names. Before they ran home to their mamma, I handed them a few bucks. Although I couldn't hear Kevin or Roger calling me, I was sure that they must have been trying to by then.

I looked at the green tile floors. I remembered seeing some large packing crates at the junkyard. I thought about how I could rip them apart and nail them to the floor. They would go great with the cable reels but that would have to wait. I finished the walls.

I found an old power drill in the basement. It had a weird raspy bit. I ran it across a cable reel and saw that not only could it serve to clean them up, but also I could make designs in the wood with it. So I did. After learning to control the drill bit, I began to follow the grain of the wood. As I did this, I began to see images emerge from within the grain. I kept digging with the drill until the image was realized, then another and another would appear. Although I didn't start out with a plan, the carved figures took on a life force of their own.

Since the door was shut and the windows were boarded, the store had a way of making time seem irrelevant. A pile of sawdust surrounded me as I stood back to see my creation. Figures of a man and a woman separated by waves of energy adorned the top of the reel at my feet. I had never carved in wood before. I marveled at how a moment of curiosity led to the obsession that caused me to carve this vision as night turned into dawn.

At some level I knew that I should be concerned about my job. How bizarre, I could not care less about that which I had always considered to be my livelihood. It seemed to be a mere distraction from what was before me.

The significance of my carving was the only thing that concerned me. The man and woman each projected a strong yet equal presence. The man held a large mass above his head. The woman held a circular object in one hand with a cross above it. On her other hand was a large perching bird. Neither figure dominated the other. Balance was achieved through equal lines of energy radiating between them. The lines emanated from each form until they met those of the other and blended into a single mosaic of harmony.

I never had any preconceived notion of that design. I was fascinated by the experience of witnessing my imagination in form. I felt as though the wood and the carving of it were introducing me to more of my unawakened self. If I might be the man in this carving, then who might this woman be? I tripped over the work light cord. The beam from the fallen light cast the cable reel's shadow on the entry door.

I took a small knife and cleaned up all of the rough edges from the rasp tool. In doing so, I discovered that I could heighten the detail with this tool. After achieving another skill, I opened the door for some fresh air only to find that the dawn had reverted to night. A sensation that I never had before came over me. Instead of feeling that time was passing from my life, I felt that finally, life was filling my time.

The basement was crammed with remnants of the different businesses that had occupied the store. There were large burlap bags filled with semiprecious rocks with faded writing that said, Prospect Park Dig. These must be what Benny had referred to.

After I set aside the more recent junk, probably from the after-hours club, more things appeared. There were some more strange tools, rusted barbells and old textbooks among other stuff. An antique book seemed to stand out among the debris. The cover had what appeared to be five words carefully scripted in a formal calligraphy style. They formed a circle around the faded figure of a woman, appearing to hold an infant. I gently scraped away the caked-on dirt around them and read the five words: Magnitude, Impact, Recollection, Deliverance, Perpetuity.

I scanned through the book, hoping to find a meaning behind the choosing of these particular words. It had only blank pages except for the first, which was written in the same style of calligraphy. It read, "Keep this journal forever. You must remember tomorrow, that which created today." There was no name for either the giver or the receiver.

Who might have been so meticulous in preparing this journal for one who would ignore and abandon it? The pages were yellowed and the edges were brittle. While I read the handwritten sentence, a delicate voice seemed to echo the sound of the words as they each entered my mind. The words preceding the blank pages sat before me as if they awaited an answer from, perhaps, the erstwhile possessor. I brought the book upstairs, together with some of the rocks.

Previously, whenever I sat in a strange room, I would always place myself against a corner; if no corner were available then a wall would do. I sat huddled in my sleeping bag in the very center of the store, my only companion being the candle beside me as it evoked the shadows that danced upon the brick walls.

The only sound that I could hear was my beating heart. The flame of the candle and the shadows on the walls seemed to join in its rhythm. Images of automobiles, telephones, televisions and employers were overshadowed by the shadows before me. It was as if the shadows were arresting and incarcerating them beneath the bricks. My eyes fluttered, but I chose to remain awake.

I took the empty book and wrote, "Who will I be and where will I sit after I fill in the last page of this journal? And what of the future of this book, will it be revered and each night be placed ever so gently, in its usual one-inch spot in a fine hardwood bookcase? Or will it be thrown, without a thought, from the window of a moving Greyhound bus?"

I had no idea what day it was. I wrote only JE for Journal Entry.

Found in September's Child's guest sketch book

Chapter Four

September's Child

"Good morning, Zach." He looked at me then turned away, so I asked, "What's the matter with you, bro', am I too ugly to look at, or should I have said, good afternoon?"

Zach's head slowly turned back toward me while shaking in apparent disbelief. His eyes were nearly popping from their sockets as he said through his restrained fury, "Mr. Kevin is going to call you upstairs. He wants to talk to you."

Staring at the Beria Building Maintenance logo stitched across his shirt and cap, I asked, "Why do you call him Mr. Kevin? Does he call you Mr. Zach? You don't want me to think you're Mister Uncle Tom, do you?"

With my attempt at humor lost, Zach shouted, "Joe, stop your bullshitting! You fucked it all up. Man, you had the world by the balls here. Whatever you wanted, they would have done it for you. But you been bullshitting on their time. They would have made you a big part of the Beria Corporation! Next year a better company car, even more money and don't forget the security that you have here. Most people in their right minds would kill for what you're throwing away."

I sat in my executive chair, leaned back and lit up a cigarette. Then I said to Zach, "Or die from it. I really appreciate your concern for me. But in my case, being part of the corporation is just being a trivial ingredient within the greater fool. For every measure of growth that the Berias see that I achieved in their company, I'm three times reduced within my own sense of self-respect. Imagine how those assholes at the top must feel.

"Zach my friend, as far as the money is concerned, they can never give me enough to cover the mirror in order to hide what I can't look at any longer. Think about what you say when you said, 'On their time.' If people allow themselves to think in terms of being on another's time, it grants them title to their fucking lives, man. Zach, all we have in life is our fucking time."

Zach knew that he wasn't going to get a word in until I ran out of air, so he put his chin on his folded hands and let me blow off. I went on, "You mentioned security before, Zach. Just how is it that the South American dictators can employ forces to subjugate people under the name of security? The whole fuckin' idea behind security is to keep the little people quietly content while the life is sucked out of them in exchange for a few pennies toward their toothless years. As far as all of the governments and corporations are concerned, the ultimate security that they give us is the grave. At least until they decide to build a highway on top of us. Speaking of highways, the car idea is cool."

My words and even the stab at humor seemed to be lost on Zach. He picked his head up and looked at me as if he knew that I smoked the roach I found in my car's ashtray on the drive over and said, "Joe, you motherfuckin' idiot! You better get your shit back down to Earth, 'cause you sound like you're still flyin' in them airplanes or your ass is stoned. One way or another, your fuckin' head's still in the clouds.

You gotta get your shit together, man. Mr. Roger saw you smokin' shit with Jamal right in front of the office last week. Joe, you gotta be goddamn crazy!"

I smoked some, and then I bought some. I couldn't tell Zach that part. I leaned back on my executive chair and cupped my hands around my eyes. At times like that there's only one thing to do. See only what you want to see. All that there was before my selected tunnel of vision was the poster that I found at the head shop.

Somehow the ancient warrior appeared to look away from his departing comrades, casting his desperate gaze toward me. I rubbed my eyes and saw him even more absorbed in his agony. His legs were completely overcome by the Earth's barbed vines. I could only imagine that his very tears had nurtured them to that level.

"Joe, if you're downstairs, please come to my office immediately!" The junior authoritarian had spoken. I completed my thought and went upstairs. Kevin's new office was a far cry from the salvaged storefront at the old building. His walls were festooned with school plaques that beyond the inscriptions all probably meant Most Influential Father Award.

I stood before the child of the man as he opened with, "Joe, we've known one another long enough for me to just get to the point. You're not the same person that you were when we hired you. You disappear for days at a time. You said that you would wear a trimmed beard, meanwhile that thing all over your face is hardly trimmed and your hair is too long for representing our company in any business environment."

I was hearing what he was saying. But what he said triggered a thought. I wondered, "If shorter hair and a shaved face made one a better business person, then maybe everyone should also shave their eyebrows and pluck their lashes. Then they would be even better business people." I may have missed some of the other things that he said in between.

My attention returned as he continued, "Furthermore Joe, I can't have you going around, calling the purchasing agents at our accounts assholes. Buford Todd called me and said that you intimidated him and made him feel like an idiot. What do you have to say for yourself, Joe?"

What I really wanted to say was that the paneling in his office possessed the greatest acoustics for a big pickled-egg-and-beer fart. Instead I began with, "Kevin, gotta tell you the latest, I've decided to be known as Kenny. Okay, when I called Buford Todd an asshole, my name was still Joe. But either way I'll take the credit or blame for saying it. Don't forget, for a guy like Buford, an asshole is a very important thing. First of all, where do you think he got the news of his last promotion? On the other hand, taking a shit might be the only exhilaration he has left in his idiot life."

I picked up Kevin's father's enormous Cuban cigar that lay unopened on the desk and asked, "Did you ever wonder if people puffed on these things because they may have been denied the breast, or might they just be in search of something greater than themselves?"

Getting back to business, I went on to say, "Please pardon my digression. I should respect your position and maintain proper decorum. Kevin, Buford Todd is a fuckin' asshole. He feels like an idiot because maybe deep down he's at least smart enough to know that he is one. You know he had me go all the way down to south Jersey to look at a piece of paper under a chair in a locked office. The punch line is, he had the only key for the fuckin' office!"

I plopped down on a chair, lit up a smoke and placed my trash-stained boots on his desk. Kevin's face reddened with contained rage while becoming framed within my smoke ring. His coffee cup rattled into its saucer to the relief of Kevin's shaking hand.

He stood and placed his hands squarely on the desk and said with a trembling voice, "Joe, or whatever your name is, your attitude verifies my father's suspicion of what he thought he saw. He said that you were smoking a marijuana cigarette with Jamal across the street. Joe, let me cut to the chase. I'm giving you two weeks notice. Turn in the car the week after next and then clear out your office."

His words made me finally realize what I had wondered about for so many years. Cutting to the chase meant going to the last scene of a movie. Why didn't I figure that out before?

Back to Kevin, all I could say to him was, "I hope that you aren't going to ask me to testify that I quit during my own unemployment hearing." His jaw dropped so I said, "If there is a hearing and if you tell me to lie, you know that I will do as I'm told."

There I was, basking in the glory of the truth that was created the last time I lied in the hearing room. Kevin was ruining my exhilaration with his shaking, so I said, "Kevvy, rest your mind at ease. The restrictive covenant that I signed protects you. I can't divulge anything about your company's practices. It did cover the lying stuff and all that, didn't it? By the way, can your father also impersonate voices like John Wayne or Humphrey Bogart, or does he only do accounts payable guys?"

He looked toward the intercom, then to the door to his father's office.

With his face framed by my boots I said, "Don't worry, Kevvy. I'll just tell them at the unemployment office that my mind quit on you months ago. All that you did was to fire my ass! Maybe we can split the difference. Seriously now Kevin, does this mean that I'm not expected to wear ties any more? I was hoping to use them to start a dog-walking service. You know, something to make ends meet."

I reached up to high five him. He placed his hands over his head and ducked. My excitement overwhelmed my ability to choose words. All I could say was, "Wow! Is my life settling into a time worth remembering, or what?"

I felt the horse beneath me shaking free from the barbs while feeling his wings. It was as though a slave was freed. Free at last! Free at last! I may not have gotten forty acres, but I had the mule for two more weeks. I could gather up the packing crates and whatever else the junkyards had to offer. If I happened to score unemployment then great, it was more money than I needed to live comfortably in the store.

When you get fired you're supposed to feel the world has rejected your very worth. Why was I only feeling that I was on the threshold of discovering it? I walked into my office and said to Zach as he caught up to me, "Now you're really the head man, man. Two more weeks and this place is fuckin' history to me."

Zach appeared unsettled. He may have thought that they were just going to warn me. Maybe Kevin had intended to warn me until I opened my big mouth. It was extraordinary how Zach was able to tap into conversations taking place in the main offices. Come to think of it, I never really asked him what he did in 'Nam.

"Joe, you really helped me here. I ain't never going to forget how you went out on the limb to bring me into this job. You helped me every day when those two upstairs would start runnin' me around with their lyin' and bullshit."

We closed the dispatch office door. Zach lowered his voice and asked, "How do I give them the right answers when they start puttin' me on the spot? Every time it happened before, I always called you and we figured something out together."

My hand fell well short of grasping the girth of Zach's arm as I consoled him. "What's to figure out, Zach? If they needed to know anything at all from me, all I ever told them was the absolute truth. It's the same thing I always told you to tell them whenever you asked me. Truth is the one thing that people like them will never understand. Given that, they can never be the authority in that realm. Those two are so caught up in lying and scamming that they could never figure out my angles especially since I never had any."

Timidly, Zach signaled for me to lower my voice. I did and added, "Their way of figuring is, everybody's got an angle and everybody's lying one way or another. Absolute truth is unknown territory to them. To them, the truth is to say something that might seem believable. If you tell them exactly like it is, no bullshit, they'll probably figure you must be one scam ahead of them. Not only will they listen to you with respect, best of all, they won't bother you."

A slight smile began to break on Zach's face as I continued to bestow the secrets of my limited success upon him.

"You keep this up long enough and they'll turn their backs and leave you alone. Just don't fuck it up like I did."

"Then how should I fuck it up?" With that question as his answer together with the broad grin on his face, I knew he would do fine. He would have the only advice that I could give him to remember me.

"What are you going to do now, Joe? If you're going to go back to teaching flying, you better straighten your shit out, man. Don't be fuckin' around with the drugs you been takin', bein' up in those airplanes!"

"Zach, I don't have a clue about my future. The way I feel about it today, flying is just another job for just a different litter of pigs. Anyway, I did that already. You know, of the five thousand or so flight hours that I logged, only twenty were for pleasure.

"What life's going to be for me now is pure pleasure and seeing what's out there in the world. I want to jump into the big picture and find out how I fit in. Or maybe know for sure, why I should punch out of it."

I felt a surge of rage. Out of respect for Zach, I continued my rant quietly, "One thing is certain. No more being some pig's hit man for what he lacks the fuckin' balls to do himself. I won't go around lying and ripping people off just to put a buck in my pocket and a thousand in Master Jeff's.

Whatever I do out there, I have to take a life's lesson from this hellhole. No more lying! Whatever is on my mind will fall from my mouth. The consequences will become my reality."

Zach looked down the hall. He made sure the door was shut tight, then he asked, "You going to leave it all to me now? How do I pass on the bullshit they tell me upstairs to these guys and stay believable myself? Half of these dudes are my friends now."

I heard the window cleaner's vans pulling into the driveway. I told Zach, "Just keep in mind, half of that half will stay your friends. They'll understand. The rest weren't really friends to begin with. In the end, they'll also see that you were just doing your job. No matter what, just always tell them like it is. You especially gotta be straight with Jamal and the militants; they can be either a shield for you, or a gun pointing at you. If you're being the messenger for bullshit from upstairs, then let it be known that it's not your bullshit.

"Whatever you do, show them that you're the leader. Don't ever let them think that you're weak even when you feel at your weakest."

I heard the sound of the electric garage doors opening, "Excuse me Zach, I have to get back to work." I put my feet on the desk and zoned out on the warrior poster.

The way life was supposed to be at best, at least the way I was taught: Learn from and model yourself after the garden variety of people and life's choices that preceded you, and repeat these patterns from cradle to grave. Get help from the appropriate authority figure along the way when in trouble or doubt. Then jump back on the train to paradise with the rest of the cows.

What if you jump from that moving train? Will the Universe unfold its secrets to you before you hit a tree? Perhaps there's a choice somewhere between the garden variety and the forest variety.

It's interesting if you dwell on a word. After you say it two or three hundred times it can sound really stupid. One word, however, sounded particularly good: adventure!

The flying horses in the poster were carrying their riders toward the place where the horizon and the sky met. Whatever the future held within that line was the advent; of this I was sure. It was not the time to declare any intentions. Instead of figuring where to go, I should see what's coming at me. I had neither wife nor kids. My only brother was busy raising his family. My father had been busy discovering himself since my mother died eight years before. Whatever I did with my life from then on would bring no collateral damage to anyone else. I felt this realization empowering my imagination to take complete charge.

"Zach, if Joe is still down there tell him to come up to my office." I looked at Zach, laughed and then said, "I heard him too, and I know the way." I pointed upward with my middle finger.

Zach slapped me a hard five. I climbed the stairs and saw Kevin nervously waiting for me at the top. He was holding an envelope in one hand and stopping it from shaking with the other. I began to run the rest of the way up the stairs, just to see him jump back.

"Joe, in all fairness to our accounts, my father thinks that maybe you should just leave now. We won't prevent you from collecting unemployment. I said that you could have the car for two weeks. He said that you could have it for one. Bring it back in a week. Here's a paycheck for two months and an open letter of recommendation."

I shook Kevin's clammy little hand, slapped him across the ass and then split.

The instant I shut the car door, I gazed at my journal on the dashboard. Since discovering it, the filling of its blank pages had become an accounting of my commitment to honesty to myself and hopefully to others. Feeling compelled to capture my thoughts of the moment, when freedom declared itself to me, I wrote,

JE

"It all begins here and now. Conventional wisdom has had its last chance with me. I won't try to fault what guided me to this crash. If I were to dwell on what carried me along on the road to my life's past mistakes, I might remain its passenger."

As I was driving home to Brooklyn, a thought occurred to me; throughout my life I always felt a sense of unfulfilled mission. Having been raised in a strict Roman Catholic environment, this concept may have been deeply embedded in my mind.

As a kid, I would read stories about Moses, Christ and other great prophets. There was one thing that each did that most early Native American boys would also do. They would go out into the desert, alone, with only their wits and their will to learn and to survive. From that experience an enlightened visionary might emerge after confronting the Great Spirit. Initially, each seeker may have perceived a different face placed upon this common understanding. But most importantly, they would confront themselves and finally see who they truly were.

I thought, "Why should I live through the shadow of another's vision when I can go and see for myself? And what can possibly be learned of the human experience being bereft of it? Missions such as these don't have to occur in a desert of sand and isolation. If one can look into a single speck of sand and see the Universe unfold, what if I dive into the desert of my unexplored self while remaining in the world's largest village, New York City? Although the whole world has suddenly become open to me, perhaps the greater journey might be to explore that question.

"Had my firing been a precursor to my rite of passage?

Was my channel to a greater understanding all lying ahead of me much like the tollbooth that I just drove through? Shit!" A hand from the booth signaled for me to back up.

"I'm sorry officer; I confused the new Holland Tunnel one-way toll with the Battery Tunnel." Unfortunately, I was at the Battery Tunnel. But fortunately for me, the cop bought the excuse.

I had one week to gather up all of the material from the junkyards. I had to take my stuff from the commune, pay them and live in the store while I continued to work on it. After the car went back, the Harley would be my only transportation. Not wanting the seat of a parked Sportster to become a springboard in the local kid's running track, the store would also serve as its garage.

To think, I was looking forward more to going home to a store filled with old cable reels, rocks and no idea of what it's going to be with more enthusiasm than when I lived in Nina's brownstone. It was her brownstone and her bed. This was my store with my sleeping bag.

When I returned home to the store, I took a large cable reel end and began carving on it. It was September, so I wrote that across the top in various size letters. I kept digging deeper into the wood than usual. I had brought various types of semiprecious stones up from the cellar. Acid bathing them brought out sparkles from the minerals within them. The more I bathed the stones in the acid the more they sparkled. I seemed to be drawn to them as if mesmerized by their cosmoslike effect.

My calf muscle began to tingle as I stared into the stone that I was twisting around between my fingers. When I looked down at my pants, I saw a large hole burned through them exposing another hole developing in the skin of my calf. I poured the rest of my extra light coffee over the wound hoping that the milk would neutralize the acid. The tingling stopped and I returned to the twinkling world within the rock.

I poured glue into the carved letters in the large cable reel side and placed the rock and many other acid-treated stones beside it. They formed the word September's. It was evident only from four points of view. Otherwise it looked like a pile of rocks. Beneath that word, the shading of the wood looked much like an embryo. I highlighted the natural essence of the embryo shape into a large letter C and completed the word Child with the rasp drill placing more glued stones within it.

"Hey woodcarver, what's that you're making?" A lit joint passed over the carving with an introduction, "My name is Rico. Que pasa, mon?"

The diminutive, dark-skinned West Indian began to satisfy his apparent curiosity by both staring at me and seeming to look through me as he absorbed every inch of the store and all that it contained. Was this guy fascinated with the place or was he what Steven had warned me about? He wandered all around the fifteen-by-fifteen feet of the store, admiring the work that I did on the walls and my finished cable reels.

Since he had no apparent attraction to my stereo or any of my closed cartons, I chose to see his interest at face value. With his mental inventory complete, he turned back to me and asked, "Hey, it's really cool what you done here, bro'. But what's that thing you're making now with all the rocks and shit?"

I had no end idea in mind about what I had been working on, only that it felt good to have wood and stone as a day's project rather than lies and deception. I knew that the thing before me looked to be finished, except for maybe a polyurethane coating.

I connected it with my day's events and answered Rico by saying, "It's my birthday cake."

I thought, "It is September and I am a Virgo. So yeah, I can say this with qualification. And if not, then fuck qualification. It is what I say it is."

Since he was looking at me as if I were an idiot, I extended my answer by saying, "I'm celebrating the fact that I will never again work for assholes who decide what I do and what I'm worth. I got fired from my for-shit job today, and I fuckin'earned it!"

Unimpressed, he looked toward the street and said, "Okay, whatever you say, mon, it's a birthday cake. You must be that dude Kenny I hear about. Nobody around here can figure out what you be doin' in this store. Tell me, mon, maybe you make a club like they have here long time ago?"

He took a deep hit from the joint and finger rolled it back to me.

The smoke flowed from his nose while he said, "Every other white dude that took a store in the Slope, they make a big sign and put things in the windows so people know why he there. You, Kenny, are the big mystery mon. You seem like maybe you're trying to be here and no one see you. People want to be unseen, so they get a crib. People want to be seen, so they get a store. You do a little of both, huh?"

I glanced outside where he kept looking. There were a few people waiting for him. One of them was the guy that was on the receiving end of the garbage can. It was then that I recognized Rico's face as the guy that was swinging the can. It would seem as if Rico had the capacity to forgive, or at least to ignore.

Since there was no fruit basket in his hand, I knew this wasn't the welcome wagon. Turn around being fair play, I asked him, "Maybe some people sell things from their cribs, if they do then no big deal. Me, I just like this store. Maybe I'll sell something, if I find something to sell. Maybe I'll just live here and think about it."

His friends began calling to him from outside. He yelled back, "Be cool, mon! I be coming right out." He turned to me, "Maybe I come back again and we talk some more. Later, Kenny."

He dropped a couple of joints on my tabletop and then ran to catch up with his friends. This was the welcome wagon after all! Before Rico entered, while he strolled about and as he left, he kept looking at the hatchway to the cellar. I would have paid it no mind, but it was as though his attention was more on what he couldn't see below than what he appeared to be admiring topside.

JE

"I always had to answer to other people all of my life as if I owed them an explanation. Now I have to make no explanations to anyone for my actions, only to myself. Yogi Berra once said, as only Yogi could say, "*If you come to a fork in the road, then take it*".

"For some reason these words now seem prophetic. Here's the fork. There are the roads. Do I think I have an answer as to which to take? I haven't got a clue. All I can do from this point on is to rationalize my choices or follow my feet. The following my feet notion is becoming more intriguing. What do I have to lose by doing this? Absolutely nothing, because I have nothing, which makes this a truly great start."

"Hey officer, can I take some of this stuff with me?" I yelled to the bewildered armed guard at the dump. I was referring to a steamer trunk, some bags of fur scrap and a bunch of old, wooden wine boxes in the city dump. The guy was guarding garbage with a gun on his hip, so I figured that I better ask permission.

"Who gives a shit? Take all the garbage that you want," he answered as he looked at his buddy while they both laughed at me.

I thought, "Who should be laughing at whom? I'm a completely free man who is filling a car with garbage. They still have some asshole for a boss that makes them guard garbage with a gun."

I made countless trips back and forth. From the store to the junkyard with plaster and debris, then from the junkyard back to the store with material. My project would have a theme. Only industrial scrap and recycled trash would adorn my walls and floors. Was this somehow a self-perception, evolving toward an abstraction of a self-portrait?

Either I had become obsessed with the store or obsessed with the store's obsession. All I wanted to do was to work on bringing whatever obsessed me or it to form. There was a strange force within that place. Somehow it was nurturing my newfound sense of creativity. I had no plan of what to do. My eyes followed my hands and feet. My mind served as a viewing device. At one point, I worked for three days without sleep. It was as if the place was constructing itself, with me as a willing medium.

Since I would work all night, my sleep patterns, if I slept at all, changed. I required sleep for only a few hours during the day. I was becoming a totally nocturnal creature. The neighbors complained about the noise, especially around 3:00 A.M. So I didn't saw wood or hammer then. That would be when I would carve small details with my knife or write in my journal.

I broke down the large crates and nailed them to the floor in the same order that they had been originally. I joined crate piece after crate piece until the entire floor looked like the sides and bottom of a large unfolded packing crate. I maintained the integrity of all of the fragile or this end up markings, and so on with extra 'urethane. The entire floor was covered with a heavy coat of matte polyurethane to match the soft look of the brick walls.

The bar and lower walls were covered with matte-polyurethaned packing crates. This gave the illusion of being within a giant open box. A large cable reel end served as a counter extension with a heavy crate beam above it as a cup hanger.

Everything was done in matte in order to not disturb the shadow effect from the candlelight. The ceiling was covered with large burlap coffee bags that I stapled to it. They retained their authentic markings. I allowed the bags to hang loosely, giving the appearance that they were still full. Within four of the bags hung my quadraphonic stereo speakers; the amplifier turntable and tape deck were set into the bar.

The bathroom walls and floors were tiled with the wooden ends of wine crates. I polyurethaned them so the winery names showed through. I stripped the steamer trunk down to bare wood and metal. Then I shellacked it. One of the boarded-up windows was still bare so I stapled all of the scrap fur to the plywood. In order for the spirit of the transformed trash to dominate, the only lighting, besides candle, was from four twenty-five-watt bulbs rigged to a dimmer and hanging from the ceiling. The bulbs were concealed in fruit baskets that served as shades.

The brands and titles that the corporations had placed upon these objects shined through the polyurethane. They had survived their discarding in a risen form. The overall visual effect of the store together with its sound system was surreal. Each level toward completion began to set the tone for further work.

The room began to take on a life in its own right. It seemed as though the shadows that once danced upon the walls had since lay claim to their positions. They had taken form and became manifested as part of the walls themselves. I began to feel as if the store was becoming more like clothing upon my body rather than a home for it.

Behind the other boarded-up window, I built a loft bed from the heavy beams that connected the sides of the packing crates. Since winter was approaching, I located it at the wall where the chimneystacks from the basement of the adjoining apartment building would heat the bricks.

It was impossible to breathe while working in that small space, unless the door remained open. I would be totally absorbed in my work and turn around only to find some smiling stranger asking something like, “Whatcha doing, Mister?” When your intentions aren't stated and your open door is a storefront, the curious will enter and ask questions. I learned to close off to them most of the time and just perform my task at hand. Somehow that brought even more of them around.

There might be anywhere between one and ten passersby just standing around, watching and taking in the music from my giant speakers. Ordinarily, I said nothing and just worked feverishly. If anyone asked me a question about my intentions for the store, I would turn up the volume. Depending upon my mood, I might answer them, "A carpentry shop," or "A crafts store," or whatever came to mind. One day I looked at the coffee bags hanging from the ceiling and answered, "A coffee house." I was astonished at my reply. But as I thought of it, it seemed like the perfect idea.

"Is September's Child the name of your coffee house?" a young woman asked as she pointed to the birthday cake cable reel hanging on the wall. A crack from the fruit basket cast a beam of light on to the name.

I answered, "September's Child is the name. Yeah, that's a good name for a coffee house." I kept looking at the cable reel, as if to convince myself of my own answer. I wondered if I was realizing what I might have had in mind all along.

I put my drill down and asked her, "What's your name?"

I had seen her walk by everyday around sundown. She would look in and smile as I worked. Then she would go to her building and disappear until the next evening. That night, she finally stopped in to satisfy her curiosity and mine. Her overpowering presence projected a personality of unusual strength. But somehow I felt that it was on the verge of breaking, perhaps from the very weakness it was trying to hide.

"My name is Kathleen; I live next door with Gordon. You might know him, the guy with the two dogs. He's always yelling at them when he takes them up to the park."

I thought, "Oh yeah, the guy who helped me finish my entire bag of reefer the night I discovered the store."

Then I recalled a day when one of his dogs wouldn't sit when he told it to. He pummeled the dog with his fist, stopping only when another dog walker called him a pig.

I answered, "I thought that he was a drill instructor, what with the military get-up and all that. So if those dogs are his recruits, then the park must be boot camp, right?"

She laughed out loud as if to agree with my assessment. Then she lit up a joint and passed it to me. She had a beguiling look about her. I felt that the next level was waiting for our exploration. But she was also my next-door neighbor who was living with some paramilitary dog beater. I knew I had better keep a safe distance.

She said, "This carving looks like a big gate that opens to nothing. Are you going to carve a scene or person on the other side?"

She kept running her fingers through the texture of the wood in my work in progress. Her eyes did the same to my thoughts.

Trying to remain objective, I replied, "I kind of let the objects reveal themselves to me from the faults and the grain of the wood as I carve them. It's difficult to put into words what I see until I'm finished."

I felt a sense of relief since she appeared focused on my carving. Then she replied, "I must say, the results make it seem easy and natural for you to put your thoughts into wood. You know, this figure guarding the gate looks just like that West Indian dude, Rico. You probably see him popping up all over the neighborhood."

I looked at the carved face. She was right. I guessed that it had to look like someone. She started to browse through my cartons of things with a graceful curiosity. She held up a record album and asked, "Can I put this on the turntable?"

The sounds of Malo Santana filled the speakers and reverberated from the walls as she began dancing. She had a quality of style that belonged on a Broadway stage instead of a packing crate floor. There was no joining in on this dance.

She threw every bit of her inner forces into every kick and twist. Her face took on an intensity that was only surpassed by her lunges and splits.

All that I, or anyone for that matter, could do was watch. I suddenly realized that I was not an audience of one. The door had been open all along. A large dog was sitting next to me, as was his even larger, combat fatigue-clad master.

"Kathleen, are you coming upstairs to eat?" he asked.

Then he turned to me with a piercing look from his half-open, lazy eye while his dog alternated between sniffing my pants and staring me down. Appearing every bit combat-ready, he extended his hand and half smiled while his other eye took an inventory of my place.

He asked, "What's happening, Dude? I'm Gordon. Where's the back door?"

"Kenny is making a coffee house from the old club, Baby. He has some dynamite cuts back here in his record box. You don't mind me dancin'down here, do you, Baby?"

He kept looking back and forth at every inch of the store. He realized that the front door was the only possible entrance and exit. As Kathleen tucked in her blouse, he glanced at the loft bed then at the open door.

One eye scanned the store while his lazy-eye focused on me as he said, "I like coffee. Maybe I'll come down some day and check out your best brew."

The checkout that he referred to would only be a continuation. With one eye scanning, he backed out of the store while the other remained fixed on Kathleen.

The cable reels would be the tables. I already had the bar and the sink was there just waiting for a purpose. There was a mattress company down the hill. I bought bundles of scrap filler and stuffed it into bags I got from the coffee importer. Prior to stuffing, the bags were washed in fabric softener. I couldn't have burlap cutting into anyone's flesh. I kept the brand names and country of origin markings on every coffee bag, packing crate and cable reel. The only brand that had been removed was the one that was on my ass.

Each time that I thought of simply polyurethaning a cable reel and just set it down as a table, I would wind up spending untold hours carving a theme or a design into it. Before applying the power drill to the wood, I would squint my eyes and allow an image to reveal itself in the grain. Then I would try to let the form unfold itself to my normal vision with the drill as the medium.

To accent the image after it was carved I scorched the high points on the wood with a blowtorch and then came the poly'. I was sure that I must have eaten something other than sawdust, since many dawns became dusk and vice-versa, all to my non-realization. My hair and beard became longer. My clothes became baggier. All of that was irrelevant. I was a living element in a work of art.

My father stood at the door. He had a smile on his face and a glimmer in his eyes. He stayed by the entrance taking in the feeling of my nearly completed creation of a coffee house.

He asked, "Did you do all of this yourself Joe, er, uh, Ken?"

He made every attempt to acknowledge my recent choice of name. Strange though, prior to my becoming known as Ken, Dad would always address me as, "Bob, er, uh, Joe," Bob being my older brother's name. Name changes were a shared experience for us since my father had long ago chosen to be called by his middle name, Otis. His given first name was Joseph, just like mine.

I explained to him everything that had happened. The smile of approval never broke from his face. Strange, no matter how old you get, you always feel like the judgment of a parent is pivotal when making your own.

Dad looked the place up and down and said, "I have to bring your brother over to see this. It's really great what you've done in here. I never knew that you could do this kind of stuff, what with the flying and the executive thing at the maintenance company. Oh by the way Joe-er, uh, Ken, call Kevin at the job. There was a message for you on my answering machine-recorder."

"Holy Shit, I forgot to return the car! I'm probably three or four days late!"

He laughed and said, "Look, you can't do it now. It's dark already. Let's go eat and then I have to go. We'll take my car. It's parked in front. Joe-er, Ken, you drive. I have no idea where we are, never mind where we're going."

I got behind the wheel of his Chevy. I had always been a neat freak and Dad was not. I immediately began straightening things as soon as I sat down.

"Joe, don't throw that leaf away! Here, give it to me," he said as he took the old dried maple leaf from me and placed it back on the dashboard. Then he looked at me. The greatest expression of composure and resolve that I had ever seen in him was radiating from his face.

He grabbed my hand and said, "Joe, that leaf is just like I am. It has finished its cycle and it is now entering its next phase. Don't be concerned about me. I'm fine about everything."

Before I could say anything, he smiled at me and pointed ahead. Then with his unending look of serenity he said just one word, "Drive."

We had supper in The Economy Restaurant at Seventh Avenue and Union Street. The rain had become heavy. I guess he remembered how I was always unprepared for weather events, so he laughed and handed me an umbrella. I held it over myself as I watched his brake lights flash two times, highlighting his good-bye as he drove away. I continued to look down the street until his lights blended into the blur of traffic.

I felt as though I had made a commitment by saying that the store was to become a coffee house. Was I ready to be a businessperson? One thing that I was sure of, I was a lousy businessperson. The thought of people being set apart from one another's humanity by virtue of money and material had become appalling to me. The concept of money had gone beyond determining net worth and claimed to define Humankind's worth.

JE

"This storefront living space might give me the greatest opportunity to sort things out and understand my own self and my relationship to others. I have to allow myself to get in touch with what now seems to drive me. The best thing is to do what I am drawn to, without question. If I allow my mind to open to what is now unfolding, I may become even more enriched by the experiences to come than by what has so recently occurred.

"On the other hand, I could blindly follow these feelings to my own demise. But who ever said that the best lessons in life were simple or that survival was guaranteed? I now salivate at the thought of the adventure of seeing my own worth through this effort. If I go for the business route all I might learn is the value of locks."

I couldn't recall another period in my life, except for a sliver of time between toilet training and kindergarten, when I felt so creatively inspired. During both times I would gather up scraps of this and that and apply color. Then I would bang different shapes together, stand back and bear witness to thought becoming form.

The commonality of these two times seemed to be imagination utilizing only what materials are immediately available to manifest a vision. The more success I had from this force, the more disdain I had for the inclusion of things gotten from money in my efforts or even in my life. The total monetary investment in the store at that point was forty dollars for tools and miscellaneous materials. The rest was trash, although rearranged to appear as art. To place a financial value on any of this was antithetical to my intent in this endeavor.

The only value that could be placed on anything that I had done in that tiny place was: It was as transitory as were the thoughts that inspired the work. To truly grasp the worth of any single work of mine, one would have to appreciate the creation that preceded it and that which followed. Since everything in the store was inspired by everything else, each piece must be seen as a component of a work in progress as was the willing tool, me.

Mirrors could only reflect what was already there. Photographs might only show what may have been there. My perception looked to the distance to that which was unfolding before me. If I needed sanction in the form of appreciation for any of my work, then the look of admiration in the eyes of the beholders of my results was reward enough.

Found in September's Child's guest sketch book

Chapter Five

Sovereignty

"When is the coffee house opening, Mister? Is this place going to be like The Machine coffee house?" The gentle whispers of my muse would be overwhelmed by such shouts of annoyance from the ever-curious as I sat in front of the store carving my cable reels. I made a sign on a piece of wood with letters of melted polyester; all it said was SOON. I would point to it whenever I didn't want to talk or if I might never want to talk to who was asking.

It was to be the last warm day in November. Grand Funk's "Closer to Home" blasted away on the stereo inside the store. I carved away in the autumn light, getting closer to a fulfilled vision on a cable reel. The rasp bit began to render a completed form just as the Sun was blocked by an alien entity that asked, "I'd like to buy that table that you're making. How much do you want?"

The Sun was fully eclipsed by the unwelcome body of obstruction. His face began to reveal itself as my eyes adjusted to the light. From the picture of a space man on his t-shirt reading, Far Out Man, to his blow-dried hair, to his designer sandals, to the painted-faced female on his arm. It seemed that what was before me was an outward display of inner shallowness.

I asked myself, "How can people that transparent still obstruct my light?"

I looked back at the carved cable reel, then back at the two of them. Pulling my hair aside, I asked, "You, want to buy this?"

The two of them nodded and giggled. Then she said, "Buy it for me, Andre!"

I thought about how I had lost an entire sleep cycle, missed perhaps a day's worth of meals and not cleaned myself for two in the making of this table.

I glanced back and forth between her and him and said, "You would put money in my hand and walk away with this creation of mine? That's what you're both saying?"

They nodded yes, and then the girlfriend said, "We have the perfect place for it."

I answered, "You do? I thought that I did."

I blew away the sawdust from where I had just finished and focused on a scalloped design near the cable holes. I remembered that while working with the grain of the wood near the hole, my carving bit hit a knot and smashed the design. I tried to reproduce the original scheme and in doing so discovered an entirely different direction to take not only for this piece but, beyond that, for my art form itself.

In some way, after that experience, I felt that this particular sculpture described my place in the Universe, albeit esoterically. I realized through that accident that every entity, micro- or macrocosmic, is itself a unique perception of time and space in an eternal expression understood by mortals only through the magic of art.

I thought, "How the hell can these Bloomingdale's weekend hippies be asking, how much? Maybe so they can present my efforts to their friends as their own, and place beer coasters or their fuckin' feet on my greatest spiritual moment."

I answered, "Five hundred dollars! If you want this piece, it's five hundred dollars," I said as I half raised my head.

Peering through my curtain of hair, I noticed Rico approaching from inside the store where he had almost become a fixture. In between carving and writing, I would brush up on my karate with him. He would tell me that "White boys are too damn uptight and rigid to be a match for a brother." It didn't bother me; I enjoyed the physical release of energy from working out with him.

Rico had been practicing his flying kicks, using my birthday cake as a focal point. He said that he felt energized by it in spite of the honkey music in the store. Although the stereo was at nearly full volume, he heard me talking money and came out for some Sun. Rico stood off to the side, listening as the negotiations went on.

The girlfriend tugged at Andre's goatee and said, "Honey, if that's his price, then buy it. I'm sure that he will take a check."

"By the way, who should I make it out to?" asked the invisible man.

I looked at the dude, and then I looked at Rico looking at me as he shrugged.

I rose from my stool and asked, "Check? Did you say a check? A check that's backed up by money that has the audacious declaration, In God We Trust, printed by a government that has no appreciation of any of those names forming the statement written upon it? The same government that suddenly declares a decades-long archenemy as a needed trading partner, after watching thousands of its young men die at the hands of this new bedmate!"

After a hit, from the ever burning, I passed the joint back to Rico and shouted, "Sir, I demand gold! No, I demand gold bullion! Yes, only gold bullion and it must be from . . . The Netherlands!"

Andre and his girlfriend couldn't get away fast enough. Rico slapped me five as we laughed our heads off. Then he grabbed my hand in mid-slap and said, “Kenny, the dude want to give you five hundred bucks! You gotta be fuckin' crazy, mon. Five hundred bucks and you turn him down and make like you're a radical.”

Rico lit another joint and fell back on the coffee bags, perplexed. I knew that what I was about to say would make no sense to a guy who was living day to day from the street.

I said it anyway, “A year ago this cable reel was rotting behind a factory in New Jersey. Now it's worth whatever I say it is, only because I turned half of it into sawdust and the other half into pictures. If he comes back, I'll raise the price and he'll probably be willing to pay it because he knows he can't have it. How is it that trash suddenly becomes treasure because someone puts a face on it? I could make two or three of these a week and sell them. But what would that make me?”

Rico turned ever so slowly to face me. There was no telling what could come from his mouth. He wasn't one to initiate conversation, his style was more to observe, and then respond. If his response was in words, then you knew where you stood, if it was otherwise you might not be able to stand.

He had been deposited on the street years ago as a child. His parents fled back to their country in Central America for reasons still unknown. He kept himself alive living in basements and in the park. A Jamaican couple later took him in for a few years. He was drawn back to where he felt best, the street.

He said, “As I see it, maybe it make you rich, mon. How can you turn that shit down? You let that sucker walk away. You made him run away! You one fucked up dude, Kenny.”

He had to sell about five pounds of pot to clear what I just scared away. Come to think of it, a few months ago I had to work my ass off, kissing ass for that. What price progress?

JE

"As I watch the shadows from the candlelight dance upon the walls of this soon-to-be coffee house, I can't help but to be drawn to my birthday cake hanging above the pillows. So much of my self is etched within those grains. The stones that form September's Child bring images not only to my mind but also to others. They say that when they stand before it, they too sense images and experience a strange effect from the piece. In each person's case, however, the images are different, as is the effect.

"Gazing at the word Child in the carving, I'm reminded of a recurring vision that I've had throughout my life. I am naked in a frozen field. Gray clouds begin to blend into a snowy horizon. I remain motionless. The snow removes all definition between land and sky. It is the same in every direction about me. I feel the icy grip of the driving snow surround my body. The cold begins to force the life from me. Sensing my impending demise, I cause myself to change back to my waking state by placing my hands over my temples and screaming, No!

"When I awaken, I imagine that perhaps diving through the blurring line of the disappearing horizon might be another option, an option that I avoid over and over again.

"Was the reason for the recurrence of this vision or thought symbolic of my fear of the unknown? Was it possibly a way of showing me my own avoidance of experiencing it or experience itself? The thought that an option might be available within the vision intrigues me. Must I await the vision, or await the option in some other form?

If I were thrust into a living situation where I had nothing but only my wits against the elements, as the vision might imply, could I survive the test? I wouldn't necessarily have to be naked in the cold, wet snow, would I?"

"Are you ever going to fix up the outside of this place, Kenny?" asked Danny the Flick after knocking at the door three times, then two. He was a walking hairball, loaded with questions and spare time. Danny liked movies, but not as much as he liked pot. You couldn't call him Danny the Pot so everyone went with the second option.

The front of the building was just as it was when I took it over. I had not opened the store as a coffee house, but there was coffee and everyone served themselves then dropped fifty cents in a jar to replace what was used. The idea of business for business' sake still didn't appeal to me. I just wanted to hang out and observe this unique perspective of life.

I explained to Danny, "I let in who I want and when I want to let them in. If I attracted attention by fixing up the place then it might be overrun by the world. I haven't decided what I'm doing here yet." I pointed to the SOON sign. Danny sat down.

Observing the way people would react to the environment was giving me a new perception. The absence of structure was allowing me to view humanity in a way that I never imagined possible. The essence within the coffee house had a way of drawing the dreams and fantasies from all who entered. The surreal was dominating the ordinary.

One great thing about the 'seventies, it was very much an extension of the 'sixties, much like the people who also grew from that magical era. Exceptional behavior had become commonplace. Ten years of social change had opened the minds of people everywhere in the process. The streets of Park Slope had become a hippie Mecca, filled with mostly young people, like myself, in search of something beyond themselves.

There was a strong diversity in both ethnicity and interests in the commune dwellers and coffee house clientele. The people that stopped in to hang out at my store were a mix of street people, writers, musicians and various types of artists. I might leave the stereo blasting and allow folks to wander in. It was as though my social efforts of the past had reversed. Instead of going out to hear music and find people, I would just stack the turntable, turn the volume to full, open my door and they found me.

When I wanted to be alone, I would lock the door. Those who knew the secret knock also knew that no response meant, please go away. Being alone in the store somehow felt like being inside my own backpack among all of the interesting stuff that I might gather on a journey. During that time I would commune with the creative force growing within me and write in my journal or carve wooden things. Or not be completely alone.

I began feeling a great sense of personal empowerment when either carving or writing. Each form of expression brought me to creative areas of my self that, until then, were never realized. Until the coffee house, I saw myself as either a pilot or an executive. In each case a servant of others. For the first time in my life, I was functioning completely at an intuitive level, serving only my whims. It made me want more.

Since the journal happened into my life, I had begun writing poetry. It was just simple verse, for-my-eyes-only stuff. Whenever an idea struck me, I would drop whatever else I might be doing and pursue it. Unfortunately, I might do this in the middle of a sentence, often the other person's. The people who came there had learned to expect this of me. When I did this, they would just continue talking with one another. I might get lost in a thought or a project for hours or days without surfacing.

I had to take three different trains each way once a week when I went to New Jersey for my unemployment checks. Each check that I received felt like one of twenty-six pieces of sand programmed to fall through an hourglass and crash upon my face, as I stood helplessly below.

I thought, "Am I to be defined by the remaining checks due to me? Will I, one day, have to depend on the coffee house to support myself when the last piece of sand falls and turns it into nothing but a vending machine with me serving as its pull-handle? Worst of all options, will I return to the commuter world and again be someone's pawn?"

The blackness of the PATH tunnel was replaced by the bleak industrial panorama of New Jersey as the speeding train emerged and surfaced, hurrying toward Jersey City like a silvery serpent with its willing prey seated in its bowels. I wiped the frost from the glass and looked out of the window.

The trees were like leafless skeleton hands crawling across the deathly gray sky. Their ghostly fingers scratched at the clouds above, the falling snow enveloping all remaining color. The late autumn freeze set it all into eternalness, my frozen breath upon the glass erasing it from my mind.

The clouds were beginning to break on the horizon. Magenta and golden rays of hope pierced the otherwise austere setting. A winged horse with its mounted warrior flew through the opening to the warmth of better things.

The train stopped at Hoboken, one station before the unemployment office in Jersey City. A sense of panic came over me. I jumped off the train and began pacing up and down the platform. I tried to gather my thoughts as I sat on a bench. All I could hear were the sounds of commuter's feet echoing through the cavernous station as they raced to their destinations. Covering my ears from the cold, I closed my eyes. I then could only hear the echoes of my thoughts as they raced toward further confusion.

I saw the tracks leading to Jersey City and my weekly dole. I looked in the opposite direction. The tracks went off into the empty horizon. I looked again toward the direction of Jersey City. The yellowing Hoboken sign hung before me like a large state-issued check, the check that Eddie never got because I was lured into lying by Roger's blood money.

Much to the astonishment of my fellow travelers I yelled, No! I cupped my hands around my mouth and screamed at the top of my lungs, "Fuck money! Fuck money!"

The echoes within the station and the bewildered looks about me sanctioned my statement to the nothingness that surrounded me about the worthlessness before me.

Had my ever-emerging true self again declared itself through righteous rage?

I thought, "Like a penny flattened on a train track, my soul will not become the same at the end of the line! I will not hear the whistle and march into an H.G. Wells void only to join the unenlightened Elois and be processed as sustenance for the mindless Morlocks!"

A feeling of freedom through defiance filled my being as the train entered the blackness of the tunnel, piercing the horizon, returning me to the Brooklynite.

JE

"You don't always decide to take a leap of faith. Sometimes you will see yourself in the leap itself, perhaps on a winged horse or on a train. Money has always been the device to settle issues in life. If a problem arises, throw money at it. Must it always be concluded that he who has the greatest amount of money has the fewest tribulations? Conversely, does he with the least money the most?

"Would the elimination of all material in one's life including money reveal the true uncontested self to itself? Would one perish from these circumstances or gain powers not yet realized? If the window opened for this opportunity, would I hold a tether line or leap free to the unknown?

"Is this trash surrounding me in its resurrection from the scrap heap daring me to make the same journey that it made? Must I venture into the human equivalent, or am I already there? What force, beyond me or within me, might reconstruct me as I did the trash, and if so into what? Why does the page that I am writing upon sometimes bring the word to my pen?

"Today I abandoned the security of money and felt liberated in doing so. Do I possess the courage to continue the process until I am without resources or direction? Must shedding the objects that I once valued be a somber, dull experience, or can it be like a New Orleans marching band dancing its way to the graveyard gates?

"Who were you who placed this upside-down card as a bookmark among these empty pages? Who is this man pictured in the card whose eyes are covered by his helmet? How can he stand in a chariot with his arms at his side, his face looking forward, confident of his direction though not attached to it in any physical way? Why do the horses appear to be pulling the vehicle in different directions under the guidance of this faceless, unconnected being?"

"Why didn't you ever do anything like this for us when we lived together?" asked Nina while looking at all that I had done not with admiration but with burning jealousy. She had finished dressing for her walk home from my coffee house.

I threw a shirt over my shoulders and a hammer at the door to stop the people outside from knocking. Then I answered, "You would have wanted me to decorate your brownstone in industrial garbage? Knowing you, Nina, you would probably put "Halston" labels on the packing crates and tell your friends that you paid through the nose for them. You made it clear that the brownstone was your home. It's quite clear that this is mine."

How things had gone full circle. There I was, the sudden meeting that she told her new lover that she couldn't miss, just like she did with her husband when I first met her. I knew that night that the last link to her had been broken. If the excitement of sex with someone diminishes to foreplay before taking a piss, it's time to leave that lid shut.

The silver lady that hung from my neck had stolen the last hit of coke from the painted lady that hung out in my store. Her overpriced fur wrap lay beneath the scraps of animal remains that hung on my wall. I pointed to them and commented, "What irony."

She looked at her wrap and asked, "What?"

I lay across the top of my Sportster and lit up a smoke. She carefully placed her six gold chains around her neck, and then talked about things she understood, "So, when are you going to be open for business? I want to bring Arlene and the gang to see this place. It's really groovy."

She took her purse and headed for the bathroom. Totally missing the beauty of the wine crates, she shouted, "Where the fuck is your mirror? I have to put my face on!"

If she has to put her face on, then what the hell was stuck on her head that I've been looking at and talking to? That's all I need, her gang of kinky, sex-from-a-manual, Quaalude-crazed, weekend bed-hoppers fucking one another all over my pillows. Imagine, my coffee house being the set for Revenge of the Body Crabs Part II.

An epiphany exploded from my mouth to her ear, as well as my own, when I yelled, "This isn't a business like other places you might think of. It is, by design, an anti-business statement! Don't you fuckin' get it, Nina? September's Child's sole purpose is to fail as a business and then go down the drain while I go into orbit."

I thought, "That's what this place is, it's like a glider landing on a distant D-Day beach, whose sole purpose was to crash while its warrior cargo escapes to the unknown. I've created a vehicle to take me to who the fuck knows what or when."

While staring at the ceiling's coffee bags, basking in the light of my inspiration, Nina, immersed in the mundane, said, "Leave it to you Joe, this could be such a money maker. You could put paintings and works of art on the walls and sell them while people drink gourmet coffees and teas.

"There is great gallery potential here too. The cups and plates could be from top craftspeople. They could be sold to the customers after they ate and drank from them. The customers could describe a theme and have a custom cable reel carved for their living rooms. There are so many ways to make money with this. The whole look of this place is very marketable. Arlene just got a job at a New York magazine; she could do a feature on 'Brooklyn's Little Hidden Treasure.' People will be beating down the door. How could this fail?"

She was ironing her hair with her hands while visions of dollar signs danced in her eyes. Whatever value Nina might find here would quickly be drained and discarded like a used lover when something that appeared better fell into her sights.

With my head still wobbling from my mind-burst, I said while straddling the seat on my bike, "First of all, the only thing that beats this door down is the front wheel of my Harley when I don't feel like using the fuckin' key!

"Secondly, Nina, you always fail to understand anything outside of your myopic inner visions. What if I don't really want to succeed as a business here? What if I only want to experience the success of failure as a business? If my goal was to fail at business and I succeed at that, the reward would be in a form that can't be money. Nina, you're not hearing anything I say, are you?"

She cocked her head sideways as she studied the marketability of refinished steamer trunks. As usual, her ears were blocked by her opinions.

I waved my hand at her in disgust and said, "When you see the For Rent sign on the door, talk to Benny about claiming all of the salable crap inside. Then you can bring it all home with you and see it for the shit that it is in the daylight."

She looked at her watch and opened the door. Kathleen was standing outside about to knock. "Hi Kenny, can I come in?" asked Kathleen.

"Good-bye, Joe. I'll let myself out," said Nina.

"Who's Joe? I don't see anyone else in here. Did I interrupt anything?" asked Kathleen while she perused the crime-scene then peeked in the bathroom.

I answered, "No Kathleen, it was interrupted a long time ago by a blinding flash of reason and an even stronger sense of self-preservation. And by the way, to explain Joe would take a lifetime."

The door clicked shut. Standing behind Kathleen, like an aura of Wonder Woman less the crown, stood an incredibly massive female form. Kathleen, together with her shadow, headed directly for the turntable and said, "I've got to put the Malo record on. I can only get the steps right in here. It's strange, maybe it's the lighting that does it, but there's a whole crazy energy thing happening to me here. By the way Kenny, this is my friend Lana. She's a go-go woman at a bar in Jersey City. You're from Jersey, right?"

The tattooed rising fist on Lana's partially exposed breast was a dead give-away. Apparently she was a victim of conflict of movement.

Lana said nothing. I looked dead into her impassive eye and said, "Let me guess Lana, you're a feminist but you have to make a living."

Lana's gentle Jane Fonda-like face was offset by an ever-present Marlboro that replaced her missing lower tooth. Ashes and smoke flew from her face as she finally answered, "If you call dancing in front of a bunch of drunken, old-horn dogs while they try to grab your ass every five seconds a living, yeah, then that's what I do."

A knife was beginning to take form within the tattooed fist.

"But that's not all that you do, is it?" I asked.

"No, I work at the Women's Center before my night job. I teach preschoolers at the single parents' day care program for women while they're at their jobs. Kathleen! Throw your leg higher and hold your arms outward, and then you go into a split."

Somehow Lana made Kathleen uneasy as she danced. She stopped dancing and looked meekly toward Lana while she used my counter as a stretching bar.

The door flew open and we heard, "Why don't you show her how it's done Lana? You're the pro. Or can't you dance with your clothes on?"

Kathleen's music had drawn Gordon out from his lair. When he came in and saw me sitting and talking with Lana, he smiled in a most curious way.

Kathleen became increasingly uneasy as Lana said, "Why don't you eat your own shit Gordon, or go back to the park where your fuckin' dog left a fresh load. It wouldn't be the first thing that you ate from that dog."

I felt certain that Lana knew the reason behind the screams that I would hear coming from Gordon's apartment after Kathleen came home. Gordon needed to change the subject, so he turned to me as his next victim and asked, "When is this coffee house ever going to open, Kenny? You keep working on the place. People are here all the time, it seems like there's a party every night. Maybe you need a business partner to give you a little push. Did you ever consider that?"

It was my turn to change the subject. I handed him a cup of Mocha Java and said, "The door hasn't been locked any time you've tried to open it, Gordon. You're drinking a cup of coffee right now, as you must have noticed. So, what's to open?"

Lost in banter with Gordon, I failed to notice the place filling with others. Rico danced his way toward Kathleen while giving a taunting look at Gordon. Danny stacked records on the turntable. Mark, a refugee from the defunct Machine Coffee House, began his orangutan dance with anyone he could find, real or imagined. Although Gordon had his ear to me his eyes were elsewhere, engulfed with flames of jealousy.

While Rico was getting closer to Kathleen, Gordon snapped to me, "So, like when the fuck are you really going to open and be a business once and for all? How the hell do you expect people to come in here and buy coffee with a motorcycle taking up the whole fuckin' floor? And when the hell are you going to get a fuckin' clock in this fuckin' joint?"

I answered, "Since I don't have to report for unemployment anymore, who needs clocks or calendars? If I need to know the date, I can get a newspaper."

"Bullshit! You never have newspapers or magazines in here other than National Lampoon. You don't even have the radio on, just your fuckin' records and tapes."

Before I could answer Gordon, he leaped up and grabbed Kathleen by the hand. With her securely in tow, they headed for the outside as Kathleen expressed a look of meek compliance. She gave Lana a last glance then held her hand up to her in a halting gesture. Lana crashed down on a pillow beside me, crossing her arms and looking away.

After the door slammed shut, their shouting faded as they neared their apartment. Lana could hardly restrain herself and shouted, "That fuckin' macho bastard!"

It seemed that she felt as if she had to defend Kathleen from Gordon's temper while it must have been becoming more and more difficult to control her own. I returned to my reefer and to my thoughts prior to the psychodramatic traffic jam that had occurred and somehow cleared itself from my little room. My self-indulgence diverted me from reacting to the kidnapping that had taken place.

With dance music and the conversations of others fading from my perception, a realization came to me that I hadn't watched television for months. I thought, "Media in any form is a distraction from life's occurrences. The Media is a device with no other purpose but to place everyone on its schedule of corporately motivated messages of consumerism. Awareness of any subject matter should not be limited to half-hour intervals interspersed with propaganda. Pure life relationships can be accomplished only through interpersonal experience rather than a sound byte followed by a laugh track."

So I was not totally isolated, "Cheech and Chong" albums provided insightful situation comedy. "National Lampoon Magazine" gave me all the news of the world that I needed. Both were without commercial interruption. One of the nightly passersby was an editor for "National Lampoon" and brought me copies of every issue published.

My reverie was interrupted by, "Kenny, are you just going to Bogart that joint and stare at the fuckin' wall or are you going to hand it to me and give me some answers while you're at it?"

I handed the joint to Lana. Her exhaled pot smoke filled my face, accompanied by her saying, "I hate to agree with that bastard, Gordon, but like no clocks? How do you know when it's time to close?"

Since we were sharing a smoke, I shared some of the thoughts that she just interrupted me from having, "In order to close, I would have had to open, wouldn't I?"

She flashed a cynical smile and showed a clenched fist to me, then asked, "Was that a door that I came through or a fuckin' rabbit hole? The next thing I know you'll be standing on your fuckin' head. No fuckin' clocks, no fuckin' television? You don't even have a fuckin' mirror in the bathroom. How do you know how you fuckin' look, Kenny?" Lana pressed her face to mine, seeking answers.

Maybe my reply was too esoteric for her when I said, "If I want to know how I look, I can see myself by the expression in the eyes of others. A mirror merely reflects and reinforces one's own delusional opinion."

Lana smiled as she held her bewildered gaze at me. When I saw her sarcastically wiping the corner of her eye, I could only think, "This has got to be the total anti-Nina!" Besides possessing a completely unsocial attitude tempered with bluntness verging on rudeness, we probably had one hell of a lot in common.

I found out how much we did have in common when she replied, "Kenny, you're so full of shit that it's beginning to pour out of your mouth. Just a little word to the wise, don't go laying that fuckin' rap that you just played on me on Kathleen. When that peach falls from the tree, it's gonna be mine to catch, bro'."

She leaned down and kissed me on the forehead, then looked up to the ceiling, laughing. The night's dancing and melodramas slowly faded into my early morning's writings as sleep approached with the rising sun. I would await the homeward bound sounds of the working world or whoever might pound on my door to awaken me.

Each evening with the setting sun, I would think, "Is this the day that I walk off, or is this another night to stay and party?" At night the door would blow open. I would not walk off since a party would somehow walk in.

One late afternoon, Danny the Flick held up an ancient record album. Through his mountain of black hair he asked, "Any of you dudes ever listen to Olatunji?"

"What the fuck an Olatunji, mon?" Rico replied as he headed outside with a bag to sell in hand.

The entire room was soon filled with the sounds of "Drums of Passion" by an African percussion group and its leader, Olatunji. The needle met the disk. The words, "Jingo-lo Jingo-Bah," grew louder and louder as they soon matched the level of the incessant, mesmerizing drumming.

Overcome by the sound of the drums, Danny brought the volume up to full then he faked a challenge at me with a volley of kicks and punches. I responded back at him and we were then sparring to the music while others, who filled the coffee house, danced and chanted to the hypnotic beat.

Again, the door swung open. An empty-handed Rico entered and saw us sparring. He ran back outside then re-entered with a conga drum around his neck. He joined in with the record as we all sang, "Jingo-lo Jingo-Bah," over and over. It must have meant something incredible in Swahili, because singing it and dancing to it was all that everyone in the room could do.

Since the door had remained open and Rico took the drum from his friend, who was jamming with a group of drummers on the corner, they all followed the music and found their way inside. Suddenly, there was wall-to-wall drumming. The center of the packing crate dance floor was filled with people dancing and sparring, all done to the sounds of "Jingo-Lo Jingo-Bah" and the combined passion of at least six local drummers.

I seemed to be the only one who realized that the record had ended. Its legacy not only continued by way of the local talent, but it intensified. We all danced, sparred, drummed and sang. People returning from work poked their heads inside. By the time they passed the store, they too were dancing. The entire street soon filled with at least two hundred people, all dancing to the sounds of "Jingo-Lo Jingo-Bah". Car hoods and roofs became the brothers of the drum.

Rico pointed his finger at me and yelled, "You!"

He threw his drum back to its owner. Rico flew forward and landed in front of me in fighting stance. He shouted right into my ear as the music grew toward a fevered pitch, "Yo Kenny, c'mon and show me your shit. It be time for no mercy, white boy! I gonna fuck you up bad, mon!"

Rico was a black belt in Shoto-Kan Karate. He had taken me on as a full-time project. I represented a challenge. For his endeavors, he could crash at the store when there was no other place available. He seemed very adept in setting the basement up as an instant pad. He had his own mattress and we ran a work light to keep him from bumping into things. I would have my privacy with whomever upstairs. He would let himself in and out through the hatch, unnoticed.

I came close to beating him once or twice or so he allowed me to believe. It was at that point that the lesson kicked in. It always began with, "Hey you, uptight New Jersey white boy!"

Everyone in the coffee house would then scatter for shelter, although the punches and kicks were meant only for one another. We were known to use home-made nunchucks that sometimes broke apart without warning.

Did the drums evoke a demon within him? I didn't know if he was serious about fucking me up or why he would even want to. I didn't know that this was just another lesson in attitude until he said to me, "Go with the drums, mon! Don't think. Just let the beat take you to the fight."

Before I could begin to think or before I could decide whether or not there was any choice, a blinding volley of kicks came at me so I countered them. As I did this, the drumming seemed to grow louder and somehow more personal as if it was being focused on me. The speed and fury of his combinations left me no choice but to cease seeking options. I threw volition aside. I felt nothing but the drums drawing movement from within me to my hands and feet as they blended in combat with those of Rico's.

Time became irrelevant. There was only the frenetic drumming, as moments became the space between the beats filled with the endless wall of chanting. Together, they seemed to penetrate me to the core of my persona. I felt as though my spirit was awakened from a trance as my body exploded over and over with spontaneous responses to Rico's attacks. I was void of thought yet my awareness had gone beyond what once were the boundaries of self.

In a frozen moment that seemed an eternity, Rico glowed red with energy before me. His form seemed to blend with his reddened aura. It was as if all of the energy within the room imploded toward him. It and his voice then became a screaming vortex followed by the focused thrust of his leg as his foot flew toward my face. I felt an explosion recoil from my arm then through my entire body. I then saw his failed flying kick locked in my hand.

As quickly as the kick came, it pulled away, while Rico spun in mid-air landing in a cat like stance. My forearms and shins began to announce their presence with the pain from blocked punches and kicks. The sweat puddled on the floor beneath my face as I rested my hands on my trembling knees. Rico clenched his fists and half bowed while maintaining a fixed stare at my eyes. I reciprocated the gesture. Neither of us had hit the other. I was grateful that it was only a much-needed lesson.

Rico ran outside looked to the sky and yelled, "Hey, mon! I think I see a ghost of a white boy flying back to New Jersey. Maybe he gonna crash 'cause his wings got too uptight."

The drummers had settled down to basic accompaniment of the dance music that Danny had put on the turntable. The intensity of the Olatunji-inspired karate drum fest was apparently appreciated only by the two combatants who were slapping five and howling, "Fuckin' incredible, mon!" and the drummers themselves. I looked and saw that the street emptied and a whole new crowd had developed in the coffee house itself. Rico and I were soaked in sweat as we laughed and mimicked Mark's orangutan dance.

"Cut the shit guys! How can a guy dance in here with all that Kung Fu shit going on?" said Mark with his eye riveted on a young girl named Karen's ass. Although he thought that she was dancing with him, it looked more like she was running from him.

"I thought you was killin' roaches, mon. You mean to tell me you was dancin'?" Rico laughed and high fived Danny. They started dancing like orangutans with Mark.

I switched to "Dark Side of the Moon," to mellow out the situation. The drummers cried out in protest and headed for the door, saying, "That psychedelic shit's too whitebread for us!" Heading for the door, they said, "Later, mon."

The lunatic became firmly entrenched in our heads from the cloud that had developed above them. Kathleen and Lana were slow dancing together in a manner that only professionals could. All yielded the tiny floor to them and watched with delight while they performed beneath the room's dim lights. Kathleen seemed more relaxed since Gordon's wandering eye had landed him and his lazy eye somewhere in the East Village for that night and who knew how many more.

"Why that dude sittin' on the floor with his coat bouncin' up and down to the music, mon? Rico asked while pointing to a guy who neither of us knew that was sitting under the loft, fixated on Lana and Kathleen. Kathleen also noticed and danced over to the stranger. His coat throbbed with increasing frequency as she approached him. He looked up her leg, then to her breasts as she lowered her head toward his. His jaw lowered, his eyelids drooped and his eyes began to roll back into his head.

She looked him square into his enamored yet startled eyes and said, "I certainly do feel flattered that you would select me as the focal point of your expression through the masturbatory arts. Please take note that upon ejaculation, slippery conditions may result that would require the need for maintenance personnel that are unavailable to us at this time. Thank you for your consideration to this matter."

Having been denied the act of showering attention upon Kathleen in the method that he preferred, the stranger in the long coat showed both of his hands and applauded her instead.

"Karen and I are going to split back to my building for a massage," said Mark with young Karen in hand, "Check you out later, Kenny. Fuck you, Rico!"

Rico was lying back, smoking one. He then turned to Mark and said, "I hope that you killed plenty of roaches, mon, just in case you get hungry later." With that remark, Mark ran outside with Karen.

Rico shook his head and said, "With all that dude's money and women, no one knows why he be fuckin' around with those young runaways. He goin' to lose his building and his business. This one, she told me she be twenty. Maybe she get younger after he give her massage. You wait an' see. He do somethin' stupid."

The coffee house had plenty of life for a dying business. People would come in after the clubs closed in the city. I left a large drawing pad and colored pencils on my trunk where artists would log their impressions of September's Child. Musicians tried new stuff out if they wanted. Most of the time they just kicked back and jammed until the Sun rose while I envisioned the march to the graveyard gates in acoustic.

Vera, a clerk-typist by day, street person after dark, had been half under my quilt for most of that night. There must have been an unwritten rule saying that any woman under the quilt with me when the music stopped remained when the door was locked. Vera held the other half of the blanket out to me whenever I left the dance floor.

Vera's knees rose alternately beneath the quilt as her jeans worked their way to her ankles. In the same moment the door closed on the last person to leave, it reopened to reveal Karen's face as she returned from Mark's massage in record time. She locked the door, walked directly over to Vera and myself, stroked my face gently and then worked her way into the quilt with us. She appeared to fancy the idea of the two of us becoming the three of us.

Vera looked across my face to Karen's and said, "I brought only two wine glasses, maybe you can take the rest of the bottle to drink on your way to the train."

While Karen rose from the bed of coffee bags, she held a fixed stare at Vera as she stroked my ear with her tongue. Then as she walked to the door with the wine bottle in her hand, Karen blew a kiss to Vera and me to bid us goodnight and left. Was it the bottle in Karen's hand that gave her the same look of rage that Jamal showed me that November night? Soon after, the last record fell to the turntable. I lit a candle and shut the lights while Vera held the quilt open for my return.

JE

"No one but Nina really knows that any given night at the coffee house might be my Bon Voyage party, and Nina wasn't really listening when I told her. There is absolutely nothing to stop me from deciding to jump through the looking glass and chuck it all at any time. My spirit and my being now thirst for an existence without any material connection. Will I become like Old 'Lung, should I get lost in the question? Then so be it if I do. If my reward is to find and accept my true self, then the journey is more than worth the risk.

"How would these people who hang out in my bedroom and drink my coffee treat me if I were a homeless, starving hippie on the street? Do the people who surround you somehow reflect your surroundings? Or is it the reverse? Am I still hearing commuters rushing to other destinations? Have I been enjoying the ride and not heard the D-Day glider crash? Have the remains somehow become a way station for my travels to come? Every answer that I find is a question that I have never asked myself, or is it?"

The evening following the Karen incident, Rico and I were working out inside September's when we heard a thunderous voice fill the coffee house, "We came here for Mark!" it said. We looked all around, then at one another. We were alone. Suddenly, the door opened and an enormous image right out of a Marvel Comic covered the threshold. We ceased our sparring.

Politely, I approached the hulking mass at the door with this question, "Who the hell are you?" Rico held a pair of nunchucks at the ready.

The voice thundered again, "We're the Justice Committee. One of our charges, Karen, was raped by your friend, Mark. He wasn't at his crib on Union Street. Maybe you can help us find him so we can dispose of this matter."

The booming voice had at least four hundred pounds of architecture supporting it. The question of we was answered by the appearance of a second head. The other head, a tall, skinny, pencil-mustached, leather-clad creature emerged from the left. A maddening, squeaky voice was heard from behind the giant. It kept talking about the surgery that the leather guy was going to perform on Mark's balls. Finally, it stepped out from behind the blob. All that the runt lacked was a briefcase and some intelligence; otherwise you might mistake him for a lawyer. The giant put his hand over the runt's mouth. Leather showed his large knife to us and smiled.

With a look that saw past you while he looked right at you, the five feet five Rico said, "Mon, you come in here saying you goin' to cut someone. The dude you want to cut be my friend. Maybe it won't be so easy to do this thing, mon."

Sensing that their mission may not be as easy as they had thought, the trio that comprised The Justice Committee made a triangle of their backs.

"I'm sure you have a name," I said while looking the giant in the eye, "I'll talk to you, not the yappy runt."

The big guy chuckled and said, "My name is Tank."

I said, "I can see why you're called that. Does your Mohel in leather, having the hundred-percent-off sale, also have a name? We already named your puppet."

I sensed that the big guy respected our arrogance. I also sensed that he would deal with anything that got in the way of his objective. He pointed to Leather and said, "He has a name, but I think of him as Trust. That's all anyone has to know about him. Look, if you don't know where your friend is, we'll go look for him now. Our time is precious."

I wondered, "How precious can their time be? Could they be on some kind of strict citywide ball cutting schedule?"

Trust moved to the side after acknowledging his introduction. Then out of nowhere, Karen appeared. She had been hiding behind Tank. I wondered if any more clowns would pop out of this taxi. I saw an opportunity to at least raise some questions. I reached for Karen's arm and gently pulled her inside the room.

With my other hand on Tank's shoulder, I said, "Take a few minutes, Tank. Come in, let's sit down and have a cup of coffee. Maybe Karen will join us." I looked to Karen and said, "Karen, you sit down too and tell us all about last night with Mark."

Karen's eyes were swollen with held-back tears. Her anger from the previous night became replaced by anticipation as she nervously sat down. Tank covered her shaking body with his massive arm. He then snapped his fingers for Yappy to get us all some coffee. Yappy proved to be the proper servant.

I looked directly at Tank and asked, "How can you be sure that this so-called rape happened at all?"

Rico sat beside me matching his nunchucks with Trust's knife. He held everyone else's attention while I focused mine on Tank.

Tank folded his arms, raised his head and said, "If Karen said that this happened, that's good enough for us, right, men?"

Much like Kevin upon heeding Roger's commands, their heads bobbed up and down with the same obligatory conviction of a toy doggy in a car window.

Not to be distracted by what was on the other end of the leash, I returned my attention to the man and said, "Tank,

I'm going to talk only to you. You're quite a good friend for anyone to have and I don't think that you're an idiot nor are you anybody's fool." Upon hearing this, Tank's folded arms tightened their grip on himself as he smiled.

I snapped my head around and said to Karen, who was hyperventilating and clutching her coffee mug as if it may be her last friend on Earth, " Karen, you're full of shit! You were back here in a blink of an eye after you left with Mark and you didn't say a word to us about any rape. Mark didn't have time to kiss you never mind fuck you. Another thing, no woman would try to cuddle up for a threesome like you did last night, with Vera and me, after having been raped."

As if joining in Tank's judgmental posture, I folded my arms and leaned my head back. We stared at Karen, waiting for a response. The energy of all in the room was directed into her eyes. Tank placed his hand on her cheek and asked, "Be truthful Karen. No harm will come to you. Did this happen as Kenny said?"

As Rico stood clutching his chucks, Trust stood holding his knife. Yappy stood, but still appeared to be seated as he tried to hold on to what remained of his dignity. Everyone looked toward Karen as she tried to hold back her tears.

Her face fell into her open hands. Through a gush of tears she said, "He grabbed at my tit on the way to his apartment. He said that he wanted to start massaging me on the way over, and he pushed me toward an alley. I didn't like him sexually. All I wanted to do was play the massage game. Really, that was all! When I slapped him, he called me a ball teaser.

"I told him that he'd be wearing his balls around his neck for grabbing me! I went back to the coffee house because I liked Kenny, but he was with Vera. She was nice too, just a little uptight."

She began crying while looking toward me with a bewildered yet still inviting gaze. Tank held her as a father would his child.

"I should cut you, bitch," said Leather. Amazed that he had a voice after all, we listened while with blade in hand he added, "I almost messed the dude up for good! You're one fucked up bitch, you bitch."

Tank put his massive form in between his friends and said, "That's enough, Trust! Put the knife away. She's just a stupid kid."

Then Tank directed his thoughts at us, "I don't think that we have reason to act on a silly argument over passion protocols. These two had a misunderstanding and that's it. We're the only ones that got fucked. Rico, you and Kenny are righteous dudes. Mark might be an asshole but he's not a candidate for surgery, at least for now."

Yappy started preaching at Karen. She continued to cry as Tank yelled for everyone to shut up. Mark's balls would remain intact. The Justice Committee departed for the train back to The Village.

"What the fuck do you want with me?" screamed Mark, as he jumped out of his bed. The hinges had barely landed on the other side of the bedroom as Rico walked across the fallen door. Mark quickly turned and retreated toward the nearest corner.

"What did you do to the young chick, you dumb motherfuckin' honkey?" asked Rico while throwing Mark to the floor by his collar.

Mark seemed confused yet remained cool and cautious with his words, "I was just walking with her, that's all! When I put my arm around her, maybe I touched her tit a little. She pushed me away and I asked her, 'Why?' Then she walked back toward Kenny's. That was it, I swear! How did you know I was in my attic?"

He seemed bewildered that we found him. His facial expressions were too contradictory with his words. I grabbed Mark's hair and pulled his head down and said, "Look down your motherfuckin' shorts Mark! What do you see down there?"

He stood up with an incredulous dropping of his jaw and held his arms out.

Then Rico said, "Do what Kenny say, mon! If you don't, then maybe I rip off your pants for you and maybe some other shit while I'm there."

Mark looked down his shorts and said to us, "Okay, I'll play your stupid fuckin' game. Okay, I see my cock and balls. So what's the big fuckin' deal?"

Pressing my finger into his neck I shouted, "The big fuckin' deal is this asshole! They're not stuffed down your fuckin' throat. What the hell did you do to that girl? She wouldn't call her friends to castrate you for grabbing her tit."

Mark glanced at the broken door, and then toward the nunchucks sticking out of Rico's back pocket. Before us was a cornered man standing in the middle of an open room.

Mark took a deep breath and looked at each of us as he appended his story, "Okay, maybe I wanted to get some head from her in the alley. I felt like I was going to explode! Man, she was coming on to me all fuckin'night. Okay, I pushed her into the alley and asked her do me before we did the massage thing back here. I thought that's what she wanted to do. I guess I must have misread her."

Somehow Mark didn't appear to fully grasp the seriousness of the situation. He didn't show guilt or remorse. He lit a cigarette and looked Rico and me up and down as he tested our reactions. I realized that truth to him was, whatever works.

I asked, "Why would anyone want their head shoved into someone's crotch? Your lovemaking technique is in serious question Mark, in addition to your truthfulness. Every time you stand up to piss you had better be grateful to her for changing her story."

Mark placed his head in his lap and dry heaved. He looked up to us and said, "You shouldn't have stopped them. I could have bled to death and it would be all over by now.

Now go play Batman and Robin for someone who gives a shit!"

Gratitude takes on strange forms sometimes.

After that night, Tank came to September's regularly. We learned that he was an ex-soldier of fortune and was once with the radical group, Students for a Democratic Society. Although an activist, he had an inner conflict with the Peace Movement.

The pacifist group's basic premise of aiding people conflicted with Tank's deep need to kill people. As a mercenary, he felt a sense of contractual anonymity in his actions and therefore he saw himself as being guilt free. Nothing personal, just business.

After Tank would tell the tales of his exploits in Iran and other exotic places as a soldier for hire, someone always asked the same question, "If you savored battle so much, then why didn't you allow yourself to be drafted for service in Vietnam?"

Tank would always give the same answer, "The Vietnamese people's cause was a just one. I would have fought right alongside of them if somehow it meant that American capitalists and the pig politicians that they owned might be in my gun sights."

He would tell us of his adventures with the Weather Underground when he was a student. He would tell us how he worked with the Chicago Seven during the '68 Democratic Convention. He would tell us of the ceremonious burning of his draft card on a national network television newscast.

Tank's life's experiences were revealed to us over and over, night after night, after night. Mark continued to descend from his Union Street loft and be a regular visitor to September's in his search for any form of dance or massage partner, real or imagined. He and Tank acted as if nothing ever happened between them. They never brought up the Karen incident again. Karen never returned to September's Child.

From the Grand Army Plaza Fountain
Photo by J.K. Savoy

Chapter Six

Options

The most terrible urge to piss awoke me one day that followed one forgotten night. Quickly, I rolled to the edge of the loft. I was about to place my foot on the last rung of the ladder when the sound of growling forced a sudden reversal of direction. I looked below me to see a mangy yet noble battle-scarred beast. His head almost reached the bed as he placed his paws on the ladder and began wagging his stump.

I twisted around in agony while thinking, "Maybe I should try to jump over him and make a run for the John." Then I realized as I looked at his teeth, "If I did that, in addition to pissing all over the floor, I would also be bleeding all over the floor." Instead, I distracted him with the remains of some old Chinese food and jumped over him to seek my reward. Afterwards I took him to the park for him to do the same.

Abandoning this Doberman pinscher in my coffee house was the single act of kindness for a dog who otherwise knew only neglect. The scars on his face and head spoke of the years of attention that he did receive. Half of his left ear had been torn away.

While one necktie made up his new collar, two others made up his leash. He seemed to bounce along as he walked with a look of challenge toward anyone that happened by as if he were claiming me as his.

I thought, "If Walt Disney can name a dog Pluto after the planet farthest from us in the solar system, then I can name a dog Terra after the planet that we both grew from. So what if the name is Latin." To think, just the day before I wondered how I might continue to feed myself.

Terra had a way about him that was a bit eccentric. With no warning or provocation, he would often snap at your throat. If you didn't grab his snout fast enough, who knows? Could this have been his way of reaching out for the kindness of strangers?

Help in modifying his mood-swings was provided from the people who came to the coffee house and shotgunned him through his snout with pot smoke. Terra took it all in and mellowed out. Then he would circle a coffee bag and fall down. His tongue would drop from the side of his mouth and he would join the crowd by staring at a spot on the wall while zoning out on the music.

"If you need this suit, take it. I won't be needing it any more. Take the ties and the shirts too," I said while Terra's head raced back and forth, attempting to make dog sense of the actions of his latest human.

I was giving my business clothes to a college kid on the block. I had given my camera to his friend. The bank had repossessed the Harley. I felt so much lighter without all of that baggage. The coffee house sign still read SOON. I had only the clothes on my back and a spare set in my steamer trunk.

"Yo, Mister Kenny, are those barbells down there? If someone cleaned them up and painted them, he might be able to work out with them," said Demetrius.

He was always there to lend a hand when I needed help. He had helped me knock plaster from the walls and load debris on to my car when I first came to this store and he always appeared when I needed a hand, no matter what. Demetrius was a skinny, exuberant kid with a never-ending smile.

I answered, “Nobody that calls me Mister has a chance at cleaning up these weights, never mind working out with them. Now what's my name?”

He jumped down to the cellar from the hatch above and declared, “Kenny, I got some black paint at my crib. Maybe I could fix them up for you. If I did, then maybe you'd let me work out a little with them. Okay?”

I laughed and replied, “If you did that, then the only way I could pay you would be with the barbells themselves, since I already gave away my money. Does that sound okay with you?”

“You got yourself a deal, Kenny.” We took the weights to his house.

I had two dollars left in my pocket after I bought coffee and supplies. Terra was fed with table scraps, thanks to Kathleen. I sat looking at the menu board at The Gazebo, a local health food restaurant. Soup was a dollar, whole grain bread was fifty cents and water was free. The rest was for a tip in order to maintain my dignity. I caught the waiter's attention. At the same time I somehow caught the attention of a beautiful smiling face, framed with a large straw bonnet.

The sky was blue like her eyes that in one timeless moment pierced my soul and in the next looked away. Her beauty not only surpassed that of all other women, but it eclipsed the very meaning of the word. The moment, although elusive in its passing, evoked memories of previous lifetimes I must have shared with her. They danced through my beguiled mind during our momentary exchange of glances and heralded an unfolding of feelings strange to me, yet memorable.

She turned to answer her friend. I turned and ordered my soup. The three of them had a look that could only be gotten through gainful employment.

I thought, "Perhaps we'll skip this lifetime and meet again in another."

Somehow each night, enough quarters would find their way into the jar to sustain Terra and with what was left, perhaps me. The night that Haamdi and his friends visited proved to be no exception to this, but the night itself proved to be exceptional.

Haamdi, an Egyptian falafeler, owned a food stand on Seventh Avenue near September's. He was sitting under my loft bed with his friends, who were visiting America from Egypt. They were drinking tea and watching Lana and Kathleen dance.

He walked over to me and said, "Kenny, I would like to propose a business deal. If you would be so kind to arrange for your dancing women to entertain my friends this evening, we will pay a considerable sum of money for this privilege."

I asked myself, "Did a cobra wiggle out of a straw basket and bite me in the ass, or did I just hear what I thought I heard?"

I answered the falafeler, "Haamdi, maybe the music is too loud. But did I hear you say that you want to pay these women to be with you and your friends, and you want me to arrange everything for you?"

The more that I shook my head from side to side in disbelief, the more his head nodded up and down in hopeful anticipation. He grabbed my hand and said, "Yes! Yes, Kenny my friend! This is what we would like you to do for us."

Haamdi was also a gifted martial artist. We had sparred on many occasions. I had much respect for him as a fighter as well as a sandwich maker. I never knew that we had such a cultural difference. We had never discussed the issue of women's autonomy. I hoped that I might enlighten him on this topic.

With the music blasting, I shouted into his ear, "You know, Haamdi, in America women make their own decisions! They choose for themselves who they want to be with, and they enter into business deals on their own no matter what kind of deals they are! Above all, they would be extremely offended if either you or I asked this of them."

He smiled and nodded enthusiastically, appearing to have grasped my message or at least his version of it. "Thank you, Kenny, I understand," he said as he shook my hand with both of his very excitedly. Haamdi then relayed my communication in Arabic to his friends who slapped my back, shook my hand and made guttural sounds of appreciation.

While they drank their tea and argued with one another, I went about my host routine until it was interrupted by a high-pitched scream followed by, "Ow! Ouch! No! No! You have killed me! My manhood! My manhood!"

Haamdi fell to the floor, holding his groin. Lana stood over him, ready with another kick, just in case the first two failed to communicate her message.

She shouted, "You son of a whoremonger! Who do think you're talking to? You're no fuckin' smarter than the day you fell out of the camel's ass!"

Haamdi propelled himself across the floor with both feet and one hand while protecting his groin with the other, to what he must have hoped was a neutral corner.

Lana pursued him mercilessly and shouted, "I'll kill you and your fat fuckin' friends if you even look at Kathleen or me again! No one has the right to assume that we're for sale because we're women! Kenny, please throw these idiots out before you have to carry them out in a fuckin' garbage bag."

She did say please. Haamdi and his friends needed no further encouragement to leave. They ran for the door, mumbling to one another in Arabic. I was sure they were enroute to their next lesson in cultural diversity.

"Lana, you decked a black belt judo champ! We gotta work out sometime," said a very impressed Rico. Lana was so much more than just a dancer to him after that.

As the Egyptian contingent turned the corner, I turned to hear a woman's voice behind me saying, "We would like to talk to you outside, Kenny, if you don't mind."

Her name was Alison. I felt that she had been giving me meaningful looks for quite some time. Maybe I would see where this thing was going. I walked out with her. Her friends followed. Her friend Ana lit up a joint and we passed it around. They kept looking back and forth at one another.

Ana pointed with her chin at Alison as if to say, "You do it!"

I looked at them as I exhaled the pot smoke and asked, "Do what? Did you drag me out here to smoke with you and watch you look at one another like you're playing some kind of mental hot potato? What's up?" I pointed with my chin at Alison as if to second the request for the potato.

Alison said, "Okay Kenny. Here goes. Like, what's your real story? You come to this block from nowhere. You say that your name is Kenny, but someone reads on some of your papers the name, Joseph. Who goes by one name while telling everyone another unless he's maybe hiding something or living some secret life, you know?"

Alison's friends nodded with her and then she added, "You suddenly appear as the center of attention, hangin' out with all the real cool street people. Like, what's up? Like, we want to hear it from you. Who the fuck are you really, Kenny? Or is it really Joseph, or what?"

She and the others looked at me even more suspiciously than before. All I could think of was that someone was poking around near my private journal. I went on the offensive and said, "First of all, I don't appreciate your third degree. Secondly, if you must know and I'm not going into the whole thing for you, I like it around here and I like the people and that's all your getting."

Even the pot couldn't slow their rapid eye movement and nodding. They seemed to be in agreement that they hadn't made their point to me yet, but I felt it coming.

Ana, the apparent leader, took the floor and asked me defiantly, "Are you C.I.A or a narc, or what? We saw your pilot logbooks in the trunk. There were entries saying that regularly, your passenger was Trevor Lasco. I mean the dude's a spook for Nixon and the whole power regime in Washington, man!"

The conversation was getting as pungent as the lingering pot smoke. She went on to ask, "Why would a pilot of his, probably from the army, grow his hair long and start gettin' down with the street people?"

I couldn't believe how two and two were adding up to six in their minds. Alison took pause as she held in a large hit from the joint. The smoke and her convoluted logic then blew right into Ana's face, "Ana, get your shit straight. Lasco is a major drug trafficker. Why would he be messin' with narcs unless they were the ones that might have turned him around? I don't think anyone got to Lasco. The dude ran off scott-free to Honduras. If Kenny or Joe, or whatever his name is, is a spook then the Lasco shit was old news. Now Kenny and the people that sent him are after whoever and whatever's left of The Movement!"

I could feel the stake at my back as the flames licked my feet. The spectral evidence was in. I was guilty by disassociation. There was nothing to do but attack.

I cleared my throat, spit a luger six inches from Ana's foot and said, "I think that you're a bunch of nosy little bitches that smoke too much fuckin' pot! Your stoned-out paranoia is dominating whatever might be left of your perception."

I took the joint from Alison's mouth and drew in a hit that left a one-inch flame, finger-rolled the roach to her and said, "Here's a real hot potato for you. You keep your fuckin' hands the fuck out of my personal belongings. Yeah I flew airplanes for that crooked bastard, and that's all I'm going to tell you. Why don't you go home and watch your idiotic soap operas and leave the living alone? Stay the fuck out of September's!"

I forgot that I had a past that might seem questionable to some, especially to the narrow minded. I thought, "When I was a bodybuilder, everyone thought that I was a cop. Now I must weigh a hundred-forty pounds, most of it hair. Where do they come off thinking that I'm a narc or a spook? Did I get a promotion in Fantasyland, or what?"

"Time will tell. Time will tell," said Alison as they left.

Maybe I should have told them about my vow to never lie. I'm sure that would have convinced them. The forces of opposing ironies were further narrowing my ever-dwindling silhouette.

I guessed the women had some justification in confronting me. But what they did was invasive. To think, my only area of privacy, the trunk, was open territory to them. At least there was some consolation to the assault upon my world; their pot was pretty good.

I walked over to the stoop next door to sit down and sort out the details of the confrontation. Wow! The pot was really good. I began to flash back to a memory of my flying a charter passenger to Kennedy Airport a few years before.

My passenger asked me, "Do you have any idea who you're working for?"

I recalled how his question threw me for a moment. I answered him, "Yeah, right now I'm working for you. You're the man who's paying for me to go to Kennedy Airport, right?"

I had so many different bosses at the airport. When I wasn't teaching flying all I cared about was logging as much multi-engine time that I could get in order to be marketable to the airlines, hoping that both might add up to one decent paycheck.

He waved his hand and said, "Not me, I mean that fucking carpetbagger that took over your airport, Lasco. I sold aluminum storm windows with him years ago when we were kids out of high school. He didn't give a shit what he had to do to get a sale. He didn't care how he got what he wanted, as long as he got it."

Until that moment, I never gave much thought to what Lasco was before he took over the airport, where I worked, with a handshake and stock options. I aimed the Cessna toward Kennedy Airport and gave my full attention to what my passenger had to tell me.

"A few years back, Lasco bilked the company where we were working for five hundred dollars. Then he split. He probably parlayed that same money over the years into creating Lasco International Power Corporation, the company that you work for. Now he's using worthless stocks and pure illusion to rip off Overland Securities of Geneva, as we speak. One day he's going to fuck the wrong people and wind up behind bars or blowing bubbles while he's kicking at the inside of his Lincoln's trunk lid. What goes around comes around."

I listened and wondered about the man whose signature appeared on my paycheck as Kennedy Approach handed me off to the tower. Wow! This pot is un-fuckin'-believably good! Now I'm having a flashback within a flashback!

Here goes the intra-flashback flashback:

The day was CAVU, ceiling and visibility unlimited. The engines roared as I scanned the approach during my clearing turn at the base of the runway prior to take-off. This would be the last time that I would have the honor of flying the boss himself. It started like all the others at our home base, Lasco-Air, in a small airport in Northern New Jersey. We were going to JFK Airport where he would leave for Europe. Lasco allowed those of us who held his life in their hands the privilege of calling him Rev.

With empty skies behind me and before me, I blasted down the runway and raised the nose high above the tree line at nearly ninety knots. The wheels began to retract.

Suddenly, I heard, "Eeeek! What the fuck was that?" coming from my right.

If it weren't for the fact that one of the only working things in that Cessna 310 was the shoulder harness, Lasco would have been in my lap as he screamed like a hysterical child. I reached across him and secured the vent window that had popped open.

Lasco kept an entire fleet of aircraft at his disposal. As compulsive as he was about flying, his bean counters were just as compulsive about scrimping on the money that should have been put into maintenance. Fortunately, the sky was clear that day, or I could have shown him how I had to learn to fly by instruments without having any to speak of.

Lasco was a man who did every thing he could to look and act like Howard Hughes, right down to the penchant for airplanes. If only he could replicate Howard's courage. Howard Hughes would not let anyone fly a prototype airplane that he conceptualized until he personally piloted it. Lasco probably employed food tasters.

Rev, his army of C.P.A.'s, and other financial charlatans, had our entire fleet shuttling their integrity-impaired souls from New Jersey to Kennedy and vice versa, night and day. It would only be a matter of days before Overland Securities would bite Lasco's well-aimed bullet.

As a highly trained, fully qualified pilot, I had the responsibility to carry Rev's bags to the cabstand where we would take a yellow Port Authority car from the General Aviation Terminal to the Main Terminal.

As we stepped out of the doorway, a yellow cab veered toward us and slowed down. Rev reached for the door handle and just before he could grab it, for some unknown reason, the cab screeched rubber and sped off. A very indignant Trevor Lasco ran along the roadway after the cab yelling, "I'm going to buy this fuckin' place and fire your goddamn ass!"

I stood there incredulous, watching the world's largest ego left powerless against a little cab driver in the midst of the world's largest airport and thought, "If he wasn't busy beating the shit out of Overland Securities of Europe, he probably would give in to his obsession and print enough stock to actually buy Port Authority just to fire the little guy who had the audacity to ignore him."

Lasco's favorite line to us lowly pilots when we asked about how long we would have to wait in the terminal was, "I'll be back when I get here!" At that point we would see only his back and the get there part might happen in hours or perhaps, days.

The last flight crew that flew him to Mexico, where he split with the loot for Honduras, may still be waiting at the terminal for his back to get there. The people who gave him the cash to finance his last trip were paid with stock certificates in his company. You can be sure that the return of Lasco and the stock's value are of equal certainty.

"Do you mind if we look around your establishment?"

I had just returned from buying supplies at the tea and coffee store one evening when two uniformed members of New York's finest found their way into September's. They must have been sure that I wouldn't mind since their eyes were already all over the place.

"Would you fellas like a cup of coffee?" I asked. Having been raised in my parent's restaurant business, I learned early in my life that you offer a cop a cup of coffee as soon as he walks into your place.

"Yeah coffee would be fine, plain black for both of us. The music seems to be flying all around the store. Where's it coming from? I don't see any speakers." asked the officer while they both were looking up and down and 'round and 'round and 'round, unable to fixate on the music and the lyrics of "Dark Side of the Moon" as it surrounded them within the softly lit room in quadraphonic.

I hoped to limit their curiosity so I answered, "Up there, inside the coffee bags in the ceiling. The amp and turntable are under the bar. Sit down, relax and enjoy your coffee. If you have any questions, I'll be right here drinking mine and doing my wood carving, if you don't mind."

Because of all of the cop stuff hanging on their belts, they found it to be impossible to sit on the floor pillows so they plopped on the bench under the furry wall. They sat and checked out what there was to see and appeared either less concerned or more relaxed than when they arrived. I could see their fingers stroking the sand finish on the coffee cups as they sipped the Jamaican Blue Mountain blend. Their other senses were busy absorbing the otherworldly ambiance of September's.

The lyrics of, "Us and Them" circled the walls and seemed to slow the earlier frenetic movement of their eyes. The peaceful message of "Pink Floyd" appeared to have captivated their spirits. Their eyes fluttered and their heads lowered as if they were beginning to realize that after all-we're only ordinary men who all have the need to touch our better selves, if only during the timeline of an album side.

I went about carving a figure of large eye into a piece of wood. Rico blended into a wall in the corner of the loft. Being the eternal looker he remained eternally unseen.

"Every Good Boy Deserves Favour" was the last album on the stack. Then, as if a DJ meshed the Moody Blues' brilliant chords with the less brilliant sound of a siren coming from outside, the officers jumped from their trances and raced to the door. We watched New York's Finest be bested by the summoning finger of a sergeant-striped arm beckoning them to its car. The rear door of the squad car swung open for them while their heads hung down as if awaiting a noose.

I turned to Rico and asked, "Did they call this an establishment?"

Every night as the Sun would set, opening the coffee

house door would thrust one surprise at me after another. Those who wandered the streets after dark, in search of others doing the same, might find September's' small bulb burning in the narrow window slit. It became a beacon for the World to find this way station, erstwhile wreckage, and deposit their emotional baggage on other visitors, doing the same.

I might remain in a dark corner, behind the beam where the earthen cups hung, as if waiting in the wings of a stage. The players and the audience would be before me, exchanging roles with one another as the night progressed, each in search of direction.

The nocturnal creatures, which frequented September's Child, were all seeking something. There were those who wanted to find it within themselves and those who actively sought it from the outside. There were those who told of receiving messages from the Great Beyond, unfortunately the messages were usually greatly beyond them. All of this created a marketplace for even others trying to peddle themselves and their muddy paths of righteousness to the wide-eyed seekers resting upon my pillows.

"Joe, I'm sorry, I mean Kenny. You know Joe, I've known you since high school and especially after being married to you, it's difficult for me to call you by a different name," said Deanna.

Then she said, "I've been an astrologer for half of my life, and in all that time I can't remember so many so-called shamans in one place other than at a convention. The problem is, most of these people here don't know what the hell they're talking about."

Deanna had to come to Brooklyn to see me sharing what she called the life style of a sewer rat. She would attribute my life change to my Moon in Gemini. But knowing also that my Mars was in Virgo, she knew deeply that I was dead serious in my mission.

Deanna and I had ended our marriage a long time before. We managed to set aside our differences and focus only on the good memories and the ideals that we shared. The result was success in a great friendship after a failure at being lovers.

She was the only other person, besides Nina, who knew that the coffee house would never officially open. Deanna knew that I was in the process of giving away everything. Once I was certain that the vehicle that was September's Child had truly crashed, my life on the street would truly begin.

"Don't let on that you're a professional astrologer," I said, "They'll either worship you or bore you to death." I had to warn her about the sharks that swam the midnight sea.

She answered, "I can take care of myself, just fine. It's you I'm worried about. Joe, your fantasy-driven way of living never ceases to amaze me."

Then she summarized my situation, astrologically, "Leave it to you and your Venus-in-Leo, Moon-in-Gemini problem to design a business with failure as its goal. What are you going to do once everything you possess is gone? Will you drop your thumb and at last head out for the great unknown?"

I guess she mentioned that because it was what I had often talked of doing while we were married. Unknown to her during that time, to me the great unknown was yet another woman that I had not found to cheat with.

In the interest of our peaceful coexistence, resulting from the divorce, I answered, "I'll have to dive through the looking glass when the time comes. There's no need to search for some faraway place to confront my demons. Brooklyn will do fine. Call it fantasy if you have to, but something deep within me has demanded this of me. For some weird reason this store presented itself to me as my arena."

The person, who knew me long before I shaved, never mind grew the beard that I spoke through, seemed to be hanging on my every word.

So I added, "I have never been in the circumstance that I'm in the process of placing myself. It's difficult to foresee the options that might present themselves, never mind which may be mine to take. I feel like I'm riding blindfolded through a cage of tigers and somehow I know that even if I put my hand or even my head between their jaws, I won't be bitten. All I know is, I have to go along with the ride that seems to be taking me along to what, I don't know. If there's some unknown price to pay or choice to make, I guess I'll find out if and when the ride stops."

She shook her head dismissively, rolled her eyes and said, "If you place yourself into the hands of Fate like that Joe, there are no more options only circumstances. Joe, why do you have to actually do this thing, and with such panache? Why can't you just imagine being penniless? You know, I wouldn't gouge out my eyes to truly understand the meaning behind Stevie Wonder's lyrics. All I have to do is close them and listen. Anyway, you never listen to anyone."

I explained the "marching band to the graveyard gates" symbolism to Deanna. She told me a story about a man who spent his life dreaming of one day being laid to rest in a burial plot that was dead center in the middle of the cemetery roadway. The inscription on both sides of his oversized tombstone would read, "I shall not be ignored in death as I was in life."

I asked her what she meant by that. She said, "Don't become so deluded by your fantasies that you might get in your own way."

Confiding my supreme quest to my childhood's best friend, I said, "Perhaps having absolutely nothing means having absolutely no options either. What does a person discover within him or herself after being confronted with overwhelming adversity? People who live through war, the extreme of adversity, survive by becoming one with the situation and earning their continuation in life through combat, unfortunately in that case, with the ruin of others.

"Maybe I have a war to fight, with myself as the only potential victim. I see this as my personal just cause. If this challenge is not put behind me, it will sit out there, forever before me."

Deanna just sipped her tea while slowly shaking her head, no. She looked at me with the dubious snicker that one might only give to a close friend and said, "Oh well, I just hope that this isn't the beginning of another political career for you. Let's get off the subject of marching to graveyards for two reasons, I'm tired and I don't want to think of death. On to tales of life! Did you meet anyone interesting lately?"

The 'seventies was a time when a handshake or a genital-shake was equally commonplace, so of course I'd met some interesting people. If Deanna meant, "Did you meet anyone that could be the one?" I would have to answer that I saw the person at The Gazebo that must have always been the one, in all of my lives before and those to come.

I answered, "Not in this lifetime, at least for this lifetime. How about you?"

She laughed and said, "You know damn well that I'm not looking for just one, never mind The One."

I was about to show her some verse that I had written in my journal, when it dawned on me that Deanna might help solve a mystery. I asked her, "By the way, this card fell out of that blank journal book that I told you about. Do you understand the meaning behind it, Mystic Maven?"

Her brow lowered as she looked at the card. She drew it closer to her and said, "Joe, this is the Chariot. It is number seven of the Tarot's Major Arcana. How strange, when I do a reading for myself, this is the card that always represents you. Did you say whether you found it right-side up, or upside down?"

I did my best to recall. I let my instinct answer her, "It kind of flipped out of the book as I turned the page. Let's see, it was upside down when it finally landed on me."

She was admiring the detail of the artwork on the card. She then put on her most strict astrologer's face and said, "Here Joe, you keep my Tarot deck and read this book on the different card's meanings. After a while the interpretations will come from within you. It's a matter of practicing and more practicing. Doing your own Tarot readings will help in gaining a perspective on your life's circumstances in general.

"About this card that you found, the significance that I see in the Chariot's appearance from this reading is, it is saying that things might become more difficult for you before they become easier. For a while, everything that you attempt to grasp will seem to be slipping away from you. But if you persist you will regain control of the elements, as the . . . "

Suddenly the God of egocentricity bestowed upon us his only son, Mark. At least he thought he was. He had been waiting for a break in our conversation for quite a while. Hearing none, he decided to create it by crashing through the middle of Deanna's sentence like an overly zealous linebacker.

Mark bellowed, "So, I hear you're an astrologer! I had my chart done once. It showed that I was formally executed as a political prisoner in at least three previous lives. Do my chart, you'll see. You know, you look like an Aries. I can always tell an Aries, it shows in their eyes."

What Mark saw in people's eyes was how they would roll them back as he plopped down beside them. Deanna, his latest victim, took great pride in projecting her Capricorn persona. To call her an Aries was an act of war! Mark thought he was putting his best foot forward. But as usual, it went right into his mouth.

Deanna asked him for his birth date and time. He supplied it. She quickly drew a circle and positioned his natal luminaries. She then exclaimed, "Oh my God, I have never seen this before!" She looked him in the eye, adding, "This is extraordinary."

Mark leaned forward and asked boisterously, "You see it? Do you see it too? I was also a martyr in my other lives! Right, huh?"

Deanna put her thumb to her chin and looked to him with great concern and said, "According to what I see here Mark, this is your first complete lifetime. Every one of your lives that preceded this one resulted in either your many different mothers each refusing to feed you, or in crib death. You did live to term however, in your many incarnations as a lower primate."

After telling her not to go for the massage option, I left Deanna to her challenge as I awaited my own. This had to be a record-breaking night. There were three different members of the newly self-realized, holding three different copies of "Be Here Now" by Babba-Ram-Das, Brooklyn's homegrown Guru of Gurus. Any page in that book you might turn to at any time would have a line that was pertinent to any topic being discussed at any time.

The initiate would then follow the master to the next level, usually at his place, to learn the mystical true nature of the enlightened organism that each of us is. Then the greatest truth of the Universe would be revealed to the naked apprentice, that being:

The ultimate enlightenment for all organisms is orgasm.

JE

"How many would-be-messiahs must come into September's before they realize that they only have one another to proselytize? If all of the hunters in the world had only one another to stalk and kill, would the eventual winner perform an obligatory suicide seeing self-conversion as the only remaining act? What if it were the first act for each?

"Why do all of these people, who dress in second-hand clothes and speak in second-hand verse, believe that they are the second coming of the guy, just like him, who left an hour ago?

"Can the Dead Sea Scrolls, the Tibetan Book of the Dead, or the Kabala be somehow deciphered to mean, 'Do you come here often?' When did spiritual issues join bellbottoms and Nehru jackets as fashion statements? Why has the dungeon that I have created, in order to wrestle with my own demons, become a place for others to meet theirs, if only in the guise of seers?

"Most of our natural predators have all but been eliminated by way of our superior minds. Yet the predators that remain are spiritual cannibals in search of other souls."

The setting Sun signaled the dawning of yet another night.

September's' door flying open signaled the challenge from yet another beast when I heard, "I want to get high, man! I want to get fucked up! You must be Kenny. I need to get some shit. Whatcha got in them bags, man, them bags in that jar?"

A strapping, head shaved creature with a roaring mouth blasted his way into my reality as he muscled his way to the bar. He had his own agenda and a prescription to fill. His name was Wow.

How does one get to be called Wow? It seems that some years before, he was having a tattoo saying Mom placed on his right bicep. After the artist finished, he raised his arm to look at it. To him it said, Wow. But that's not why others called him Wow.

He floored the tattoo artist with one punch and demanded that he get another tattoo and see it as Mom. This however, would be on his left bicep. The tattooist complied. Of course everyone else read the new tattoo as Wow. He was initially offended until he looked again at his right arm and agreed with the nickname. Wow's eyes were red from rage and stimulant deprivation.

He leaned on the counter, pushing his face toward mine. Both Wow and Mom flexed before my eyes. Then he said in a deliberate and threatening tone, "I came here to get fucked up, man! You goin' to help me or what? Ain't all you be having is coffee here. Maybe that shit in the bags ain't tea either."

I leaned my hands down on the counter near his. Looking him straight in the eye I said calmly, as I saw Rico standing off to the side, "Maybe you said enough, man. Maybe what you see is what it is."

Terra jumped up to counter height and placed his paws next to both of our hands. He joined me staring into Wow's eyes as he drooled on his hand.

I said, "If you want to get fucked up, maybe Terra can accommodate you. Should I give him the word?"

"No, no, man! That's not what I meant. I want to get high, that's all. Tell your dog to get back. Call him off, man! Dogs, they fuckin' creep me out, man! Call him off!"

Terra drooled at Wow more and more as he matched him step for step, both running toward the door. Terra headed Wow off at the door, barked and jumped up, snapping twice at his face. Wow fell to the floor as Terra tore at his shirt. Wow got up. Then he hit the door shoulder first, burst through it and ran up the block.

"If the dude wants to get fucked up, maybe he get off on the Dog Yummy I drop in his shirt pocket," Rico said as we all joined in, laughing our heads off.

"If Wow keeps getting tripped up, it's a good thing that he'll always have his stupidity to fall back on," I said as I gave Terra six Yummies and told him what a good boy he was. Terra then went back to sleep after we all gave him a well-earned shotgun blast to the snout.

Yet another sunset came upon September's' with Rico pointing his thumb at the door saying, "Kenny, I got to go to Intelligent John's place. Later, bro'."

That night, doorknob in hand, he paused and said, "Take a break from the coffee house bullshit. You take a walk with me, mon."

I joined Rico in a walk up the block to meet the mystery people he had often visited and rarely discussed.

It was rumored that Intelligent John was once a marketing executive for a large pharmaceutical company. He was married to Cindy Burp. She was called this because she believed that a woman should be free to articulate her primal feelings as loudly as any man could and with the same value of content. Although she did express herself from both ends, her moniker came from addressing the issues face to face. I was curious to learn if each person was worthy of their title.

They shared a renovated mansion at the top of the Slope, near Prospect Park. The entire house, both inside and out, expressed the power of the old money that created it many years before, and the new that brought it back from its near demise.

Rico and John exchanged some words in Spanish. Cindy looked at them and burped. She was downing one beer after another. There was probably a lot that she had to get off her mind. Rico stashed a bag in the back of his shirt, and then tucked it into his belt. There was something that I couldn't figure out. If Rico was receiving product, then why was he also taking money in the handshake with John?

I walked toward the door. While passing the gallery, I thought that there might be a deeper meaning, besides the obvious, in a painting signed by Cindy. In vivid red, underscored with magenta, a hooded woman stood on the gallows about to be hung by an oversized jock strap while tightening the noose herself.

Cindy burped at us as we were about to leave and then asked, "What's the rush? Before you came over, John said he was going to make some tea. Rico, you know, that very special blend. So listen guys, share a little tea and hang out for a while."

Rico rolled his eyes back while John took some powdery stuff and placed it in a white paper towel. Slowly he raised the kettle. The water trickled over the powder and the room began to fill with the smell of dirt.

"John, mix some Red Zinger and honey into that shit, will ya?" asked Cindy as she pinched her nose and made a waving motion to John with her hand. John dunked the Red Zinger bag in and out of the monstrous cup and squirted some honey from the smiling-faced head of a little plastic bear.

John threw the teabag across the room toward a waiting trash bucket. As if the paper tag at the end of the string on the teabag suddenly became a key to the deepest vault of my unconscious, I exclaimed, "Holy shit! I had a flashback already!"

Cindy's burp of surprise nearly blew out the candle that she was placing on the table. A spark jumped from the last glowing ember. Shooting along the wick, it returned the flame to life.

"Tell us your flashback," said a curious Cindy.

I answered, "Oh wow! I must have been, maybe two or so. I was playing on the kitchen floor, when someone at the table above me dropped a hot teabag right on my leg. All I can remember, before I filed it away in the Permanent Repression Files, were my own screams filling my head just before a nipple was shoved into my mouth. I guess that's why I never drink tea. Now I guess I'll have to."

John passed the tea around for all to share in the communal cup. It wasn't half bad. I knew about Red Zinger and honey, but I wondered about the dirt part. When I looked to Rico, he just laughed and said, "Go with it, mon."

The candle's tiny flame evoked the same look of introspectiveness from all as it flickered slightly from the breath of our casual dialogue. It was the only light in the room while the soft sounds of Ravi Shankar's sitar spilled through the slightly opened window from the building next door.

Morpheus was denied our entry to the gates of unconsciousness when in a voice just above a whisper, the good hostess blurted, "Uuuuuurp!"

Cindy placed her hand over her mouth, smiled and said, "John! What's your earliest memory? Kenny told his. Now let's hear from someone else. How far back can you go?"

John hardly moved. His glassy eyes remained fixated on the candle. Then he spoke, beginning in a low monotone, "The white ceiling seemed to move away, while the rocking caused the wall to fall into my range of vision. I wanted to cry, but my mouth wouldn't open. A lantern sat on a shelf halfway between the ceiling and the floor. There was a steady flame from a white wick behind the glass shield surrounding it."

As if startled by the escalation of his own voice, he said, "My eyes couldn't move! The rocking was all I knew. It took me from the ceiling to the flame, then from the flame to the ceiling, on and on and on. I could hear voices and laughter from far behind me. If only I could cry! Over and over I tried to, but I couldn't."

John winced repeatedly and seemed more and more agitated as he went on to say, "The rocking stopped, very suddenly. My body was motionless. All there was in the room was the flame and my realization of it. If only I could move my eyelids, then I might blink and hold back the tears that had since magnified it to the blaze before me."

John's face became completely contorted. His speech became almost distant as he said, "Incredible pain was rushing through my entire body! I kept trying to cry out to the laughing voices so they might come, but my jaw was paralyzed. The pain grew more intense while the flame began to grow larger and brighter.

"I tried to transcend the pain and summon any remaining strength that might be within me to force my mouth open that I might cry out! Then, I felt the smallest tingle of energy enter my mouth. My lower jaw opened slightly and my denture fell to my tongue. I pressed my feet hard to the floor hoping to rock, allowing me pause from the flame that was overwhelming the room. But I couldn't sense my feet, never mind the floor. The pain began to feel as if it was the cry that wouldn't sound as it and the light melded like one distraction, engulfing me!"

Only the whites of John's eyes could be seen, the candle's flame swaying to the breath of what had become an almost serene voice, "The laughter faded from my consciousness. There was only the blinding light. It seemed to both overpower and soothe me. I would like to say that what was me became one with the light, but by then I had lost any sense of my self. There was no pain, no sound, no up nor down! All that there was, was the light. The light was all. All that there was, was the light."

John looked away from the candle and pointed to a bookcase. He made a back and forth motion with his finger to a shelf filled with folders and notebooks with various loose papers stuffed into them.

He asked, "Do you see all of that shit from one end of the shelf to the other? It must measure three feet and twenty years. I'll never stop trying to describe what I truly felt then. But as life would have it, I'm left with only words."

With her eyes swollen with tears, Cindy handed him her cigarette. He took it. She asked him, "John, don't you think that you went back a little too far?" John's eyes suddenly brightened. The corners of his mouth turned up slightly.

Cindy grabbed his forearm, and asked, "What's wrong John?"

His eyes glowed almost as brilliantly as did the candle. Then he smiled nearly fully and said, "Nothing! Nothing, at all."

Our saying, goodnight to them was in vain. Cindy and John lay tangled in an embrace, the flame's reflection dancing in their eyes that stared upward toward the wall, where it met the white ceiling.

The frigid night breeze reassured me of my own consciousness. Standing on the limestone steps, the sound of the sitar music from the neighbor's window found us from the alley. The brass lock of the mansion's door clicked shut behind us.

Rico turned to me and said, "That why he be, the mon."

I answered, "Huh?"

Rico began laughing and pointing to the mansion window. He then said to me, "John always gives the answers just before the questions come to you. We just all got hit in the face with the same shovel load of bullshit the mon throw at Cindy."

"Huh?" I exclaimed. Rico's words felt colder than the air itself. I turned to him and asked, "What the fuck are you saying? You can't mean that the son of a bitch was putting us on? Before I could reach the bottom of the stairs, a window slammed shut, the sitar sound dying in mid-chord.

We walked down the hill. Rico fixed the bulge from the stash in his shirt and said, "Mon, he put the peyote in Cindy's head, then he fuck with it. That motherfucker, maybe he see that poor bitch make that picture with her neck in the noose, or she stop shaving her legs and 'pits. So he pull the brain outta her head and put it in his pocket, just a little different this time. Now he have her where she lick the sweat from his balls. Next thing, mon, she be scrubbing the toilet and singing a song."

As one door closes, the paranoid might hear echoes of distant portals slamming shut. Perhaps it was a residual hallucination from what I had just experienced or ingested, but I couldn't shake the vision of the coffee house door locked from the inside by a crazed madman serving tea to all who may have entered.

"Rico, I don't like to leave Danny the Flick looking after September's this long. We've got to hurry back, man."

I listened to my own words. Never, did I imagine that a sense of proprietorship toward September's Child would overcome me, but it apparently had. One can only have this feeling if he is possessed by something outside of himself. Perhaps the public's acceptance of September's as an institution was permeating my mind. I could not allow this business to succeed in giving me any sense of security. This would mean the same as if the money and property that I had shed returned in another form.

Unaware of my change of heart, Rico said, "C'mon, let's track! It won't take us no time, mon."

Being new to the neighborhood, I asked, "You mean run, don't you?"

He shrugged his shoulders at me and laughed. I was running, he was tracking and we were both moving along lock-stepped with the N.Y.P.D. Anti-Crime Squad undercover yellow taxi that had placed itself at our side.

One week on the street and anyone could tell that this wasn't really a cab. The same three passengers every night kept all the windows down with their arms hanging out. Their heads and eyes would sweep the neighborhood and one of them would always sit to the driver's right in the front seat.

Then there was a short siren burst, "Where are you two going? We're police officers! Come over here!" yelled the plainclothes officer-passenger.

The cab had driven halfway up on to the sidewalk in front of us while knocking a dozen garbage cans down in the process. As we approached the cab, Rico systematically righted the garbage cans and placed them back at the curb, lids attached.

We made it a point to act perfectly calm and normal, while I politely said to the officers, "We're heading back to our crib. We were just getting a little running in on the way before we work out."

They looked all at one another. The cop in the back seat started to signal for us to come closer. He shined a flashlight in our faces for a better look. Just what our peyote soaked brains needed, blinding light. Their radio blasted garbled sounds that only police academy initiates could understand. In the midst of the enlightened questioning, the cop in the front seat reached for a red rotating beacon and stuck it on the cab's roof. They sped away before our answers could reach them.

I asked Rico, “Why do the cops seem to come to you, then they seem to pass right through you? Something else always draws them away. Maybe the budget cuts have reduced their numbers and they're spread thin. Whatever it is, it's like you're living in a “Road Runner” cartoon. Whenever all seems lost, somehow an open window is drawn and you jump through it to safety, or somehow a tunnel is drawn and the coyote crashes into it.”

We went back to the garbage cans. Rico lifted the lid of the can where he just stashed his stash. After he recovered it we continued toward September's.

Rico kiddingly feigned a volley of punches toward my face and asked, “How you think I stay alive out here? It always be like you say, mon, a window opens. I don't question nothin', mon. I just go with it, whatever it be. Why try to figure it out? If you gonna be out here on the street, mon, what you owns is what be on you. You got to be ready to run at any time an' not be holdin' nothin' to weigh you down or that you need to go back for.”

Rico pointed upward to an apartment window and said, “Nobody draw no window for nobody, mon. You just got to keep a little light in sight in the corner of your eye all the time an' know you can get there with one jump no matter what.” I never saw him so animated; he practically danced as he talked.

“Remember, mon, don't attach you' self to no people. Never get to know them too good. When you gotta split, you gotta go with the wind. There be no time to break away from anything or anybody when the mon be doggin' your ass.”

Then he laughed and slapped my back as we approached First Street. He said, "Maybe now you know how a black man feel if he don't walk nice and slow wit' his head down an' his feet a'shufflin'! Hey, catch you later, mon. I got to go change some of this Gold into gold."

He began blending into the street crowd. As he left I yelled up the block, "Only from the Netherlands, mon, don't forget!"

Dusk or dawn, I was always in for a surprise when the door to September's opened. The biggest surprises were often when it was I who was entering. After leaving Rico on Seventh Avenue, I entered September's and I was hit by a waft of pot smoke as the door closed behind me.

My immediate thought was of Wow and how people must think that this was a place to get high. The quality of the waft that hit me proved this to be correct. I took a few deep breaths, fell back on a pile of pillows and watched a hand strum the most incredible chords from a six string that I had ever heard in my life. The entire room was filled with people who were as fixated as I was upon this gifted guitarist. He looked up at us. His eyes were as bloodshot as the best of ours.

He slowly strummed on the Martin and said, "I would like to play my latest composition. It's called, "Every Time I Kick the Habit, A Nun Rolls Down the Hill." He began hitting the strings with a passion equaled only by his musical skill.

Everyone was swept back by his talent. Comments exploded from the audience as the music exploded from the Martin: "That's some heavy fuckin' shit man!" "Oh wow!" "This is gonna be like, really relevant, man!" "Totally right on." "Far fuckin' out, like with the nun and stuff, man." "Hey, I gotta hear this message!"

Just then, the musician's chords became as scattered as his focus. He looked up then he looked around at his captivated audience with his bloodshot, drooping eyes. He began to strum the same riff over and over, more and more slowly, more and more quietly and then, silence. His head fell on his shoulder. It looked as if he had stopped breathing.

In an instant, he picked up his head and said, "Oh wow, man!" The crowd sat paralyzed, hanging in anticipation of his every word to come.

He placed his hand over his mouth, strummed a chord and then said, "Shit! Like I forgot something, man! Like I got the title down and the music, but I didn't like, do the words part yet. So like, that's all I got right now. Bummer, huh?"

He put his guitar in the case and headed for the door. Mark and Sally were in immediate pursuit. Mark placed himself in the musician's path.

Mark said to the guitarist, "I must affirm my interpretation of the title with you."

The musician forced his eyelids up and looked at Mark. Then he said, "Huh?"

Mark pulled the musician down on to the bench by the door and asked, "The objects within the title of your song were all symbolisms for various forms of spiritual domination. Am I not right?"

"Huh?" asked the guitarist.

Mark persevered, "Look, the nun must have symbolized the individual's slavery to tradition. The habit was the veil of oppression that imprisons free expression within it. The hill was the hierarchy in established religion. The kick was an unanswerable question that when asked pierced the veil, right?"

The musician's eyes opened fully. He reached into his pocket and pulled out a pack of E-Z Wider. He looked at Mark, tore out a sheet, handed it to him and asked, "Hey, man, like could you write that all down on this rolling paper, man? Like they could be the words and stuff 'cause like I already have the music and the name. Hey, man! Uh what are symbolisms? Or like, would my drummer know?"

The musician found his guitar and after a few attempts, found the door. Then he was gone. Everyone echoed his words, "Yeah, bummer. Yeah, right." Then with unanimous conviction, they declared, "He was just testing what he had on an audience."

"Mark, don't you see the connections?" asked Sally. "Rolling-Paper! Hill-Hierarchy! When he asked you for the rolling paper, he was telling you that the Establishment will be brought down by the force of Marijuana! That's why he winked at you with both eyes."

Mark looked up from the still blank E-Z wider and said, "Huh?"

My instinct toward self-preservation saw the conversations that followed, ascending into a funnel cloud skyward to Oz. Every one of these message-seeking assholes was busy trying to attach hidden meanings to some stoned-ass guitar player's brain-lock. I was sure the bullshit would somehow lead to, "And Paul is dead!"

I said a silent fuck this shit to all and began carving. A few hours slipped by unnoticed as the night crawlers all talked while I carved. I heard a demanding voice coming from my loft, "Kenny, turn off that drill! We can't hear each other talk."

Mark was hitting on a lonely, vulnerable Sally while she imitated the guitarists sounds. He was preaching his usual line to her: that certain prime numbers noteworthy to their respective birth times meant that sex with one another was predestined.

Being sick of reruns, I shouted, "Mark, you really have a lot of balls and you know who to thank for that! Why don't you shut your fuckin' mouth. The sound of your bullshit ruins my concentration. If you don't like it, finish your lecture on the stoop."

I thought, "If the crowds keep coming in, then the way to get them going out might be to start cutting a wooden beam with a power saw. And the time to try it is now."

Success! The shrill blade noise quickly emptied the place, except for one. Then upon opening his eyes from an interrupted chant, Mark ran for the door while calling for Sally to wait as she escaped up the hill.

With a running power saw in hand, I yelled at the crowd as it escaped up the block, "It's all a fuckin' work in progress! Don't expect so much. If you don't like the noise then tell the fuckin' boss!" Just another element in failure's grand design.

Terra leaned his head to the side and then pointed his nose to the door. I stood in disgust of those pretentious fools. I wondered as they fled, "Was their perception altered or aided by the pot that we smoked? Does their own depth of thought go only as far as the first conclusion they jump to? What motives do they attach to my actions if the tangents that they went off on are now how they perceive the guitarist?"

I knew that I had no one else to blame but me for allowing myself to be buoyed by a false sense of security by way of public recognition. My only course of immediate action was to place wax in my ears as Ulysses would instruct his crew to do, and block out the incongruity of those voices about me. No matter how hard I chipped away at my life to try to discover the true self within me, people kept shaping sawdust into idols.

I was feeling rage toward the world. My pent up anger toward those invaders of my refuge sought its animal release. I placed my nunchucks up my sleeve and locked up. Terra and I headed for the lightless abyss of the inner walkways at Prospect Park.

Terra ran through the bushes to the side of me. I walked along the pitch-black pathway, holding the handle of my concealed 'chucks. Although muggers filled the park during those times, they must have sensed that I would have welcomed their attempts. Sinister shadowy beings moved out of my way as I walked directly toward them.

My wrath dissipated through my own footsteps as I pondered the thought, "The path that I walked along and the path of my life must be free of bridges to any form of sanctuary."

JE

"How does a business that was designed to fail, find a way to prevent its very demise by offering a sense of security to its creator? Has the illusion of décor that the trash was intended to give taken on a life of its own? Does it draw others and myself within its presence while offering us only one another? Are these others causing me to see myself, if only with the hope of being unlike them? Will I accept the risk and the consequences and step off the precipice of choice that lies before me, to either begin a new path or fall to oblivion? Must I await a push or cause it? Are the dynamics of choice merely impetus toward greater levels of inertia? Can the seduction of the spirit be somehow more captivating than that of the flesh? How can concepts so abstract, as those of lives once lived or those to be, be so audacious as to attempt to usurp the absoluteness of the eternal now?"

Drawing of Terra, Found in September's Child's guest sketch book

Chapter Seven

Chariot

"Joe! Joe, open up!" I nearly landed on a sleeping Terra as the pounding at the door drove me from my dream to the floor below the loft. I looked to see Nina's ex-husband Harry's face appear in the peephole. He had the expression of a magistrate re-folding the little note handed to him by a jury.

Harry received a call from Deanna, while he was visiting his sons at Nina's brownstone. All that was left for him to do was to deliver the message. This might all sound complicated, but these were after all, the 'seventies.

The news that he brought was as bad as news can get. Harry said, "Joe, Deanna asked me to tell you this as simply as possible. Okay, here goes. Joe, someone told your father a joke and he died while laughing."

I could only imagine that punch line. But the joke would have to be on Fate itself. Dad dreaded a protracted, agonizing end. Could his laughter have been an expression of relief as he saw the quick way out?

Upon hearing Harry's message, my eyes drifted to the

water heater that my Dad had given me to make the hot drinks. It had become the heart of the coffee house. If only it was that heart that failed and not his. I held on to the cable reel where he sat when he visited. I thought how he was the only person that I allowed to sit on one of my carved cable reels. I wouldn't ask him to sit on the floor pillows unless he saw fit to do so.

Denial of the news of his passing would not allow my grief process to begin. I ran to the Stack of Barley Bar next door and called Deanna in New Jersey. My only hope was that someone was playing the cruelest of jokes. Deanna answered the phone on the first ring.

I immediately knew that her answer would corroborate Harry's words as she choked upon hearing my voice and said, "Joe, I loved him as I would my own father. I'm so sorry for you. Will you be okay?" We agreed to ride together in the limo at the funeral and said goodnight.

Would anything have changed if I ran through the rain to his car the last night I saw him? Was I being summoned by his brake lights or was he bidding me farewell?

My father was a member of Alcoholics Anonymous, but he was far from anonymous about his alcoholism. He wore his membership in his group as if it were a badge of honor. He knew of no greater strength than to overcome one's own weaknesses, in his case by choosing to do so one day at a time as if each were a lifetime.

He took on the task of bringing other alcoholics into his own apartment where he would dote over them until they chose to take the first step. His reference to them was, "They were a bunch of drunks, like me." His reason for doing this was, someone had once done it for him, so it must be the way it's done.

He would try to help others realize that their first step toward recovery was admitting to themselves that their lives were out of their own control. These people were termed pigeons. The endless roll call of those that he helped to return from the brink of self-destruction honored him for his efforts time after time with testimonials and plenty of simple respect. Of course, afterward, they would celebrate with endless coffee.

Ironically, he was working his latest pigeon's shift as a short-order cook in a local restaurant while the pigeon slept one off at Dad's apartment. He did this after working ten hours at his own job. It was there and then that he was stricken.

My father and I had a running dialogue about the "Serenity Pledge". The wall plaque in his small apartment read: "*God Grant Me the Serenity to Accept the Things I Cannot Change, The Courage to Change the Things I Can, And the Wisdom to Know the Difference.*"

I would challenge those words with my own adaptation: Accept the Things That You Cannot Change, And Change the Things That You Cannot Accept. We each realized how we differed, and we each accepted our differences.

My vision blurred, and then cleared as I wiped the corners of my eyes. They filled again with tears upon seeing the smile lines still near the corners of my father's eyes as he lay beneath the Serenity Pledge plaque placed in his casket. My brother Bob and I knew that it should always be with him as a fitting tribute to his life and his true vocation.

My father had only two things left in this life to leave to my brother and myself: the insurance settlement and his car. Bob was raising three kids. We agreed that he should keep whatever money there was from any insurance there might be. All I needed was a ride home to Brooklyn. I kept only the car and what might be in it.

The car contained the answer to another need. It was December and I had only a thin jacket. I found my father's old coat in the back seat. In addition to a half-pack of Pall Malls, it provided immediate warmth, four silver dollars and three two-dollar bills.

As I smoked the last of his cigarettes, I pledged that the car would never be liquidated for cash. I could not allow my father's memory to be cheapened by anything as transitory as money. I knew that there must be a reason for this car to enter my life. I was sure that it would reveal itself to me in time.

I returned to Brooklyn from the funeral and entered the coffee house to find it to be pitch-black and without its constant music. The fuses were okay and all the bulbs looked fine. The sunlight from outside revealed that a notice of termination of service from ConEd had been slipped under the door.

No payment, no juice! I guess that this was to be expected. The first rule in the design of a business that is destined for failure is, "Don't pay rent or utilities." The rest of the rules are easy. Indiscriminately bed down female patrons that you're attracted to, and throw out everyone else in order to do so. If you see that something that you're doing is drawing the public to your door, then lock it.

Perhaps if I weren't in a state of shock and grief, the shut-off would have signaled "success at last" and initiated my entry to the unknown. The two previously mentioned states have their way of placing one into a third, limbo, even if it might be temporary.

"Yo, Kenny! How are the lights and music back on in the coffee house? The dude shut you down right after you went to New Jersey for the funeral," said Rico. He and Fireman George hung out with me all of the previous night when I received the news about my Dad. They were nearby at Kathleen and Gordon's watching for me to return, so they could tell me about the shutoff.

After leaving them in a flash, I returned from the cellar of the apartment house next door in another and told my friends, "Rico, George, I decided that I could deal directly with the utility company," I pointed to the circuit room in the building next door where the jumper cables from my father's Chevy brought life back to the party.

I spent a long time with the doors locked to all but Rico

and a select few. I would allow my thoughts to spell themselves out in my journal. Every line that I wrote echoed the message of the one before it. They demanded that I abandon all forms of security in order to discover true freedom of spirit, whatever the consequences. It seemed like an easy enough request. To abandon all material surrounding me, so my spirit might soar was nothing compared to what my father had just done.

Deanna reminded me at the funeral about the Tarot deck and book she had given me. I told her that Melanie, a Theosophist friend, was teaching me how to read and interpret the cards. Deanna was happy to hear just how right she was. They did help to put things into a more meaningful perspective.

With the passing of my Dad, he and his apartment were no longer there as safety nets for me should my ride reverse course. I saw that any tether line back to the World was no more to be found. Like it or not, I would soon be thrust headlong into the emptiness which I sought. The memory of my father's approval of this living experiment that I chose gave impetus to my determination to continue what I began.

The grieving process, mixed with the need to survive, can both slow down and accelerate time in the strangest of ways. I chose sidereal time, the time value of the Universe, as my only reference to events.

The position of the Sun and the Moon was noted daily. My occult clientele saw to that. I allowed the coffee house to progress toward oblivion with neither my help nor hindrance. I had become a recluse within the crowd that filled September's Child.

Will was a neighborhood psychologist who hung out at September's nightly. He enjoyed taking charge of things and playing the role of host while I blended into the décor where I did nothing but read my cards and write in my journal.

Will's after-hours application of his vocation seemed to be geared toward one end only, finding women who would soon find his couch becoming a bed. Psychology must be similar to proctology, since either end that you enter will take you into some deep shit.

Could September's Child actually have begun setting a path of its own? Did the force that was within September's allow Will to take the helm knowing that I had set the course for the rocks ahead?

"Raphaël, qué pasa? Come in and have a cup of coffee. I haven't seen you since The Machine closed down. Is this your new hangout?" asked Will, greeting an old friend. I had seen Raphaël around the neighborhood. We kept crossing paths, but never met. He seemed to know me; at least he acted that way.

Raphael replied to Will, "I'm with a bunch of people. They're waiting up the block. I told them about this place and they're dying to check it out. Is there room for about five of us?"

Will told Danny, Mark and the other all-nighters to jump up on the loft-bed and make some space on the floor. He then returned from his authorative voice to that of the good host and said, "Any friends of yours are always welcome. Bring them in."

My demonstrations of spontaneous machine carving or combat with Rico during business hours had paused since Dad died. The curious were coming back, Will was having a social life, and I was contemplating the step before me.

"Renaissance" was playing through the speakers as Raphael came inside. I was walking toward the stereo when he came over and said to me, "Kenny, this is Apples."

I came to an immediate stop and looked at her. Quickly, I glanced at my carving of the man and woman. I thought back to my first days at September's as the flames of two candles on that cable reel cast Apples' shadow, combined with mine, upon the door.

The mysterious blue-eyed woman that I had seen at The Gazebo restaurant weeks before was within September's, smiling at me. I knew that I must have smiled back because my upper cheeks caused my eyes to nearly shut. Raphael stepped back asking, "I get the impression that you two met before. Right?"

Apples and I kept looking into one another's eyes. I nearly answered Raphael's question by saying, "Many times." Fortunately for me, I was speechless. Everything else in the room faded from my perception, except for the smile before me that was speaking volumes to my soul. A small glimpse of eternity enveloped us as all about us was equally diminished to irrelevance.

Life seemed to return to the distant shadows that were my friends. My ears filled with the returning sounds of Renaissance and Annie Haslam's singing and the realization that all I had been doing was staring into Apples' eyes. I hadn't yet said a word to this woman who just walked into my world.

I took her by the hand, the good host that I was, and immediately introduced her to a person that she already knew and to whom she wasn't speaking. Small world isn't it?

I wanted to throw everyone out and just be with her, but good behavior was the order of this night. I sat with her and her group. We exchanged smiles while her friends sang songs in Hebrew. There were times between songs that we chatted. I described the different features of September's to her, feeling at ease while basking in her smile. Her fingers were gliding among the energy lines that I had carved upon the cable reel of the man and the woman. I placed my hand on the table near her hand. She drank tea. I drank in her presence.

Her friends put their guitars away and I was delightfully surprised that Apples remained seated next to me as we waved good-bye to the evening's troubadours. The last record fell from the stack. Rico opened the door and waved his hand for me to leave with Apples as he and Will practiced Tai Chi.

From the moment I first saw her, I felt that I always knew her. We walked toward her apartment on Polhemus Place. I felt as awkward as a school kid. Somehow, being outside of the coffee house environment, I found it difficult to initiate conversation.

Suddenly, words worked their way around the lump in my throat as I asked, “Do you work around here?”

Having heard myself, I asked myself, “How the hell did those words sneak past the censors? Of all the possible openers for conversation, a guy like me who rejected the working world breaks the ice with talk of work.”

She answered, “I'm teaching English in a ghetto school during the day, at night I'm studying for my exams.”

“Your exams for what? You don't mind me asking do you?”

“No. I'm studying for my doctorate in Comparative Literature. I have to write a thesis but first pass an oral exam by the department heads.”

I guess that I must have been in a big hurry to show off my ignorance as I asked, “Can't a note from your dentist qualify as an oral exam?” She pushed me away, laughing.

“After you become a Ph.D., then what? Do you get raises and recognition from The Board of Ed? Or do you go on to something else?”

We were approaching her apartment building. I guess we both wanted to spend more time talking, so we sat on some stranger's stoop.

Then she answered my question, “Probably something else, somewhere else. I always wanted to be a professor in my field. These jobs are usually out of the area or even in Europe. Who knows where I'll land?”

She suddenly grabbed both of my hands with hers, and exclaimed,"I don't usually discuss my ambitions with strangers, but I sort of feel at ease around you. Let me just air this out on you. After all, what you described in your coffee house essentially showed it to be your career choice of passion."

Her blue eyes looked off into the distance within her mind as she elaborated, "I feel that I have to finish my doctorate in Comp Lit, but perhaps it's because I am now so close to the end. It is a field that I love, but as I close in on finishing, I see that I may have lost my enthusiasm for it."

Although I hardly knew her, I saw sadness as an unwelcome participant in our first evening together. I looked at her and asked, "And where do you see that your passion might have flown and one day nest?"

She looked away briefly. Her eyes again shined, but with an explosion of inspired brilliance. Our clenched hands jumped up and down on her lap as she said, "It's as though an idea was traveling through the air and found me sitting here! Since you asked, here goes. If at some point, if I could redirect my efforts, it would be to help immigrant kids somehow continue to grow academically in their native language while they also develop their abilities in English."

She was happy again! Then she said,"What I'm studying now seems like a job. But come to think of it, yeah! That might be where my passion will land. I don't want to talk about that any more tonight. Now I feel happy. So Kenny, have you always been in the coffee business?"

She asked me this as we took up our leaning positions on the stoop. For some reason, I sensed that she would understand what I was really doing with September's, so what the hell.

I told her, "What you saw at my place on First Street was pure illusion, for lack of a better explanation. It's a waiting room before the exit door leading to my life without any physical possessions."

Every other time I tried to explain my motives to others, their reactions would seem dubious. I was taking a chance here.

Her head tilted in a way that suggested interest. She smiled at me and said, "When I saw you at the Gazebo, a while back, I pictured you as a successful business person with a firm hold on things. How can September's Child not be successful?"

I couldn't believe that she remembered that moment and me. I returned my jaw to my head and said, "September's Child's success will be when it fails. The coffee house's form will become that of confetti. When it settles, the crowd will fade down the street and I will be living on it."

She didn't get up and run. She actually saw merit in what I was doing. "Great!"

She answered, "I wish you every success in your search for failure. But what will happen after the door opens and the empty world stands before you? Did you plan that far ahead?"

Looking into her eyes was having the effect of sodium pentathol coursing through my veins. My answers preceded their very formation in thought, "I want to know the feeling of life with no plan at all, only a sense of urgency. Like that of a skydiver landing in Hell. I crave desperation as the litmus test of my very being. Security, planning and structure are all part of a cage that I see myself breaking free from."

I went on as she listened, "I had enough of the structured world of business and all forms of controlled, predictable behavior. It's time for me to rely only upon the absurd and the outrageous as my guides. It seems to be the only way to make sense of things."

There! It's out in the open! Instead of "I think you should leave now", she said, "You want to see your true self revealed by eliminating society's physical and ideological shelters. I would keep some record or even a journal detailing the experience. Do you foresee a direction that you might choose after the flakes settle?"

I still couldn't believe that she remembered me. While I thought of an answer, we had found our way into her apartment and we were holding hands across her table. Before the teacup found my lip, a fantasy adventure from the far reaches of my mind surfaced. I responded to her question from before with it as a possibility.

"I have a car now. I may do day labor as I drive southwest through Texas, learning Spanish along the way. I might like to volunteer to work on The Mayan Indian excavations in the Yucatan Peninsula. There are many exciting mysteries just waiting to be revealed beneath the ruins."

She held her cup to her mouth as I continued, "After Columbus, the European Inquisitors stripped an extremely civilized Native American culture of its identity. They destroyed every last fragment of written records, most of which the Inquisitors didn't understand, and any other evidence that showed that these people were culturally equal or superior to the Europeans.

"The Indians were brutalized. Their most intransigent leadership was killed off. Any survivors were completely dehumanized and reduced to human debris."

"The Conquistadors brought some of these people back in Spain to show the Royals. The caged Indians were perceived as naked savages. The Jesuits then stepped in as their saviors. Jesuits would accompany all future expeditions to force their beliefs upon those who survived the slaughter." Her eyes lowered as she placed her cup down.

"I'm sorry, I'm rambling. I guess I have an ax to grind, or at least a tomahawk."

She looked to a tattered picture of five people on her mantle and said sadly, "That's not the last time that someone tried something like that."

I squeezed her hand gently. Our eyes met and that changed the subject. Words would have to wait. As I was about to leave, she stopped me. While handing me a book she said, "I think that you might like to read this. Let me know what you think of it." Her library would have to miss "Siddhartha" for a while.

Every day I would look at her phone number on the

piece of paper that became a bookmark, though stuck on page one. My moods during the coming weeks ranged from grief for my father, to rage for allowing myself to prolong the coffee house's life by connecting the jumper cables, perhaps missing my window of opportunity.

Between those moods was a sense of longing to be with Apples. I could neither foresee nor dismiss the remote possibility of something meaningful developing between us. If there was a mirror around, where I might see myself and my state of being, I would have to choose dismiss.

Rico and I returned to our martial arts and increased the intensity of violence in our workouts. Out of some sense of respect for Will we limited this to the late afternoons. We would nearly collapse from the spent energy. Will took pleasure in seeing this. His fear of my sudden outbursts at night in September's subsided. My unwelcome entourage would still flock to the door nightly and I would routinely ignore them.

JE

"I reach out from the window of a train carrying me off to battle. I grasp the hand of a woman that I met, but hardly know. Yet I can only hope she will be here if I return. The battle is within my own soul. The destination is here at its start. I know that I will be detached from all of my resources soon. I welcome the climax of whatever process has taken me this far. Might the empty vessel that is my soul be filled or shattered? Could my dreams discard hope as their anchor as I float free of the weight of material? The chance to learn which it will be is in and of itself, incentive to go on."

"Will, are you setting up for your night job?" I asked while sitting on the loft as he entered carrying some little cakes and other supplies. He ignored me and went to work setting up the tea racks and lining up the cups. I kind of expected a paper hat and a Fries With That? lapel button to come out of his shopping bag.

He answered, "A lot of people have learned to depend upon me to keep this place going. It's your right to grieve, but you should see a time coming when you resume your responsibilities."

"My responsibilities to what or to whom?" I asked as I jumped to the floor from the loft. Then I closed my journal and placed a white paper coffee filter on my head while singing, "Special orders don't upset us!"

Will aimed a scolding finger at me and said, "This is all up to you! It's your decision whether or not September's Child continues or disappears like all of the other coffee houses did around here."

Will kept wiping the counter and the tables as he gave me a pep talk. I held my chucks over my head then at him in a facetiously threatening form. I asked, "Are you going to lay that towel over your arm as you show the folks to their tables? Should I get some of the guys from the schoolyard to park cars for our guests?"

"Kenny, you can throw all the sarcasm at me that you want. But if you keep treating everyone the way you've been, you will only be hearing echoes in here!"

Poor Will, there he was, a psychologist trying to save a suicide jumper. Could it be that he didn't recognize that I was in mid-flight, and he was with me hand in hand?

I laughed and said to the poor fool, "Will, the echoes might be coming from the iceberg dead ahead."

He looked at me intently, silenced by the crashing symbolisms. The roar of the pouring rain announced itself and then quieted with the door opening and then quickly closing.

I heard a nervous, yet concerned voice say, "I was so sorry to hear that Terra ran off. Some people think they saw him at the park walking with a guy with two other dogs. Should I ask them to check it out for you?"

Kathleen stood by the doorway. She was soaked from the rain. "Get over here girl!" I said, "Put your wet coat near the radiator and pour yourself some coffee. Look Kathleen, I can't afford to feed Terra anymore. If he hooked up with a dog lover, leave them be. Anyway, it's about time he puts his pot habit behind him."

I really missed Terra but I was glad that he may have made it big.

Kathleen asked, "Do you mind if I put this tape on and try out some steps before the crowd comes?" I pointed to the stereo and nodded affirmatively.

Will interjected, "You should have come over earlier to do that. People will be coming in soon and all of the tables are in place." He was plugging in the little beacon light in the window. Somehow, the whole world had learned the secret knock.

I asked myself, "Just who the hell is he to talk to her like that?"

Then I said to him, "Kathleen can dance whenever she wants and to whatever music she chooses! Maybe you can't see the stamp on this black woman's hand. It says, 'permanent rights of re-entry'." I kicked the tables aside in order to give her room.

Will looked toward the door nervously. I guess I was hoping that he would run out. Instead he said, "Maybe it's still a little early. I really like your dancing Kathleen, go ahead."

He liked it even more since she left Gordon after he slapped her in public. I watched my friend dance while Will set his sights on her butt. Every night she had to blow off steam with a dance on this floor before she faced the world.

She said, "Thanks, Kenny, I hope you're feeling better. Thanks again, Will. I have to bring my sister around to meet you. She wants to be a psychologist too someday."

She blew a kiss and waved it to us as she left. I went back up on the loft. The bricks were nice and hot from the furnace below. I placed myself in my corner and began writing in my journal.

Will had mentioned to me that one of his therapy groups would meet there that night, before his regular group of friends arrived. Instead of their usual structured encounter at Will's Formica-paneled, fluorescent-lit office, the ambiance of September's might inspire the exploration of therapeutic paths yet untaken.

This was to be a casual get together, maybe some music and poetry. No hard emotional confrontations or psychic torment. Will would orchestrate the spontaneity. I saw no role for myself to play in his pending psychodrama. Squeezing my body deeply into the corner, I lowered my pen to the journal.

It sounded like the rain was mixed with the cackling of whining hens as they congregated outside the door. I heard one of them say, "This can't be it, it looks like an abandoned candy store."

Another one whined, "Maybe Will meant First Street in Manhattan." Will ran to the door before his group might turn themselves loose on the neighborhood and showed them in.

Surprisingly, as they entered the store, they appeared to be sane. One of the girls was nearly cute. She climbed up to the second rung of my ladder and said, "Hello." Since there was no evidence of drool or foam coming from her mouth, I smiled politely. There was no interest coming from any part of me so I went back to writing my poetry.

It only takes a minute to show people a fifteen-by-fifteen-foot room. With the orientation tour over, Will's group gathered around the largest table and began bickering. Will reminded them, "Tonight, only music and written works are the agenda."

The guitars and flutes sounded pretty good as they worked into some Beattle's riffs directly from tuning. They all wanted a guy named Damian to sing an original song of his that they all seemed to like. Damian was recently released from an upstate facility.

After a few moments of struggling, Damian realized that since he couldn't do both at the same time, he must either play the flute or sing. So he grabbed a guitar from the unwilling hands of one of the girls and obliged them with a ballad called "Damian's Song":

"You made me love you from your window
Your silhouette would speak to me
I cry at night, where did our love go
Your blackened shade a memory"

Then the chorus joined hands. Swaying back and forth they smiled and sang,

"There's a sad and untold story
Of panties hanging from a tree
A deadened heart lies in this city
I'll follow you eternally"

I don't recall whether or not my feet ever made contact with the ladder. I do know, that as they landed on the floor below, I yelled, "You fuckin' people are truly fuckin' nuts! And you Will, are the craziest! Listen to this fuckin' maniac's words, man! How can you allow that sorry-ass fool on the guitar to reinforce his delusion by singing about it with your approval, and then transfer it to the chorus?

"What's next on the agenda, Maestro? Maybe they'll all listen to "Helter-Skelter" and you'll pass around the knives? Let me get the fuck outta here! There's only one padded wall in this place."

I knew then that Will had spent eight years in training just to drive people crazy or maybe to misunderstand them from a different level. I grabbed my jacket and quickly left Will's asylum. The sound of thunder was a welcome relief from the echoes of Will's snake pit. I yearned for the feeling of the deluge outside to somehow cleanse my senses of the senselessness occurring within what was once my place of refuge.

My wish was granted. A heavy sheet of rain pelted my face as soon as I opened the door. As grateful as I was for my escaping to the elements, 'Lung, who stood by his grocery cart across the street, longed to escape from them to the warmth of the place I had just left.

I thought that I saw him pointing to the basement hatch. I caught the door from snapping off from the wind. After closing it, I was about to run across the street to ask him why he always pointed there. The rain became so heavy that I couldn't see the other side never mind him. When I could finally run across to him, he was nowhere in sight.

I ran from First Street and found safe haven nearby at Minsky's Pub. I placed my open pad on the top of the barrel table hoping my pen would join the paper and tell me that what I had left was only a hallucination. The bar crowd must have recycled three times as my pen raced across the paper; my mind following its guiding force.

Warm soft skin suddenly brushed past my cold wet ear that heard an even warmer voice ask, "What do you mean by,

> 'Hearing my name not sounding the same,
> As it's sold like diesel, Jesus or pork chops
> At a Kentucky truck stop . . . ?'"

A woman's hand was reaching over my shoulder, pointing to the page that I was writing upon. I closed my book. I followed the hand then the arm. As I suspected, it led to a face. It was void of make-up yet filled with curiosity.

I looked at her and said, "I imagine that you would have had to have been there from the beginning to truly understand."

She asked, "Where?"

I answered, "Hell, I guess."

Of course Hell could have meant anything from serving in Vietnam to living with one's parents, as far as she was concerned. I didn't feel like elaborating.

She placed herself alongside of me and said, "I write poetry too. My name is Kanika. I've seen you around First Street. Do you live there or nearby?"

I don't know why, but I answered, "I used to. Now I'm just hangin' out." I saw that a puddle was developing beneath where I was sitting. I said, "Maybe I should hang out to dry while I'm at it."

She read some of her poetry from a thick old diary with a little broken lock. It must have been with her since she was a kid. Her writing was unlike the street poetry that I heard at September's. It was very structured, nearly of the level of a trained writer. She had drawn a cartoon and inserted it three quarters of the way into the book. It was of her, standing on the shore of Brighton Beach, while holding up a stop sign at Europe across the sea to the east.

She placed herself back in time with Pre-Columbian Monterey, California and its rugged coast at her back and her present-day living in Brooklyn at her feet. Human history as she saw it was an irrelevance, against the endless power of the sea.

"Are you from Monterey?" I asked.

"No, I've never even been there. It's supposed to be a beautiful place on the Pacific coast and Brooklyn is the coolest place in The East. I just see Middle America and its pathetic history being crushed by its waves as everything in its path yields with the European Westward invasion, drowning in the tide. If that might have occurred, then maybe the enormous sins of the time between then and now may never have taken place."

I couldn't decide if she was reading my mind or had read more from my journal than she admitted to. I said to myself, "Who cares? I'm half-dry, half-drunk and since I'm here, I'm not where I just left."

I emptied my glass and let the conversation take its own course. I asked, "By sins, I gather that you mean events such as the enslavement of the black people and the subjugation of the Indians in order to benefit so-called Civilization's voracious appetite for resources as it marches forward in its timeless quest to convert the noble human creature into loyal consumers and corporate goons."

The bartender handed us the two Black Russians that Kanika sent for. Then she said, "Very good, let's not leave out the motivating force behind it all, the insatiable appetite for consumption of property and people by the Eurocentric authors of History. Wasn't the eternal domination by force, of third world souls begun by the Vatican's army of Jesuits and their accomplices, the ruling royal families? "

I nodded in affirmation of her statement and added, "And the image of God that they brought to those people was nothing but a reflection of their own agenda."

Two more Black Russians found our hands and even more quickly our mouths. Her eyes drifted, melding with her inner visions. I awaited their return. With my insides thoroughly lubricated in alcohol, I said, "I see that we have a shared perspective on these issues. Isn't it amazing, the entire wave of domination of both North and South America began with the total commitment by the Spanish royals to the greatest blunder in the history of navigation?"

She wore either a look of bewilderment or intoxication. I raised my finger before she could ask for an explanation and added, "Columbus approached Ferdinand and Isabella, the king and queen of Spain. He said that the world must be round and if they provided him with funding and personnel, he would sail westward. By doing so, prove it to be round by landing on the shores of India."

Her intoxication was surely approaching my own when she asked, "So, what's your fucking point?"

I continued, "Well he did sail, as we now know. When he met the first people, he was so sure that he was right and that he had arrived in India, that he called the natives Indians! Just imagine what we would call them if he sold the royals on the notion that if he sailed westward, he would land on the shores of Poland."

She laughed and said, "You're right. You're just hangin' way out there."

After much talk and many Black Russians, I guess we left Minsky's and hung out at her little room at a commune in Crown Heights, because that's where I woke up the next day to the sounds of people talking loudly at a kitchen table.

I walked toward the sounds through a hallway lined with posters. One had a red fist holding the words, Power to the People! Another was of Che Guevara looking bravely to the future while the people looked to him. Then there was one with Chairman Mao's fist clenching a red, green and black A-K 47 held above a crowd in triumph. Then there was one with a gigantic Afro superimposed over an atomic mushroom cloud, as it protected a group of black children from the fallout-laden rains. That one was too much for my pounding head to bear so I followed the sounds.

I covered my face from the blinding kitchen light bulb and heard, "Hey everyone, this is Kenny. We were doing poetry down at the Slope last night. C'mon over Kenny, sit down and eat."

There were at least ten people at the kitchen table. Little kids were chasing one another up and down the stairs that led to the bedrooms. I could hear loud adult voices coming from the floor above. The words cause and movement were mentioned dozens of times in their dialogue, the volume of which was escalating with each word.

The heated conversation above had caused concern to the people at the kitchen table. Not wanting to seem as though I was privy to their business, I pretended to be lost in the act of eating the food before me. This was not difficult for a starving man to do.

Suddenly, the combatant conversation upstairs was overpowered by a single voice, "Fuck that shit! I'm out of here after breakfast! You motherfuckers stay the fuck up here 'til I'm gone! The only bread I wanna break with you will be across your face! You do what the fuck you want! I want no part of that kinda' shit again. You be goin' too far this time! Fuck you! Motherfuck you!"

He put his intentions bluntly to his dubious comrades. The force of his pronouncement of indignation through righteous rage let all within earshot know that he had arrived at the point where the self declares its separation from the mass.

The content of his tirade may have been unfamiliar, but something about him registered in my mind. Suddenly, a cold chill ran up my spine as his tone, and above all his fury, matched a face and form in my memory.

By the time he said his last fuck, the voice that had become so familiar to me joined us at the table. His enraged demeanor became less threatening as the sounds of his cursing melded into the chomping of his toast. He took a long, loud slurp of coffee while glancing between Kanika and me.

Like the sudden silence that comes when you least expect it in a game of musical chairs, he fixated on me. He stared directly in my eyes, and then he squinted his. Looking back at Kanika he said, "Kanika, I see hair on that person. It be long like a woman's hair might be. But unless the circus is in town, and I know it ain't, I see a beard like no woman I ever seen."

He yanked at my beard and said, "Kanika you bitch! You been messin' with a boy this time. Damn! You been messin' with a white boy. I don't know if I should curse you or congratulate you. Never thought Whitey would be puttin' a fire to this place, 'specially under your ass."

My face was half-covered with the girly hair he was talking about. I must have changed a lot to the world outside of me. There I was in the den of the dragon that once nearly slew me and Jamal didn't even know who I was.

How ironic, to witness him breaking away from the cause that once held him so strongly that he would have sliced my throat. As he reached over the table to slap me five, it was refreshing to see no weapons in his open hand. I had thoughts about introducing myself, but these were the circumstances of a world new to me and of one that would soon be new to him, at least after breakfast. Why bring up old times when he's apparently on the threshold of self-discovery. It was best that we took it all from there.

Kanika looked at Jamal from behind her folded arms. With her head moving from side to side she said in an almost motherly tone, "Why don't you shovel some more free food down your throat and shut your never-ending mouth? Jamal, this is Kenny. Kenny, this is Jamal. Now play nicely boys."

Jamal shut his mouth while smiling like the toast was the canary that had his tongue. The silence lasted for a split second as he said to me, "Good goin', white brother. If Kanika say you're cool, I'm cool with it."

I thought, "If only I could remember what it was that I did that changed history here." Whatever it was, I was cool with it. Kanika walked me to the door after breakfast. I told her that I had no phone and maybe we would see one another again at Minsky's.

As I was leaving, I stopped in my tracks. The dim hall lamp revealed a copy of the Pegasus poster taped to the wall. The winged horses and warriors that helped me begin my evolution were hanging among the symbols of the Revolution.

What would I say to those who would fly toward the horizon that I had crossed? Would I beckon them to leap over, or would I paint them a picture from the other side where dreamers might seek the barbed vines of deliverance from dreaming?

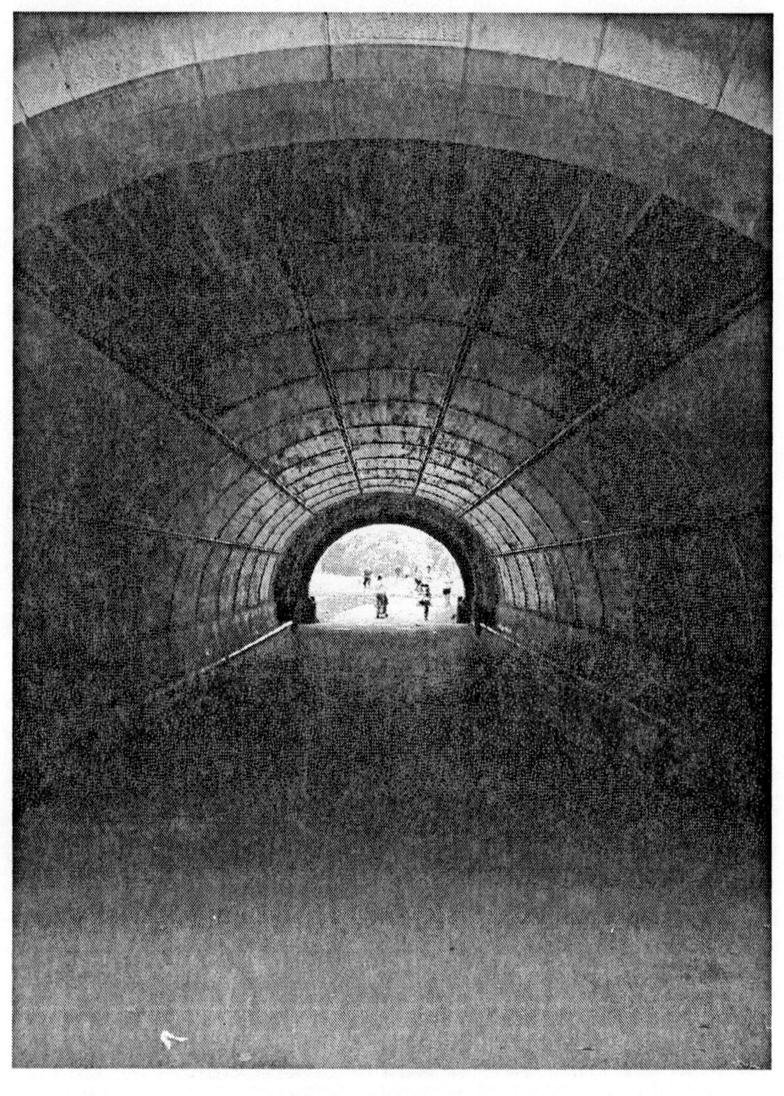

Tunnel in Prospect Park

Photo by J.K. Savoy

Chapter Eight

Impact

With my denim jacket covering my head from the rain, I began my long walk to the Slope from Kanika's commune in Crown Heights. My reward for years of cigarettes was to walk the hill when I tried to keep up with the runners in Prospect Park.

I was soaked to the skin as I neared the coffee house. I turned the corner only to see Benny, the landlord, holding an umbrella over two women. They were standing at the curb in the midst of pillows, cable reels and everything else that was September's.

As they walked beneath the shelter of the umbrella to the shelter of what once was my store and home, Benny said, "Kenny, I never saw you with the rent for months. I figured that you split. It was a lousy hundred bucks a month, you idiot! Where the fuck was your head, Boy? Sorry about the mess, but these people took the place over."

A growing torrent of gutter water washed my coffee bags down the hill like so much afterbirth. Finally, I had been reborn unto the street. I sat in shock on one of the three cable reels that remained on the dwindling heap that was once my work of art.

Somehow I pictured that my leap to the other side would be much different, perhaps even somewhat ceremonious. Things might have seemed a bit more worthy of my dream if I were at least still dead drunk instead of having a hammers-of-hell hangover.

I stuck my foot under a cable reel rolling toward the curb and thought, "Oh well, wheels that you put in motion can crush you, especially if you turn your back on them."

I could see only the rain that enveloped me and September's Child's triumphant moment of failure. I heard only the sounds of my pounding head and of the two women who had gone inside with Benny saying, "We must sheetrock these walls and cover those ugly bags on the ceiling. Better yet tear them down and those ugly fruit baskets, ugh! Maybe we can lay some nice linoleum for the floor. We have to brighten up this dreary look. Did you say that the boy outside had a coffee shop here? No wonder he went out of business. He never even put up a sign or had tables and chairs."

From the curtain of rain, a figure appeared and said, "You look like you just got thrown off the "Magical Mystery Tour" bus, or maybe it just crashed into your ego."

I looked up through the downpour and recognized Will's beaming rays of self-righteousness casting their condescension upon me.

I looked through the rain and his arrogance and asked, "Will, are you gloating? If you are motherfucker, your ass will be floating down the gutter in one of those coffee bags! I ought to fuck you up on the spot. To think, the last thing that I had to see and hear in September's was your group of sick bastards singing about panties in a tree. So tell me, where's Svengali gonna hustle chicks now?"

Cupping his hands from the rain, he lit a cigarette and said, "I tried to help you come to terms with your circumstances, Kenny. You never listen to anyone. It always has to be your way. No matter what anybody else did to help you, you went off in your own self-destructive direction. People depended on you and you let them down."

I took the cigarette from his mouth and smoked it. I stood up and said as the remnants of my life's experiment floated away together with his attempt to assign guilt, "If I allowed myself to be helped back to normality by you, then could I write a cute little song too? You don't help people Will. You just help yourself to them through their vulnerabilities. You transform their maladies into a dependency on you in order to gratify yourself. You're the one that needs help, you fuckin' parasite! Now sit down and join me at the curb. Let's see what opportunity may float by to change your life's direction."

He took his little bag of teas and crumpets and headed toward his office.

JE [Mental notes]

"Is this raging gutter water the river where I am to sit, to fast and to wait? Has my life now been scripted by Herman Hesse? I have no direction, so I must sit. I have no food, so I must fast. I have nothing but time, so I can only wait. If I crossed the street, would I see the course of my life change much like that of the torrent, or would both continue downhill? While I envision my self, sitting on the opposite curb, seeing me, am I witnessing the ideal of "Siddhartha" in his quest for self through enlightened denunciation? Am I witnessing Old 'Lung in his days before the shopping cart became his refuge? Our shared laughter is the only answer to our mutual quandary."

"Kenny, stop laughing like an idiot and bring your stuff up to my crib. Here, let me help you carry some of your shit," said Gordon from next door as he picked up a cable reel and began walking toward his building, down the street.

I did the same and followed him to his apartment. He was coming from the park with his dogs when he saw me. There was no second option to consider. The only thing greater than my shock from hearing him offer me help was my haste in accepting it.

The door closed and the dogs scurried to their water bowl as Gordon said, "You can sleep in the hall tonight. There's an inflatable mattress in the closet."

I was too hung over, cold, wet and confused to question or analyze his motives. My life was much like the flow of the gutter water, diverted and ultimately dammed.

With my soaked still hung-over head spinning, I answered, "Halls beat curbs anytime Gordon. Thanks, Man! I have nothing left but what you see on your floor. If can keep my shit here for a while, I'll get it as soon as I figure things out. I can't fit it all in my father's car. I guess that'll be my bedroom when it dries up out there."

As I leaned my birthday cake reel against the wall and placed the remaining cable reels in the closet, I noticed that there was something different about the place. The last time I was in this apartment Kathleen had made a dinner for Vera, Gordon and me.

Then I realized, since then, Gordon had carved designs on his doors and burned them with a torch in a similar manner that I had done with the cable reels. There were three pillows made of coffee bags stacked in a corner and I saw two of my missing cups on his windowsill. I felt barely enough energy to question his intentions. I allowed myself to accept it as flattery, together with my gratitude.

I made it a point to check that my father's jacket was in the wooden trunk. It was. I couldn't wear it any more. I felt like a grave robber since the time I smoked his last half-pack of cigarettes that he left in his pocket the day that he died. Gordon liked the trunk. I told him that is was my last bastion of privacy where I stowed my personal shit.

He rubbed his hand across the shellac finish with admiration and said, "You can crash here for a while. There's no particular hurry for you to leave. I'm all alone since Kathleen split for California."

Gordon's lazy eye dwelled on my trunk while the other looked at me when he said, "I guess she didn't tell you. She took off and went to Santa Barbara to live with her sister. She got a gig singing and dancing at some club. I thought for sure Lana would take off after her, but lately she has her eye on some Commie bitch."

Gordon fixed both eyes on mine and said, "You help me out here whatever way you can, when you can. Just remember this isn't a permanent gig. You know, I'm not working either. So we can share any resources that we each grab along the way." We would have to start grabbing immediately since the pantry shelves were empty.

There was a knock at the door, followed by an announcement, "Kenny! Here's the rest of your shit from the store. I really should have kept it as payment toward your fucking up the place like you did."

Benny brought my stereo and whatever he couldn't sweep from the floor to the apartment. Gordon hooked up the music at once and began rifling through my boxes and said, "You have an incredible record collection. Did you buy all this stuff?"

Jim Morrison sang "L.A. Woman" while I told Gordon how people would bring a record to listen to with their friends at September's, then leave it there as a tip of sorts. It seemed like the gift that would keep on giving. We scavenged all of the pot fragments that we could find in his ashtrays and managed to roll one healthy joint from it. The record finished, so did the joint.

The ever so faint hiss of the air mattress lulled me into a zone of comfort while it also signaled its own end to come as support. My quilt had survived the Great Expulsion by hiding in the trunk. It felt like both a receiving blanket and shroud as I wrapped it tightly around me and peered over its perimeter. Its boundary seemed to both define the world around me while it allowed me to hide from it.

I drifted off to a twilight sleep only to hear the last note of the New Orleans jazz band turning the corner as it left the graveyard. My ancestors faces emerged from behind their tombstones, singing in chorus, "Be careful what you wish for."

Was that the deafening crash of the iron gates shutting? Or was it me tripping over my own headstone? Maybe it was it just a cockroach falling from the ceiling and into my ear. The sound of hitting bottom can come in many forms.

I burst awake with a question, "Is this finally rock bottom or is it the first trap door in a series that precedes a bottomless pit?" I was left with only one answer; "A life of unpredictability is no way how I imagined it to be."

JE

"Could I have thought, at some level, that a magical portal would exist to jump back through, should I not like what I find here?

Could I have thought that I could dive through the edge of the horizon, gather some knowledge into a basket and quickly return to life as it was, only wiser?

Is being homeless, penniless yet free, the power that I sought when I was comfortable, affluent and enslaved?

Will the spirit and intellect's thirst for knowledge and understanding soon be eclipsed by the overwhelming needs of the stomach?

Will I have the courage and strength to remain on a path toward enlightenment as I become humbled along the way?

If I pointed randomly to a page of "Be Here Now", what could it suggest, having never been here itself?"

"The fruit and vegetable store throw this shit out every night, mon. You peel away the rotten shit and the rest be good! Gordon, boil up some water in that big pot. We be having a nice soup today," said Rico as he walked into the apartment with bags of half-rotted food, compliments of the Korean grocer's dumpster. The landfill would be denied that day, but not our stomachs.

Hardly shocked by how Rico could enter the locked apartment without even the dogs barking, Gordon said, "You know, I pay shit here, thanks to rent control. My family has had this place for ages and as long as I come up with the knot every month, I'm in. I have room here. You guys can both crash as long as you kick in somehow, but don't ever call our shit a commune! I had enough commie bullshit in the jungles of 'Nam. Okay, let's do this thing and get over together."

My question concerning Gordon's sudden hospitality was answered when Rico reached into his never-ending stash and rolled one fat healthy joint. Gordon quickly lit it as I seasoned the soup in progress. The kitchen, like the rest of the place, smelled of ancient grease spray clinging to all surfaces, highlighted by the essence of roach poison. I cleaned enough of the room to make a token acknowledgement to my restaurant upbringing. We discussed how we would pool our resources toward our mutual survival without calling it communal living over some USA-made soup and USA-grown herb.

The grocery stores would become our mainstay for edible trash. Restaurants were not as good. They would mix leftovers with spoiled food. You had to be careful: the food might be covered with floor sweepings. They could contain pesticides or even rat shit. Not too many businesses stop to separate clean solid waste for the pickers.

Speaking of rat shit, if you hit a restaurant dumpster, you have to be there when the garbage lands or the rats could get there first and you could get bitten. To avoid a rabies treatment, you would have to bring the dead rat if you're lucky enough to catch it and kill it. Since emergency rooms wanted means of payment before service, they were not about to do rodent post-mortems.

Italian restaurants and pizzerias always were good for day-old bread. Rico sometimes came in early in the morning with fresh rolls from the bag left in front of the deli. He would only take a few pieces so they wouldn't notice anything missing. If you're greedy or demanding, you can lose a life-support stop or worse yet get caught.

The blinding ray of sunshine through the hole in the curtain in Gordon's living room would be its last of the day before it set behind the tenement across the street. As it had for so many identical days before, it signaled the coming of yet another night. Our first stop was always the schoolyard across the street.

The thumping sound of a basketball would be followed by a moment of stillness, followed by the crash of rubber to backboard, then always by, "Yo, yo! Over here! Yo!"

The games in the schoolyard were fierce, but not nearly as violent as the sparring that would follow between my street brother, Rico, and me. Gordon would know that we had finished our workout, because one of us would grab the broom handle from him just as he was about to send a Spaldeen three sewers down.

The streetlights would glow, and then brighten, as did the first stars. The cries of parents seeking their children to return home for dinner reverberated from the walls of the five story buildings that lined First Street. While most children fled to their homes, a meal and the end of another day, those who heard no call might gather their own children for another night of scavenging.

Somehow, the derelict survivors of life's separate storms managed to find the street as a common safe harbor and feeding ground. At first, street living seemed to be anarchy. As I lived in it, I began to see us like the remains of broken people somehow managing to fit together and form a caring community of outlaws.

The Establishment looked down on the hippies. The hippies looked away from the Establishment. Both would see the outlaws of the street as outsiders looking in. The outlaws would see all others as interchangeable characters in different costumes all cut from the same cloth, hanging from the same rack.

Living a street existence bears a striking similarity to living in jail. You spend most of your time confined to your area of life support and defending it, possibly with your life. But the main reason it seemed like jail was that most of the people you deal with have been in jail at one time or another or would soon be returning.

"Bro', I hear drums! Let's head up to Second Street and check it out," said Rico, speaking from his uncanny sixth sense for finding a party. Slope parties ranged from commune happenings, where the two bags of chips and two bottles of wine were gone in the first two minutes, to the mansion dweller's bashes where there were always plenty of women, good smoke and food. Fortunately for us, Rico was sensing the latter.

Like a hovering night-hawk, Gordon was obsessed in his search for new female prey. Perhaps it was his hatred for Communists that fostered his sole criterion; she had to be loaded. For some reason he thought that some rich woman would be just as obsessed with being snatched up by a guy who was destitute but free-market oriented.

Isn't that what parties are for, a place to project your motives on innocent bystanders? Fortunately, the noise is so loud you can't always hear the rejections.

"Rico, did you hear the music or did you smell the pot first?" I asked as we slapped fives while running across traffic, over parked cars or around anything in the path of the sound of the drums.

"Mon, it be maybe a little bit of each. I know if there be one, there be the other," answered Rico"

The closer we got, the hotter the party sounded. We ran toward the music from the two five-foot speakers that were aimed out of the open windows blasting "Freedom" by Ritchie Havens. The bass was set to summon all but the dead. We were the ants scurrying up the hill to the sugar pile.

"Hey! What's happening, brother? You two aren't together or anything are you?" Gordon said to the guy half of a couple as he placed his arm around the woman half. All the poor fella could offer was a meek shrug as Gordon walked arm in arm with his acquisition heading with her toward the building.

Rico and I started walking, talking and then mingling with a group on their way to the steps. You would never know if it's an open house or if someone is checking at the door for uninvited guests. Chances were that a large group was invited so it was always best to latch on if you could. In spite of all that, Rico seemed familiar there as usual.

The mountains of food and the endless supply of pot at that bash exceeded our expectations. The upper floor was for acoustic music for music's sake. The parlor floor served as a discotheque for dancing's sake. How so many people could crowd into four floors of a brownstone without imploding the structure was beyond me. We always headed straight for the food and loaded up; this kind of meal could be made to last two days. That's what backpacks were for.

"If one more person sings, 'We Represent the Lollipop Guild,' I'm going to throw the fuckin' tank out the window and shove the balloons up his ass!" said the party's host, Jeff, as he passed the helium around to all the more-than-willing takers.

A longhaired woman reached from within the crowd of heliumites and grabbed the valve. While filling her own balloon, she said to Jeff, "That's fine but only if you promise to then kiss my ass and blow up the fucking balloons yourself, after they're up there."

Her name was Terry. She came from England with the music wave of the 'sixties. The wave crested and her life went directly to ebb. She put her balloon to her mouth and sucked in the gas.

She began slamming on a guitar that she took from a guest and assembled the pieces of the puzzle. Like an English munchkin, she sang to Jeff's face:

> "I had something to live for,
> 'Til all I dreamed of became mine,
> You fed yourself to me, line after line,
> You are the nothing that once filled my life,
> I was less than you were 'cause I was your wife,
> Kidney stones, marriage and all things must pass,
> So take your balloons Jeffie and blow 'em up your ass!"

After pounding out some sounds that would normally precede Pete Townsend's turning his guitar into toothpicks, she held short and threw the instrument back to its hippie owner. Then she laughed.

Turning to Jeff she said to his reddened face, "That's pretty fuckin' good for on the spot lyrics! Hey Jeff, you bastard, aren't you glad you invited me to put your life into perspective for all your new little friends?"

Jeff looked right into her face, turned to a wall and spit on it. Then he said, "I've never been serenaded by a stoned-ass chipmunk before. Go sit on a pickle you fucking British bitch from Hell! For the record, you crashed this gig the same way you did our Mercedes, and our marriage."

I was sure that this was the best that they ever got along. They laughed and carried on with what probably were their mutual friends from better times, separately of course.

Terry's long blond hair covered her ass, as did Gordon's eyes. He read the situation, ex-husband with a mansion-ex-wife on a mission, plenty of possibilities to move in on. The woman that Gordon came through the door with was probably looking for the guy that she left outside. When it came to opportunity, Gordon was like a three- stage rocket, heading for the stars as he leaves everything else behind.

Most people become introspective from pot. Terry was the ultimate exception. What was in her mind rolled off her tongue as fast as it could get around her censors, which were nil. Gordon got real close to her real fast. He had her giving up her past as fast as he could roll her another skinny. With the heart of a pawnbroker, he appraised her assets. Like an armed torpedo, he set course for her libido at full speed ahead.

She confided in Gordon saying, "I told that bastard Jeff that I wanted him to piss off. Then he yelled right back at me . . ."

Terry went into her Jeff voice, after she sucked on a bong saying, " . . . Piss off! You want me to piss off? Okay here you go, here's a piss off, you Limey cunt!"

Her face changed form as she reverted to her own voice and said, "Then the bastard tied my hair to that circular staircase pole. He pissed all over my face and said, 'Always do as the fuckin' lady asks!'

"Then he told me to 'Get the fuck out of my house you Limey bitch!' I had to go to Sheila's and wash up. She gave me clothes and put me up 'til I got on my own. He's a bastard I tell you, a real prick!"

The ashes from her joint fell on Gordon's pants. Slowly, she wiped them off while saying in an exaggerated Cockney manner, "Now Gordon, that is your name isn't it? You have better things in mind for me than that, I hope!"

She grabbed him by the hand and they disappeared through the crowd.

Rico shook his head and said, "Gordon goin' to be a busy mon tonight! Maybe more busy if Jeff still gettin' visiting rights to his ex-old lady. The old mon, I bet he still be checkin' her out. She be here for more than to play with things like Gordon Boy."

Rico had a keen sense for seeing ulterior motive. He read people as easily as he read the street. I had a feeling that he knew more than he let on, as usual.

I said to myself, "There's a big party to explore, so piss off Gordon!"

We left Gordon to his project. But still, I had to ask Rico, "Something doesn't make sense. He tells her to get out of his house and she's back here visiting him after he assaulted her. Doesn't the victim usually get the house?"

Rico looked at me as if I should have an understanding of some common knowledge. Then he spelled it out, "Jeff, he be a music producer sometime, and he do other shit most of the time. He be a real smart dude, mon. Nothing he do go back to him where it might hurt him. This house? It be his momma's. She live in the basement apartment. She do what he say 'cause he bring home big time cash. He got two more ex-wives. They can't get shit from him either, everybody know him, but nobody know him." Rico was looking to the side of me, by then I knew this meant that he was holding something back.

"You're telling me that you figured this out by just looking at him? Rico, you're smart, but no one's that smart. Hey, if you don't want me to know, I'm cool with it."

Rico looked straight at me so I felt he knew me well enough when he said, "Okay bro', this be the deal. Sometimes I take some shit over here to Jeff from Intelligent John's place. This dude Jeff, he give me music cassettes and a taste of what I bring him here and there for tips. I turn them over later on the street for cash and favors."

Rico's attention turned to a pair of breasts, swaying to the music. As he walked away he said, "Kenny, I check you out later, mon. There be somebody maybe I get close to. Wish me luck, mon. I been there before and I think she want me back, maybe a little."

"Luck, mon," I said as Rico headed for the dance floor. The lady that he had his eye on jumped right on him as they took off to places where they must have left off. I left the noise and went to the soft music and sofas upstairs.

Sally, fresh from being fucked over by Mark, her latest mistake, was busy singing and playing her guitar. Sadly, her bunched up sleeve revealed a series of fresh tracks. Sean and Billy backed her up, like always with guitars and friendship. The whole room joined in singing "Southern Man". Their talent and energy could stretch a guitar riff through the entire night on this song, and they didn't disappoint.

I found an empty place on a couch and sat next to a shorthaired, bald-faced, half-familiar being that said to me, "I went to check out your coffee house. At least I think I went to the right place. Two older women were fixing it up. They said you disappeared."

It was Howie from the commune. I had to do a double take, and then ask him, "Did a lawnmower get mad at your head? Howie you look like a fuckin' Brylcream ad in search of a barber shop window somewhere in the nineteen-fifties."

I had to allow my imagination to reinstall ten pounds of hair on his face and head. Upon doing so, the echoes of the words of this people's advocate of old returned. I could only wonder how changing his hair would change the world.

He extended his hand and said, "Congratulate me Kenny, I finally got my degree and passed the Bar Exams. I'm working downtown. You might have guessed it. Guilty as charged, I'm a lawyer. I guess I must look a lot different to you people. The head honchos at the firm said the freak flag had to go."

I sat amazed and asked myself, "Was this person next to me the same laid-back disciple of Cesar Chavez and Bobby

Kennedy who would speak of accepting a home-cooked meal as a fee, only if he could first save that home from foreclosure? Who was this imposter with a solid gold chain in place of love beads? "

So I answered, "Okay, congratulations Howie. By the way, are you lawyering for Social Services, or are you just being Robin Hood on your own, or what?"

This was the law student who said that he wanted to do nothing but learn how to slice through the system to better help the Revolution. Upon passing the Bar, he would join a vanguard of legal eagles that would help change the laws to help the little people who had no means to help themselves. I could only sit and await his answer.

Then he said quite modestly, "I'm just clerking right now."

Then he said quite proudly, "But I got with a firm that has a rock solid history and an even better future ahead of it. When I get my bearings they'll move me into mergers and acquisitions. That's the future you know."

True, I was talking to a genuine establishment lawyer. But even truer, he was still one very perceptive person. He must have read my mind because he offered me an argument of justification for his diversion from his alleged philosophy of old, "Kenny, I have to put certain things, that I really want to return to, on the back burner. I have incredible student loans to pay back and some great opportunities have come my way that will allow me to do that more quickly. But we're still cool, right Dude?"

He was so proud of how his feet had landed beyond his dreams, or at least the dreams that he said he had. Had a comb and razor unearthed the true being within? All that I saw before me was a mountain of bullshit, so I let him have it. Just for all the little people that he left beneath his climb up the ladder.

"Wow Dude! One nation under litigation, with libertines and junk bonds for all! When they swore you in, or whatever lawyer guys do at their initiations, did you light your cigar with a burning picture of Abbey Hoffman? When you sat around the table smoking dope with all the commune people, did you forget to inhale?

"Right on! Power to the people! Howie, maybe the people that you're sucking up to now will see your bullshit after you get to the next level, whatever the fuck that is." Then I messed his hair and wiped the grease on his shirt.

I added, "Those women by the store were right Howie, I did disappear. As far as you're concerned Dude, if this is the real you, then you never met me in the first place."

Do people wake up and say to themselves, "I have a great idea. I think I'm going to buy tons of food and allow the entire neighborhood to come into my house where they can eat and drink all they want. Then they can spill things on my furniture, and then raid my refrigerator when the party food runs low. In the meantime, they should feel free to drop cigarette butts on my oriental rugs and grind them in as they dance and break various things in the process.

"The real lucky ones can get to place fuck-stains on my sheets. The sick ones can puke on any surface available. If enough people don't show up, then those who do will reject my hospitality and seek those people who passed me by and went elsewhere."

I sunk down into the couch and thought, "And people think that I'm crazy?"

Rico entered the acoustic room as I was returning from my soliloquy asking, "Hey, bro', you ready to split? Ain't nothin' happenin' here I ain't never seen or done before. Kenny, you seen Gordon anywhere?"

I thought back to when Gordon was softening the beachhead like the Marines preparing to invade the canal and answered, "The last I saw of him, he was making his way through the crowd of people to go up those stairs. He was pulling that English chick along. I get the feeling he won't expect us to wait for him. Yeah, let's split. We got enough shit to eat for at least a week."

We hung out on a stoop across the street from Jeff's. Once a few people headed for the door, the multitude began to follow. Rico pointed with his chin at the bottle neck sticking out of my pack and asked, "Where you get that wine, bro'?"

"It was sitting alone at the table. Everybody was doing the punch. This poor bottle must have felt like an orphan. I guess somebody had to take it," I answered while passing the bottle of Mateus over to Rico. He passed a joint over to me.

"Watch out for the car, man! What's the matter? Hey, bro', you okay?" I asked some kid with nearly waist length hair trailing behind him like a horse's mane as he darted between passing cars.

I never saw him before, but who could miss him as he came stumbling toward us. We were washing down the superheated smoke from the last of the roach with the last of the Mateus. The kid opened his eyes, and then he squinted them. He looked at us briefly and then tried to focus away from us.

He pulled his hair over the front of his face and screamed, "I didn't mean to burn any of that shit, man! I'm sorry! I don't want to look too hard at anything, man. Like if I do, it will all catch on fire! I'm coming over by you dudes but I promise I won't stare, 'cause like I don't want to burn you down, man."

Then he began smacking his arm, shouting, "Oh shit! My sleeve is burning? I can't feel the flames or anything, man! Am I dead? Do you guys see any flames? Throw some water on me. Please help me!"

Both Rico and I grabbed the kid and sat him down. He kept his hands over his eyes. Then he screamed, "If I can't feel the heat, then I must really be dead and burning in Hell! Please don't let me give confession. Satan will then know all that I ever did and hold me here forever. Shit! He probably hears us right now. Help me, please."

His breathing was heavy and rapid. As we held him down we could feel his heart nearly exploding from his chest. This boy was having one fuckin' bummer of a trip.

Rico tightened his grip on the kid and said, "No, mon. There no flames here. It all be in your head. Soon the bad dream be over, brother, and you see everythin' okay. There be no Devil here, mon. You be in Park Slope now, not Hell, little brother. Maybe you just a little fucked up from the acid, mon. Hey, bro', you been drinkin' the punch, right? Tell me how much you drink, mon."

The kid parted the hair from his face and looked at Rico as if he were truth incarnate. Rico kept talking to him in a lullaby voice, assuring the kid that this too would pass. It worked. This new side of the Rico mystique came as a complete surprise to me. Rico sat next to the kid's towering form. They were somewhat close in age. Yet Rico was very paternal toward him.

The kid began answering Rico's questions, "I don't know how much I drank, man. It tasted good so I kept drinking it. That's all I drank all night."

Suddenly he began to focus and he shouted out, "Fuck! Did I burn down my old lady? Where's Donna? Where's Donna?"

The kid began swelling with extraordinary strength. He tried to break free from us and nearly succeeded. We could barely hold him down as his eyes scanned the street.

Rico placed himself in front of the kid and said, "You don't burn nobody or nuthin', mon. You just be trippin" from the punch. You just hang out and ride this thing. Every breath you take, it go away a little more. Go easy, mon, inhale, exhale. Mon, people pay good money for what you just got for free."

A car screeched to a stop in front of the stoop where we hung on to the dude. A chick stuck her head out and yelled to the kid, "Tommy, are you okay? Why did you split from us? We've been looking all over for you, Sweety!"

Donna, his flame-resistant old lady, jumped out of the passenger side of a car. We lifted Tommy gingerly, reassuring him that this was all real. He told us that he thought that the fire had stopped, but he felt a burn on his arm. We sat him in the back seat of the car with his friends.

He must have known that he was back in reality, as his old lady said, "Didn't I tell you not to drink the punch you stupid bastard? Why do you think we brought those bottles of Mateus?" We covered the empty bottle with our backs as he covered his eyes.

Tommy said to Donna, "I remembered what you told me. I didn't drink the punch at all tonight. I just ate all the fruit that was floating in the bowl." Tommy quickly turned to us with his finger over his lips and winked. His secret would be safe.

I ran back to the car and said to his girlfriend, "Take him down to the Methodist Hospital Emergency Room. Tell them that he's hallucinating from a bad trip. They'll probably give him Thorazine. It can bring him down a little from the acid and time will do the rest. Just don't let him run out of the car and into the traffic."

She patted my arm and said, "Thanks a lot for helping him, guys."

After they had safely headed for the hospital, I turned to Rico and said, "Good thing there were no oil delivery trucks out tonight. He might have blown up the whole fuckin' neighborhood."

Sporadic yelling and the pounding bass from the dance floor was all that could be heard for the next hour. We finished a couple more joints. I pronounced the party officially dead as the boom-boom-boom from the speaker towers was followed a long hiss then by a one-minute flat line of silence.

The last of the crowd left the mansion. The speakers left the windows. Indistinguishable words mixed with laughter were all that was heard as the party dispersed, its people heading in every direction.

Rico pointed to a group and said, "Yo Kenny, check it out, mon. Ain't that Apples leaving over there? Why you don't go see maybe you walk her home? She be with a whole bunch of people. Maybe you go put your arm around her. She maybe want to rap with you."

As much as I would have liked to be with her, I couldn't imagine why she would want to be with me as stoned and drunk as I was. It would be the wrong time to explain to her how the noble experiment that was September's and my life washed down the street.

I said to Rico, "No, I'm just going to the crib and hang out until I fall out. You got the key to Gordon's?"

Rico slapped one pocket, then the other. He shrugged as he pulled out his knife and said, "Who needs a key to a door when I got the key to the whole fuckin' city, mon?"

We walked down the hill toward Seventh Avenue. As we neared the corner, we looked down the street after hearing a bread truck pulling away from the deli.

Looking at one another, we said simultaneously, "You thinkin' what I'm thinkin'?"

The smell of warm, fresh rye bread overpowered the smell of the truck's exhaust that had signaled our opportunity. With the Sun just starting to break the horizon, we slapped five and headed for our waiting breakfast. Our hands each drew a loaf from the large paper bag and we placed our loot into our jackets.

Rico elbowed me and said calmly while pointing down the street with his chin, "Shit! Get the fuck outa here. I saw, a cop car hit his lights. He make a u-turn, now he be coming back toward us, mon."

We ran down Second Street with our bread and backpacks bouncing along.

"Quick Kenny, roll under the fence, mon! Get in the schoolyard fast and lay flat on the ground. Eat the fuckin' bread, don't throw no crumbs nowhere. If they catch us then we say we don't take nothin, 'cause by then we got nothin'."

A searchlight flashed above us from the First Street end of the schoolyard as a car skidded to a stop. I whispered, "Yo, Rico, did you call a cab?"

The anticrime taxi had joined in the hunt. I was waiting for the Rico magic to kick in. We wolfed down the bread and even blew the crumbs away as the spotlights crisscrossed over our bodies. Maybe they thought we would steal their cars if they actually got out of them to look for us. The cop's laziness was Rico's magic that time.

After they drove away, we waited ten minutes and then headed for Gordon's. Quickly, Rico slipped the lock with his knife as I pressed the door with my ass. We were home at last.

"Hey guys, get a couple of plates and have some eggs, compliments of a slow-moving milk truck."

Another layer of grease was about to find its way to the kitchen wall as Gordon cooked his breakfast. The shit-eating grin on his face foretold that there was a happy pecker lying beneath his pants.

Falling upon the trash-strewn futon, I said, "Save ours for tomorrow, bro'. We already grabbed something on the way over."

While stuffing the eggs down his throat, straight from the pan, Gordon listened to our adventures. Before our story could get off the schoolyard ground, he dropped the fork and began to unravel his own odyssey, "She told me about a bedroom on the top floor. It was hers while she still lived with the dude after their marriage went on hold. After you saw us leave the party room, we ran up the stairs and went there.

"She was like a fuckin' animal, man! She tore off my clothes and hers almost in one move. Somehow, these intense bright strobe lights went on in the room. Like, it totally highlighted the punch I drank. The whole fuckin' room almost came alive with pulsating color mixed with the strobes.

"She took off her two garters and made me use them to tie her hands to the bedposts. There was this strange music playing in the room. It was like Bolero but it was done with sitars and synthesizers. Whatever it was, it got her fuckin' crazy! She kicked the back of my legs black and blue. We were at it for a while then something strange, well maybe it was nothin'."

While gulping down another load of eggs, he paused as if to replay a missing scene through his memory.

"C'mon Gordon! You didn't stop like this with her, did you?" I asked as Rico kicked him in the back as if trying to get him jump-started.

He went on to say, "Okay, the music stopped, then I swore that I heard a floor board creak from above. I figured, all that could be above her room was a crawl space, 'cause we were on the top floor. Anyway, at the time I paid it no mind. Then something strange, a different kind of music came on. It was hard to describe, maybe it was disco.

"She squeezed me so hard with her legs, it felt like my back would break. Then she grabbed my hair and said, "Everything's cool, Gordon Boy. Hang in there 'cause I'm almost there. If you fade out on me now, boy, we'll just have to start all over again."

He threw the frying pan in the sink saying, "I got my mind over it and then I was cool with it. I ain't never been with anything like her before. I think that I'm addicted to her, bro'. I haven't washed my hand since last night and I don't plan to ever again."

Gordon grinned as he sniffed his fingers and his eyes rolled back ecstatically, and then he licked the remainder of his eggs from his beard. Rico had a suspicious, as always, look on his face. For some reason he wasn't impressed with anything.

He brought Gordon back from the clouds for a moment when he said, "Bro', when you get it on with Terry, you just better make sure that what you think you getting, is all there is. She be comin' to you from a dude that's into a lot of shit. Don't forget, she be with him a long time. Different strokes for different folks."

Gordon grabbed my last cigarette from my ear, lit it and sat down, then asked, "How complicated can a chick that just likes to fuck get? I mean, like what could she be after in me? All I own is the cigarette in my mouth and the lint in my pockets." Gordon gestured by blowing smoke and pulling his pockets out.

Rico leaned back on his chair and pissed on Gordon's fires of passion when he said, "Maybe somebody eatin' popcorn right now watchin' your white ass bouncin' like a basketball in the strobe lights. Act one-scene one honkey now a movie star! Mon, you can almost hear the sound of one hand clapping when the leading mon finish her off."

I could only fall to the floor laughing as Rico put it all together. Rico soon joined me. Gordon threw what he thought was an empty egg carton at the garbage. He missed and two raw eggs joined other misdirected objects on the floor.

With his dog cleaning his mess, he said, "So big fuckin' deal, so what! What if the old man is peepholin' us and gettin' off on watching? Everybody likes to watch other people fuck, don't they?"

We turned to each other with puzzled looks on our faces. Gordon tried to save face and went on the offensive, "The dude looks like shit. I couldn't imagine me watching him doin' her, but if he grooves on seein' me do Terry, I can be cool with it. Maybe he'll pay me."

Rico would never tell anyone what to do, directly. Even if he did, Gordon's brain was dwelling in the head of his dick, far away and unconnected to his ears. Rico tried again, "What if he be doin' her after he see you do her? Maybe seein' some young dude shakin' her up while he hold himself back, be the thing that turn them both on. Check it out, bro', maybe you just warming up the audience and leaving before act two."

Rico's challenges were galvanizing Gordon's defiance to them. Rico looked at me and turned his mouth down and shrugged. Gordon had the stage. All we could do was watch and listen. What the fuck? It was his crib.

The glimmer in Gordon's eye spread to his tongue and then for all to hear as he declared, "If that was a screen test and I passed, then I want a raise! If I have to fuck both of them on the way to some good fuckin' money, then I'll do what it takes. After she experiences me enough, she'll stick her finger into the peep hole and tell him to fuck off or piss off or maybe just to jerk off."

I had to either relieve my conscience or go on record for having told him off, so I said, "Your little head is making shadows on your big head. Jeff is into other shit that you never dreamed of. He's the invisible man. He makes a lot of money I hear, but he doesn't exist if you try to track him down. Gordon, do what you gotta do, but just open your mind at the same time you open your zipper."

I just wanted Gordon to be careful, but I couldn't tell him the specifics that Rico told me in confidence about Jeff. Gordon sensed an opportunity to have the last word and he took it, "One lay at a time. One day at a time. I'm going to her pad in SoHo tomorrow night. We'll see what's up. Hey Rico, pass over that joint, bro'."

Rico complied and Gordon immediately did a thirty second inhale of Columbian magic. Somehow he managed to hold the smoke in and at the same time ask, "Hey, man, how do we start a secret society?"

Rico grabbed the joint from his hand and replied, "First thing you do, bro', don't tell no one." The subject never came up again.

JE

"Have I become like a child who, when beleaguered by the world around him, might go beneath his bed with only the company of dust balls and broken pieces of toys? Has the human race around me, with its relentless influence through every form of media possible, driven me to seek a hiding place within it? Has my soul become so skewered by the endless flames of outside influence and imposed values that it finds sanctuary in drowning? Has the super-tribe of Humankind become so overpowering that it chokes its members by its very existence? Why do the meager pickings of the rat pack that I now run with have greater value to me than anything that I've known before?

Has the corner that I've backed myself into become another form of support from which I must one day soon break free?"

Found in September's Child's guest sketch book

Chapter Nine

Circumspection

With a fully deflated air mattress beneath me, I woke up and picked up exactly where I left off as a flame found the burned end of the roach I had been smoking the night before. The sun was setting. We were rising, like vampires making ready for the night. Rico and I began our workout ritual of stretching then sparring. Gordon tried to join in but it wasn't his thing.

Rico laughed and said, "Gordon Boy, you supposed to hit the other mon with the chukka sticks. Maybe you show him how they hurt when they hit you and he run away."

Gordon slapped at his own face and then played like someone had hit him from behind. We gathered around the table and emptied our pockets of whatever change we may have found on the bar floors during the week. It was shopping time. Rico threw down two ten-dollar bills.

It was Gordon's turn to be the philosopher, "Man, you're gonna get yourself ten years of gettin' your butt fucked in Attica if you keep sellin' on the street, Rico. Remember the fuckin' Rockefeller Law, ten years mandatory, man."

Rico would always look ten degrees to the side of your eye when he answered. He looked off to Gordon's lazy eye and said, "Bro', I knows my shit out there. Nobody be getting' anythin' from me who I ain't done business with before. I do enough just to get over, then I cut out. We be livin' a whole lot better if I could get some help out there with my business. Just as many honkeys out there that only wanna buy from a honkey as there be that get off buyin' from a black dude!"

Gordon almost weakened a bit, and then he replied, "I got my own way to get over. My plans might take some time. Some day I might become your best customer when my shit all comes together."

Rico gave a barely audible laugh. There was an undertone of the unsaid when he said, "Just like a fuckin' honkey. He think he get more at the front door by askin', than you can grab from the back. Have a good time tonight, bro'. Don't do anyone that may do you in."

With all that said, Rico and I left for Gwillie's Store, at least that's what the Spanish dude named Willie called himself.

As Gwillie pressed the little white keys, ringing up each item, the register numbers changed. While the price of each item was recorded, I kept wondering why it seemed to me that there was some personal significance to this activity. We left the store with our small but meaningful bag. It then hit me like a freight train.

When I was married to Deanna, we would go to the supermarket and gather up a cart of groceries. While the checker hit the keys, I would add the sum in my head as she did this. Before she could hit the total button, I had the amount plus sales tax already calculated. This had been one of my disciplines that kept my mind sharp for instrument flying.

"Why you stop, mon? You look like you just see a ghost," Rico asked as he looked back at me. I stood frozen in my tracks, feeling the impact of the freight train that just passed through my mind.

"I'm cool; I just had a thought, that's all," I said, realizing that the thought that I just had was a memory of the thoughts that I was once capable of having. Like any other glimpse through one's own denial, issues of immediacy would soon block any insight. I took a hit from the joint that Rico palmed over to me and went off on my own while he walked back to Gordon's.

I felt like I had stumbled into a darkened hall of mirrors in my mind. I knew what surrounded me and that I had to look, but I couldn't or I wouldn't find the switch. The neighborhood that was once the sanctuary for my reborn spirit was becoming like a worn circle in a prison yard that I paced constantly with no sign of reprieve.

Things were not making any sense to me at all that night. Then, as I turned the corner I stopped in my tracks and saw it before me. It was a bumper sticker, but not just any bumper sticker. It sat there on a VW Beetle. It read, My Boss Is a Jewish Carpenter. The car was parked in front of a shop with a sign that read, Sheldon Fein-Cabinet Maker. This made perfect sense.

The Chariot's movement was being denied by its very own absence of effort. Its vision and control of the very forces that it employed were frustrated by the concession of principle. No matter how many times I spread out the Tarot, the same unwelcome story would tell itself before my eyes. I placed the cards into my backpack.

I saw myself becoming a parasite and freeloader. My noble experiment had been grounded by another form of security, routine. Although basic survival had been accomplished by our mutual efforts at the crib, I saw either repetition of the same lessons or total surrender to outside influence as my course ahead. Neither option was acceptable. I could not abandon my friends nor could I walk in their paths. Until a decision was formed as to my own direction, inertia would prevail.

If you order a Black Russian straight up the ice won't dilute the strength. You can then nurse it. No one's going to throw you out of the bar for just hangin' with a drink in hand. I had my regular spot at Minsky's Pub where I would go and either try to write stuff or read my Tarot cards. I needed insight during my time of personal inaction.

I saw my life much like that of a derelict ship with its tattered sails hanging in the dead air. Its desperate lethargy reflected by the sea, like a mirror, surrounding its stillness. Had an albatross hovered above during that allegory, it would have been felled from the consuming stench of Shalimar perfume. My head raised itself from my cards lying across the bar and I saw that two chicks had placed themselves on either side of me.

Words actually managed to emerge through their constant gum-chewing as one of them asked, "Can you tell people's fortunes with those cards? Maybe you can tell ours. Please, we'll pay you. Just tell us how much do you want."

I glanced down at the arrangement on the bar. My cards told me that I should be open to change. Half-heartedly, I gave the chicks my argument, "I read the cards for my own personal enlightenment. I never do readings for others, never mind for money."

As the bubble from her gum grew larger, one of the girls rolled her eyes to her friend. Simultaneously, the bubble and the question popped, "Okay, what if we tell the bartender to fill up your Black Russian glass. Will you read our cards then?"

My glass was halfway down. I quickly gulped the rest and replied, "What the hell! Sit down. Let's see who you really are." I never even got their names. I made mental reference to them as the Scissor sisters.

Did they tell me that they were hairdressers, or did I

read it in their cards? I was a little drunk at the time. In spite of that, I did see unimaginable depths of shallowness in the cards that lay before me. After three drinks and two sandwiches, I managed to tell them enough to satisfy their curiosity without divulging the tragedies that I foresaw.

After the bar closed, I walked with them down Seventh Avenue, telling everything that they wanted to hear, "In the near future," I prophesied, "people will have their hair cut again. Everyone, everywhere will want manicures. The era of the hairdresser will be upon us!"

This drew cheers from the girls. They seemed to possess the first rays of hope for their profession since the musical Hair landed on Broadway.

One of the Scissors said to me with shear panic, "I need a joint! Like it's 3 A.M., where the fuck can anyone cop some reefer at this hour? Shit, I wish I was back home in Bensonhurst, I could cop any time." She pointed to the Tarot deck and asked, "Honey, is it in the cards for us to score some pot tonight?"

Since they were sharing their deepest thoughts with me, the least I could do was to share some reefer with them so I said, "I guess so. Will this do?" I whipped out two joints from my shirt pocket.

They jumped up and down with joy. Each girl grabbed one and lit it. Passing a joint to me in between hits, one of them said, "Okay Honey, now you gotta take this. Here, don't give me any bullshit either."

She shoved a five-dollar bill in the pocket where I got the joints. They both kissed me and split for their car. I heard the sail above me catch the wind of an idea. This wasn't so bad, read cards in the bars and hustle loose joints after closing time. Everyone at Minsky's was always asking questions about the cards while I sat reading my own.

People would come over to me and ask if I came there often. The food was good. Booze wasn't my real thing. But if somebody filled the glass, I would empty it. After all, I may have been destitute but I still had my principles. I guess there were worse ways to get over. At least I would be helping others in their midnight hour of need for personal illumination and hallucination.

With respect to my effort to remain non-reliant on money, I could score a nickel bag from Rico, roll three or four skinnies then flip them for what I paid and barter the rest for food and booze for my own needs. Nobody ever went down for selling or trading a loose joint. If I happened to sell dope to a cop at that hour, they too were grateful.

With my plan underway, on weekends I crashed picnics in Prospect Park. People were always a little high and willing to share their food with a longhaired fortuneteller who could read their souls and later fill their stash boxes. We would part afterward, each of us more fulfilled than before in every way. I would often get tipped with shirts, other articles of clothing and often, sex. Rico's end of the deal would be covered, as cash would find its way into my pocket as loose joints found their way out. The rest of my end would get me fed and be able to bring food and bottles of beer to Gordon as my rent.

Long after my inspired thoughts became my means of survival, it became apparent that the rat-pack life style at the crib had evolved to a different level. Gordon never really missed my company or Rico's. Rico and I would divide the reefer, set our separate courses to meet our clientele's needs and life went on. Regular food or booze was left for Gordon as my rent for the hallway. Regular deposits of pot were left by Rico as his payment for passing through as necessary. Rico and I would usually run into each other around sundown and work out.

Sometimes we would take our sparring to the park or improvise as we saw fit. Rico would say, "You gotta land balanced, mon. Every time you change your spot to the other dude, it gonna become a stance to strike from. Ain't be no time to go into some silly-ass position you see in a book. Don't think about just blocking his arm or leg when he strike at you. The worst that could happen is you block it an' he come again. Strike at his arm or leg to break it! Do that and you take it away from him. No time to play like you in a Dojo if the dude be tryin' to kill you for your stash."

Rico emphasized that every position you might be in, even while sitting on a train, has to be a stance to attack from. There is no defense, only attack or counterattack.

"Mon, you got some bread for tokens? You be a big time drug dealer now. Buy us a ride on the subway. I give you a good lesson, Kenny Boy! When we get back, we hear Gordon Boy tell us about his good fortune."

Rico wouldn't elaborate on the reference to Gordon. I had to spend the next few hours trying to figure out his riddle. But when it came to Rico-speak, why even bother trying?

We boarded the I.R.T. heading toward Manhattan. The train's route had a stretch where it rode along at top speed for about five minutes. It would rock violently during that time. That's when we sparred.

Every time each of us missed the other, we had to land balanced regardless of the movement of the floor below. If you fell on the floor or on a seat, you had to land ready to strike. Rico made his message clear to me. This lesson was on attitude, both mental and physical. The city's streets, alleys and its very bowels were his Dojo. Nothing was academic to him when it came to staying alive.

Fortunately, for our immediate purposes, the budget cuts had reduced the number of transit cops on the trains. Seeing no threat to them, after a while the other passengers just watched us as if we were a floorshow.

I learned, "If you sit on a train seat then you should rest the weight of your body only on one point. Put one foot up on the seat. This foot, although appearing to be at rest is in the ready to strike position. One hand, while covering the other, must be thought of as a serpent, coiled for any target of opportunity."

The ride home was both rest and practice. I sat with my eyes appearing to be shut. Forms moved about me visible to me through the narrow slit of my still open eyes. I envisioned myself, the serpent. I believed I was a serpent, sitting coiled and ready.

"Don't sit by the bum! Slide over here by your mommy."

I opened my eyes to see in full focus that the whispering was coming from a phony, apologetic smile. The body attached to it was gently pulling her small son away from me. I looked around to see who the bum might be. I, the serpent, was alone on the bench with the two of them. This was not the attack that I had prepared for.

My sense of indignation responded with its usual rage. Before my wits could prevail I ranted, "Just what the fuck makes me a bum? What the fuck makes you any different? You have ten dead rats that make up your coat collar. Your own fuckin' ancestors probably helped crucify that poor Jew hanging from your gold chain. You stink like you drank your fuckin' lunch. Five people could eat on what you paid for the fuckin' clown paint on your face!

"Furthermore, you take your fuckin' son on a train with all the bums, so that makes you an idiot. I might look like a fuckin' bum Ma'am, but I'll sure outlive a fuckin' idiot."

I changed my seat to the one next to Rico and said to her kid, "Please excuse me son. I don't sit next to idiots."

How can anyone draped in the trappings of decadence be so audacious to assume that I was a bum because I wasn't in fashion or reeking of sweet-smelling chemicals? I was not a bum! I was living a noble experiment. The train car darkened momentarily and I saw a flash of my reflection on the window.

I thought, "Had I become as she saw me? No way, that's bullshit. What's a bum anyway? She's the bum."

Was I being equally presumptuous to assume her to be

decadent because of her outward appearance? No damn it, she started it!

Rico stood in front of me and said, "Yo, bro'! I never hear you talk like that before. She get the fuck up and run out the next stop, it be downtown. I hope the dumb bitch don't talk no shit to the brothers like she talk to you, huh?"

We ran down Seventh Avenue, laughing and sparring with one another as we headed for Gordon's. We ran up the stairs only to hear screams and pounding noises coming from the apartment. We nearly flew down the hall, anticipating the war we had trained for. We opened the unlocked door to see a distraught Gordon as the apparent source of the commotion. Rico ran to Gordon while I searched the place for possible intruders.

Rico called me back saying, "It's cool! He be beating himself up. Ain't nobody else here but us."

Rico held his hand up to me as if to say, "Let him finish," then he said to Gordon, "Bro', calm down! Don't be doin' Kung Fu all over your walls like that. You gonna hit a stud and fuck up your hand big time. Mon, let me guess. You checked out one of the porn joints down on Forty-Second Street like I tell you to, right?"

Rico held him back as he finished his fifth hole in the plaster wall. Gordon said, "I'm gonna find that son of a bitch and fuckin' kill him! Imagine this shit, I go to a fuckin' peep show and see me starring in Jumpin' Jack Flash-Big White Ass! That fuckin' bastard ain't gonna be makin' bread off me ballin' his old lady while I collect shit for pay."

Nothing is worse than someone who points to the obvious with, I told you so. Rico couldn't resist doing just that as he rubbed his advice into Gordon's face, together with an oblique warning, "I hope you don't drop too many quarters down the hole, before you see your big part. Don't you be goin' after Jeff. He expect you to do this, mon. You do that stupid thing and that ugly old dude have you hurt real bad.

Stay cool with it, Gordon Boy. He get you when you don't see it comin', and maybe from someone you never expect to do it to you."

Gordon picked up his head and shouted, "I should have known something was up when she grabbed me and said, "Hang in there 'cause I'm almost there!" She had to know the old man was filming us. Damn good thing that her hair covered my face when she went on top. I hope you guys are the only ones who know about this. Keep your mouths shut, alright?"

As good advice took root in Gordon's mind, he began to calm down. Rico must have had enough fun by then so he again became the philosopher, "Don't worry, mon. Nobody here gonna say shit. You tell her that you only see her at your crib. If she be cool with that, then she really dig you for you. If she say she only see you at SoHo or back at the room at Jeff's, then you know she still working with the dude. If she be with him then you dump her. But don't you go and hurt her or him."

Gordon was too self-absorbed in his indignation to even appear convinced. Rico added his last line of advice to his fallen comrade's fallen ego, "Mon, you do what the fuck you want, but that be how I see it."

Gordon slumped down into the corner, puffing away on another cigarette he took from my ear. Rico and I headed up to the top of the hill and parted like two sidekicks in a western. Remember, this was the era of the anti-hero.

There is nothing that can cast a shadow of grief over a Brooklyn bar crowd more than a loss by a New York sports team. Had the players on TV listened to the drunken advice of the mob at Minsky's Pub, I'm sure that the outcome would have been far different.

In need of something more uplifting, I wandered down the block to The Iron Horse whose ambiance was dominated by an old player piano rather than old players on a television. I found a booth and attempted to write some poetry in my journal. It didn't matter to me that the place stayed almost empty for two hours.

The silence was broken by an exuberant Sally. She seemed to be either high on something good or straight on something better. I assumed it to be the latter, since the smile on her face seemed stronger and fresher than the scars on her arms.

She said, "Everybody's at Ryan's Pub, Kenny. They're having a talent thing in the back room. All the people from the old coffee house are there. C'mon, stop playing the hermit. After the gig you'll be able to do business at the bar. In the meantime listen to me read some stuff and some live music."

Ryan's Pub had been Ryan's Bar up until just a few weeks before. The addition of plants in the window, some textured wood and stucco and voila, Park Slope has yet another pub. I couldn't care less what they called it. If after the show, I was lucky enough to find a card customer and if they had a grille to make my usual fee, a sandwich, they could call it anything.

The back room was filled with, as Sally promised, all the people from September's and everyone from the other coffee houses past and present. The musicians that showed up there were the same musicians that showed up everywhere. They did the same stuff that everyone had heard every time, and then quickly headed to fulfill the free-drinks-for-performers promise. An audience, less entertainers, was what remained.

As the event's organizer, Sally felt that she had to take immediate charge of the situation. She saw the microphone pointing from the makeshift stage and whispered to me that it was calling her by saying, "Someone talk to me before they pack me away."

Heading for the stage, she said, "Billy, Sean, bring your guitars up and back me up. I'll read one of my poems."

Sean and Billy picked and plucked while Sally read something she wrote about someone who screwed her, in more ways than one. She realized, as the voices around her drowned out her own, that one could only get screwed so much before no one cares. She finished and came back to our table to the sound of polite applause.

I guessed that Sally didn't want to be the last one to jump from a burning stage as it headed out of town. I poured the last of my drink down my throat. Through the bottom of the glass I saw her pointing to me. I lowered the glass in time to hear her ask the crowd, "Didn't I see Kenny writing something at the Iron Horse?"

Then she said, "Folks, fresh from Kenny's journal, 'the thing he was writing' just before I hauled his ass over here! Somebody grab his other arm and pull him to the stage before he can split. Kenny read that thing that you were doing at The Horse."

I sat on the little stool between Sean and Billy and tapped the mike. Hearing the thud sound, I said, "I won't quote Lenny Bruce."

I looked at the crowd then I looked at my journal. I never read anything to anyone from this book. Until then, its blank pages filled themselves with my hand and mind as its willing instruments. The pages fell open to the latest entry. I took that as the book's permission to me to read aloud.

As the guitars strummed, I wondered what an audience's reaction to my own creation might be. Although the place was filled with people that I knew, I still felt uneasy. I looked around the room as quickly as one could after downing two Black Russians. Then I saw her face. It glowed at me like a beacon within a hostile sea.

But Apples barely noticed me. I hoped that my poem's statement would catch her attention. If it did, I was sure that she would not take it personally. I began reading:

Who are you? You, who stand out there, spread all around me
You who circle time from all directions
You who prey upon my senses so I might nourish your body
And when I do, you offer me your feces as my reward. Who are you?

I give to you in regular payment, all that nature has allotted to me, my time
For this you return to me, a statement showing your right to claim my life
When I feel that I know you by sight, by name, by reputation or by your essence
You change and say that I was right and there is something better for me to serve
Until I see it is only your reflection

Others have named you and called you out as they left your fold
But they would have been better off dying of starvation
For cattle are always returned by virtue of their brand
History has always proven you to be right, as time has laid its path before us
But you have either written history or turned it to ashes

You have scripted the words that I speak, for you are the author of my knowledge
I am a mere product of your schools, your religions, your media, your languages
If I speak from my soul to a canvas or carve the sights of my mind's eye in any form that you won't accept
I must risk being thrown from your mechanism into the abyss of scorn, to die of disassociation

If I think first of all that is acceptable to you and your servants
Then I shall be rewarded for my compromise
For then I will be helping you to better control my brothers and my sisters
If I cry out that our world is but a machine that creates us, that nourishes us
Then bleeds and discards us, I will be told that it never has been any different
And that nothing can be done, ever, to change it
If I say nothing, then I will be crushed by its wheels
If I strike out at it and try to destroy it, my body will rot as a warning to any others who would do the same

When I harvested your crops with my hands until they bled
I told you that my mind was capable of better
You then gave me a machine to harvest more for you
And my mind bled from repetition
If I proved to be a leader, you gave me a gun to hold on others as they served you
And I thanked you for my power

You have given me Gods to love, Devils to hate, but none has ever shown its face
All you have ever taught me were words to which I react
And you speak them to me when you want a reaction
For you know me better than I know myself

Who are you? You are the sum total of the efforts of my kind
You are the machine that man has built that outlives its builders
You are the world that forever promises the security of tomorrow
For only the surrender of today

I looked down at Billy. His jaw was open and his hand rested on the neck of his silent guitar. I said to him, "Billy, relax, I wasn't talking about you. It was either I read that one or, 'Shake, shake the ketchup bottle, none'll come and then a lot'll'."

I walked right past Sally and planted myself next to Apples, who was sitting with a small group of her friends in the back row. I looked at her and asked jokingly, "Do you come here often?"

She half-smiled at me and answered, "Sometimes."

That would be the last word that anyone would hear at Ryan's that night. The latest incarnation of Jimi Hendrix attempted to separate the mortar from the brick with his twelve-string. The fading sound of "The Star Spangled Banner" was replaced by the groaning of my stomach as Apples and I hurried for the door. Unfortunately I never got to earn my supper by reading Tarot cards that night.

As much as I could use the bread, if anybody were to ask me about loose joints, as I walked along Seventh Avenue with Apples, I would have say to them, "For that, I would see a doctor."

"Have you been successful with your business plan?" she asked, with a facetious look on her face.

There really is truth in, "If you have nothing, there's nothing to lose". If I had a choice in losing any one thing at this time, it would be the emptiness in my stomach. Instead of risking the loss of what dignity I may have had left with an ego-saving answer, I took a deep breath.

I recalled how she saw my experiment as a righteous one. Could I have lost sight of my own deepest motives that led me to that moment with this person? Finally, I replied, "Yes, I'm basking in my failure. Things went better than I could ask for. I left September's Child with nothing but the cable reels on my back. As far as the coffee house business is concerned, I sold it for a song. I told her about Will's outpatient-care night, this drew laughter.

Tentatively she answered, “You seem as though you've gained some perspective. The poem that you read sounded like a lot of water has gone under the bridge.”

The fact that it was a lot of gutter water including the bridge that had gone down First Street, seemed unimportant then. I didn't want to look back at any of that. As much as she was once open and forthcoming, she seemed that much distant and cool with me.

So I broke the ice with, “I think about you every time that I look at “Siddhartha”. I really want to thank you for hitting the nail on the head when you loaned the book to me. I read it twice. I keep it in my backpack right next to my journal.”

Her pace began to slow down, and then we stopped. She looked at me with in a most serious way and said, “I guess you didn't read the bookmark either time that you read the book.”

I remembered that her phone number was written there. I choked. But she didn't choke as she continued to read me out with, “I'm very annoyed with you! You said you were going to call that Tuesday after we last talked and you didn't. Not that Tuesday nor the next. In fact, I didn't hear from you at all. You just disappeared. I have no idea why I'm talking to you now. But here we are. So, why are you talking to me? What do you want?”

I asked myself, “What is going on here? Where do I start? I've experienced two lifetimes in what may have only been a couple of months. My life was supposed to be about truth. I couldn't give her any less than that.”

When any woman in my past would challenge me, I would just move on. Then it hit me. In addition to being drawn to her, the difference with Apples is, this was the first time in my life that I could say, I cared how the woman felt.

All that I had left in the world was the truth. And that's what I offered to her when I said, “I wanted to call you, but everything in my life kind of went downhill after I was unceremoniously exited from September's. I really didn't want to see you until my head was clear. I don't like laying my personal shit on people that I like." I could feel the handle of the shovel in my fist as I dug myself deeper with every word I spoke.

"So that's why you ignored me when I left that party on Second Street? I saw you pretending not to see me. You could have waved, you know."

I thought, "How many more bullets for me are in the chamber? I better take these shots one at a time and just answer straight out."

So I did, "Apples, I was really fucked up on everything you can think of when you saw me on the stoop. Rico and I were nursing some tripped out guy back to Earth. Rico pointed you out as you left the party. I knew that you were there. I just hoped that you wouldn't see me as wasted as I was that night."

There was something different about how I felt when she spoke to me. I was marveling at how I really cared about how my actions affected her feelings. Whatever this feeling was, it was a new one for me.

She tugged my hand abruptly. Looking me dead in the eye she said, "Okay, this is how it's going to be. We could walk separately beginning right now, or we can walk together. It depends on how you answer me right now.

"When you say you're going to call, I expect a call. If you're not going to call don't tell me to wait for a call. If you want to say goodnight right now then say it, and make it goodbye. But Kenny, you better mean what you say. I can't deal with empty promises."

I really liked how she made herself perfectly clear. I knew exactly where I stood with her. Unfortunately for me, it was on the spot. But my position was also clear.

I reached into my pocket and withdrew all that I had and said to her, "Apples, do you see this dime? I'm putting it in my change pocket. I will call when I say I will. Count on that! I'm very sorry for screwing up before."

She gave me a curious look from the corner of her eye, followed by a half-smile, and then she replied, "Okay, let's see how you can keep a commitment. Call me tomorrow at four-thirty, that's when I get home from work."

She held out the key toward the lock to her apartment. Suddenly, the door opened. An old woman wearing a large lime green fedora with a cape and skin to match greeted Apples with, "I hope that you aren't having any overnight gentleman guests, Dearie. There are rules in this building that forbid this type of behavior, you know."

The owner of the building was on her way to her job at the laboratory. She was an eccentric doctor who spent her off hours sitting in her tenants' apartments while they were out. She used this opportunity to listen to the activities of those who happened to be at home. She would note the level of noise that they made.

She would time their showers: "We mustn't waste water, you know!" was typical of the Official Letters that she would tape to the violator's doors. While trespassing in the apartment that she used as her listening post, she would wash the dishes and fold laundry. She had her good points.

Apples told her, "Kenny is going to install the new shower head for me. Have a good evening Dr. Renfield."

I thought, "Wasn't that the name of Dracula's servant?" Since the doctor's reflection had appeared in the hall mirror, I put my mind at ease.

Maybe it was just a coincidence. Apples put a plate of crackers and cheese-spread on the table. I politely dipped a cracker into the cheese. I was hoping that the drool that I felt rolling down my cheek wasn't noticeable. I ever so delicately nibbled on one cheesed cracker at a time while my mind consumed the rest before me. The last meal that I had was the day before.

I couldn't let her know my level of desperation. She might think of me as an animal that she took in from the street. She would have been right. While we snacked on my supper and drank coffee, Apples continued our conversation from where we left it, "The last time I saw you, you said that your goal was to deplete all of your resources down to your backpack and yourself?"

I nibbled on the cracker and began to realize that my street life was nibbling at my identity. Had I become part of the question to which I only sought an answer? Somehow my conversation with Apples was giving me a reorientation to purpose that I realized had been missing.

My stomach continued to growl, but my mind began to churn. I answered her by saying, "All that you see before you is all that there is left of me. I'll know if I own the next moment if I happen to exhale, then I'll hope to take the moment after from there."

She looked at me over her hand as it held her cracker and asked, "So what makes you think you can call me tomorrow? Never mind, don't bother answering. I have another question. Now that you're free of your business obligations, are you going to head south to Mexico and your quest for the Maya?"

I realized that my present resources would probably exhaust themselves at the Verazzano Narrows Bridge tollbooth, if that. There was enough gas in the Chevy to allow me to change street sides on alternate parking days. How do I answer her question truthfully without revealing the fact that I am truly a penniless street rogue who is selling reefer for rent and fortunes for food?

"I can't go anywhere until I finish reading your book for the third time and return it to you. By the way, do you really need a shower head installed?"

She held up a wrench and a packaged shower massage and said, "Actually, yes. Here it is. If you are successful in this task, then you can be the first to try it out."

She handed me a towel and reminded me that, "The ears have walls. Don't use too much water." I quickly installed the showerhead then double-checked my work by looking at the directions.

The ice-cold, pulsating water covered my body. I felt a strange tingle rush over me as if a force was emerging from beyond my goose bumps. An aura enveloped me as if to demand my recognition of my own existence. I stood naked in this downpour of my own creation. Self-inventories can choose the strangest of times. Would this one be fearless?

I reflected on how most of my showers had been in the apartments of women that I would meet. My motivation while either at September's, where there was only a sink, or while being on the street was, "If I don't meet someone then I can't shower. If I don't shower, I'll never meet anyone." How long could one live within that irony? Was I prostituting myself for cleanliness, or just being a real stinker?

There I was, rewarding myself with that which I had earned. I didn't scheme, read cards or see that moment as a ploy to take me to the next. I could only hope that Dr. Renfield was not timing me because I was enjoying the realization that this cleansing of my body as well as my spirit was a genuine repayment for my plumbing efforts.

Had I truly become my own animal while living like a rat? Might my journey toward self-realization end at a mirror that showed only an opportunistic beast?

As the water's flow ceased, I watched the drain, symbolically, accept my denial into its spiral. The smell of the street would remain on my clothes because they were all that I possessed. I remembered how I felt the day that I tore the shirt and tie from my body after I betrayed Eddie at the hearing. I would never remove that guilt as easily as I could the polyester. I dried myself and applied all that I owned to all that I had become.

Apples waited for me by the table and asked, "Well, did it work?"

My immediate thought was she was reading my thoughts

about my revelation. I stood there with a bewildered look. I felt both awkward within myself, yet somehow renewed.

"I heard the water running; I see that your hair is all wet. Please tell me that I have a new shower massage."

"Oh yeah, I'm sorry. Yes, congratulations, Apples. The surgery was successful. There now is a new shower message! It works fine. I know that you have an early day tomorrow. Thanks for the shower."

"There's no need to thank me. You earned it, remember?"

"Speaking of remember," I said, pointing to my change pocket and the dime that was the key to my salvaging any hopes of any kind of contact with this woman.

She smiled and answered, "Yeah, right! Four thirty. Until tomorrow, good night."

I closed the doors of the ancient mansion turned rooming-house and my thoughts went to those doors that lie before me on First Street. I left the key to Gordon's in his apartment. I could only hope that Rico was around or that Gordon was home.

I turned the corner to First Street and saw Gordon standing on the stoop, looking up and down the block with a dazed, confused look on his face. I asked, "What's up, bro'? Did something happen on the block?"

It was early for our schedule, nothing usually happened until after the bars closed. He held his arms out, signifying emptiness. Simply and plainly he said, "They grabbed Rico, bro'! They fuckin' grabbed Rico."

I thought of all the times that Rico had saved our asses and said, "Well let's not just stand here! Let me get my chucks and we'll go fuck them up whoever they are."

I started for the door. Gordon grabbed me by the jacket and said, "Ain't gonna help, bro'. The fuckin Feds have him. They're sending him back to his country, wherever the fuck that is."

I could not get past my disbelief of Rico being grabbed.

Somehow, deep inside, I truly thought that he could not be held even if captured. Looking down the block, I asked, "How do you know this for sure? Is someone fuckin' with your head or what?"

In answer to my question, Gordon could only shake his head. Rico was a man who could become a tree in a forest or a grain of sand on the beach if it meant becoming invisible in order to avoid arrest.

Gordon then delivered the next set of shocking information, at least the next in a series, "His old lady came by here for his stuff. She said he was starving and freezing at the lock-up, wearing only blood stains and the shorts he had on when he was rousted."

My mind raced with thoughts of busting him out. I knew that he would have done this for either one of us. I continued to pump Gordon for any information. "Down where? Where did they take his ass? Is he at the Brooklyn House of Detention, Rikers or where? He might still be at the Seventy-Eighth Precinct if they just grabbed him."

The other part of Gordon's statement finally hit the processor. I exclaimed, "Hold it! Did you say his old lady? Since when does he have an old lady?"

I reinserted my eyeballs while Gordon explained the mystery to me, common knowledge to all other details, "You mean you never saw him with that blond Spanish chick. He would see her in the park, near the picnic house and play with his kid. That's probably where he would go when he disappeared, if he wasn't runnin' for Intelligent John."

The processor was sure busy that night. I responded to the news of the third detail, "He had a kid? Right here in the Slope? Holy shit!"

Gordon filled me in on what he knew about our enigmatic partner, "He went to Maria's crib, probably to see Little Rico. The Feds must have been tipped off somehow. Immigration's been kind of after his ass since his parents went back home.

Until now, he managed to keep two steps ahead of everyone.

"They got him after he dove through the second floor window. Maria said that he tucked and rolled so he would land on his feet. When he started running for the fire escape across the yard, two Feds downed him and cuffed him. Then they beat the shit out of him and threw him into a van only in his fuckin' shorts, man."

I remembered how I said to Rico, "You always find the open window."

The irony of that memory was overshadowed by the recollection of Rico's message to me, "And above all, don't attach you' self to no people, mon. Never get to know them too good. When you gotta split, you go with the wind. There be no time to break away from anything or anybody when 'the mon' be doggin' your ass."

I joined Gordon in silence. We looked to the corner that would always produce Rico. This night, we would be denied. Gordon jumped as if he sat on a third rail and said, "Oh shit, I forgot all about her!"

Gordon bolted up the stairs as I followed in hot pursuit. I couldn't imagine whom he could forget. Perhaps he left someone hanging on the phone and he was paying for minutes. The screams from within the apartment soon answered my questions.

At the end of the hall I heard, "You fuckin' bastard! You could at least wipe my face before you run out like a goddamn asshole! Now drop your drawers and finish what you . . . Oh, Hi Kenny! Gordon, I thought that this was going to be just the two of us."

A naked Terry was tied to the radiator pipe by her hair. Gordon managed to find enough of it to loop around her wrists so that she was completely immobilized. He looked at me and said in a matter-of-fact tone, "Catch you later at The Horse, bro'." I guessed that she had set her hopes on things to come, or whatever.

I left Gordon as he sought the answer to untying a square knot. I ran down the stairs asking myself, "How does one mourn the living?"

I felt the chucks that I had placed up my sleeve and the unquenchable thirst for vengeance burning within me. Fortunately, for anyone who might have walked my way, my need for solitude prevailed. I headed for Prospect Park.

Could I be so lucky, if I walked through the park, that someone would try to mug me? I pitied the poor fool who would go for it that night. But no such opportunity presented itself, only the dimly lit path that drew me to the meadow. I pulled my chucks from my sleeve and began smashing trees, benches and any apparition that might accept my challenge. I was answered by the echoes of my own actions and the sky above in its eternal indifference. I launched the sticks toward the heaven's black abyss and filled the night with my scream of hopelessness.

Exhaustion caused my collapse upon the meadow. The only sound I could hear was that of my own labored breathing as I lay flat on the grass. Planet Earth was like a wall to my back. I clenched the grass, looked out to the paradox above me and said, "Eternity, a void filled with infinite worlds, mysteries and potential."

My breathing slowed, as did my thoughts, until a sense of nothingness yet oneness with all about me prevailed. There was a serene awareness of my connection to the Universe. My body was enveloped by the silence of the moist park grass while that of the starry sky stilled my mind. I was both humbled by the sense of my own insignificance to everything about me and inspired by my perception of it all.

Found in September's Child's guest sketch book

Chapter Ten

Awakening

A slobbering tongue slapped against my cheek, "Terra, good boy!" I said. My eyes opened to see the rising Sun's corona radiating around his big Doberman head.

Since he had placed his two paws on my chest in domination, I wasn't going any where, until a soft voice called out to him, "Bobo, come Bobo! Sorry about that, Mister. Bobo sit."

The footsteps stopped just short of my head. I heard the sound of a leash clip attaching to the dog's collar. The woman inquired, "Why did you call him Terra? Did you own this dog before my husband found him?"

I looked at a fatter, happier and straighter Terra than I've ever known. I said to the woman, "A dog like this is never owned, he just allows you to serve him. No, I never owned him. But please don't apologize; it was time for me to get up anyway."

I wrestled Terra out of my way. There was a stick nearby, so I threw it down the Sheep Meadow. Terra chased it and I walked toward Seventh Avenue.

I thought, "If you wake up on top of the ground, then you know you're not beneath it." I wondered, "Did I just think that, or is it something I once heard?"

I sat on a bench and lit the last cigarette in the pack. The buildings before me evoked thoughts from having read Ayn Rand's initial perceptions of New York when she arrived from Russia as an immigrant child. She referred to the skyscrapers as stone monuments to the enterprise of Humankind. Since I was looking at meager brownstones and apartment buildings, I guessed that they were simple headstones, at the very least.

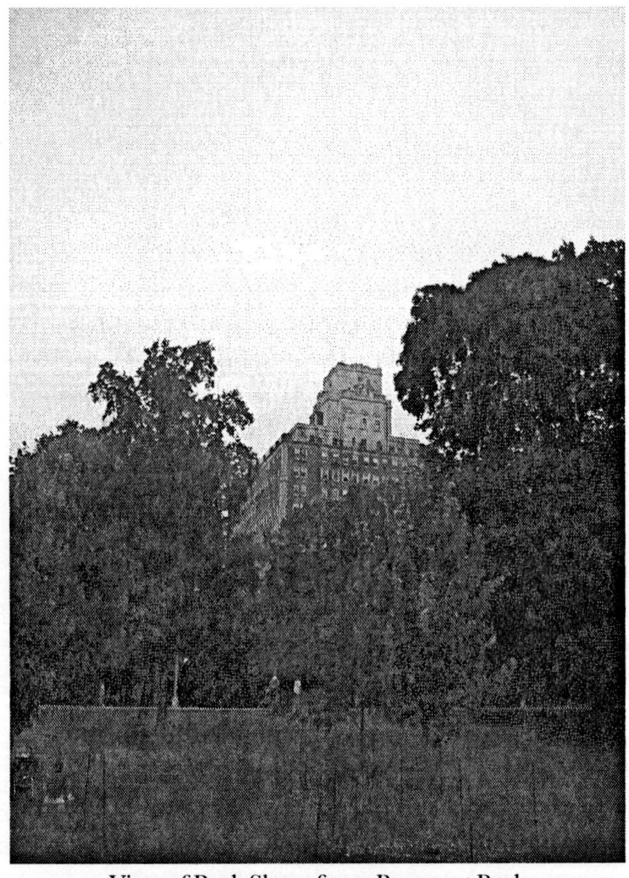

View of Park Slope from Prospect Park

Photo by J.K. Savoy

Throughout her novel, "Atlas Shrugged", she would have her characters constantly say to one another, "*Check your premises!*" I'm sure that she was referring to the foundation of their thoughts or actions. I saw myself above the ground and standing upon it. My epistemological wits were about me. I felt worthy of those premises.

The problem with relationships that are made on the streets is they are fleeting at best. We aging urchins of the street were all caricatures of ourselves to one another. We became one another's opportunity for the moment, and then the moment passed. Another opportunity somehow presented itself, and perhaps we went on for the next moment.

I never truly knew Rico, I guess. On the street, the people that one befriends can be characterized better as stories than as lives. A life has position and direction, usually accompanied by a first and last name. The names of people on the street rarely went past their first name, if it were in fact their name.

Any surname or title that might result was a product of appropriateness to something that set the person apart from others. For example: Frankie from Bay Ridge, Intelligent John, Cindy Burp, and so on. I was Keni September. It distinguished me from Kenny the Cop or Crazy Kenny, to some at least. In any case, it told the story. So who needed to know your real name?

I felt that I would never see Rico again. What he taught me, however, will always be part of me. After all, I am but the sum total of my knowledge and experiences. I can live off the land and defend myself against anyone because of Rico and his teachings. During my tour of the sewer of life, he was instrumental in helping me to overcome some of my greatest fears and to endure them. If only he listened more carefully to himself.

I threw my cigarette butt to the ground and a song came to mind, "Every Time I Kick the Habit, A Nun Rolls Down the Hill." Then I remembered there were no words to that song, so I put it out of mind.

I saw a familiar form walk past me and I said, "You never paid me for the last cup of coffee when you split from September's, Freddy!" He didn't roll down the hill as I kicked him squarely in the ass.

He looked at me all startled and bewildered and said, "Kenny, I thought you left the neighborhood after the coffee house dissolved. I'm heading for The Economy. Do you want to join me in a cup?"

I thought, "If I got any skinnier, I could probably join him in a thimble."

He was called, Freddy Fantasy. His trademark was that he dressed completely in black regardless of the time of day or season. It was said that the neighbors near his family's mansion by the park, of which he and his sister were the sole occupants, thought that his clothes symbolized the mourning of his parents' hopes and dreams for him.

His sister was known as Feathers, because of her trademark earrings. She spent her time actually developing a career in art. Freddy spent his waking hours in an endless pursuit of extending his developing years. In his defense, he did, however, have an enterprise of his own: a throwaway newspaper called Selective Reality. Freddy sold advertising space in it to the local merchants. He would then publish photography, small articles and poetry from all of his hippie friends.

After a month of accumulating material and maybe two days of preparing it for production, Freddy would drop it on the publisher's lap and hope for the best. The New York Times' slogan was, "*All the News That's Fit to Print*". Selective Reality's slogan could have very well been, "All the Print That's News to Fit". His friends would happily accept the free paper. Unfortunately, and of little concern to Freddy, the rest of the public would allow the paper to live up to the throwaway promise.

"How long can you make a cup of coffee last?" This was the question posed to me by Freddy. I guess that I caught on quickly, I answered, "As long as it takes to keep them from throwing me out!" Freddy raised his fist in triumph as if to say, "Right answer."

I ordered a cup from Bessie, the waitress. The Economy was the only place where ten people could sit at a booth designed for six. At our weight there was no challenge.

Freddy Fantasy was like a guiding black light in a fog of desperation. All of those with no direction of their own seemed to sense his resignation to dereliction and thus, gather within his flow.

The Economy was not the ordinary neighborhood restaurant. Its location was central within the traffic patterns of the city bound. To them it was a launch pad to their daily mission. I saw it as a modern-Greek tragedy. It was as though, there, within the never ending flow of coffee, was a bend in the stream of life. The driftwood could accumulate in the corners, while the current carried the fish to the nets.

I sat in the midst of the ongoing accumulation of human wreckage that was making an attempt at intending to have thoughts of employment. This was a step above having no thought at all of endeavor. Some of them had frequented my coffee house. Others were local hippies that I never met. Others were alternative life-stylists, a euphemism for the chronically unemployable.

"What is, is! What isn't, isn't!" Michael shouted the obvious to all who would listen. It was impossible not to listen since she had plopped down at our booth. Michael had been attending BEST (Bearhard Seminar Training). The words blasted from her mouth like detonations! The power of her proclamation was like a rushing diesel locomotive! Her ability to defend her position was nonexistent! At BEST, they promised that upon completion of the course, she would see the whole picture.

Bessie had the most incredible waitress skills on Earth.

She could carry four cups full of hot coffee or tea in one hand. She would appear to walk past your table as she placed the right cup in front of the right person. While still walking she would begin to take the orders from the next table. The other hand would then drop three plates of food next to the cups already placed. After a roll to the right her pad would be out writing up the other table's orders. Nothing was ever spilled and no one was ever missed.

As the crowd in the restaurant became noticeably thinner, the crowd at our table became that much more noticeable. Guest checks flew at us from Bessie's pad as fast as she could write them.

Spiro, the third generation owner of The Economy, would sit at the register all day encased in a cloud of cigarette smoke. He would be collecting cash with one hand while with the other; he called his long list of tenants living in his endless list of properties, seeking rent payments. I thought that the extent of Spiro's communications to the world beyond the phone was limited to ahem until I heard him ask, “Are you people going to eat anything, or what?”

Pocket change found its way to the center of our table from all of the pockets present. Some paid and left. We stayed and shared two bagels. My contribution for the feast was to give all the details of, The Fall of September's. And this too will pass, or at least run out of time. We managed to stretch our unwelcome presence into the early part of the lunch hour. I could almost feel the booth tip and catapult us through the window.

“See you tomorrow.” “Yeah, see you at the Old PU.” That day must have been the tomorrow that yesterday promised, to the dismay of Spiro and Bessie. As one whose days usually began at sunset, I realized that life in the AM had its share of street people too. We parted ways and went on to the pursuit of our misfortunes.

I thought, “If their common goal were procrastination, they would surely find a way to put that off.”

I wandered along Seventh Avenue, marveling at the daylight world. While passing the store windows, the image beside me matched me step for step. I glanced at the face only to see it reflecting my own astonishment. The windows turned into brick façades and then alleys, thus momentarily relieving me of my unavoidable confrontation, until I walked past the next window. I paused and so did the reflection. We stared at one another, both realizing that what the woman on the train saw, was so.

My last memorable encounter with a mirror showed a snake that was to shed its skin in order to find a beginning from within itself. If what I saw before me was my beginning, what I was seeing in the window appeared to be at its end.

My fingers touched the dime in my pocket. All I could think of was, "What words could that thing in the mirror say at four-thirty when it makes the call?

After Apples picks up her phone and I say, "This is Kenny," will she see in her mind what I see before me? At four-thirty I will speak to her. At this moment, the thoughts that I have would serve me better to find a pen than the ears of another."

The Seventh Avenue Merchants Association never provided benches for the weary shoppers. The stores all had stoops that afforded multi-level seating for consumers who needed rest between purchases, not for those of us who were pausing between lives. I would beg, only to differ with any of those who might challenge me. I sat down on a stoop, took my journal and pen in hand and wrote:

> New York City, you are a finger down my throat
> You can snatch a young boy from the bosom of his
> mother
> Then change him into a man! Or a woman
> As you look upon us all with your mesmeristic eye
> That sees a market in anything

You create the orphans that you claim to nurture
If only by beckoning them to your seduction
When held within your embrace
We are forced to achieve our ultimate potential
Even if it is death itself or living while in our tombs

Here, within your overshadowing presence
Do we truly see ourselves, as you ignore us
We who gather beneath you in our isolation
Become lifelines in your hand.

"Well, it must be four-thirty because Kenny is calling," Apples said laughingly after picking up the phone.

I meekly defended myself with, "I told you that I would call. This proves I can keep my word."

My claim was met with a silence that seemed to invalidate hello itself, followed by, "This call proves only two things, three if you count the dog house that you're still in. One, you can actually tell time, at least when challenged. Two, you do know how to use a phone." Once before she said that she would put up a pot; somehow I felt it banging me on the head.

"Apples, I'm almost finished with "Siddhartha". I would like to return it to you. Maybe we could hang out afterward." She seemed to be exceptionally generous with her use of silence.

After enough of it went by she said, "How will I know if you're really coming over when you say you are? Will some unforeseeable circumstances overwhelm you and keep you glued to a strange stoop?"

I knew that any woman in her right mind might have second thoughts about someone like me. She was in her right mind and I was as close to like me as one could find. Perhaps it was not the right time to try to prove my merit, so I said, "I will call you tomorrow at the same time as today, I will confirm our agreed time to meet, and I will meet you then. Is that okay with you?"

I heard a faint laugh. Then she said, "I don't want you to rush through a book just to run to a phone. You may miss something important. Why don't you stop by tomorrow night at eight o'clock and we'll discuss what you read?"

How could I say no? So I said, "See you at eight o'clock, tomorrow night."

I had to check my reefer inventory back at Gordon's. Whatever I had left was at the apartment. Until I could hook up with Rico's source, then that was it. When it came to the affairs of that world, all I cared about was cutting what I bought from Rico down to joints and then turning it over to meet my needs. Rico never mentioned who his supplier really was and I never asked, but in this case an assumption was safe. Intelligent John seemed like the reasonably sure call to make.

The more that I thought about John, the spookier he seemed. John could take the road less traveled and at the same time the road most traveled, while collecting tolls on both. A vision of him slowly describing the Eternal Light in the form of a hot poker enroute to my eye came to mind. Someone at one end or another of Rico's business may have felt fucked for who knows what reason. Could Rico have stiffed his supplier for money, or a customer on a short weight?

Sometimes Rico would boost weak pot with angel dust. If you weren't expecting anything, you might feel your spirit leave your body and do tricks. Someone may have thought that they had a score to settle with Rico. Not many people could go one on one with him, but a dime could take any enemy off the street pretty fast. I felt like a drowning man might feel when he finds that survival is his, only if he can first patch the lifeboat that might save him.

My trunk was undisturbed. I checked beneath the false

bottom and found my stash. I could roll this over, literally, into a bridge over the next couple of days. To a man blindfolded by his own sense of denial, a gangplank might seem like a bridge.

"Gordon, here's the rent for the next week!" I threw the stash to the welcoming hand of the needy. Was I throwing my lifeline to him or my anchor? I had to escape, not only my dilemma, but also those dogging nauticisms.

Gordon was happy with the deal. I guessed that he would truly begin to miss Rico after he smoked it all. I felt a strong sense of relief seeing the pot fly out of my hand. I looked forward to reintroducing myself to any of my brain cells that may have survived the cannabis wars.

What I once felt as a mysterious force drawing me toward the adventures which would ultimately redirect my life, had become one with my internal compass. My direction was, anyplace but there. It wasn't difficult to make a fearless self-inventory. All I had to do was see the pot disengage from my hand. What remained from the hand back was what was left of me.

My foot exited the door as my entire world accompanied it. Of all the times that I walked past what was once September's, I would just do that, but that day I paused. Whatever drew me from within the small store, which was once my haven, burned within me as fuel for my passion.

The sidewalk beneath my feet was the riverbed where I was purged of the superfluous. The door that stood beside me was once the exit that became my entry to the Eternal Now. Those things once revered by me were the wreckage from which I had emerged. I was left with the question, "As what and as whom?"

I had no past gnawing at my conscience. All of my debts were paid. Those who survive the street are those who pay who they owe upon receiving payment themselves from others. We may only keep the change. Repaying the hand that once helped you helps to keep it from your throat. If there were to be a future for me beyond that of the street, it would have to be an ongoing product of the ongoing present.

"Hey there! Now that September's is gone, you're oot and aboot I see."

Only one force from the north was more powerful than a glacier when it came to destroying all in its path, in this case a language. That force would be a Canadian.

Right from the stoop where I sat while writing, I gave him a perfect opening with the worst answer possible, "Don, so what's new?

As soon as the words left my mouth my hands should have held my ears as he answered, "Oh, New York, New Jersey. New Mexico's so far away, you'd be old when you got there, ay?"

Why did, "Workin' hard or hardly workin?" invade my consciousness as the next thing Don might say if I didn't head him off the road to knee slappin' cliché?

Diplomacy had left my life at about the same time that farting in public had entered it so I said, as a good neighbor in the south should, "You're dripping sweat all over the stoop Don, and you really stink. I guess you've been working all day?"

I thought, "Now he'll either be pissed and leave me to the stoop alone so I can write a little, or at least not get hit with another chestnut."

Instead, I was treated to his rambling, "Well I just finished a job. I moved a bunch of art over to Williamsburg. The artist people were forced oot of their broonstone. They said something aboot the building being converted, ay. What can you convert a building to? You would think that it would always be a building, ay?"

I had absolutely no idea what he was talking aboot, I mean, about. I was only sure of one thing, neither did he. I asked, "Do you mean that people pay you to take their paintings and art work in that rat's-ass, piece-of-shit, open pick-up truck?"

There was a certain resiliency within Don that allowed insult to pass right through him like beer at a border crossing.

He smiled broadly and answered, "It's not that they pay me a lot. I get my gas and something for my time, ay. It all started with helping friends, now everyone that they know calls me when they're moving."

It's been said, if you're with a dog long enough, you may begin to resemble one another. Given enough time. I guess this could also be true of Canadians and their trucks.

We walked over to his pick-up. Don would slow his walk slightly and then lurch as if he were changing gears, followed by eventual acceleration. His mouth did resemble a grille, always curved up at the corners with broken teeth. His oversized eyeballs had such an infectious high-beam quality, that you automatically would look to the right when approaching him head-on. Although I knew Don, I could only recognize him by his profile.

"Don, what do you do when it rains? I mean like, your truck has got an open back and you're moving fuckin' art. Doesn't this create a logistical problem for you?"I totally underestimated Canadian technology.

Don answered with his solution, "I got a tarp, ay. If it starts raining, I throw it over the load, if there's enough time, ay. The oil paintings are usually okay, ay. On a rainy day, I probably qualify for a by-line for the watercolors. I used to partner with my friend Lonny when it rained, ay. He had a closed in van. Lonny went back to Canada a while ago, now I only have the tarp. By the way Kenny, why do you always call me Don?"

I thought, "Perhaps because Shithead is taken?" Instead I remained diplomatic, "Because you're the head of the fuckin' Canadian Mafia, why else? Or maybe because, like, it's your name."

At first he blinked at me, as if to pass. Then he dropped the bomb, "My name is Dawn, D-a-w-n. Not Don."

I answered, "Honestly, I would have gotten it the first time if we were using cue cards. You just said both names the same way; the only difference is that you spelled the first one. Are you sure that you didn't understand your parents correctly? Didn't they have the same accent as you? Anyway, isn't Dawn a girl's name?"

I was hoping that I didn't ask too many questions at once and overload him. When we approached the van, we slowed slightly. He pulled alongside of me and explained it all, "My parents were from Minnesota, ay. Their accent was completely different from mine. I was named after my aunt, who also left me this truck and that box of mallard decoys in the back. In Canada, Dawn can either be a boy's name or a girl's name, kind of like Michael is doon here."

As he left I said, "It was really interesting talking to you, Dawn. Good luck with all your moving jobs. Try to keep your low beams on at all times, except when passing."

"Thanks Kenny. But I won't be doing any more jobs doon here, I'm heading back to Manitoba in a week or so, ay. I have a hard time understanding the way things are in the States. Anyway you people talk too funny for me, ay."

When traveling through distant lands, we may take on some of the characteristics of its people, or at least we may learn from their ways. The same might be true of invaders who impart their wisdom on us, in lieu of pillaging or plundering. I envisioned a large Canada goose landing on my father's Chevy.

Dawn sputtered toward the north. I looked down at the gutter where he was parked. A portrait of Alexander Hamilton lay there surrounded by the word ten. I darted over to it and quickly shoved the bill into my pocket. I felt like a dog when he takes a scrap to a corner, growling and prepared to snap at any possible challenger.

I suddenly realized that if I had rolled the reefer, my

evening routine would have begun. I would have walked in a different direction after I left Gordon's. I wouldn't have talked to Dawn and I wouldn't have found the ten.

I would have risked my ass, and at best sold the pot and ate and drank from fortune telling. Who knows? Maybe it was my time to get busted too. Shit! Never get busted on a Friday night in New York. They hold you in The Joint until Monday and good-bye hemorrhoids, hello doody-babies.

Feeling like a gambler might feel, when his horse comes in and he can miss a day's work, I looked to the left towards The Horse, and then to the right towards Minsky's. I had made my day already. There was no need to punch in.

The setting Sun's last light fell on the final page of "Siddhartha". I could take my Tarot cards to one of the bars and sing for my supper, or not. Ten dollars is a lot of money to have at one time when ordinarily favors and barter get you through. But ten dollars in hand, in my case, might allow me to make new choices and by-pass the favor and barter routine that was taking me nowhere but back again.

In spite of my disdain for money, I saw something special and very symbolic in that particular U.S. Ten. Exceptional or heroic people who have become presidents adorn other bills. Hamilton's presence symbolized more than an office or patriotism. To me he symbolized the concept of the moment of choice.

Hamilton was a man who might have become president. Instead, he made a critical choice to take a stand and defend his honor. To Alexander Hamilton, there was nothing to live for without having honor. He truly put his whole self behind his last decision as he looked down the barrel of his pistol only to see the flash of another's.

My thoughts drifted to Rico and how he had been a great and honorable friend. All that life ever gave him was a choice to make in order to survive. His heightened intuitive awareness, except for the one time that he blinked, made him a true professor of the street.

But he had become a crutch for me that only aided me along his path. His help, as necessary as it was at the time, allowed me to procrastinate in my dealing with the issues that had caused my latest quandary. A nearly empty pen found an empty page as my thoughts took form before me.

JE

"Why, during those times that I had chosen isolation, has my need for human interaction prevailed? My need to communicate has language as its medium. Could my need to trade and bargain have money as its? Have I taken my conflict with money as far as it could go only to conclude nothing?

"Could I have oversimplified corruption as a concept and saw money as being the foundation for all that was corrupt and not the hands that might be upon it? How many experiences does it take for me to see that the Trevor Lascos of the world and the street rats, who would kill for ten dollars, are a cut of the same cloth? Can one who says that he never assumes, attempt to live with the assumption that, 'corruption exists within the soul of the species' and not within its symbol of common value? Would life in the world be bearable knowing that the same degree of decadence is within a pauper as well as a prince? Is there somehow, the same potential to change, within each?

"Had my dive within a speck of sand to know the Universe, not revealed to me that gravity is that which unites the stars? Therefore, can money serve as the bond between people and their promises to one another? Can money symbolize honor between others and myself if I see it as only a tool and not an objective?

"There was a time that I would give away everything that I had to anyone in my way. That ten would have been no exception. I decided to give that particular bill a chance to possibly teach me something. I took a ride into the unknown by trying to eliminate money from my life. The ride would continue, but by giving worth to my choices and actions.

I added to my journal, "I will place every penny of this ten behind my intuition. It may have fallen into my hand randomly, but I will honor it with purpose in my choices.'"

Like a kid would see a strip of tickets that you get in an amusement park, I looked at that ten. I wondered, "Am I holding the simple power in my hand to set the course for the next moment or my destiny, or what is the difference?

"How many and what kind of rides will this bring me? Which one will I go on first? The haunted house was always free; I just had to reflect on my childhood for that. Until now, thrill rides came in capsule form, or on a blotter. Enough of that! How many times do I have to run barefoot in the snow hoping to become aware of my feet before I realize that the same numbness has occurred within my perception?"

The menu board before me at the Gazebo was evidence that a choice had occurred. Was I hallucinating from hunger, or was Apple's smile summoning me to join her at her table? Whether this was a mirage at an oasis or a vision of hope at the Gazebo, I followed the dream without hesitation.

I walked over to her and said, "I finished "Siddhartha" for the third time. Now can I eat?"

She laughed and said, "You can also just think about it. So sit and order up." She slid the chair out for me with her foot and I replied, "I can hardly wait." She kicked me ever so slightly with her returning foot.

I probably earned another kick by asking, "The past two times that I've come here, I've seen you. Do you always eat natural food?"

Instead she kicked me right in my cerebral ass and answered, "If the only other option would be to eat unnatural food then the answer to your question has to be, yes."

I justified my being at the Gazebo by answering in my usual feeble manner, "I also know how to use a calendar. I was supposed to come over tomorrow at eight. I assure you, I wasn't following you here."

I glanced at the counter where I first lost myself in her eyes. Was this the other lifetime that I thought there must be in order to meet this woman? She lifted her sleeve and my hopes and said, "And you see, I thought that you were taking the opportunity for us to synchronize our watches so neither of us would miss the call."

I placed my empty pen between my fingers and pointed to the shadow on my hand. Her eyes danced between mine and the show on the table as I said, "My sundial works only during the day. At night I rely on my team of spies to gather time information for me."

Her brow lowered as she checked her watch, but for a different concern.

"It's very odd, you begin to show yourself to me as being reliable. At the same time my friend, Annette, becomes the opposite. She was supposed to meet me a half-hour ago. She probably got knocked off course by a gust of wind or whim."

"Was Annette with you at September's the night that you first stopped over?"

"Yes, she was also with me the time that I saw you here. She is kind of short. She is also very assertive. She kept jumping in front of me whenever we tried to talk at the coffee house."

I said to myself, "The Jolly Green Giant could have walked between us that night at the coffee house and I still would have been lost in the same blue eyes that I am now." Then I said to her, "You know, I never noticed, I mean, I never even noticed her let alone remembered her. She must have been extremely short."

Apples laughed then placed her chin upon her folded hands. Our surroundings again faded to irrelevance as we were encapsulated within the sense of our mutual presence.

She asked, "So tell me, how's "Siddhartha"? Did you enjoy reading about a fellow seeker although a fictitious one?"

I was flattered that she would consider me to be a seeker. I slid the book over to her and removed the marker with her phone number and put it in my pocket. My mind and body again, feeling at ease in her presence.

I allowed my words to just flow, "The book's protagonist needed to experience the type of world that I rejected, if only to reject the excesses of that world. It apparently validated the life that he left originally. There seems to be a universal need for a rite of passage either to discover one's self or to re-enforce a belief."

From the moment that I walked in, she had been smiling. Come to think of it, she always smiled. How does one know what another feels if a smile never leaves her face? I answered my own question by listening to her soul while remaining lost in her eyes.

She leaned forward and tilted her head slightly. I was enveloped by the essence of her persona as it radiated before me, saying, "Most people who consciously enter some form of voluntary life transition go about doing it in a way that allows them to make changes more gradually. Although the character in the book was different in his motivation from yours, both of you immerse yourselves in your search."

Listening, I thought, "One who thinks that he's shouting in a vacuum welcomes an echo as a form of self-validation. This is the only person that I have met who not only appreciates why I did what I did, but understands the effort and can foresee a goal."

I began to feel as at ease being with her as I was with the thoughts that took form. I said, "I guess I have always been unaware of my being radical, I've been realizing this progressively. Unless you finally become one with the thought that obsesses you, procrastination will rear its ugly head, and you may live in the shadow of your own ignorance.

"The same may be true of fear; it sometimes represents ones own unrealized potential. Unless you dive into its face, it will haunt you in your own reflection. In either case, at some point one must act as his own salvation, or die in reruns."

The smile never broke her face. Her eyelids lowered, then she said, "I'm sure that you're familiar with the saying, when life begins to imitate art. Of course this is a play on the axiom, art imitating life. Suppose the two were one of the same. Just suppose, for instance that theater had no actors, no script and no predetermined conclusion. What might it be if those conditions existed?"

She smiled throughout her statement and afterward. I found my hand resting on hers, and better yet hers remained with mine. I realized that her smile might have been out of politeness since the last thing that she said was in the form of a question. I replied, "I have no choice but to answer, life itself! Another maxim, the world is but a stage, would come to mind."

She nodded in affirmation and I continued, "Consider for a moment, media, television in particular. The news has become no different than a play. The difference here is that it is ongoing and product driven. Every night at six o'clock we're shown to our seats. The talking head pops into view and tells us of the half-dozen selected topics of ultimate importance to the world, probably because their sponsor's messages could be most easily linked to them."

"Kenny, what you say is absolutely true. Our common reality is nothing but an illusion that is agreed upon by popular opinion. What if there was pure theater with no ulterior motive, no script or no director? The only foreseeable thing there might be is the spontaneity of the next response. Perhaps it comes in the form of a statement, an expression or a gesture. The audience and the players become indistinguishable from one another. All participants develop an ongoing collective movement."

I realized how great it is to be with someone that you can really talk with. Better yet, someone that's really worth listening to. She added, "You said before, life itself. That's exactly right. People today are conditioned to scripted behavior, so "Living Theater", as it is known, has found a tremendous audience. On the other hand, who can tell the audience from the players?"

"Come to think of it Apples, the need for this type of storytelling falls into proper progression. We had CBS and the rest of the networks write history before our eyes for ten years with Viet Nam. And then it became eclipsed by the other half of the double feature, Watergate. People must be sick and tired of our scripted reality. Doesn't it stand to reason that their need for storytelling should summon up the unpredictable?

"Ancient storytellers would wander from one tribe to another, telling tales of social and political import. They described to the different tribes, as listeners hung on their every word, where they were before or where they're going next. The next day they would tell others about them. Besides traveler's tales, this was the ancient's only connection to the outside world. The original media!"

I added, "What if the leader of one of the tribes became for some reason intimate with the storyteller and they united? Could this have been the onset of the great government-media conspiracy that bonds the world in universal thought, motivation and paranoia?"

Her head tilted the other way and she asked, "Is this why you turned your TV and everything else off?"

I felt that I should announce that our food might be getting cold. But since we were both eating salad I just replied, "Since TV completely turned me off, I retaliated. Any conclusion regarding the events of those times that I might draw was based upon information from the media in all of its other forms. The sum total of both electronic and print news is drawn from the same mother lode.

"The more exposure that I had to this one-dimensional perception, the more I found myself seeing the absurd in the same light as the reasonable. For instance, I concluded that in Richard Nixon we finally had the ideal president."

I was delighted to see that she knew that I was about to put her on.

"Okay, I'll bite. How can a president who was forced out of office be the ideal?"

"Thank you for biting, Apples. The reasons are twofold: first, he is a known schizophrenic. This allows his multiple personalities to be both the candidate and his own running mate. Therefore no need for an annoying vice-president."

"Alright, you said two things, what's the other?" Bite number two.

No sooner than the second thing formed in my mind, it escaped from my mouth, "Well, he's a megalomaniac. If he were to die while in office, since he would have no second in command, he could succeed himself with his own resurrection."

We walked up and down Seventh Avenue, talking the entire night. We could have had desert at Gordon's by lying on the floor and letting the roaches fall into our mouths. Her apartment and coffee was the better choice.

"Okay Kenny, since you returned "Siddhartha" on time and in good order, perhaps you might enjoy reading this."

I looked at the title as she passed the book from the shelf to my hand. For some stupid reason I referred to the author of "Siddhartha" by the wrong first name as I said, "The Life of the Theatre'? I'm sure I'll enjoy reading Julian Beck as much as Rudolph Hess."

Being the English teacher, she took immediate but polite aim at my syntax, "By that you must mean that Rudolph Hess had read "The Life of the Theatre" while serving a life term in Spandau Prison."

How can one's own foot, so easily find one's own mouth? After kicking the ass-end of my own sense of discretion, I answered, "The last thing old Rudolph read was his horoscope, before he stole the plane from Adolph. A study in the spontaneous may have been a better choice for him. I did mean Hermann Hesse, I'm sorry about that."

I had to apologize to her for saying the name of a Nazi, let alone Hitler's top deputy. She laughed at my error, but I sensed uneasiness in her upon hearing that name. The pictures of her refugee family on the mantle spoke for her discomfort.

I can't remember ever feeling as good as I did during the weekend that Apple's and I hung out together. The days and nights that we shared were like one unending conversation, interrupted only by laughter or an embrace. I have heard of people being able to finish one another's sentences, after spending a great deal of time together. Apples and I were actually able to begin one another's.

There were moments when I saw us not as beings, but as the pure spirit within our incarnations having managed to break free from gravity and float together through our perceptions. We would soar to the pinnacle of idea. The mundane whirled about us like dancing horses on a carousel. The world became a carnival bestowing cotton candy unto our souls.

Apples said that she needed that kind of weekend to relax because she had to spend every minute of the following two weeks preparing for exams. This would require her to seal herself off from the outside world. She made it clear that she wanted to see me afterward. When I asked, "Who is Ward?" she kicked me.

It was pouring rain that Monday morning as I left Polhemus Place for First Street. The rain was less dampening to my spirit than Gordon's Do Not Disturb sign on the door. Terry's hair had some time to grow. Who knows what uses Gordon had found for it? It was too cold and wet to hang out on a stoop.

The back seat of the Chevy would have to be my reading room that day. No big deal, it or the Prospect Park bandshell had become my choice of residence since Terry moved in.

The roaring sound of the rain on the roof diminished in my mind. It was as though I was observing my spirit travel through Julian Beck's thoughts on theater and reality. I approached the last page and it occurred to me that I hadn't had a cigarette nor eaten all day.

I thought about how many times I had resigned to starvation during those months. I could accept not eating; it was merely a physical requirement. I often enjoyed the mild hallucinations that occurred when a couple of days went by without food. What truly amazed me was that I managed to maintain a thought long enough to neglect an addiction.

How can a distraction such as a habit overwhelm my senses to the point that I could disregard my very survival in order to feed my addictions? If I were down to my last dollar and I had neither food nor cigarettes, what need would I choose over the other? I guess the thought occurred to me because that choice was made by me recently.

I had walked into The Economy just a few weeks before, after Providence blew a dollar my way. I stopped short of the counter and said, possibly aloud, "Shit no! I can't eat. I have no cigarettes." After slapping my own forehead, I sat at the counter and wrote:

JE

"Does one remain insane if one becomes aware of his insanity? If one allows that behavior to continue, can one cling to insanity as a basis, or is he now only stupid? Is one's descent from insanity to stupidity a major loss of status for the newly stupid? Or is he oblivious to the difference, albeit on a different level? How long can a life continue if preference is given to that which will cause its demise and not to that which will give it sustenance?"

Did I, that day, truly breach my denial when instead of buying a pack of cigarettes, I bought loose tobacco and rolling paper, leaving me enough for a bagel and a glass of water? Did bargaining count as a breakthrough if it preceded anger?

I thought, "The Chevy's window is covered with pouring rain. But why do I see only drifting sand? I feel as if the Sun is burning me, yet I am surrounded by torrents of water. Can the oasis that I would search for escape my discovery, because what I seek, I am within? Has my search for answers ended with only more questions? If I were to take a fearless self-inventory, would I list only the paper which I would write it upon?"

I wrote, "At what point, is there one . . . ?"

Suddenly, the moment my pen, again, ran out of ink, a large Doberman ran past my car toward the park, "Is that Terra?" I asked myself.

I hoped that the Chevy would start. It caught on the last click. The dog was running up the block. He leaped over the gutter rivers on each side of Seventh Avenue in his pursuit.

"Pursuit of what?" I asked myself. I soon found myself and the Chevy joining the hunt.

The traffic that crossed the running dog and pursuing car went through their green lights. I felt a sense of mission as I ignored the red ones in my chase. Somehow we were being spared collision.

At Eighth Avenue and Union Street, the mystery Doberman rested at the feet of its person. Terra had not suddenly become a female. I, on the other hand, became aware that I had very little gas left in the car.

My guilty feelings from having run all of those red lights caused me to think that the police presence was in my honor. They were directing traffic up the hill, toward the park, away from some rained-out event. I followed the traffic and found myself thrust in the three-mile inner roadway of Prospect Park. If my name was empty, then the fuel gauge was calling me. I found a two-dollar bill under the seat, but not a thought of where a gas station might be. Rather than search the streets aimlessly, I pulled over to think.

Pathway within Prospect Park
Photo by J.K. Savoy

"Get out of my way, you stupid goose!" I never saw one like that, except in pictures. It flew in front of my windshield as I pulled into the lot. I wondered if it was coming here from Canada or returning, much like Dawn.

Then a thought dawned on me, "Am I sitting in what may become my only home? How many times will a bolted door require me to sleep with my knees bent for the entire night? If I decide to head south to the Yucatan, a car could not double as a bedroom."

I pictured my father, shrugging his shoulders, signifying, "Whatever."

Fortunately Dad's lawyer had transferred the title of the car to me. I felt an idea forming as a van passed me. I left the parking lot and followed the van. The radio in my car was blasting in my ears. I opened the windows and sang, "If I only had a van," to every tune that came up. I added my own stupid words to all my favorite classics: "The Lion could keep his heart; I could use a fuckin' cart. That would work too!"

I knew all the same people that Dawn moved art for. With a van, I wouldn't be as creative with their watercolors. But I could put an end to having to sell pot or tell fortunes and get some spot cash moving art.

"If I only had a van!" I got so carried away with my singing that I missed the turn at The Grand Army Plaza, "Shit! You stupid self-absorbed asshole!" I cursed myself out while looking at my reflection in the rear view mirror. I saw a different person than the one who looked back at me the day of Eddie's hearing. Fear and self-doubt dominated Joe. Uncertainty mixed with unfulfilled mission was foremost with Kenny. Joe always had enough gas. Kenny had become the seeker, if for nothing else then, of gas.

I felt a sputter as the turn for Fourth Street came into view. Fourth Street is a downhill street. I hoped that if I run out, I could at least roll into a parking space on the Monday side of the street. My luck was on a roll. There was a Mobil station sign at Fifth Avenue. I thought that I was the luckiest person in the world at that moment. That moment would be upstaged by what I was about to hear in the next.

A raging man in a VW Minibus yelled, "Man this shit is fucked up! I get a job, Lucy's sister moves back to P.R. Lucy can't drive me to the train and the kids to her mother's 'cause the fuckin' Minibus got a stick shift. If I only had a car, maybe one with an automatic. See if you know someone with a fuckin' car, Ramon."

Ramon, the gas station attendant, told the infuriated man in the VW Minibus that he would see what he could do. I felt Fate move my window back open, in addition to my mouth. I shouted, "Yo! You want to trade? Even money, the car for the VW. I need a van. You need a car. Let's talk."

The man exited the Minibus. He locked the doors as his very pregnant wife sat alone in the back seat. He looked me dead in the eye and said, "Man, you must be smokin' some mean ass shit, or you stole this fuckin' car. Why would anyone want to trade a 'sixty-nine Chevy for a 'sixty-four VW even money, if it wasn't hot or he wasn't stoned?"

I wondered, "How do I explain that I don't recognize common value or that I'm following Fate and the pure force of magic without him calling his friends over?"

I showed him the paperwork for the car and my license. He looked me up and down, and then looked back at pregnant Lucy. The gas attendant was busy shaking his head as I signaled him to give me two dollars of his finest no-lead for my empty tank.

The man, although appearing puzzled and overwhelmed by his wish coming true, said, "I don't know, man! You sure you didn't fall out of that car headfirst? I gotta talk it over with my woman. You got a phone number where I can find you?"

I wrote down Gordon's number. He snapped back when I told him to ask for Kenny. I guess that he saw the name,

Joseph, on my license. He seemed satisfied when I pointed to the middle initial, K.

"Okay, bro', my name is Carlos. I gonna talk it over with my woman, like I said. You sure you ain't gonna come back and say some shit later like, 'I don't remember any Carlos.' 'Cause if you run that shit by me if I call you, then we gonna be gettin' down!"

Carlos took the stance of a fighting rooster about to protect his hen and egg. I handed my last two bucks to the confused gas jockey. I turned to Carlos and said in my best street macho, "Carlos, it's cool, bro'. I got my reasons. All I want is the van so I can earn a little bread doing hauling work and sleep in it out on the road. The car's title is clean and it's ready to sign over."

I didn't want to part on an apparent note of weakness, so I added, "Don't you be coming back at me with any shit, either! You better have solid paperwork, too. I got no time for fuckin' bullshit, bro'!"

We swapped phone numbers and shook hands. His wife smiled at him. I don't think she understood English. As I left I could hear them arguing in Spanish.

I thought, "Magic is illusion. Illusion is a product of perception. Choice is awareness of circumstances and a selection. Mistakes are subjective."

I realized that the World had pulled me through another of what had become a series of vortexes. For once, I submitted and allowed form to truly shape itself before me. If I could easily supply words for a Tarot card arrangement, could I just as easily supply action for circumstances as I saw them before me? Could life become more rewarding by following a running dog than a thought-out plan? I guessed that it would depend on the outcome of each. This outcome was in Carlos' hands as well as mine.

My mind awoke to the sound of John Lennon imagining no possessions.

I imagined, "Easy for him to imagine, having all the possessions imaginable."

My eyes opened to see a roach working his way along the ceiling. It paused when it was confronted by a loose paint chip directly above my mattress. It seemed determined to move straight ahead, so it chose to grasp the chip rather than go around it.

I became absorbed in the bug's plight and somehow predicted just when the chip would break away from the ceiling. The paint chip fluttered as the faint breeze from the open window carried it randomly. The roach fell straight down and landed on its feet and continued walking along the floor. Although its path may have changed before it, it didn't lose focus. Onward to the crumbs and grease.

I asked the ceiling, "Which is more oppressive, the heat or the thought of tomorrow repeating today? I can very easily control the heat by lying here and breathing very slowly. How has it all come down to this? The most interesting part of my day is taking a shit. Has the attainment of my goal of the abandonment of all of my worldly possessions only served to bring me face to face with my bodily functions?

"Is my way out of this inertia to accept the first job offer I've had since my journey to the center of a question mark? Huh! Not just any job, but a job guarding a whorehouse with my nunchucks and what's left of my wits. Yeah, right!"

"Kenny, stop talking to the fuckin' walls. There's some dude named Carlos on the phone. Talk to him, but don't be too long I'm expecting a call from Terry's old man," said Gordon who was waiting to learn what I had already found out from rapping with Jeff's new live-in lover, Celia. I was hanging out with her and some other locals when she mentioned the job openings.

As usual, Celia was decked out like midnight at noon. Who would guess that she began her career covertly as a whore while she was an aspiring author? Celia had descended from her cloud of curiosity only to be consumed by it.

As a columnist for a local paper, she set out to write a novel called The Hooker Chronicles under the nom de plume, Jenna Taylia. Diving full force into the life, a daily diet of lines kept her from getting past her opening line, "I really suck at this job." Could the constant fear of being discovered as a spy make riding under the covers win out over writing while under cover?

She told me that Jeff wanted Gordon and me to guard the hall at his downtown fuckatorium. He needed bodies with martial arts or military training to keep the girls safe. Gordon was a combat-trained soldier. I kept a trick up my sleeve and my hand was always on it.

I saw tightening barbed vines growing from the whorehouse walls. The job wasn't for me. If my life had come to that, I would rather be disemboweled over an extended period of time with rusted tweezers.

Then it hit me, "Carlos! Oh shit! He's the dude with the Minibus!"

I interrupted my recollections of Celia and ran to the phone to hear my transportation fate. My ass landed on the desk chair and at that instant, I caught both the receiver and the "hurry the hell up" look from Gordon as he pointed to his watch.

"Yo, Carlos, what's up? Make it quick, Dude," I said.

He answered, "Yeah okay. Yo Joe, or whatever your name is. You still interested in the swap? I mean, like trading the cars." I could hear by the changed tone in his voice that his wife's foot was up his ass for this deal.

I could only answer, "Yeah, bro', I'm down for this. I wouldn't have asked you if I wasn't. Let's do it! Bring the 'bus over to First Street, right next to The Stack of Barley. You'll see me there with the Chevy."

With plates and title swapped, the Chevy headed around the corner and disappeared from view with a very happy, very pregnant lady at the wheel. I thought of the last time I watched its brake lights blink. A vision of my father smiling to me from the VW lent credence to my actions. His old jumper cables will have to add power to my new endeavor, whatever that might be.

The roar of the departing Chevy's engine was soon replaced by Gordon's roars of indignation as he greeted me at the door with phone in hand. He smashed the receiver back to the cradle while his other hand pointed to my face.

His eyes were filled with astonishment and disbelief as he asked, "What the fuck is wrong with you, Kenny? The dude offers you a job and you turn it down? We could have been a team. You hit 'em high and I hit 'em low. This kind of job isn't one that you do alone!"

Gordon's libido was pulling his strings, as usual. And just as usual, he tried to pull mine. There was no penetrating his pre-opinionation. He was blinded by the same garter belt that always covered his judgment. Anyway, I gave reason a try.

"Gordon, I don't know what kinda dudes Jeff has working inside. But think about it, man, there might be more shit to deal with from the staff than from the clients. It's a fuckin' whorehouse, bro'! It ain't no daycare center."

Rather than arousing his sense of reason, his sense of manipulation showed up. He said, "By the way, Rico's not around any more to break up ounces for you to sell. You're gonna have to come up with some bread for my rent, don't forget that!"

Suddenly a thought began forming. I stalled him a little when I said, "Maybe neither one of us has to work for four bucks an hour and all the blow jobs we can get. I really don't like the idea of working some guy over because he comes up short on the cash or some crab-infested bitch yells foul. I saw that kind of shit go down with Mark when The Justice Committee showed up at my door. Do you want to be on the cutting end of a switchblade if some shit goes down?"

I could see apprehension in his eyes. Still, he wanted this gig. But he felt he needed my back to his in order to make it work. I was Gordon's friend. I knew him well enough to know that he could not comprehend why I walked away from the kind of money that I once made because I wouldn't be compromised. How then, could I expect him to understand why I refuse to work in Fellini's Satyricon as a tormentor?

Gordon tried another approach, of course assuming my motives to be the same as his, "Dude, I don't get where you're coming from. We have a chance to make some serious bread here. Jeff might pay you shit for regular money, but the hookers kick in if you look after them. Think about it. What guy in his right mind could turn this down?"

I didn't want to acknowledge his logic. A distraction was in order at that point, "Okay, I have to pay you rent. I told you right from the get-go that I would do my part."

Suddenly lights and whistles went off in my head. I looked at Gordon and said, "Bro'! You and I have the ingredients for getting over without fighting the pussy wars. Listen, I have a van now. People all over the Slope need shit moved from here to there."

I tried to get as many of my words in before Gordon could invalidate any argument that might keep him from his destiny. I continued, "Dawn from the coffee house went back to Canada. He had a really great gig going on moving art. There are plenty of people fleeing the neighborhood, who can't afford to hire regular movers.

"Then there is a need for transporting art exhibits to SoHo. Don't tell me you wouldn't like to jump the bones of most of the women artists around here. You'd make money; get all the pussy that you want, and have no fear of sex leading to death.

"You have the phone and the little desk that could be the start of our office. I have the vehicle. We could partner and split what we make down the middle. Think it over. You know where to find me. I'll either be locked in my new cell that's parked at the curb, the old one at the end of your hall or under the stars in the park." My alternative gave him pause and me a needed reprieve from the pressure of the corner that I was suddenly squeezed into.

As if all of the cards that were laid out on the table were his to fold or hold, he said, "Kenny, you're right. You don't seem to be going anywhere too soon. Okay, I will think it over. Meanwhile, Terry wants me to help Jeff at the whorehouse for at least a while. We'll talk more about your idea after I check out this new gig. By the way, this is the last of that pot you threw at me. Got any more, Dude?"

After pointing my thumb down to the empty position, I gave Gordon the pass sign when the joint in my face seemed like just another pill to make me feel larger when it might be time to know the power of staying small. Maybe it was time to not need anything at all that would hold me among the ranks of the delirious led by the oblivious.

Like an internal compass, my thumb returned to the ready position then quickly pointed north. Was it time to break out and land on the shores of a place where echoes of my cries for freedom could land upon my own ears, not just on the bars of my self-imposed cell of security?

I always wanted to feel the wind that blew across the sea to the shores of Nova Scotia, where my French-Italian ancestors were greeted by my other ancestors, the Native Canadians. Since I had no clue about the strange Minibus' performance, my thumb and the wind would be my means of transport. My idea of a breakout wasn't to have a breakdown.

Chapter Eleven

Odyssey

Ayn Rand was not alone in marveling at how Manhattan's wall of skyscrapers was a gathering of monuments to the human mind, resting on the bedrock that is New York. But what of the reservoir of brilliant potential lying untapped beneath the bedrock of assumptions and unchallenged beliefs?

The F train brought me through the rocky underground abyss whose construction was inspired by visionaries of another time. I wondered how some people could drive their ideas through the Earth's mantle, yet others bury their dreams beneath a veil of fear and self-doubt. Is the fine line of difference called decision?

The train bumped and swayed. My eyes fluttered and then shut. The curtains of remembrance parted. The stage before me revealed my Confirmation party. I was twelve. The essence of some poor dead pig's boiled carcass encased in the funerary shroud of its own intestines overcame any breathable air in the room. Garlic and spices adorning this kielbasa could not dignify its killing nor camouflage the stench of the pig's remains.

A friend of the family, who had been a nun since she was sixteen, kneeled at the other end of the room with hands clenched and eyes tightly shut. The entire family lived in fear of her Church-sanctioned judgmental demeanor. She was praying at me because of my refusal to partake of the prey before me.

I held my nose and gagged when she opened her eyes, walked to the table and exclaimed, "Joey! Don't you just sit there and waste the food in front of you. God wouldn't want you to do that. Eat your meat or you'll be punished in Hell for sure!"

The year prior to my Confirmation had seen me grow to where I matched her height. I knew that it might be the time to show that I could match her intellect. This was my opportunity to show my stuff and postpone another moment when a piece of animal flesh would look at me and cry, "Don't let me go to waste, I died just for you!"

I hoped that a good question and the conversation that would follow might somehow ward off the inevitable feeling of some once-living creature's muscles and organs falling into my stomach acid. I leaned forward while covering my plate with my arms. My hands were held in a traditional praying pose when I asked, "Sister, does God really become angry if we waste what He provides for us?"

She gave me her sternest of looks, and then replied, "Of course, and you shouldn't question things like that. There are things that you should just do because it's the way it's always been done. Just eat what God gave you and don't waste. It's about time that you stop questioning everything. You are now a brand-new soldier of the Church."

As a child, I hoped to one day understand Humankind's eternal quest to reveal the true genesis of our purpose within this Universe. With my immediate challenge lying before me on my plate I thought, "If I had joined the ranks of a noble crusade, then why must they murder a living being in my honor?"

Could the dilemma that faced me then have been a result of perhaps my life's first exposure to irony? When I was little, I would sneakily preview my older brother's Early Reader. Was it during my first experience of relating letters to words that my mental filter for all teachings to follow was formed from a dyslectic vision of G-o-d and d-o-G? Did I, from then on, view both with equal relevance and reverence?

I looked at the pig's remains, feeling only empathy toward the table's other victim. Then I looked at the Sister and asked, "The Catechism said that God made each of us in His own image. Is this true?"

Her habit draped her shoulders like the hood of a cobra as she leaned over me and responded with her ever-present sanctimonious certainty, "Imagine, the Confirmation boy is asking a question to which he has been given the answer! Now what if the bishop asked you that one? If you answered with a question, you would have embarrassed the whole family. Yes, we are all made in the very image of Our Lord, Jesus Christ."

Upon saying the name, she bowed her head and did various things with her hands and thumb that I never could quite comprehend. Of course, this was followed by her mandatory kissing of the giant crucifix that was attached to her holy ammunition-belt.

Could that have been the moment when I first thought that we somehow always know all of the answers, and that life is but a process of revealing the appropriate questions at the appropriate time? The people around the table paused in their conversations and looked at me and then they looked toward the nun.

No one, but my dog, Rex, looked through my praying hands at the meat falling from my plate and into the mouth of one lucky carnivore. I took a deep breath and focused my thoughts. They became like a torch cutting chains that, until that moment, held back the questions that weighed upon my mind.

I said, "Okay Sister, you say God is angered by people who waste. You also say that God made us in His very own image."

She looked at me proudly and nodded, yes.

Then I asked, "Since we are made in the image of God, wouldn't God be very angry if we wasted the minds that he gave to us, that must also be in his image, by not asking questions? Oh yeah, another question. If God made us in his image and all of God's creations are perfect, how do we know the difference between us and God?"

I'll never know whose hand found the back of my head. I'm sure it wasn't God's. Possibly it was just his image slapping me. But then again, what's the difference? I only remember the nun telling me that I was thinking too much, as she left the room.

The absence of motion and the sound of the opening doors signaled the end of the line. Hoping to hear the sounds of crickets in the night, instead of screams and sirens, I made my way to the entrance of the New York State Thruway and dropped my thumb.

The best thing that a hitchhiker could hope for, of course is a ride. My best hopes materialized in the form of an old, black Cadillac limousine. The door swung open and I climbed into the back seat. The couple in the front must have sold the funeral parlor and kept the car because it seemed like the only communication that they ever had with anyone in the back was to hand them a Kleenex.

The burned out tenements of the South Bronx faded far into the distance as we rushed headlong into the red and golden foliage of the Catskill Mountains. My city-weary eyes felt soothed by the ever-increasing panorama of forestation before us until they saw those of a predator lurking from within the rear view mirror. For nearly an hour the driver's piercing eyes darted between making contact with mine and the road ahead.

The sound of the tires striking the roadway cracks was all that could be heard until the eyes fixed a stare at my face. The driver then turned to me and said, "You know, son, a boy like you should be thinking of getting a haircut and a shave. Perhaps then you could get a job with a nice company. If you have anything on the ball, you might one day become an executive or at least do something to bring some security into your life. Try to learn to take orders. It's not too late for you to, maybe, join The Army to get the necessary discipline."

The head of the toy dog sitting on the rear window shelf, along with the head of his wife sitting alongside of him, kept bobbing up and down in agreement as his diatribe intensified. Again, his cold gray eyes stared at me through the mirror as his hands emphasized his every word. I thought, "Good thing Caddies kind of drive themselves."

He pounded the dashboard repeatedly, and then added, "You hippies didn't make it easy for real Americans to try to win the war, you know. Your kind can't be bumming around the country like a bunch of worthless vagabonds, living off welfare forever. There comes a time of reckoning!"

A large, shiny, plastic crown on the dashboard with an even larger cross atop it bounced with his every strike as it reflected his wife's passively, and with each nod more aggressively, smiling face.

I couldn't slow down the car, so I did all that I might do to slow down his mind. I lit a foul-smelling, thick as my thumb, roach that I found in my jacket pocket and blew the smoke into the front seat area as much as I could. While the folks in front grappled with the choice of holding their noses or rolling down the windows, the car careened along the shoulder with the view of the trees ahead becoming less than soothing.

With the door handle in hand I said, "Yeah, that's cool. Just pull over anywhere." The moment the car stopped, I flipped the handle and yelled, Okay, I'll jump out here!"

Doctor Death and his smiling angel were as silent as the bobbing head of the doggie in the back window. With the safety of a car door between us and hallucination as my guide, I added, "Hey, listen, thanks for the ride. By the way, do you keep the pitchfork in the trunk? I sure didn't see it in the back seat. Do you just have to buy a new one each time?"

I let go of the handle to the door and placed my feet in a ready to run position. His wife rolled down the window completely and finally spoke. She asked, "What pitchfork? We don't carry pitchforks. Each time that we do what?"

I was far enough away from the car with my hands outstretched when I exclaimed, "Oh I'm sorry. No, wait a minute! Do you mean to say that you're not the couple in the picture that stands in front of the barn with a pitchfork in the old man's hand?"

They looked at each other with total confusion. This may have been the most conversation they'd had since they fell out of their coffins.

I then said, "By the way, when you do find the pitchfork that you pose with. Why don't you just stick it up your old man's self-righteous ass? Judging by the look on your face, that's probably his punishment whenever he fails to convert a hippie. Again, thank you very much for the ride. You better hurry so you can catch up with the flower car."

I put my driver's license between the pages of my book, dropped my thumb-sized roach to the pavement and my thumb toward the north. At least I had something to read to distract me from the company of the criminally inane. I found it hard to believe that we had covered eighty miles without me jumping from the open window of their car.

The great thing about hitching is you open the doors to a new reality upon hearing just two words, get in! If the person behind the wheel has no intention of using your head to warm up his shovel before he buries you at roadside, then those words are magic.

"Jump in on the roll, brother! Our brakes really suck," the driver said as a van door slid open and I rolled into the arms of Annette on the other side. She had a Carly Simon smile, framed in a Julie Christie hairdo. She and her old man secured me as the van coughed, then accelerated. The door slid shut with a kick from Annette.

The inside of the truck was covered with floor-to-wall-to-ceiling green shag rug. The speakers were blasting "Court of The Crimson King." A hookah pipe found my mouth. Immediately, I joined in with everyone else singing, "*Aaaah-Aa-Aaaah, Ah-Ah.*" This would repeat and repeat as we held one another while swaying along the green shaggy walls. We became one in mantra and in whatever the hell it was that we were smoking.

"Oh wow! Carlos Castañeda's Don Juan! Can I check this out? I started reading my friend's copy back at the dorm, but she split with it," said Rita, another hitchhiker, as she put her head on my lap and started looking through my book. She flipped around the pages, hoping to find where she left off with her last borrowed copy. Rita got picked up two exits and twenty tokes before me.

Suddenly, I had a flash of clarity and I remembered where I got the thumb-size roach. I found it under Gordon's refrigerator and at the time, had second thoughts about smoking it because of the presence of roach poison. When my clarity began to resemble a rapidly approaching stone wall, I could only think, "Shit, now that's roach poison!"

I wish I could say that it was at that point that everything went black, but I would have had to remember a point. All I do remember, after having held a hookah-toke down for some unknown duration, were the sounds of my head crashing into the van door, Rita flipping through the pages of my book and her asking, "This dude's for me, okay?"

After returning to consciousness, I heard Rita say, "Hey listen, Brooklyn, I didn't hear your name. But I heard you say you came from Brooklyn. So, like, do you mind if I call you that? These people are going to jobs in one of the hotels around The Finger Lakes. They asked me to go with them and work for a while. The hotel needs to hire more people. Like, why don't you come, too? You and I could hang out, or something. Maybe you can change your plans and come along."

Annette and her old man seconded that by saying, "Yeah, we can have a blast. It's real loose out there. We work the lunch and the supper hours, and then we party all night. The place is totally cool and it's co-ed. Come on with us, Brooklyn."

I looked around and saw that everyone's face had become green and shaggy with their heads nodding to the affirmative and to the music. I looked into Rita's stoned-out, amorous green, shaggy eyes as she said, "Far out, man from Brooklyn. Hang with us."

I asked her with my stoned-out, numbed lips, "Where are you from?"

It wasn't the response she had expected. She answered my question with the apparent anticipation of another, "I'm from Buffalo. Why?"

All that could come to my mind, besides seeing that the clouds on the horizon were turning into a magical mushroom marching band was, "Okay, I'll call you Rita."

The New York Thruway changes direction from northbound to westbound at Albany. Rita took me by the hand. A month before I might have said, "Yeah, that sounds great. Let's go!" Instead I heard myself say, "Let me out at the tollbooths. I've gotta get to Canada."

Found in September's Child's guest sketch book

Rita squeezed my hand and pleaded, “Can I keep the book, please?”

I released my hand and answered, “Yeah, keep the book.”

We all kissed and hugged. We had passed through one another's lives and we went on to our separate unknowns. I rolled out of the van like a paratrooper from a plane as they headed down the shaggy green highway, sputtering and I'm sure singing along. I could only think, “Shit! My driver's license is in that book.”

I stood there without a thought or a provable identity. The world was buckling and waving around and under me. What looked like a large truck suddenly appeared in front of what I saw as my outstretched thumb.

I exclaimed, “Oh shit! That's cool. I'm hitchhiking again.”

I slapped the truck's frame and my hand hurt. Either it was real or I just slapped something or someone that looked like a truck. I heard the chirping sounds of either a bird or a window handle. I looked up to the window and saw two large red lips protruding from a collar. They were covered by “Elmer Fudd's” very own hunting hat.

The lips leaned out of the window, and then spoke to me, "Hey good puddy, if you want a ride then grab on the ladder and haul your ass on up here!"

I took the chance that it was really a truck. I was further convinced upon seeing that the ladder led to where the lips were seated in the cab. My body's ability to even accomplish the simplest tasks apparently was left back at the hookah pipe.

I tried to haul my ass on up, as the lips instructed me to do, but I kept stepping on my own hands when I wasn't grabbing at my feet. The result was falling to the ground repeatedly from what then seemed to be an attack ladder. Somehow, I distracted the ladder with a half-eaten ear of corn that I found at the roadside. I then managed to ascend to the passenger seat. When I looked at the rear view mirror, I saw that the ladder had clung to the side of the truck and was following us. I locked the door.

Either I was really in a truck or I was flying above the Northway at seventy miles an hour, ten feet over the pavement. I think the driver's name was either Pill or Bill. A large red nose had evolved and placed itself over the lips. Then I remembered hearing that truckers had to keep their eyes on the road. That thought almost undid me.

My senses were functioning in total distortion much like the rest of me. My vision, when not kaleidoscopic, saw everything as the result of a dam burst of light and color. The approaching cars passed through the windshield and then through my eyes. After circling the inside of the cab, they would somehow exit by way of the truck's rear vents. Pill remained oblivious to all of this activity while continuing to drive right into it.

All sounds were both baffled and echoed in convoluted waves. I somehow rallied enough composure to be a good guest and listen to my host as his ears became wormlike and knotted themselves above his "Fudd" hat.

Pill must have had a routine monologue for hitchhikers.

Everything that he said to me seemed to be one word short of a sentence. He told me of his plans for his future. I believe he was going to attend The Billy Bob College of Knowledge, and get a degree in Barbeque or something.

I got lost in his continuous loop tape of Tammy Wynette, singing the same song over and over. Pill and I would wait for the musical lead in, and when it arrived we would both bang on the dashboard and then join Tammy and sing out at the top of our lungs, "Stand by the Band!" Pill had an obnoxious way of crashing into those words by making up his own, or it just might have been the lips crashing into one another.

Pill let me out at the last exit in New York and then drove off. Canada was so close that one could see it. If it weren't for the fact that it was pitch-black outside, or if I could figure out which way Canada was, I might have seen it. Instead of overtaxing my mind with issues of reality, I dropped my thumb in the same direction that I had been going and looked up at the midnight sky.

"Far fuckin' out, man!" I was unsure whether the heavens were exploding with the most incredible shooting star show imaginable, or my dissipating inebriation was giving it one. In either case I stood there in awe of the splendor, real or imagined.

My head was leaned back and glued to the sky. It wasn't really glued, that's just a figure of speech. I began to feel the cold air on my neck. This was a sure indication that I was beginning to feel my neck.

There were the constant sounds of approaching then receding cars. The last car I would hear, however, redirected me from my sound and light show to his sound show of siren and overhead lights. He made a u-turn and drove back toward me. Enough sobriety had returned to make me realize that this could really be happening. I wasn't sure whether or not my backpack contained any drugs so I ran through the woods toward the distant lights of a town. I vaulted a deer fence and disappeared into the bushes.

I found a hiding place in the tall grass where I waited, hoping for the cop to give up on finding me. I covered myself with my jacket and placed my stoned head on my backpack as the sound of fading footsteps in the grass was followed by an engine's roar.

Thud! I opened my eyes to the blinding Sun in my face and found a bunch of bananas resting on my chest. I raised my head to see a waving hand in the back of a departing Highway Department work truck. The State of New York was providing me with breakfast, less the jailhouse dining room of course. I guess it must have been feeding time in the hippie patch.

My short walk to the Thruway entrance and the road to Canada resulted in a u-turn when I realized that my driver's license was marking a page in Rita's new book. With shoes in hand, and the tall grass that surrounded me submitting to a gentle warm wind, I walked across a golden meadow. The sound of the air rushing across my ears triggered the cornball side of my brain to strike up the tune, "Zippity-Doo-Dah". The functional side immediately declared war upon it. Brer Rabbit and Uncle Remus were quickly defeated and replaced with "Question of Balance".

If I ever thought of returning to the aboriginal ways, it would have been right there. I knew that the Indian summer weather was what made it possible for me to be sitting nude in a tributary to Lake Champlain. The thought of winter's approaching ice age abridged any thoughts of staying. Naked in the cold in the metaphorical sense was quite enough for my head to handle.

I could feel the stench of two days on the road leave my body. I would soon have to return to my one set of clothes. Some other people downstream, doing the same thing, waved hello. It must have been the place where road-weary hippies did their body maintenance.

A bare-ass charioteer was centered in the Tarot arrangement spread upon the rock before me as the water rushed around my own. He looked toward his future. There sat the Empress card, beckoning him to stand before her. The reading spoke of a union. The union would be both eternal and fruitful.

The Empress was a Libra woman who could help set his life's direction through appropriate verse. I held the card up from the rock. As I did, I imagined that I saw the Empress's eyes slowly turn. Instead of gazing off to the distance, they looked directly into my soul. Her taciturn expression had become an unending smile. Indistinguishable, yet comforting words filled my mind.

I thought, "How was this possible? I'm sure that she and I both take comfort in knowing that things are day by day at best. How can there ever be a union of two people so completely different?"

The vision within my mind's eye became the face upon the card. No matter how many times I rubbed my eyes, I would reopen them only to see the change before me.

I felt a chill throughout my body causing me to leap from the stream. Was the water suddenly cooler? Was I suddenly seeing my future within my grasp, yet completely out of reach? Was it no longer possible to be objective reading my own cards?

Could my truest feelings from deeply within me be shouting from a card? Was it projection or interpretation? I could neither believe nor discount what I saw before my eyes. I began taking simple comfort with this thought and at the same time having contempt for allowing just another form of media to invade the sovereignty of my feelings.

The Tarot had been my guiding light as it was for others through my readings. Was the Tarot contradictory to the unfolding of ones experiences? How can experience itself be experienced if a guide is relied upon? Can one truly evaluate life's moments if not through perception itself, but through a set of formulas?

I thought, "Whether my life or that of anyone else is a product of preordination or pure happenstance, there can be no true realization if through the filter of foretelling."

With the Sun's reflection dancing upon the water flowing around me I said, "Farewell Chariot. My thumb will take over now. Goodbye Empress. The real thing may be waiting for me. Hey Hanged Man, sorry I couldn't cut you down. So long Emperor, you might have a fool for a son, but even you can learn from him."

If only I had a bow and a flaming arrow, I would have given my Tarot deck the Viking-style funeral that it deserved. One by one, they proceeded downstream, twisting and turning in tandem. Their faces looked to the Universe that they spoke for, so many times and with so much clarity. Empty handed, I thought, "As they flow to whatever or wherever life's force might lead them, then so will I."

I walked with the lodestone of Canada to my rear and the Brooklynite before me. I gave pause and turned toward Canada, reflecting upon my paternal ancestors and my denied visit. Francois Savoy landed in Nova Scotia in 1641. For some unknown reason, this young prince was swept away from Italy to France, and then to Canada. Upon landing, he would be swept away again by his true love Catherine Lejeune on those frozen Acadian shores.

If I were to cross the border in pursuit of my ancestral homeland, it might only hold me from my destiny and the hope of true love on the shores of Brooklyn. One cannot reenter The States without proper identification.

A small herd of cows rushed toward me from behind a corral fence. It was at a point where five dirt roads converged to form an intersection. My internal compass was at an impasse. Just then, the cows rushed toward the south. I asked myself, "Is this how it's going to be, follow running dogs, rushing cows or just my own true feelings?"

That road took me to the road that took me to the Thruway. My thumb knew the drill, as it summoned anything homeward bound.

If a car door would open with Grand Funk Railroad singing "Closer to Home," synchronicity would have then outdone its greatest of expectations. "Let It Be" was nothing to settle for. I lay back as we drove south.

"Most people freak out at the sight of a Doberman. You and the dog seem to like one another," said the driver.

I was scratching the dog behind the ear as I once did to Terra. He brought the Datsun up to sixty-five at which speed the blown muffler hit a harmonic level where the noise lay behind us. The Doberman became relaxed from the scratching. His tongue exited the side of his mouth where once there were teeth.

I answered the driver, "To me a Doberman is just a big puppy. I guess the way people react to them is much like the way they judge one another. One look and they know everything."

The two guitars occupying the back seat forced the enormous dog to lay his body across the center console. His head rested on my leg where his drool puddle spread. The Sun shined brightly. A pair of dark sunglasses lay unused on the visor. The usual joint found fire. I cracked my window to the surprise of my host. He grabbed the dog's snout, thus finding a taker. Alas the dog's name, Doobie.

Without a bit of smoke escaping, the driver asked, "Have you ever been to Woodstock, Kenny?"

I flashed back to '69 and answered, "No. I missed the whole thing, although I had a shot at being there. We would have been as close to the stage as possible, I imagine. A couple of music producers came to the airport where I worked as a pilot and asked me to fly them to Sullivan County Airport, right near the festival. The chief pilot saw that they were wearing bell-bottom pants and refused to rent an airplane and a pilot to mustachioed hippies from New York City. He probably didn't like Dobermans either."

The driver laughed, and then appended my Woodstock files saying, "Not the festival, man! I mean the town. By the way, the festival was in Beth-el. I'm sure that old man Yasger has corn and soybeans sprouting where hippies once grew. People constantly come into the town of Woodstock looking for the festival site. Once they find out it wasn't in Woodstock itself, they check out the town and seem to fall in love with the place anyway."

Seeing that there was no threat of any attempted religious conversion I asked, "Do you live in Woodstock? By the way, did you say that your name was Dave?"

"Yeah. I mean yeah, my name is Dave. No I don't live there. I live in West Hurley, or at least I crash there. I go to Woodstock and kinda do a gig. The slicks come up from the city, looking for Bob Dylan or other ghosts from the Movement."

Dave took a roach clip from the ashtray and sucked the last spark of life from the joint. Doobie was drooling at the ready for his shotgun.

Doobie fell back to my lap and zoned out on things that Dobermans zone out to while Dave continued, "These dumb ass people are living in the memory of music that for the most part was never played there. They expect to go and find a river flowing through the middle of town with naked hippies bathing and fucking in it. How fucked up is that?"

As Dave downshifted, the exhaust sound caught up to the car. He signaled toward the shoulder and said, "I do my thing and give them a taste of what they want and what they expect, without the river of course. The exit's coming up next. If you want to check out the town, stay on board. You can always grab a ride back to Brooklyn from there."

The center of town was pretty much most of the town. Dave parked his car north of the main intersection. I closed the door and saw that he got out of the car wearing the dark sunglasses from the visor and waving a white cane from the trunk.

Doobie was close at his side clad in a short metal-framed harness. Dave's guitar was slung across his back. He held his face skyward and said, "Follow me." The uninitiated followed the newly sightless to the little park at the main intersection.

His head would leave its skyward pose only to move from side to side as if in search of Stevie Wonder or Ray Charles while Dave slammed out a few chords. I stayed close enough to watch and listen and far enough away to not be thought of as an accomplice. Then Dave sang Dylan's, "Blowing in the Wind," for the ears of all who would listen as he rocked back and forth for the eyes of all who might see.

Blowing smoke up everyone's ass, never mind in the wind! This guy was incredible. Doobie even had little tin cans attached to his framed harness. He would either stand on peoples' feet or if they were sitting he would rest his giant paw on their legs and drool until they coughed up some money.

Quarters, dollar bills, everything you could imagine found its way into Dave's open guitar case. Dylan's songs were followed by Joni Mitchell's then some old stuff by Pete Seeger. Dave even had the crowd shelling out bucks for his album of originals on eight-track called, Get Some Sense, Amelia.

He played whatever they needed to validate the tourist's quest for remnants of the Movement. Right there in Woodstock. Right near Beth-el.

I thought about Dave's pompous litany about the tourists on our trip into town. He referred to them as zombies. They would walk up and down the streets, looking into the shops, buying anything that looked as if it were crafted in the nearby rustic villages by hand. It didn't matter to them that there may have been a Made in Formosa label. Any hands would do as long as the name Woodstock appeared on the object of their fancy.

Dave felt no remorse in swooping into town like a buzzard and picking at the bones of the zombies. I understood his resentment and what these people represented to him. He saw their behavior as mindless. They characterized blind obedience to self proclaimed prophets, who nourish themselves with the lifeblood of their herds. Dave's cynical slap was for the blindly obedient to blindly pay the fraudulently blind for providing memories of what never was.

I wondered, "Could the blue jean-clad, weekend hippies before us be the very corporate robber barons who would devour our life's efforts and leave only a bill for their services? Did they wear the cloth of their vassals in order to blend in with the crowd? Will they later exploit us as they sell back to us the message that we gave that was beyond our own articulation?"

Dave set his guitar across his lap and said, "Thanks folks. I've got to take a little break. Don't run off. We have the pleasure and good fortune to now hear the original poetry of Keni September, coming at you from the bowels of Brooklyn!"

I was totally surprised. I told Dave that I was writing some personal stuff while I hitched. We commiserated about how we felt similarly toward the world. He never once asked me if I would mind reading to a bunch of strangers. I was undecided whether I should walk away, or dig around for something to read.

The crowd looked to me, anticipating my message of street grit. I was about to slap my exposed belly repeatedly while screaming, "Attica! Attica!" Then I thought, "Hey, what the fuck, they're only strangers."

I held my head to the sky and poked my finger between the pages in my journal. Wherever it landed was what I would read. I read:

Dreaming of paradise, living in Hell
Greeting the hangman, wishing him well
Feeling the truth that no one would tell
As brothers and sisters toll the bell
Gone from the drama that saw no end
Hung an actor who wouldn't pretend to be a friend

While speaking the lines of living's play
No one believed what he would say
Until he spoke in his own way
His conviction's reward was his last day
Of being a puppet in a show
Where puppets should speak but shouldn't know
The meaning of the lines in their parts
For puppets have strings holding their hearts
To the one above that stays unseen
Using them to sell his dream

From this puppet's own dream came his word
"No strings attached" was what was heard
"I'll stand alone on my own ground
The lies of others will never sound
From my lips, for my heart is my own!"
But his heart was stilled much like the stone
That bears no name since none was his ever to claim

Doobie's head rested on my leg as he drooled all over it, as usual. I looked down at my feet to find that close to ten dollars had fallen from the clapping hands of the audience to the top of my backpack. Dave asked for a copy of my poem. It would become one of his original songs.

I wrote it out and while no one was looking, shoved it into his pocket as he looked up and down smiling at space. Doobie retired to the lawn to work on his ass. Dave and I shook hands and said good-bye. Doobie lifted his head from his life-long project and blinked adieu. After filling up with hummus and falafel, I left Woodstock.

JE

"Were those people, who I judged so immediately, the mindless creatures that my conjecture had projected them to be? What could I learn of anyone if I am to judge others by virtue of another's speculation? Could they have been the end result of their own tearing away at the shrouds that conventional behavior may have wrapped around their souls? Could all, or at least some, or possibly one of them have jumped through the looking glass to confront their private monsters? Did they emerge reconstructed in their individual design living a book that only time itself may write?

Why does every thought of late have Apples' smile beaming from the Empress' form? Why does every song that I hear or every idea that comes to my mind project that image? Is every glimpse of my own self within the universal synchronicity that once was my magic, now ours? Has my mission for a sense of possessing nothing left me with nothing but a new sense of quest?"

My walk from the train to Gordon's apartment was spent watching my one foot advance beyond the limited reach of the one before it. The indolence within me bore witness to this as being my sole effect upon this reality.

Had I attained the sense of my being as the egg that Julian Beck described in "The Life of the Theatre"? He compared the kicking free of the shell by the chick to a person's breaking free of his limitations, self-imposed or otherwise. The first step that the chick takes upon the Earth was that which sets the course of what will be.

I asked myself, "When will the next step that I take be

the first in a new direction? Has my shell of inertia become a form of security in and of itself?"

"Hey, bro'! Where have you been?" asked Gordon through his usual shit-eating grin. I knew that his question on the subject of what I may have done was out of politeness. He wanted me to tell of my things only to get to the important stuff, his. Knowing this I summarized my entire odyssey with, "Here and there."

He immediately took the floor and said, "You'll never guess what happened, bro'! This job as a bouncer is so fuckin' cool! I check in at eight o'clock. All I do is hang out at the door. The dudes come in and they pay up at the desk. Nobody hassles anyone. It's like so cool, the dudes come in joking and talking shit. Then they choose a bitch. They pay up front then they do their thing. They go into their room for about ten minutes to an hour. They leave when they're done. I hang out looking tough, and that's it."

"Okay Gordon, so you said something happened. What was it?" He was so busy smiling, mostly to himself, that he forgot his point.

"Oh yeah, right! Something happened; I did say that didn't I? Yeah, it's not what happened as much as what always happens. What happens is this. The dudes, like they mostly totally turn the chicks off, 'cause like they're gross and shit like that.

"But sometimes, if they're halfway decent, then they halfway get the chicks off. Then they split, 'cause who cares about the whores after they pop their own cookies? Then the bitches call out, 'Oh Gordon, I need you!'"

The grin had grown beyond his own shit and was consuming the room.

"And let me guess, then you run coming to help them," I winked internally.

"Huh? Oh yeah! I come running to do whatever it takes. I either get laid, or we swap a little crotch candy. Either way, whenever this happens I get tipped. Man, talk about a win-win deal! Kenny, you gotta come to work there. It's the perfect job."

I could only think, "Why must I always bear witness to this poor schmuck covering what's left of his hundred-acid-trip mind with the soothing rapture of denial?"

I asked, "What about Terry? Won't word get out to her? I mean her ex-old man or husband or whatever he is this week, you know who I mean, Jeff. He might catch wind on what you're doing and tell her just to get off on seeing how she reacts. Don't you think you might be pushing it a little? Remember, these people are sick bastards, bro'. They still have a thing going on with each other that no one else understands, even if you choose to overlook that point."

Gordon was busy in his head convincing himself of his own genius. No words of advice or challenge were to find a way inside. I turned to him and said, "Brother, you seem to have found your personal Nirvana. But it isn't my idea of heaven. I couldn't deal with the crowd-filled clouds. By the way, are you still interested in doing moving jobs with me?" Deep inside I hoped that he would decline. This must have been an overture of politeness.

He clasped his hands behind his head and yelled, "You fuckin' gotta be kidding! Why would I want to hump furniture all day, when I could be humping hookers for pay? No way, Jose! Hey, that rhymes. Now I'm a poet, too. Hey, Bud, dig the rhymin'stud!"

Gordon didn't need any outside help in that conversation. I was confused as to whether what I felt toward him was anger or disgust for his absolute disregard of others. He was truly worthy of both. I allowed my indecisiveness its time and quickly realized that anger and disgust belonged with all of the other negative energy I wanted to leave behind. I could only deal effectively with the resentment that I was feeling toward myself for being in a position of vulnerability to the whim of this person.

Instead of thoughts of Gordon, I allowed the long-awaited gathering force of choice within me to take form and a direction. I said good-bye and I was about to split when my eye caught a glimpse of the classified section of The Village Voice on the table. I picked it up to take with me. Before I could get the door, I saw a listing for an answering service exclusively for artists and writers. Since I was rooming with a new poet and I wrote some stuff too, I probably qualified.

Just five bucks a month and nothing up front. I felt the force of self-respect explode and fill my being. The shell that was surrounding my apathy broke away and fell to the floorboards below, joining the remnants of Gordon's discarded meals. My right foot landed on the floor followed by my left. Could my new path begin there at the desk?

My trail of footsteps lay behind me along First Street as my pace quickened. I saw my big toe poking through the hole in my shoe. All that I could think of was the bouncing ball in a "Looney Toons" musical animation. The ball would break free from an object in the cartoon, fly around the characters and then bound above lyrics that would form at the bottom of the screen. The kids would then either sing along or run for some popcorn.

I paused. My head began to move from side to side as my big toe wiggled through the hole. Only the *"dah-dah-dah, da-da-da-da"*, from "Hey Jude" accompanied the toe, as it appeared to dance before my eyes. Then it changed into a whistling ball with the face of "Bugs Bunny".

"Is this an aftershock from whatever was in the hookah pipe from my road trip? Okay, so what if it is? Everything has its place within the Universe. Illusion can be a glimpse of the reality that waits behind the veil of the moments that stand before us. Is this vision choosing me, the observer, to give it first recognition and then form?"

Like the magical hand that would appear from nowhere and erase "Elmer Fudd's" bullets as they left his gun, mine would draw "Bugs" and me a getaway car. I sat down on the nearest stoop and took the sketchpad from my backpack. I drew a large picture in black marker of the VW Minibus.

I wrote the word, MOVING within the borders that defined the Minibus. I extended the O, as if it were a bouncing ball popping out of the driver's door window. The bouncing ball evoked the words, CALL KENNY as the musical message below took form. The answering service's phone number added itself out of necessity. I drew a smiling face in the middle of the O. Somehow, I would always see the smiling face within the O as not only "Bugs", but also as a reminder of my ignorance of the untapped potential within me before Julian Beck's words cracked my shell.

Thanks to a cheap rate at the copy store, I was able to hang signs on every bulletin board in the neighborhood. After checking my messages the next day, I was rolling in it! My investment for the signs doubled. Imagine, ten bucks for just moving a couch one block! Five would be to live from, five would go right back into perpetuity. More signs!

"Do you hang signs here often?" asked a voice from behind me. The mere sound of the voice of the woman that I knew was my eternal partner in the dance of time caused me to turn from the bulletin board at The Economy Restaurant and engage Apple's mouth to mine as the world around us took leave.

We withdrew from our minutes-long kiss after finding that we were pressed to the wall from the ever opening restaurant door, at which a small crowd was gathering. I held her tightly. The words, I love you, nearly escaped from my mouth.

Instead of revealing my true feelings, I said, "I figured that you'd still be drowning in books and paperwork. But I'm glad that you came up for air."

My signs and tape lay all over my feet. I began picking them up as we worked our way from the vestibule and into the restaurant.

I hung my backpack over my shoulder while she said to me, "So, I guess if I come for air then someone will try to take it away from me. You know, you look even skinnier than when I saw you last. Didn't you at least come up for food? Let me guess at the obvious; you're going to do the moving thing. The question remains, with or without Gordon?"

We moved from the busy doorway to the shelter of the hanging plants. My thoughts descended to the mundane. Cutting to the chase I said, "Gordon has a job. He told me all about it. Let me spare you the details and just say that I'm going to do whatever jobs come my way by myself. If he changes his mind about his gig in the City then I'll have to see how I feel about involving him if that time comes."

I answered her so where is this leading look by saying, "I think that I'm going to stick my toe back into the waters of the World, just to see how it feels. Maybe I can steer clear of the Lascos and Berias. Whatever money I make with the moving jobs, I'll set aside, buy interview clothes and see if I can find work in the World that I can deal with. What's the worst that can happen; I fail and live like I did one day before I tried?"

I envisioned the aura of the Empress card around Apples' face. The appropriateness of Julian Beck's words that she brought to me came to mind. We headed for a table. Bessie saw us holding hands and smiled. She sensed that food was only in the back of our minds. She signaled that she would be back later for our order.

The moment we sat down, Apples said, "Kenny, remember what you said before you went on your trip, 'If I've learned nothing else from all that I've gone through, it is to deal with the World on my own terms.' You can put your toe back in the water, but don't troll for sharks with it."

Before I could answer, the booth cushions beneath us rose as two bodies crashed down on them. From across our table we heard, "Do you mind if we join you?"

It was Freddy Fantasy and another refugee from September's, Danny the Flick. Since the coffee house dissolved, Danny switched realities to the A.M. crowd along with Freddy. Together, they filled their time in the never-ending quest of new movies to see and new or old drugs to take while watching them.

Freddy was wearing a ten-gallon hat, a scarf around his neck and a shirt with little arrows stitched around the pockets, all black of course.

Danny asked, "The truth now, Freddy. Who's your color coordinator, the family undertaker?"

I'm sure there was a mouth somewhere within the talking hairball that was Danny. Danny's persona lay somewhere beneath his enormous black mass of hair and beard, interrupted by eyes that would locate any drug around, a large nose that could sniff out any drug around and two protruding lips to partake of any drug around or the food from any plate in sight. If you wanted to get rid of him, you would have to give him the price of a movie ticket. Providing he was adequately stoned, he might use the money for the ticket.

He seemed to have only two purposes in life. One was to get high; the other was to get high and go to the movies. Since that would make him constantly high, he could then draw from the vast resources of his cinematic view of reality and abuse Freddy from the perspective of the many characters he saw himself as being. Once the process began, there was no end.

"Kenny, you're all clear," answered the blissed-out voice telling me exactly what I didn't want to hear. I slammed the receiver into the cradle and yelled to the air, "I don't spend ten cents just to hear that there are no calls for me!"

I walked away from the vestibule mumbling aloud. I was in mid-rant when I came back to the table ventilating from my periodic message check-in.

Apples bounced up as I landed on the seat cushion beside her. I continued my rant, "What the fuck is this shit? Is there some kind of Scientologist at the fucking switchboard? Every time I call my answering service, this guy says, "You're all clear!" Does the fuckin' idiot think he can see through people over a phone line?"

"Why do you need an answering service? Do you actually know anyone outside of the neighborhood?" Freddy asked as he leaned into the booth with his ten-gallon black hat lowering like an umbrella over his eyes.

"For your information Gunsmoke, I have a little gig doing moving jobs. That's my sign in the vestibule. Fuck with it and I'll shoot your hand off!"

Freddy threw a copy of his monthly across the table to me and asked, "Why don't you stick an ad in my paper? If you take me downtown to the print shop once a month in your Minibus, I'll give you a free half-page ad. If you get any moving jobs where you need some help, call Danny and me. We can always use the bread. 'Cause we always need the weed."

Apples gave me a, how can you lose, look while jumping our clenched hands up and down on the table. She reassured me by saying, "You see that Kenny, an hour ago all you had was your signs in your hand. Now you have media advertising and a labor force. Just think good thoughts and it will all fall into place."

We walked toward Polhemus Place. She had to go back to the books. I had to go back to making a name for myself. I showed her that the dime was still in my pocket. She said that she knew I would call.

"I want to leave a message for Kenny," I said as I called my own number and asked for myself.

"Kenny who?" asked the bleached brain at the answering service. I furthered the inquiry with, "I saw a sign on a bulletin board for moving jobs and I want to speak to Kenny. That was the name on the sign."

After a pregnant pause I heard, "I'm sorry Sir, I can't

take a message without a last name. Have a nice day." I heard a click, and then silence.

I thought, "This explains why I'm always clear, except for when someone's call sneaks through the censor."

I called back and said, "This is Kenny. Any messages for me?"

An all too familiar voice asked, "Kenny who? We have five Kenny's at this board?"

I knew why there were no messages. It stemmed from my acquired outlaw behavior, not longing to see my real name on wanted posters never mind bulletin boards. I let my mouth surprise my ears with my intuition's response, "My last name is The Mover! Yeah, my name is Kenny the Mover! Any messages?"

"No Mr. Mover, you're all clear. But I think there may be something later."

Who was I to argue? The World saw through my story and named me what it saw. I called back later and found two calls. I wondered where they came from so suddenly.

"My name is Kenny the Mover. You called me about moving some stuff?" Wow, what a sales pitch! What technique. Who could refuse an opener like, "You called me about moving some stuff?"

I figured that after hearing me speak, the guy on the other end would hang up. Instead he asked, "How long before you can get here? I don't want to stay in this place one moment longer than I have to! How much will you charge me?"

The dude sounded frantic. I asked about how much shit he had to move. It sounded like it would fit in the VW. I told him a number that just came to me, "Flat rate, fifty dollars." The dude agreed and asked me to get over as fast as I could.

After roll starting the VW, I doubled back to The Economy and picked up Freddy and Danny. When we arrived on President Street, I realized that the guy's apartment was in the building next door to Nina's brownstone where I once lived. Talk about coming full circle. No one ever stayed the length of his or her lease in Park Slope during those times. Nina was long gone. Dude must have moved in next door after I had left her. He's going on to new horizons already. Might there be something in the Slope's water?

The door opened. We were hit with a wall of patchouli aroma, then strawberry, then vanilla and so on. The answer to our olfactory dilemma was laid about the floors in broken bottles of body oils and love jellies.

We gave one another a "to each his own" look, and smiled. I began the formal introductions plus a careful analysis of the scope of work to be performed. Bluntly, I said, "I'm Kenny. This is Freddy and that's Danny. Is this the stuff you want moved?"

The customer had gathered what was to be taken into the middle of the living room. The cartons must have been stuffed in a grand total of five minutes. What didn't fit in a box found a place either on the floor or the wall, in pieces. The only large item of furniture was a single bed. There was a hint of dried mascara that had run from the customer's eye.

He looked us over and answered, "Yes, and please be quick about it! I want to be out of this shit hole of a place yesterday."

The situation spoke for itself. There was a small statue of Michelangelo's David, resting in the corner surrounded by plaster shards. Its crotch area showed evidence of a recent hammer strike. Where once there were genitals, there was a void. We were told to leave it as a warning to the prick that owned the statue.

Freddy and I carefully wrapped the bed in a tarp and took it to the van. Danny stashed the 'Ludes that he found under it into his pocket. We were out of there in no time flat. Arthur, the customer was moving around the block to Carroll Street.

Upon arriving on Carroll Street, I wasn't about to let the guy get over on us. I asked him, “How can a first floor be on the fourth floor?” Arthur agreed to another ten dollars for the stairs.

With the VW empty, and the last piece on the top floor, Arthur said to Danny, “Now put that chair over on the other wall, young man. I told you that before! What's the matter with you, can't you take instructions?” Danny could listen all day. In addition to at least a half-dozen 'Ludes, he later found a vile of coke and two giant sized joints.

Arthur lowered his brow as he looked at me. He held his arm out as his finger rotated and pointed down the hall and said, “Now you Mister Boss, you're a different story. You just don't want to hear anything. I think that bed would look better in the little room. Now please put it where it belongs. I am the customer and I have the right to change my mind as often as I want!” He held our money like a whip handle, clenched in his fat sweaty fist.

“Kenny, cool it, bro'. Don't let the dude get to you, just chill out, man!” Freddy said, seeing my face reddening from anger. He knew me from the street as one who knew no diplomacy, only the immediacy of my fist to the face. I chilled out for the moment and then we moved the bed.

Arthur held his arms folded while his finger rested on his chin. He leaned his head left then right and finally said, “I think I want it back in the other room, come to think of it. Don't you all agree that it looked better in there?”

Freddy saw that my face had become nearly purple with rage. He waved his hand back and forth at me as if to beg, no. I paid no heed and stalked at Arthur while saying, “Look Arthur, you get one more fuckin' switch and that's it! Then we get paid what you owe us, and we're outta here. You got that, Dude?”

Danny put his body between mine and Arthur's while Freddy held me back by my shoulders. Arthur then said to my restrained enraged face, “No one is getting paid anything until I am completely satisfied! Do I make myself perfectly clear on that, Mister Boss?”

I broke free from Freddy's grip. Within a nanosecond I had Arthur by the jacket. I lifted him off the floor and smashed him against the wall. I thought I heard his back crack. I looked at his sleeves tearing in my hands as his weight settled him downward. For a split second I thought that I killed him.

Then he smiled at me with a look of pure ecstasy. His eyes were lit up like bonfires of delight. His body went completely limp. He let out a groan, and then a sigh followed by a whimper. Our contract was fulfilled. He was moved and completely satisfied. We were paid in full and we left.

Sixty dollars! I had to keep things in perspective. This money had to mean more to me than dollars. It had to make sense. Freddy and Danny saw their share as the means to visiting the third ring of Saturn, nothing beyond that. To them it was an end. If I were to avoid the traps that money could become on my recent path, I had to see each penny as a meaningful tool. Once money achieves an end, its product can decay with its recipient.

After paying my friends, I allowed enough money for fuel for the VW and food as fuel for myself. The rest of it was to go toward perpetuity. My goal had to become one of having my own resources and not feeling like a bum while being with the woman I loved.

That thought in mind, I realized that perpetuity might be to use this tool of money as another form of nourishment, a form that might enable me to grow to the next level from the energy of my present circumstances. My circumstances seemed easily definable. The direction for growth was the choice that might have needed the ingredient of time.

"Or did it?" I thought as my sense of momentary contentment was swept away on the crest of a wave of urgency.

I said to myself, "Hey, what the fuck! After surviving the street all of this time, I can handle anything. Maybe even the World, if I keep things in perspective. Oh shit, did I just decide to take another shot at the corporate world? Well, it's just a shot. If I miss, I don't have to keep shooting, do I?"

That being said, or thought, the immediate objective had to be buying a job interview suit. My hope had to be that I could live in that world and keep all that I had learned and my self-respect intact. Suddenly, a picture of a chain and lock across the door to Gordon's' apartment came into my mind.

Again I thought, "Who am I kidding? I do one lousy moving job and then I have grandiose ideas about becoming an executive again. I'm still a bum on the street or in the back of my Minibus or in Gordon's hallway, when he lets me in. Either way, I'm one locked door away from the fuckin' gutter where I landed, never mind the street."

I shook my head, no. Then I had a vision of a different door that I might one day be behind. It would have a sign saying, PRIVATE or at least saying, Kenny. Maybe the frog wasn't ready for his own castle, having been kissed by the princess. But perhaps just having his own lily pad would be in order, at least at this point along the fantasy.

Chapter Twelve

Perspective

The pounding bass and the cries of Sly Stone's, "Dance to the Music", beckoned all to Mark's weekly party at his Union Street loft. If someone gives a party, they usually invite their friends and maybe some other people for variety. Then you all get down together and just have a good time.

Mark had a variation on that theme. At his parties, everybody paid two bucks at the door. If you had a history of saving his vital organs, he might look away. For your two bucks you got all the watered-down Kool-Aid that you could drink and if you got there early enough, some pretzels. Most importantly, you could dance all night, hang out with the whole neighborhood and find where life may lead you for at least a weekend.

What was in it for Mark? He got away from his latest old lady's place and got to pay his bills without working. In addition, he would usually find someone stoned out on his bed after the party. This could be a play toy for him for either the remainder of the weekend or until one of them saw the light of day, whichever or whomever came first.

Mark had an interesting theory about the 'seventies. He believed that the entire decade was a product of people diverting their lives after misinterpreting the song lyrics of the 'sixties. If audio reproduction back then was as clear as it became in the 'seventies, and people heard the real words, there may have never been a Movement after all.

The gathering at Mark's always reminded me of a wrap party for a film. I would see all of the characters from the trauma of the drama that was the week that was. Regardless of the level of their role in the various pecking orders, whether it was hippie, train commuter, shop owner, vagrant, professional, craftsperson or poet-mover, the set would be struck and all would dance!

A new set for the play of the coming week would create itself as the hunters, the stalkers and the gatherers would seek out one another either for closeness or anonymity or some combination thereof. The drums of passion would strip away all thoughts, titles and prejudice in hopeful anticipation of the stripping away of clothing.

I was in the midst of the bouncing bodies as we bumped and gyrated to a tape of West Indian drum and flute music. No one was dancing with anyone in particular. There was a freeform of movement to the Voodoo drumming of the local group. Strobe lights replaced the red lights as our only source of illumination. As the trance from the lights and drums supplanted the waking state, I saw only freeze frame glimpses of form and expression. A flash in the distance that repeated as it and I moved toward one another was replaced by the steady beaming of Apples' smile, apparently nurtured by my own.

We grabbed one another and we danced together. We kissed and laughed, realizing how we seemed to be drawn to one another wherever we each went. As we danced and turned, we saw an empty corner and fell on to a pile of giant pillows. I looked into her eyes and asked, "What the hell is your real name?"

"It certainly took you long enough to ask. Suppose I were to tell you that my real name is Apples? Would you then say that it must be something else? Might you then be saying that my parents gave me a funny name?"

"Okay Apples, if that is your name. Apples is a perfectly normal name. At least it's normal for this neighborhood. I mean, look around you. We have Freddy Fantasy, Kenny The Mover, Bob The Cab, Lenny The Loser and of course, Intelligent John.

"It stands to reason that Apples had to be a given name. How could it be a moniker? You don't sell apples. I never see you eating an apple. On the other hand you do have those rosy cheeks."

I was immediately kicked as she laughed and pushed me to the floor.

"Okay, it's Appleman. That's where my friend got the name Apples."

"Your parents named you Appleman?" I asked as I returned from the floor. I was immediately dispatched back to the same.

"No, you silly goose! My parents named me Ann. But there were too many Anns where I worked so I became Apples. Someone else became Smitty and the winner remained Ann."

And I thought that my life was complicated. I summarized, "Now I have it, your name is Ann. This is the name that your parents gave you, right?"

"Well sort of." She looked at me with kind of a facetious smile, and then said, "I was born a month after my parents emigrated from Europe. They named me after my great-grandmother, Anya. Their friends, who came here a week before they did, and had a stronger command of the language, said that Anya translated to Ann."

I pushed her to the floor in astonishment and yelled, “Anya is a great name! How can you pass on a name like that? Women would kill to have Anya as their name. Do you mind if I call you, Anya?”

She gave me the biggest of smiles and rapidly nodded to the affirmative while saying, “Actually, I've been thinking of going by Anya. So okay, call me Anya, Kenny. By the way, Kenny is your name, isn't it?”

Oh yeah, it was back to me, the one with the egg all over his face. I said, “Well sort of, I guess you should know that Kenny is my middle name. When I came to this neighborhood I decided new life, new name, consequently, Kenny. Now of course I have a trade surname, the Mover.”

Her turn to push me to the floor and ask questions. “Now, let me get this straight. I've been calling you by a moniker? What is your real name, mystery man? If you tell me it's Monica, I'm outta here!”

Another push, another trip to the floor. I guess confession comes easily to people with my Catholic background. I told her the simple truth, “Ever since I saw the movie,“Joe”, the movie where Joe, the bigot hippie-hater and his buddy kill the hippies, one of which was the buddy's own kid. Well, since that movie, I had it in mind to go by my middle name.” By this time I was smart enough to just stay on the floor, good thing.

All expression left her face. Her hand covered her mouth and she asked, “Oh no, your name is Joe? Please don't be serious. I almost married a guy named Joe. I never date Joes. You sneaked into my life by changing your name! I can't believe it.”

I looked up from the floor and said to her, “And I was in a marriage where my name was Joe, such irony!” I expected another shove back to the floor, so I remained there. Surprisingly, she started laughing. We joked about Park Slope as the land of the moniker. The Foreign Legion for the nameless.

Then a large figure appeared before us and said, "Whenever you need another mover, better yet a driver Kenny, you can call me. I can move furniture or anything. Don't forget!" He said all that he had to say and then he walked back into the crowd.

"Who was that character? He's scary. If he came into my house to move my furniture, I think I would just give it all to him and run away," said Anya.

"Anya, that's Bob the Cab. Remember I mentioned him before, monikers and all that? He's one of the people that isn't a life anymore. He's become just another story"

We watched the top of Bob's departing head weave, and of course bob, above the crowd.

"So then tell me. What's his story?" asked Anya.

I then began telling the tale of Bob: "Bob was once a high-ranking leasing executive for one of the big three auto manufacturers. By high ranking, I mean he contracted bulk leases of thousands of cars to auto rental companies around the world and to large fleet purchasers.

"Bob was elevated to his executive position during the times when companies were pressured by Affirmative Action policies to show racial diversity. At first, Bob felt that life had given him a jump-start. After a while, he saw less qualified white people pass him by for promotion. He felt like he was adrift, not sure of whether he became an executive only for his blackness, and not sure if he was later passed up because of it.

"He became cynical and then of course, rebellious, followed by immersion into a serious identity crisis. The story has it that one day he was on the brink of chucking it all and walking away. Instead, out of habit, blind loyalty or simple procrastination, he went to work, although extremely late.

"A group of honchos from a company like Hertz, Avis or something was waiting impatiently for him. They wanted to check out a new model and Bob was the man in charge of their contract. Bob finally arrived. As apologetic as he was, the honchos had become just as much rude and demanding.

"Bob tried to close off to their nagging him about how long they had to wait. He just wanted to get through this day, so he could go home and think things out. He straightened his tie, swallowed his pride and grabbed a demo. The executives kept on bitching about the time of day and how hungry they were while they all piled into the car with Bob.

"Bob was doing the demonstration driving while the three execs that were with him were all bombarding him with questions about every little detail about the model. Apparently, the questions were coming at Bob so fast that there was hardly enough time for him to find an answer, when another guy would shoot out a different question.

"Bob's patience with the situation and the disgust that he had for his life as it was, shared the same breaking point just when one of them asked how the car performed in the independent crash tests. This was the straw on the camel's back that broke Bob.

"Bob said, 'I don't have a fucking clue how it did. But let's all find out!'

"The story has it that Bob aimed the car at a corner of the corporate headquarters building while explaining to the startled and silenced executives that this is the same angle that the independent crash tests were conducted. After accelerating to exactly thirty-five miles per hour, he then drove the car right into the building's cornerstone.

"He casually detached his seat belt and got out. He looked the car over and said, 'Gentlemen, I certainly hope that this answers all of your questions regarding the passenger protection features of this vehicle. This concludes our safety demonstration for today, as well as it does my fucking career. Good day, gentlemen. As you can see, your injuries are minimal as are those to the vehicle.'

"And then he walked away from it all. He left everything at his apartment exactly in place from the day before. His only explanation to his old lady was to say that his home, his job and she were no longer part of what he was becoming. He told her that she was just a hood-ornament on the Edsel that was his life and that she could keep the money from everything that she could sell until another ride comes along. Now all that Bob has is an outlaw car service. You know all cash, and no receipts."

Anya held the same astonished look throughout the story of Bob. She then said, "Wow! Talk about an off-the-wall story. He's lucky to only have that limp when he walks. You said that he has a car service. That would mean that he doesn't drive a yellow cab. If that's the case, then why don't they just call him Bob the Car Service?"

I rewound and said, "That's another story, and I guess the limp also goes back to that one. A while ago Bob did drive a regular yellow cab. It seems that a female passenger had no money and offered to pay her fare with trade. While they were enroute, she jumped into the front seat and proceeded to give him head. Bob got all crazy with passion and lost control of the cab.

"Oddly enough, Bob crashed into another yellow cab. Her head got slammed between his crotch and the steering wheel. She recovered from her injuries. What about poor Bob you ask? Let's just say, he should avoid any unnecessary excitement."

Anya had placed herself on the floor. She held her index finger up and said, "I know! Now you're going to tell me that he received a head injury!"

The crowd had gone on to their adventures and surprises to come. The more conventional incandescent bare bulb, suspended from the ceiling, replaced the flashing strobes. The Stones sang of their demand for shelter. The otherwise empty dance floor revealed only a black cloak covering two clutching forms that hovered above it, motionlessly. As our awareness returned, it allowed us enough focus to distinguish them as Freddy and his new girlfriend Maureen. Mark pulled the needle from the record.

"Hey! Who the fuck stopped the music? Can't you see we're dancing?"

We walked toward Anya's apartment. I was relating the story of Arthur and how his bizarre behavior evoked my own. I must have revealed some uneasiness as I discussed my concern regarding the concept of money and issues of human relationships. I told her how difficult it was for me to be arbitrary, yet my need to work within my own terms was vital. The problem was dealing with the arbitrary terms of those who may oppose mine, particularly if I were subordinated to them.

We stopped beneath a streetlight where she looked me in the eyes and said, "Let me guess Kenny, you're agonizing over re-entry to the World. You see yourself at a crossroad where one choice has you continuing to live on the street, learning nothing new, but not violating your principles. The other, puts you in a position to test what you have learned but in doing so, possibly being put in the position of being a hypocrite."

I must have seemed like the reluctant skydiver, who stares at the ground below for such a long time that when he finally steps out, his foot is on the runway. I replied, "Yogi Berra was so goddamn right when he said, '*When you come to a fork in the road, take it*'. The only thing he left out is the process of choosing which."

"Kenny, I want to throw some of your own thoughts back to you. You keep talking and writing about how your street experience has taught you to act within the moment. Then you say that you witness your own persona reacting to a situation instantaneously, sometimes to the astonishment of your very perception.

"Don't you think that what you're witnessing is the true self that you search for still being one step ahead of the seeker? Being able to move into that one step might be what your whole journey was and is about. Maybe what Yogi meant was not so much, to follow the foot, but in your case, to join it."

I feigned tripping over my own foot and thanked her for the mirror to my soul.

JE

"Of whose weaving, if not their own, is the web that the spiders of the world rest upon waiting to prey upon the pure of heart? Can the initiate run the gauntlet and emerge unchanged having been battered by those who would tarnish his own nature with his very rage? Might he then be enticed to join his tormentors and await the next victim? Can a blindfold of truth upon the eyes and the cap of trust within the ears keep him balanced upon the razor's edge that is this path? At what point in our passage within this reality did we lay claim to the path we walk and to the very Earth that bore us. During the history of our kind in this life, in whose blood was the sword of property not tempered?"

I leaned on the buzzer impatiently, after nearly breaking my key in the apartment lock. I peered through the lace curtain and saw Terry's form at the top of the stairs.

I could hear her, through the glass, shouting as she ran down the steps while clutching her robe, "Sorry Kenny, Gordon changed the locks. It's not about you. Someone lifted his wallet and keys at the whorehouse."

She paused on the last step and as if questioning herself asked, "How is it that they could get the keys? It's not as if he would carry them in his back pocket with the wallet. Wouldn't they stick him in the ass? Hey, but knowing Gordon, maybe he kept them there just to do that? Ha-ha!"

She opened the door and added, "Here's a new set and this is the new phone number. Like I said Kenny, it's not about you. By the way, I see the Sun's shining. Where the fuck is the bastard? He should have been home from work by five."

Terry tightened her robe as she fumbled through her thoughts for the phone number at Gordon's job. Gordon gained a much needed reprieve by running up the stoop and saying, "Hey, brother, long time no see! Man, you're getting muscles on those arms 'Couch ahoy' and all that! Good morning Terry. Sorry I'm late. Overtime at the plant you know."

Gordon gave me a knowing wink as he grabbed Terry and said to her, "Wow, talk about toilet breath, go brush tour teeth. You got morning mouth like an open sewer."

He gave her a tender slap to the ass. She giggled and went for a toothbrush. Gordon turned to me and confided, "Bro', I can't believe how much fuckin' money, and I mean fuckin' money, I made last week! I come home so fuckin' played out; then Terry wants me to do her too. I must eat three-dozen oysters downtown everyday. But who's complaining? Not me, except for one little problem. I left my fuckin' pants on the doorknob in one of the whore's rooms the other day. Someone lifted all my shit. Did Terry give you keys?"

I held them up for him to see, as I left him to his Heaven on Earth.

"Kenny, good morning!" Michael screamed to me as I searched for a seat at The Economy. Finding none, I sat in the booth with her and asked about all the writing and cross outs on the many pads before her. I was supposed to meet Freddy Fantasy at nine o'clock to do a job. It was early, so I figured I'd have coffee with Michael.

She tugged at my sleeve and yelled, "Kenny, I found the greatest shrink ever! He's right here in the Slope. His name is Will."

Then she said proudly, "I convinced him that I'm a schizophrenic and that I must come to terms with my other personalities. So you'll never guess what he has me doing. Don't guess, I'll tell you. Dialogue! He has me writing dialogue. I communicate with my other selves in our writing to each another."

"Michael, are you sure that it was really you who convinced him?"

She held her finger up as if to ask for pause, then she continued, "It's not like I'm writing a book or anything. It's just that writing dialogue allows me to create an ongoing encounter between my personalities. The various sides of me go at it on paper with one another. I simply sit back and enjoy watching them as they struggle for control over me in their conflicts."

"How many coffees do you want?" asked Bessie, the waitress. I looked over at Michael and her ever-evolving expressions of quarrel as she wrote first on one pad and then another and answered, "Maybe you should just leave the whole pot. We'll see how many of us develop as the day progresses."

Michael wrote away, sowing the seeds of trees that I was sure she would crash into in the future. Freddy Fantasy squeezed himself into the booth with us. Michael closed two of her notebooks and shoved them into her bag. At first she smiled awkwardly at Freddy. Then suddenly she appeared to become angry, then just as suddenly, she looked almost petrified. Freddy turned from her and then looked at me, then back to her. Finally he came back to me and asked, "What's on the schedule, Boss?"

At long last Freddy acknowledged Michael's presence at the booth by saying, "Hi, Michael." Michael went back to her awkward self. She rolled her eyes nervously then became petrified, staring at her sandwich that she upheld to eclipse Freddy's face.

Freddy began to fumble for words and then he said, "Michael, I can never figure you out. One moment you call me over to your booth to show off what you wrote. The next moment you act like you're a Soviet spy carrying bomb secrets. I never know who I'm talking to when I think I'm talking to you. You know what I'm saying?"

With Freddy venting his frustration with Michael, I looked into her bag and thought, "Maybe he should jump into her notes and join the crowd." Suddenly, Michael gathered the rest of her notes, stuffed them into her bag and left our booth after throwing her sandwich in Freddy's face.

Freddy pieced the sandwich back together then looked at Michael, who had taken a vacated booth, and yelled, "What? What the fuck?"

I guessed that there was something more going on as Michael's eyes had swelled with tears. She turned away and signaled for Bessie to bring her coffee from our table. Freddy looked at me saying, "I'll tell you about it later in the truck."

Whatever was going on between them was their business, so I got right down to my business, "Good morning, Freddy. We have a little job for some guy that cuts people's hair in his apartment. Have you ever moved a barber chair before?"

Freddy got a little twisted in the mouth and replied, "Those things are fuckin' heavy. Is that all he wants moved?" I had only half of his attention. The free sandwich and Michael who had turned her back to us had the rest.

"Freddy, if the thing was fuckin' light, he wouldn't fuckin' need us! So let's fuckin' go and fuckin' move the fuckin' chair!"

Freddy devoured the sandwich, slurped his coffee down and ran after me to the van. His first task of the day was to push me to a start. Having done that, we left.

While heading down Union Street, Freddy whacked me on the shoulder and said, "Kenny, that fuckin' bitch Michael is like, totally bizarre! Can I tell you something that happened between us last week? Promise me that you won't repeat it to anyone."

I looked at Freddy, shrugged a little and answered, "What do you think? It's not like I'm writing a book or anything."

Freddy put a cigarette in his mouth and began his story, "I was carrying a bag of groceries to my crib when Michael passed me and gave me this intense look. I stopped and asked, 'What's happening?' She started talking in this real girly voice, and then she stroked my Johnson while saying, 'Maybe us', then we split for her place."

He lit the cigarette and went on to say, "So Kenny, you think that she is who she says that she is? If you do, then you're a bigger fool than you give yourself credit for being. I thought I was talking to the person that I knew in the first place. Then she said to me, 'All you're going to feel is a mellow body high, Freddy'. We dropped what she said was Purple Haze and sat on her couch. I felt nauseous and ran to the toilet. Then I remember my reflection spewing vomit into my face, before everything went black.

"When I came to, she was standing over me and asking in this strange voice, 'Do you feel anything?' I couldn't speak. I could only lie there and watch. Her jaw shut like a bear trap around her voice. I could only hear, 'ing-ing-ing', from her last word as it bounced off the bathroom walls.

"Her lower jaw was the first to go. The skin tightened around it quickly, then became leathery, then cracked like clay in a desert. As it dissolved and fell upon the tiles, the cracking spread to the remainder of her head leaving only echoes of laughter from memories of times gone by.

"Her body dissolved within her clothing, providing a resting place for the dissipating bone of the skull that it cradled. A cold breeze from an open window swirled around the gray dust from her remains and brought it upward as a form of its previous life took shape and thanked me for its resurrection.

"The next thing that I remember was her telling me to drink tea from a white cup. I became suspicious and refused, because I will never do anything to alter my perception. When I asked her if she was herself or the woman from the dust, she told me that I was crazy and that I must leave. I told her, she was fuckin' nuts."

Freddy lit up another cigarette, took a drag and placed it next to his other cigarette that was burning in my ashtray. I asked him what happened next. He said, "I took my shit and split. Kenny, let me tell you, that fuckin' bitch is nuts!" Freddy lit up a third cigarette as we rolled up to the boarded up barbershop on Fourth Avenue.

"Oh wow! I could really do wonders with your hair. When's the last time you had it cut?" said Jim, the customer, while snipping at me mentally.

I answered, "What year is this, 'seventy-five? I think I had a haircut in 'seventy-three, could have been before that. I'm not quite sure. Don't get any ideas Jim. I tie the pony-tail around my belt to keep my pants up."

I had to flash a smile. Jim was looking at my belt with disbelief.

Since the chair was in a store, it was loaded quickly. The apartment on President Street proved to be more challenging. Looking to the top of Jim's building I said, "You know, every third floor in Park Slope always winds up being on the fifth floor. Usually one flight takes you to the second, two flights to the third. Now, I count four flights; that makes it what floor?"

After carrying the chair two flights I asked, "Who told you that your place was the third floor, the realtor? You should have asked my fuckin' legs, man!"

The barber chair had to weigh three hundred pounds, at least to me. When we reached the top, Freddy sat on the steps coughing up everything, except his previous incarnations. Jim apologized to Freddy by giving him an extra five bucks and two joints.

Then Jim said to me, "Kenny, I can't insult another entrepreneur with a tip. If you want, we can inaugurate the chair with your shorn locks falling to the floor as barter for the extra flights or as a gracious gratuity."

Jim stood with scissors in hand. I thought of the interview that I had coming up with The Aaron Aardvark Aagency. Not too many employment agencies had spots open for personnel directors flying a full-blown freak flag. Then I thought of Hypocrite Howie. Then I remembered what Anya and I discussed about choices and Yogi Berra.

"Go for it Jimmy. And the little beard too!" I looked across the room at the mirror. Except for occasional glances at my passing reflection in windows, it was my first complete look at myself since I could remember. I felt as though a temporary veil was about to be lifted from that which I hadn't seen since I stopped looking.

Jim asked if I wanted a Polaroid of my before head. I declined telling him that I don't want anything to make me look back. He set his clippers. I asked to face away from the mirror until both hair and beard were in my past. Soon I would face my face. I thought about how Anya would be surprised. But first, would I survive the shock?

"Voila! Heeere's Kenny!" said Jim.

The room spun around me. My head shook as the chair came to a stop. I gazed into the eyes of someone in the mirror falling off a barber chair, pointing at me and laughing his head off. I realized that I looked as I did prior to my entire experience on the street. I had never really looked into a mirror in all that time. My recent past lay beneath the barber chair. I asked the mirror, "Is this my future?"

"Kenny, you look like a Kennedy! Holy shit! Wait till Anya sees you. She won't even know you!" Freddy said as he waved off Jim's advancing scissors.

I asked, "Kenny Kennedy? Is he one of the dead ones or just another savior in training? If someone takes a hot poker to my eyes, then you know the whole temple's gonna cave in on everyone."

The air from four open windows flowed unobstructed over my face and neck as I drove back to First Street. I wondered if long hair protects your hearing from high pitch sounds like the floppy ears on a dog do for the dog. If this is true, it may explain why people in the corporate world are so crazy, and longhaired rock musicians, whose hair would enable them to handle noise, are not.

I parked the VW and drew all of the window curtains. Gordon's apartment had the odor of the grease of something that once lived, freshly splattered on the kitchen walls. Judging by the smell, it had to have been for free. I took a deep breath and ran past the kitchen and down the hall toward the closet, just to be sure that my thirty bucks worth of used business clothes were still there. There they were, and somehow they resisted the stink from the kitchen.

I paused for a moment, surveying my fine threads. I knew deep down that if I didn't buy this suit first, someone would be wearing it to the big sleep at Potter's Field. Instead, it was for my resurrection back into the World. Lucky me, I had been the fleetest of foot at the used clothing store. Quickly, I shook the ghosts of days gone by from my head as my face looked back to me from my shiny vinyl shoes. I surveyed my new used wardrobe hanging at the ready. Closing the closet, I imagined Old 'Lung as having been my personal shopper. "Yes! I am ready to ring the World's doorbell."

I found it impossible to stop looking into the store windows at my reflection while I walked to Anya's apartment. I kept licking at the hairlessness around my mouth. Some passersby licked back at me. There was no time for an explanation. I paid no attention to them. I just couldn't wait for Anya to see the me from the bottom of the hairball.

I knocked on Anya's door. She opened it and smiled. Then she pretended to close it in my face saying, "Please leave my hallway and go witness Jehovah by yourself! Excuse me; you look vaguely familiar. Have we met? Seriously Kenny, I always knew you had a face and I like it. Now you have the shiny shoes, the suit, the bald face and the ass-kicking haircut. What time is your interview tomorrow?"

For a person who couldn't give a shit less of what others thought of him, suddenly it meant so much that Anya was pleased, as well as myself. Deep down, both of us knew that it was impossible for a serious relationship to develop between two people from such different worlds. For that reason, perhaps, we felt totally at ease with one another. I guess we knew that one day, maybe soon, we would awaken from the dream, and part.

But not that day, so I pointed to the space on my wrist where a watch might belong and answered, "There really is no set time for the interview. I just jump on the F train to Manhattan tomorrow morning, find their office and line up, I guess."

Chapter Thirteen

Metamorphosis

Like cattle caught in the vortex of a Texas twister, the early morning crowd from the F train was swept up the subway stairs to the join the rest of the herd as they rushed along the Manhattan street above.

I fell from the throng to the safety of a notch between two buildings. A gray trembling hand reached out to me accompanied by a blast of warm air from the sidewalk vent.

"Where there is a trembling hand, surely there must be a trembling body," I thought. There he was, huddled within a tattered army coat, sitting atop the vent.

Hurriedly, he looked at me and said, "Hey kid, come here! Give a veteran some loose change. I'm kinda hungry and between checks, ya know."

As quickly as I could drop a couple of quarters into his palm, he turned and reached with his other hand to the passing crowd, ignoring me in the process. Could he have fallen from the eternal rush of passersby years ago and found that all he needed would come to him by just sitting on the vent? I saw the sign for The Aaron Aardvark Aagency above his head.

I wondered, "Will my journey back into the World begin here, where his seems to have stopped?"

"Am I, already, being re-molded to fit into the World?" I asked myself as the rock hard plastic bucket chair at The Aaron Aardvark Aagency waiting room cradled my ass. Then I wondered, "Would it be the first thing to change?"

The walls seemed to be closing in on my head a little more with each throb of my pounding heart as I stared blankly at the application on my lap, "Would my head follow my ass in the transformation? Were the gas chamber green walls like the planks that covered my own telltale heart? Here I sit, within the Halls of Poetic Justice, located full circle from an unemployment office, just like the one where I helped in the transformation of Eddie. Is gas chamber green the official color of places for dehumanization?

"Could this office be the mouth of the machine that swallows the living as the first step toward corporate absorption? Is this stupid-looking suit that I have on something like a taco shell that surrounds meat as an aid in digestion?"

I hung my head down to look at my reflection in my shiny black vinyl shoes. I saw my reflection staring at me in my left shiny shoe saying, "Brain! Stop the paranoid bullshit; you just came here to look for a job."

I looked up and took a few hits of cool air from the hissing vent above me, hoping to slow my racing heart. I glanced back at my feet only to hear the reflection in my right shoe say, "You haven't learned anything at all, asshole!"

The reflection in my left shoe countered with, "You're only putting your abilities on the market, not your soul."

My right foot placed itself across the top of my left. Its reflection shouted, "What's the fuckin' difference, asshole?"

I placed my feet under the chair and turned my attention to the doodles that those before me had drawn on the clipboard that was resting on my lap. I wondered, "Why did they all draw nothing but circles and boxes?"

The stick pen that was provided for me began to run out of ink as I tried to incorporate the doodles into one large circle. I alternated my attention between my project and the mixed brown and green linoleum that spread throughout the general office area until it met with the frayed shit-brown carpet beyond the partitions. With the ink gone, the broader perspective prevailed.

"Ah, the carpet!" Like the satin lining of a casket, it surrounded the lifeless forms of the managers who were interred on the other side of the partitioned border that separated the upper and lower classes within this bleak capitalist cathedral of servitude.

"Kenny! You're only here to find a job! Cut out the overanalyzing bullshit." There goes my left shoe talking again. My right shoe consoled it and me with, "Okay, We'll try! Yeah, like we mean it! Ha!"

As soon as the floor dialogue passed, I looked across from me. There sat the worker class. Housed beneath the mesmeristic flutter of fluorescent light fixtures were the secretaries. They seemed to come in two distinct varieties. One variety consisted of contestants for the Farrah Fawcett look-alike prize. Another might be competing for the Pam Grier equivalent.

Like galley slaves would pull on their oars, the secretaries clacked away on their typewriters with the chains of unquestioned duty linking them by their ankle bracelets. Silent stares from their supervisor's eyes set the slaves' mindless rhythm while the overseers with folded arms, goosestepped slowly down the aisles.

The remainder of the staff was a bunch of munchkinlike creatures with pursed lips and squinted eyes. They were probably the same people you curse at while they drive those little cars in the left lane with their bright lights on while going ten miles an hour slower than the speed limit. Between the offices, they scurried about, like squirrels gathering nuts, each in their seclusion, accumulating the indifference of one another.

Then there were the managers. The managers were those privileged few whose eyes peered over half-glasses that were about to fall off the tip of their noses, but were spared by virtue of the ever-present black mole.

As much as the secretaries smelled of bubblegum breath, the managers reeked of bad breath. Could it have been the result of all of the shit they had to swallow from the executives whose marble floors were locked behind mahogany doors? There seemed to be a correlation between the size of the mole and the degree of bad breath of the manager. Does bad breath breed nose moles?

The managers wore their bad breath like a weapon of distinction. They held their hands to cover their mouths only out of respect for one another, while always appearing to be mumbling together.

The managerial breath would be unleashed upon any member of the lower class that might enter their small unventilated offices. Upon removing the hand shield from their mouths, the manager would say to the serf, "Please sit down, on the uncomfortable chair, while I lean back on the nice one, because I have the carpet."

Since no one could hold their own breath for longer than one minute, one would only listen, nod in agreement, and then run outside the office to inhale. Power takes on many strange forms.

My reflections in my shoes were eclipsed by the shadow of a figure named Ann Saleri, who said, "Mister Savory, please walk this way."

She wasn't a serf, nor did she hold her hand to her mouth. I determined that she was a hybrid, some unusual form of middle management or a hologram.

I figured that I may as well go along with her, but I didn't have massive hips to flip, nor did I wear office slippers to slide across the floor as she did. So I walked in my own way. There was no time to tell her that my name was not that of a spice, but it was that of a cabbage.

She took me to the linoleum-carpet border and instructed me to sit down. I picked a little plastic bucket that looked perfect for my re-formed ass and complied with her instruction. Then I heard a voice that was characteristic of neither man nor woman say, "Mister Savoy, please remain seated."

After having just sat down, why would I suddenly have any thoughts of standing? And why would I stand up for someone who resembled a dandruff-adorned, last surviving judge of The Salem Witch Trials?

The creature's voice was mezzo-soprano. There was a single eyebrow that dissolved into shadowy sideburns. There were random patches of facial hair that seemed almost pubic. I was as confused as was its gender. Was this life form in need of a shave or was it between electrolysis treatments? It was impossible to determine whether the rounded lumps below the belt of its black smock were her breasts seeking her kneecaps, or his fat rolls covering his thighs.

The sound of an extended fart filled the room from the air gushing out of the vent holes in its executive chair, as he, she or whatever it was plopped down. The thing then peered, just as expected, over its half-glasses and then half-smiled. It looked back and forth first to me and then to my application. After a few glances at both, it leaned back and took aim through the glasses and over the mole and said, "It states here that you are seeking the position of a Personnel Director. Is that correct?"

I thought for a moment, and then said, "I came here wanting a job as a personnel director. Now I'm curious to know what position one has to be in to get it."

My words seemed to bounce right off the thing's ears faster than the dandruff could fall from its face. I could feel the polyester that cloaked my street-purified body beginning to smolder. Somehow I managed to restrain my gathering rage.

I guess a message of second thoughts from my self-control must have bypassed my self-esteem, since I said to the it, "That's basically correct. As you can see, my last job was as an Assistant Director of Operations, which had as a subcategory that of Personnel Director. Here's a letter of recommendation from my previous employer."

The half-wit with the half-smile and half-glasses suddenly lit up as if a personality actually existed within its androgynous form. Its face began to quiver as it broke out into a full smile and asked me, "Do you know that you misspelled the word personnel? You had it spelled as personel. We are specially trained to catch errors such as this. In order to prevent this problem in the future, think of a person named Nel. Got it? Person-Nel- personnel!"

My ass quickly removed itself from the grip of the plastic bucket. I leaned over the desk before me and said, "Excuse me Sir, Ma'am or Your Holy Flatulence or whatever the hell you are! Didn't you say that you're trained to catch things?" I held up my middle finger and added, "Trained to catch things like this?"

The thing's smile seemed to be stuck on the thing's face. The head nodded affirmatively like a wind-up toy while attempting to process my statement and gesture. To my amazement, words that I hadn't even planned to say suddenly rushed from my mouth as the hermaphrodite's and my ears recoiled in mutual astonishment.

The typewriters in the office area became progressively silenced as I yelled, "You're trained to catch fish on your fuckin' nose! Your fuckin' head is so far up your own fuckin' ass that it's sticking out of your fuckin' collar! Don't worry; I'm done."

I walked toward the door. Then I turned and said, "Excuse me; I guess I'm not done. You know, I don't even have to tell you to go fuck yourself because you probably have all the necessary plumbing in one place!"

As I found the door I added in my best Liverpool accent, "Thank you and I hope I passed the audition."

I wondered, "What sort of headstones for the living are those monoliths called skyscrapers? Are they all filled with the numbed remains of what once was the human spirit? How could I have become so delusional to think that my identity could withstand one minute of reabsorption into the ubiquitous monster that is the corporation? If the individuals within the corporate body are its very elements, then which of them comprise the ass and which of those are the stools?"

The steel and glass structured world that was Manhattan left my sight as I descended the subway stairs. My hair and beard thirsted for their free flow of growth so they might again frame a face of dignity. My soul thirsted for the freeform that was Brooklyn and the force of the Brooklynite, whatever it was or wherever it went.

The wind from the subway tunnel wafted toward me carrying with it the smells of burned electrical insulators mixed with a hundred years worth of stale human urine. A blind man would know that this heralded the approach of the train. Happily, I placed myself within the first Brooklyn-bound. The soothing roar of our passage under New York Harbor gave impetus to a much-needed meditation.

I stood with my back to the door of the F train as it surfaced and greeted the daylight at Red Hook. It was then that a uniformed New York cop looked at me. I was ready to turn and become spread-eagled against the door. Instead of frisking me, he smiled and asked, "We really got lucky with the weather, huh?"

I was speechless and void of thought for a moment. I had become accustomed to only hearing a cop's voice coming from behind a flashlight, flashing back to my nights while on the street with Rico and my friends.

The cop had an innocent and benign look about him. I thought, "Would he react differently toward me in my prior to the haircut context? Does he have the prejudices that always evidenced themselves toward me and mine so recently? Is he capable of surrendering to his pre-conceived notions about people and acting out through them? Does he have those prejudices at all? Perhaps he's just a nice guy commuting to the job or coming home from it."

Why does a black or a long-haired white warrant greetings like, "Assume the position!" or "Freeze or your dead!" while a suit, even a cheap one, gets "Nice weather, huh?"

I gave him the benefit of the doubt as the train rolled over Cobble Hill. I answered, "Sure is a fine day officer. Brooklyn looks especially good, doesn't it?"

I held the overhead handle while the train entered a tunnel and its lights blackened. The lights went back on. Lying beside my shiny shoes was a stuffed toy dog. I bent over to pick it up and was greeted by the smiling face of a little boy around four years old reaching out from behind a woman's calf.

I handed him the toy. His fur-clad mother said to him, "Don't forget to say thank you to the gentleman, Christopher." Then she placed him on the seat next to her and said to me, "There's plenty of room for you to sit too, Sir."

"No thanks! I get off here," said the hairless hippie in the bad suit.

The Sun beamed on an old commercial building. I stopped at the top of the stairs of the station on Ninth Street. Standing there, I tried to decipher the ancient lettering that the Sun had blistered away on the weathered building from another era across the street. The sole surviving letters of this war with nature, oddly enough, had conquered the world with its slogan, "Have a Coke!" I was sure that the reference during those times was to the soft drink.

Corporate feudalism aside, my imagination superimposed the name, Gladys Glover! Who is Gladys Glover? "Everyone knows," was everyone's answer in the nineteen-fifties movie bearing the same name. She was a famous celebrity. Her name was everywhere you looked. She endorsed products and her support could elect or bring down the power elite. But who was she, anyway?

I recalled the story behind this movie from my childhood. Gladys was an office worker who was smitten with the idea of placing her name in a position of prominence, just to see it there. No other reason. She directed all of her meager salary and every bit of her resources toward that end. She succeeded by purchasing billboard spaces saying simply, Gladys Glover. She repeated her success, again and again until all knew her name and sought her out to lend credibility to theirs.

I thought, "Little posters on bulletin boards and an ad in a paper that no one reads have brought me to the point where I am able to control my destiny, at least with train fare and occasional meals. What would happen if I saturated the neighborhood with my simple message, "Moving? Call Kenny?" Would those who are moving become those who will call me simply because I asked? Could I position the suggestion in the public's mind by heralding the message from every place possible?"

While I stood at the top of the stairs, gaping at the building, the throngs of commuters flowed around me like a stream around a stone. I joined their movement and walked from the top of the stairs on to the avenue ahead. Just as soon as I turned the corner, two Jehovah's Witnesses held copies of their magazine, Awake, right into my face. Quickly, I grabbed a copy of The New York Post from the newsstand and held it to theirs. They fled.

"That's it!" I exclaimed as an idea exploded in my mind. Place a sign where the line of sight falls, after walking around a corner or when walking up from a train staircase. Place ads, not among other companies offering moving services, but put it in places where people might look for an apartment. Maybe among the real estate bulletins that people hang in store vestibules. Why not go all the way? Buy space in the real estate pages in the neighborhood newspapers.

Beat the drum and all will dance! Create the form and the masses will demand the substance. Talk to the body and at some point the face will appear to seek you out.

On the other hand, I will need helpers and in time maybe another driver. Good thing that there are people like Freddy Fantasy and Bob the Cab who can't cope with the World like myself, but could handle quick in and out of the World work.

As the demand for moving increases, I can increase my list of non-conformist workers and meet the demand of the public without overworking anyone. Could this become my ideal world, one of my own making? Imagine that, a world on my own terms and at the same time still respecting the terms of the worlds of others.

I said excuse me to the people who piled into me as I stopped in my tracks with this extended thought. I stopped again with another revelation and was promptly rear-ended. Could there be conflict ahead for me? Am I jumping into an arena where my obsessive personality might take me to the brink of becoming a pig like those who once enslaved me? Will I be able to forever hold their images centered on the dartboard of my mind as a warning to any of my own underlying warped ambitions? I grabbed my journal from my pocket.

JE

"Only by trying will I ever know. The only vision that I have before me is to keep a few steps ahead of that which I left behind. The warrior in my poster, who is attached to the land that will soon consume him, has become that way because his focus failed in remaining as one with the horizon.

"If I could look ahead to a conflict that I might have with the concept of property or money, then from that point I must look back to myself, now. How can I, simply an idea in form, possess anything when my very existence is transitory at best? I will never be dominated by the tools that I employ, nor will I be by those who might employ me."

I turned the corner to Garfield Place only to be greeted by Anya doing the same to Seventh Avenue, "Hi Kenny! Come with me to the supermarket and tell me how you did today."

We gathered groceries at the Bohack and placed them into a shopping cart. I told her about my desperations at the employment office and my inspirations at the train station.

"Oh, I saw that movie! Gladys Glover declares herself to be famous and succeeds. That's a terrific motivation. If you feel that you're comfortable going for it on your own then make yourself comfortable. Just remember what you said to me when we first met, I think you were paraphrasing the chief pilot from you're flying days when you said, 'I would rather be the captain of a hang glider than the corporate slave that sells out just to pilot a 747'."

I had to stop dead in my tracks as she placed herself in my path to say, "And don't forget how you characterized your life, when you were working for Kevin, as 'being less significant than the cold sweat between someone else's crossed fingers'.

"Kenny, I like being with you for who you are not for what you do or don't do. To hell with money, just do something that makes you feel right about yourself."

Talk about words you long to hear! I looked at her looking through me. The groceries, the dairy case and all around us blended into a fade away. A symphony by way of Muzak surrounded us and swept us along in dance.

Like Ginger and Fred, bad suit and all, we waltzed around store boys and shoplifters alike. We held one another as we danced through the aisles while the lands of condiments and incontinents whirled about us.

I placed my cheek upon hers and we looked away from the meat morgue with its array of body parts nestled in bloody cardboard and cellophane. If only Busby Berkeley had choreographed a ballet of rolling shopping carts, falling canned goods and jumping jelly jars, our flight of the imagination would have been complete.

While blurred images of Kellogg's, Kraft, Cornchips and cake mix were blended into the sounds of The Boston Pops meeting The Beattle's, I saw only the depth of the soul of the essence of the Universe completing me. I hoped that I did the same for her.

I felt and knew that I was being seen only for whom I was and nothing else. A feeling leaped from the depths of my soul, and the words escaped from my mouth. I finally said what I thought I would never hear myself say to another, "I love you, Anya!"

Her arms pressed my body closer to hers. She answered me by kissing my neck then my ear, softly. Our fantastic journey through the world of Green Stamps ended only when an announcement warning of, "Slippery conditions in aisle six," interrupted the music. The checkout girl asked for cash rather than for our autographs. I obliged our audience by singing as we departed, "The hills are alive with the sound of mucous".

Trevor Lasco had built a multi-national financial empire from five hundred stolen dollars and the exploited services of the souls that he would later abandon. Could I somehow build an island of sovereignty for myself and for those whom I may subsequently employ from my investment of five dollars worth of paper signs?

Could I deny the magic or coincidence that brought my father's Chevy to Providence's door in the form of the VW?

That chariot was not meant to deliver me in daily pieces to a slow agonizing assimilation into the corporate body.

The VW would build the structure, not of property, but of an evolving tool to permit my participation in the world. The first rule of the street must prevail foremost in my mind with any endeavor that follows: "Pay those whom you owe in full and then move on."

I always kept looking straight ahead while living on the street since I never had to look back to see if anyone I owed was chasing me. A very simple philosophy, a prime directive kept me alive: "Whatever the need may be, if you can't pay for it on the spot, then get it when you can pay. Never owe anyone for tools that may only break in your hand. It may then be you, breaking in the hands of others."

I had to remember that on this new path, the world that I might find myself dealing within would be nothing different from the street that I dealt with and survived. The world ahead would be an open avenue, where the street behind had proven itself to be a dead end.

I removed my shiny vinyl shoes from my feet and held their toe boxes to my face. I saw only harmony in the eyes of my two reflections. After tying their laces together, I threw the shoes to their final resting place, an oak branch high above First Street. After they twisted themselves around the limb for the last time, I walked away.

Chapter Fourteen

Temperance

We approached Warren's Bookstore on Seventh Avenue. I saw a man leave the store and nearly walk into a tree while both reading a book and walking his dog. If it weren't for the dog pulling the man with the leash, after darting after a freshly laid hot one, then the man would have walked into the tree.

Pausing momentarily, I asked Anya, "Could a man, who walks along reading from a book while his dog sniffs the shit of those dogs who passed before it, perhaps, be sharing the same degree of inspiration and enlightenment?"

What once were poetry readings that occurred spontaneously in September's, and the other local coffee houses, or even on street corners, became contrived events to draw consumers to the new wave of book stores that grew along Seventh Avenue. Could inspiration endure under the yoke of creativity's bold new patrons?

Anya pulled me down to a cushion that we would share next to the mandatory coffee pot as Park Slope's poetry elite fought for last place in the order of readers.

"Well of course I'll defer to Henry. All the caffeine in the world won't keep these people awake after he gets done with them," said Paul while conceding to read first.

Paul and Henry had been battling at readings for years. If there were a contest to see which one was more the egotistical and obnoxious, then Paul's poetry would prove him to be the winner. A study of his writings might show that reality itself was nothing but a reflection of his opinions. Henry took great pride in his more humble approach.

Everyone in the neighborhood wondered how they could remain friends while articulating the slings and barbs that they hurled at one another. Until recently, it had been done tongue in cheek. Some said that this interaction was a necessary element in the motivation of their individual and collaborative works.

"Ladies and gentlemen, I give you Paul. He and his thoughts are to poetry, what Doctor Mengele's surgeries were to twins," upon saying that, Henry bowed sarcastically and waved Paul to the stage.

Paul walked toward the podium, stopped and stood stoically before his antagonist and drinking buddy. While leaning forward, with a piercing stare, he said to Henry,

I look within your mind and see
That which only death can release
From the form that stands before me
This very thought my very peace
Vengeance upon you, unnecessary

Upon delivering his message of good will and cheer to his rival, Paul walked toward the door. He took one last look at the room and left while holding his middle finger to Henry.

Henry seized his opportunity and dashed to the podium to have the last word. With his index finger pointing to the closing door, he delivered an impromptu limerick.

There he goes! Another pretender to the throne
Of the kingdom of the mind
It takes all kinds
But he's just another disillusioned Messiah
Who defended his ego, ergo a liar
So he puts on the air that it's his cross to bear
As he joyfully burns in Hell's fire

The door swung back open and Paul responded, "Henry, I will leave you now to your small world of small words that fill the small minds that sit before this small stage. I have greater things to do than this. Both you and I know, a great novel is within me."

Henry answered the closing door saying, "Thank heaven for medical science! Who, until now, would imagine anal probes being that far reaching?"

Mel, a friend of Anya's, was working that night as the event manager at Warren's Bookstore. He got up from his chair and announced, "Ladies and gentlemen, please help yourselves to some free coffee and cookies, compliments of the profits from your purchases. Feel free to browse and bring your selections to me at the desk. This, of course concludes our brief poetic journey for this evening."

"Didn't you say that these two poets were friends?" asked Anya.

I had told her about these two who historically would feign fighting in front of a crowd, then leave together and head for The Iron Horse where they would try all night to outdrink one another. Afterward, they would stagger out screaming verse to the stars.

Anya tugged at my sleeve and pointed toward the front of store and said, "Take a look on that counter. Warren has books and cassettes from both of your friends sitting right next to one another. I guess they've now become competitors in the marketplace."

Just then, Mel, a dude with an Afro out to his shoulders, landed beside us and summarized the poetry war situation for all to hear, "Isn't it disgusting how the pursuit of wealth and self-glorification destroys the soul in all involved? If those two spent their time promoting brotherhood instead of their fucking half-ass enterprises they'd be hoisting vodka right now instead of their fingers at one another."

Mel paused long enough to pluck the sugar lumps from his Streusel cake out of his beard, then added, "One of these assholes gets the idea to sell his poetry. The other finds a way to plagiarize even that. Now each will have the other as the demon in all of their works to come. Then Warren, the capitalist pig that owns this place, puts their work head to head on the sales counter and takes a piece from both of them. Big fucking deal, the pig in the back office makes a few pennies from all this shit. Now the two schmucks that do the actual work hate one another."

I reflected on the time that I was introduced to Anya at September's and promptly introduced her to someone that she wasn't talking to. This wasn't the case as she pointed with one finger to me and with the other to Mel. I guessed this was so we wouldn't get confused.

She said to Mel, "I would like you to meet Kenny. Kenny, this is Mel. He's studying for his doctorate in political science. Can't you tell?"

Mel and I shook hands. I couldn't help but notice that his grip was like a vice. He gave me a curious look, and then he asked, "Are you the Kenny who had the little coffee house? Yeah, I recognize you now! I went there to see a poetry reading once. I listened to some of your stuff. You trash American corporatism, and the profit for profit's sake mindset, which I love to do also. Keep it up, brother!"

Mel stood, then pointed to the podium and shouted for all to hear, "Hey, man! Since the door just slammed on my evening's agenda, maybe Keni September can read something of his."

Mel's death grip on my hand tightened in silent persuasion. I felt too laid back to do anything myself. I looked toward Freddy Fantasy and said, “Freddy, I wrote this poem for your paper. Go up and try it out on these people. If they like it then publish it. Okay?”

I reached into my shirt pocket and gave Freddy some lines that I had jotted down during the commotion. He took it and dashed to the podium.

“Hi, I'm Freddy Fantasy. I guess I'm fulfilling one now. So I'll pretend that I wrote something on my own. Keni actually wrote this, but he's too fuckin' lazy to get up and read it himself. Here goes,

From a gentle whisper, a message seizes the mind
With the power of seduction
Venturing to depths of thought, forbidden
All that was perception crystallizes then shatters
Grains of ice shroud memory 'til they are one
A spark in the distance ignites a blaze
Consuming all that lay frozen

From the settling mist come beads of idea
Nurturing the newness of thoughts to be
Like a flower reaching to the light of life
The beauty of form is revealed, the petals unfold
To hear thunderous exaltation of its splendor
The gentle whisper of inspiration goes unheard

“Okay Kenny, I'll put it in the next issue. Be cool, bro'. Later!” Freddy walked to the door. He raised his two fingers in a peace sign as he left the bookstore, laughing.

Mel just said, “Cool,” then nearly killed me when he slapped me on the shoulder.

Then he asked, “Aren't you doing little moving jobs these days?”

“Do you need some stuff moved? You seem strong

enough to do the job yourself," I answered, while still shaking my hand around in hope of returning the blood flow from Mel's grip demonstration.

"No, man, I thought that you might need some help now and then. I'd rather be out doing something physical than collecting dust behind that desk. Look, I live right across the street from Apples. Here's my phone number. Call me if you need help with the moving thing. I've got to get back to the register now and rip off the proletariat."

He seemed like a rather cool person. Also, he would be interesting to talk to while carrying furniture and boxes up and down stairs. I put his number in my pocket. Since we had been properly introduced, I figured that I could chide him a bit.

Mel was getting up to return to his register when I said facetiously, "Okay worker of the world, arise. Go on to being exploited by the war-mongering pig that sells his capitalistic propaganda to the unwitting masses that would thus have their souls usurped by his message of greed."

Mel looked at us laughing and answered, "I can see you met Warren. Catch you all later."

"So tell me. Is he a life or just another story?" I asked Anya.

It was her turn to be the storyteller, "Mel's thesis is on the application of Marxist theory toward shifting America from a country whose focus is on serving its corporations to one that would preserve its environment. Mel sees American Corporatism as the exploiter of the natural resources of the planet toward its own gain under the pretense of serving the people, while at the same time enslaving the people.

"Mel comes from wealthy parents. Oddly enough, his father is a union official. Don't ask! His parents continue to support him, although he hasn't spoken to them in years. If you do let him work for you, it might be best to never ask about his father."

Every light post, every bulletin board and every real estate page in the local newspapers carried the simple message, "Moving? Call Kenny!" The Poet and Writer's answering service reminded me that they objected to nonliterary uses of their number.

My new answering service suggested that I carry a beeper. This was an innovative approach toward instant message delivery that I once championed at the building maintenance company. In between carrying furniture, I would be answering pages and lining up my next jobs.

The more jobs that I did, the more signs I had printed. Simple! More signs, more calls. The system worked. My idea of keeping a large list of potential worker's names with me proved to be a good one. Not one of the helpers ever felt overworked. I would go from one job to the next with a different person to help and a different story to hear.

I sat at The Economy, waiting for Mel. I took my sketchpad in hand and I drew a large rectangle. Within it, I drew my simple message, however much bolder than the first vintage. The pencil-necked driver whose head protruded to form the O was more confident in his appearance. I added Piano Specialist to my list of services. I knew that if I said that I was capable of this, larger jobs would come my way. If they did, then I would have to become capable of moving pianos.

The new sign would require me to obtain a vehicle to match this magnitude of service. Mel told me about a place on Coney Island Avenue where he had seen large step-vans for rent. We took a ride there while enroute to a job.

"I get twenty dollars a day," said Tony, the station owner. "Bring it back with the gas filled to where it was when you took the truck; any damage to the vehicle is on you."

For some unknown reason, he never asked me for any identification. He probably thought that he had seen it since, having memorized my driver's license number, I had filled out that line on the forms he had given me.

I thought of Carlos Castaneda holding my identity as Don Juan traveled the Universe with my operators papers stuck between the pages. Until I could go over to New Jersey and get a new copy of my license, Tony's Truck Rental would be my only possible deal in town.

"Okay Tony, whenever I need a van, I just call you and it will be ready, right?"

Tony added the gasoline totals to my rental bill. I signed my name and he said while laughing, "Hell no! First come, first served. If one of them is here, it's yours. Your name is on file now. Just get here real early in the morning whenever you need the truck and there should be one available. But I ain't promisin' nothin'!"

With the cavernous vehicle under foot, we headed out to meet the day.

I couldn't decide which I enjoyed more: Mel's incredible strength or the endless discussions that we would have with one another. We would argue incessantly over Mel's belief in the virtues of Communism pitted against my belief in the sovereignty of the individual.

When we saw that there was no convincing the other, Mel and I would become of one mind and feed one another's unquenchable thirst for evidence of corporate dehumanization of Humankind for the sake of Humanity. There was never a question concerning his ethics as a worker or mine as an employer, we just did the job at hand together.

Finally, the day came when I had to be the boss. I said to him, "You and I have to talk, Mel. Bro', you're a real pleasure to work with. I'd rather have you on the other end of a piece of furniture than anyone. Plus, you're as strong as a bull."

Mel gave me the "okay why are you patronizing me" look, and then he said, "Okay, now comes the but talk. Everything's cool, buuuut! Dig it, but talk."

I put on my most serious face and said, "But talk? Okay, here goes."

Before I could say anything, Mel leaned over and let out the biggest fart that I have ever heard. Then the other end of him spoke saying, "Now that's butt talk! Wow, I might add, it's kind of like scratching your ass from the inside. Seriously, go ahead Kenny. I couldn't pass on that one."

I opened the window and said, "Mel, straight out, when we do a job and you ask the customer what he or she does for a living and they tell you, well it ain't cool to tell them things like, 'Your profession is morally corrupt.' For example, you told Ed the lawyer that he's a parasite, sucking the blood of the unaware and culturally challenged.

"You have told at least three different people that they were, 'Draining the resources of humanity', because they worked in the financial district, and that when the Revolution comes they will see their possessions distributed to the people. You've got to lighten up on trying to convert my customers, man!"

Mel's face became flush with blood-red indignation. I pulled the van to the side of the road. He placed his hands in a Buddhist like position, then after a deep breath and while his normal color returned he said, "I can't fuckin' help it Kenny. These people that I say this to are fuckin' pigs! They're only concerned with how much they make and how many things they're going to buy and how much they're saving by hiring us instead of union movers. You tell me how they're not fuckin' pigs."

His folded hands became clenched fists that shook together as he ranted, "The way of the pigs will one day yield to a true universal collective of Humankind. For this vision to take place, we must learn to trust the will of the people! When the Revolution has cleansed us of the pig's value system, all will be divided and shared among the masses. Then and only then, there will finally be no exploitation. Everyone will contribute equally and our resources will be harnessed to serve the good of all!"

Mel punched the dashboard to accent his point and sat back. I put my feet up on the center console, folded my arms and while looking him straight in the eye, I asked, "So tell me Mel, am I making you a pig when I pay you for moving the pigs? Do they make you a pig when they lay a tip on you after you move them and you curse their existence?

"Why is it that you don't give your tips and pay to people that we see living in cars and in alleys? And maybe you can tell me the answer to something that never seems to add up. Who is going to do the collecting in this universal collective of yours? And who will give up their stuff without a fight, and who will fight to force them?"

As soon as he tried to answer, I held up my one more point finger and said, "Furthermore, the only workers that I can see at my little level of the Universe that are being exploited are the ones who break their asses, and then have to split their tips with the other ones who half show up 'cause the rest of them have their heads up their own asses, looking for their brains."

Mel smiled and gave me the "fuck you and your point finger". I told him to put it back or I would rip it off and stick it in his eye.

"Fuck! Fuck! Son of a bitch! Fuck! The open window at Gordon's apartment was like a loudspeaker, not only for his cries, but for the noise of his crashing and breaking household articles. I quickly finished parking the VW and ran up the stairs to see what was happening. Shattered pieces of the lock and doorframe lay all around the entryway.

I ran into the apartment ready for anything, except for what I found. Gordon was pulling his bloodied hand from the hole that he punched into the wall. A fist-sized clump of hair was missing from his head. His face was swollen around his blackened eyes. When he limped over to me, crying, he held his side and wheezed. This was one fucked up dude. I had one burning question, by whom or what?

"Who did this to you Gordon? Let me call Fireman George. I can cash in some favors and get some other people together. We'll get the bastards!" I took my chucks and bayonet from my steamer trunk in the hallway.

When I returned and said, "Let's go!" Gordon pushed my weapon-loaded hand back down and told me, "We can't do shit about this, bro'!" He leaned against the wall adding, "Here's what went down."

He licked some plaster from around the bloody opening on his hand, and then went on, "Terry and her old man had his goons throw me into the back of the limo. The two of them were sitting there. When I asked them what was up, they looked away and Jeff said, 'Shut the fuck up! You'll see soon enough'. They took me into one of his screening rooms."

Gordon grimaced, put his hands to his face and yelled, "Shit, my head hurts!"

Then he held his head on his lap as he choked on his pain. This time it wasn't physical. I placed my hand on the shoulder of my pathetic-looking friend and said, "Just, like, keep quiet and try to compose yourself. I'll hang here with you, bro'. Tell me when you're ready to talk."

I lit the half joint in his ashtray and handed it to him. One end of the joint glowed red from the flame while the other end almost matched its color from the blood eking out of his torn lip. I declined on my turn to smoke.

Gordon began to let out all of the sordid details, "Okay, I'm cool now. Here goes. The two goons held me down in this pitch-black room. Jeff turned on this projector and then these big black numbers, like from the beginning of a movie, jumped all over the screen. They like, counted down from five to one and then immediately into a scene with me naked as a jaybird in Irene's room, pissing in her face. Sonia

Blownya popped out from under the covers of Irene's bed and went down on me. Then in the next scene we all partied, doing all kinds of threesome shit. Man, they had me fuckin' cold in the fuckin' act!"

Gordon took another hit from the joint and went on, "I didn't know that I was doing sequels for Jeff. I thought that I was just bailing out the hookers when the Johns didn't make them come. The two bitches probably knew about the cameras all along. He probably paid them slut scale for their work and they paid me chump change for my end. Fuckin' Jeff told me that he's been showing my ass all over New York since I got the job in the whorehouse.

"Then the bastard signaled his brainless shits for goons to rip my pants off and take all my money and shit. I went ballistic on one of them and then everything went black. When I woke up, I was in a fuckin' dumpster with no clothes on."

Gordon then pointed to a pair of orange-and-black-tiger-striped toreador pants on top of his kitchen table while saying, "I found those fuckin' hooker's pants lying on my face. I don't know if it was a favor from one of the girls or Jeff's idea of a joke. I had to run to the train station wearing just the fuckin' pants. Not even a shirt or socks, never mind shoes. The Transit cops went after me when I jumped the fuckin' turnstile. I kept running up and down staircases until I saw an open door to the I.R.T. train. For some reason they stopped and didn't chase me into the train."

Gordon's speech was slurred from the blood-soaked towel holding the ice cubes that were failing to stop the bleeding. He insisted on continuing, "People on the train kept looking me up and down.

"You see this bald spot on my head? A bunch of tunnel and bridge boys from Jersey yelled, 'Hey faggot! What's the matter, your boyfriend fucked you up and tried to throw you on the tracks? C'mon guys, let's finish the job!' Then they all jumped me right on the fuckin' train in front of everyone."

I brought a fresh towel with a bunch of new ice cubes for his head and lip. Some pieces of the story didn't make sense, so I asked, "Gordon, I don't understand something. Since Jeff knew that you were filmed all along with the hookers, then obviously he was making money on it. Why does he have his bargain-rate star fucked up like this? Also, wouldn't he have gotten word back to Terry about you sooner if he wanted her to know?"

Gordon sucked the last of the blood-soaked roach as it rolled off his finger and said, "A while back, Terry had Sonia beaten up by Jeff's goons for saying some stupid shit about her hair. It wasn't so much an issue of her hair; Terry likes to set herself above Jeff's girls. I guess, since they get paid for it, they're just whores. Terry's a lady 'cause she just gives it up.

"Anyway, Sonia thought that she would have the last laugh and told Terry to catch her golden boy on whatever reel number it was in the film library. When Terry saw it she knew that I was bullshittin' her all along about my coming home late, so she asked Jeff to do her a payback.

"Ain't payback a bitch, especially from a bitch? Jeff just assumed that I came back to Terry with stories about what I did at work, like to turn her on, like he would."

"Gordon, I don't understand something, bro'. Why the loyalty toward Terry from Jeff? He knows that she was with you all along and we saw them always fighting. He even had his mixed bag shit going on at the mansion with young boys. What gives?"

Gordon gathered all of the roaches from every ashtray in the house; the skinniest of skinnies emerged as a result. I left it all to him as he continued with his story, "The two of them have, in reality, been together all along. What happens in each of their sex lives is spice for when they get close again. Their separate shit in their separate lives turns them both on. This has been going on for years. What I did behind her back went outside of her personal rules of engagement. Also, I guess I must have told her that I was keeping the pissing thing special for her.

"The fact that she felt screwed was enough for Jeff to hear to order me hurt. I guess that I deserved this. By the way, you probably figured by now that I got fired. Maybe if I put up a better fight they would have kept me on the payroll, huh?"

Gordon pointed to the entryway and said, "Oh yeah, there's an envelope that your ex-wife sent you on the desk. It's been here for a while. Sorry that I didn't get it to you sooner."

I shoved the letter into my backpack. I didn't want to detract from Gordon's despair. He did just that on his own when he said to me, "Kenny, I have been checking you out, even while I was doing my shit in the City. You really got it going on with the moving business. I now see that you are genuinely worthy of my partnership in the moving thing that you asked me about. I would now like to accept your offer."

Did his ceasing to feel his immediate pain have anything to do with the thought of his impending poverty? I was taken aback about as far aback as my chair went when I said, "Dude, when I made that offer, you and I were totally without shit for prospects. I mean, all I had was a van that rarely started on its own and a little idea. I asked you to contribute your phone and the desk that we're sitting at and you refused me, flat out!"

My sympathy for the pathetic lump sitting before me exhausted itself by the audacity of this petty opportunist. I added, "Gordon, I went out and put a whole enterprise together from just the air that I breathed and all that was left of my dead father's meager possessions. How do you come up with the fuckin' balls to ask for an equal share after your Heaven on Earth becomes nothing but you greeting the new day, naked in a dumpster? Maybe you were somehow reborn today, but I wasn't born yesterday!"

As his finger burned from the roach in hand, his imagination cooked even faster, "You really got yourself into a commercial trip, Kenny. You talk a lot of shit about giving away everything that was material so that you can see the pure and spiritual. Maybe that's all a crock of shit. Push comes to shove; you want to keep it all."

There's a certain feeling that occurs in the pit of your stomach when your mind suddenly, and you know permanently, changes toward another person. It happened to me at that moment toward what was once my street brother.

"Gordon, you're just running another con game with your mouth. I don't have to justify anything that I did out there. You know goddamn well that you're trying to manipulate me into making you a partner after I did all of the work. You have no fuckin' right to assail me or what I did with my life on the street.

"You had a choice when I offered to go fifty-fifty with you. You can't climb on board a wagon that you had no hand in building and then lay claim to it. If you need to work, you can help me from job to job. But remember, this production is totally a creation by my efforts and if you want to see where your own efforts got you, look in the fuckin' mirror, bro'!"

I couldn't control my reactions to this outrage. On the other hand, he wasn't making any attempt to consider my sensibilities either. Somehow I spared him what was foremost in my mind, "With a partner like him, all I would ever be left with might be half of a good idea and a bunch of spent roaches in the ashtray as our legacy."

I told Gordon that I would cover the rent in full for that month in order to help him get straightened out. I would make sure that there would be something extra, just to satisfy my conscience for his letting me use his hallway as my halfway house.

What the fuck? Since Terry came along, I slept either in the VW or in the park if I happened to fall asleep while hanging out there. Still, maybe because I never hit on Kathleen, he did help me when I really needed it. I would give him installments every three days. I knew that this would guarantee that what was left of my shit wouldn't be on the curb where he once found me.

"Why is there always equally bad news to every bit of good news that comes along?" I thought as I opened Deanna's letter. Good news, inside the envelope that she sent me was another envelope with my driver's license. Bad news, within that envelope was a note from Rita from Buffalo. Not that this qualified her genealogy, she actually did live in Buffalo. But so did hookworms. Anyway it read,

> Hi Brooklyn,
>
> Silly me, I think that I get swept off my feet by a mystery man named, Brooklyn. But he turns out to be Joe from Jersey! Anyway, that's no big bummer. Why do people make it such a point of pride to say, 'I'm from New York City'? You wonder if those same people said that while they were living there.
> Anyway again, guess what, Joe from Jersey? I don't know if I ran into this problem that I have before being with you, after you or even from you. Plain and simple, I got the clap. So I'm trying to be a good citizen and spread the bad word.
> Good luck. I hope you somehow come up clean. Here's your driver's license. Come up and see me when you're sure you're uncontaminated. Bye 'Brooklyn'
>
> Love, Rita from the van.

I tried to make a play on the words in Bogies' classic line, "*Of all the gin joints in all the world, she has to pick mine,*" but I came up dry. I thought of how finally, I met Anya, someone who makes a real difference in my life. And to think, a stoned out ten-minute stand, I couldn't even recall, with some stranger in a hippie van could fuck it all up. Though I strongly doubted that anything ever happened in the van with Rita, nothing could take my mind from the task before me. I had to get checked out anyway.

There must have been at least three variations on Gordon's new toreador pants parading around the free clinic on Flatbush Avenue. Of course there were some ordinary folks sitting among the transvestites, hookers, heroin addicts and just plain old victims of passion.

Then there were the other victims, like myself, seated around me, suffering from real or imagined collateral damage. The only positive hope that I could muster was that my news would be negative and that the incident was a product of Rita's imagination.

"You certainly take yourself to the nicest places," I thought. I would have to clobber anyone who might ask me, "Do you come here often?" Although I did get the impression that that place had its share of regulars. They must have been the people who remembered to bring a newspaper to sit on. At least my little fling might have been with someone from Buffalo. Some of those people looked like they had theirs with buffalo.

When my scores came in, I imagined a yellow smiling face in a petri dish declaring, "I pronounce you free of V.D.!" Hearing that, I felt that my past was cleansed. Though prone to dance in supermarkets, and other public places upon hearing good news, I chose to hurry to the nearest exit. There appeared to be a roomful of willing, albeit undesirable, partners to my tendency toward spontaneous celebration.

Chapter Fifteen

Emergence

Danny would sit across from Freddy and snap a balled-up soda straw paper through Freddy's upright fingers. His attainment of his objective was announced by crying out to his fellow movers while we gathered at The Economy, "Goal! You suck, Freddy!"

Others might do the "Mumble Jumble" quiz in The Daily News. The more intellectual's heads would be buried in the crossword puzzle of The New York Times. The zenith of cerebral breakfast banter, however, would come from those who managed to stumble upon the most newsworthy topic of the day.

"The bagel was named after the manner in which it was cooked. Prior to baking, bagels are boiled. Be, means in in Hebrew, gal means wave. Since the dough floats in the boiling water's waves, we have Be-Gal, now bagel. I know this because I lived on a kibbutz for an entire month," said Mel as we sat in The Economy awaiting our be-gals.

The learned Freddy Fantasy interrupted his championship game to challenge Mel by saying, "That's total bullshit,

Mel! Here's how it really happened. A long time ago, in Eastern Europe, there was a horrible pogrom. A pogrom is like a raid with the intention of slaughtering Jewish people.

"Unexpectedly, heroic Cossacks rode into the village and saved the Jews from the perpetrators. They were riding horses with very ornate stirrups. The Cossack word for stirrup was bagel. In commemoration of this event, the Jewish bakers fashioned a type of stirrup shaped bread in their rescuers' honor."

"You people are such idiots!" Michael screamed from the next booth, "According to Will, in ancient times, the Mohel carried a ring of leavened bread with him to every circumcision, or Briss, even during Passover. This was the only leavened bread to be found during that revered time.

"After the Mohel finished his cut, he would place the ring of bread around the baby's penis in order to protect the wound and to absorb the blood. When a safe period of time had passed, he alone would ceremoniously consume the bread to the sounds of, Mazel Tov! All of the other people would have to await the end of Passover in order to finally eat leavened bread. The modern bagel, according to Will, therefore symbolizes the original penile envy!" On that note our bagels arrived yet, somehow, remained uneaten.

A new head-count revealed Danny to be among the missing. I had two jobs that morning and a diminishing work force. The VW and a rented step van sat in front waiting for their as of yet, unrealized crews.

In the midst of my despair, the sound of a friend grabbed my ear as a hand turned my shoulder, "Kenny my man! Do you need someone to hump furniture today? I can hump better than the next guy." It was Lana!

Lana was immediately kicked in the shin by her latest love, Kanika. Kanika remained seated. Her eyes peered at us from over a book called, Men and Other Vaginal Irritants. She did pop her head out to wave hello with her tongue while Lana landed in my booth with her trademark Marlboro, planted in her tooth gap.

She explained, "I gave up the dancing gig. Too many years of having my ass pinched. I wound up punching some asshole out when he went for my tit. I actually got fired because it was the boss doing the grabbing."

She sat across from me waiting for my answer. If her arms were as strong as her mouth and her snap-kicks, how could I refuse her the job? I answered, "Your pile of victims grows and grows. Where will you strike next?"

The men's heads were leaning toward our conversation. I addressed their curiosity by saying, "If you guys work with her, keep your minds on business. The only balls that Haamdi has left, after Lana got through with him, are in the falafel sandwiches that he sells you."

Lana shook at my sleeve and said, "So that's a yes I take it. Who do I go to work with today?"

I pointed my thumb at my own chest and answered, "Lana you get to work with the boss. Too bad, first day lousy luck I guess."

Somehow Danny finally found his way back to the restaurant. Freddy bowed out of work in deference to the stronger, although staggering, being. I was sure that Danny would agree to Mel's converting him to Communism if it could somehow fulfill his dream of a daily bottle of blackberry brandy and a bottomless bag of reefer.

Every other mover that I worked with would cause the furniture to twist with their own body movement as we carried it together up or down the stairs. Not Lana. She could sense the other person and move with them. It was amazing to see how years of dancing and mugging could result in such incredible strength and balance.

Our customer was pleased with the job. Lana got tipped. I got paid. I waited to get into the step van to pay Lana. I held the money out to her and said, "If you think that I'm going to stick your pay in your bra, then you're fuckin' nuts!"

I kidded her as I handed her the money that we had worked our asses off for that day. She answered, "The flames went out on all of my bras ten years ago."

Then she said, "Hey Kenny this was great. Let's do it some more. By the way, some dude named Jamal at Kanika's place, said that you looked familiar. You saw him the morning that you messed with my woman. That's my woman by the way, you prick! Anyway, did he look familiar to you?"

"I guess I have that kind of face. Kind of like bad news, it's everywhere."

Mel was to pick me up with the VW after his job wound up at the Mobil Station on Coney Island Avenue. I was sitting in the rental truck about to kill some time and allow my feelings to flow into my journal. I began reminiscing about my time at the maintenance company and the profound impact that Jamal and Eddie had upon my life. I always wanted to know what had been within the mind behind the broken bottle that was held to my throat.

Considering all the radical changes that I have been through, I might enjoy speaking to the radical, Jamal. But before I might approach him, I needed more inner perspective. His challenge to me so long before, still burned in my ears.

I thought, "I'll never know what it is to be black. Even if he did burn my office and cooked me, what would my dead, charcoaled ass know anyway? Come to think of it, I don't think that I'll ever know what it is to share his perception of white either. What I'm probably interested in determining is, whether he feels that his being black is his weapon or his shield."

With the setting sun blinding Tony, he waved for me to move off to the side of the station. I rolled the window down to hear him say, "You know, I gotta start adding maintenance into the rental rate from now on. You guys are always jumpstarting that piece of shit Minibus with my trucks and I don't like it. You know my electrical system's gonna get fucked up if you keep on doin' that."

Just as the VW appeared at the park exit, Tony grinned and said, "I gotta get forty a day from tomorrow on. Sorry about that, but you been makin' out pretty good, Boy! You can afford it now."

I threw him the keys and a twenty and for that day. Tomorrow would never come for his fucking maintenance.

Before the VW could roll to a stop, Mel came storming out from it and into my face. I never saw him so enraged. He said, "That fucking scumbag bitch! She's a goddamn rip-off! Kenny we got super fucked over! That bitch!" Upon securing the parking brake, Danny followed suit with his head bobbing in agreement.

"Mel calm down, tell me what happened."

"I'll tell you what happened, in just as few words as possible! The fucking bitch said, 'Everybody's ripping me off and fucking me over! It's about time that I start fucking everyone back. And congratulations, your boss is the first one! I'm not paying him one red cent'. Bro', all the bitch gave us was our tip."

All that I could say at that moment was, "That fuckin' bitch! Scumbag bitch! Nobody's gonna rip me off and get away with it. Take me to where you moved her."

The workers of the world did not arise, at least to the situation. Like, holding back her TV until the bill was paid would have helped. But that may have ruined the fuckin' tip. I guess the buck stops where the buck starts for Mel as far as Mel's concerned. As far as the Universal Collective is concerned, just as long as he collects his, then it's fine.

The door fell to the floor and my foot returned to the same. Politely, I said, "Will you please excuse me Ma'am? I don't often kick people's doors down, except when they rip me the fuck off! How stupid can you be, not paying the first person who knows where you fuckin' live? Put forty dollars in my hand right now, asshole, and add another ten for my inconvenience. If you want to call the cops, I'll be happy to wait with you, but the clock keeps ticking."

Everything in the apartment was placed neatly. All of the cartons were stacked in one area. Those fellas really earned their tip. She gave me a pouty, submissive look with a touch of come on attached. I didn't see beyond my extended arm and open hand.

"Kenny, I used to come to your coffee house and hear your poetry. How did you get into such a macho commercial trip? You were such a mellow dude back then."

I vaguely remembered her. She would talk and talk with everyone, acting as if she was with them while nibbling on their food and sipping their coffee. When the time came to order up herself and drop fifty cents into the jar, she was gone.

I answered, "Yeah, I was as mellow as a rotting cantaloupe. Why is it that every time a freeloader like you wants to rip off people like me, you start out by trying to put them on the defensive with remarks like, commercial trip and macho? Pay up you parasite bitch! You can start getting even with the world with the next sucker."

The fifty dollars was after consideration for the repairs needed for her door. Since she had no idea of fairness, whatever concern I showed toward her was enough and my conscience was clear.

I opened the VW door and said, "That's it Mel, I'm raising my rates! Why should I run all of this risk of getting fucked over for forty bucks? If I charge a hundred for the same job, look at all that's made before the next time some asshole fucks me over." I never thought that a statement like that would bring cheers from a Communist, but it did.

The words coming from the mouth of the salesman at the Hertz Truck lot on Fourth Avenue were, "I can't go five cents lower than a thousand."

His words were quickly challenged by my own, "Okay, so what if you go five hundred dollars less"?

He shook his head in disbelief but soon after said, "Sold for six hundred dollars," and shook my hand to seal our deal. The step-van had become my flagship. I took my roll of twenties and hundreds from my sock and peeled off the payment.

He asked me, "Haven't you ever heard of banks?"

I answered, "Yes, I've heard of them, and so did Jesse James." He smiled and handed me the keys and title.

The words, _ _ _ _ Sample Card Company, were all that was left on the side of the truck that showed any connection to its past. I'll never know what the rest of the company's name was that had been sanded away. I couldn't care less who they were. I was rolling down the street in a force to be reckoned with. My paper signs had performed their job and projected the necessary new reality.

Would any of my clientele care if an inappropriately or even an un-marked truck rolled up to their home on moving day? Shit No! I had a following of people who would let a total stranger, whose name they found on a paper sign hanging on a light pole, take all of their belongings to an address that they usually yelled from their car window as they raced ahead, to a hippie in a Minibus that wouldn't start. Compared to that, a truck with a name readable or not, was a definite improvement.

Tony's greed had forced my hand to wave the magic wand in order to manifest my next vision. I parked the truck and went to The Economy and sat down with pad and pen. If drawing a step-van could conjure one up, together with countless hours of backbreaking work, then let me begin laying out the next form to one day be realized.

I drew a sailing ship with me at the helm. Instead of flying a flag of the skull and crossbones, "Bugs Bunny's" face rested upon our sail underscored with crossed carrots. We were in chase of a galleon laden with a bounty of household goods.

Aboard my ship was the first mate, Freddy of course, with a black scarf wrapping his head and a black patch over his eye. Danny was chasing my parrot with a fork in his hand while Michael screamed to us from the next boat, "Please leave the waters of my fantasy or I'll be forced to fire one across your bow!"

A ketchup bottle returned to my table from the next booth as I returned from my daydream. Michael leaned into my face and thanked me for the use of the condiment. I thanked her for sparing my ship.

I knew then that I must always remain in pursuit of that which was beyond me and use what I had already attained to chase the dream. I then drew that which was to become my quest. The cargo box was separated from the cab of the truck. The M for the word moving was situated on the peak over the cab. The peak would prove to be necessary for all of the shit that customers forgot to mention. The face inside the O smiled with unshakeable confidence.

The new phone number from the answering service would stand out with its four sevens bearing the European-caned look. I held my pen to the ceiling of The Economy and thought, "I must place this image of what will be in every periodical, on every bulletin board and all light poles that I find. My pen will set the course. My back will bear the weight. My crew and I will never starve again!"

My seat cushion rose as Mel crashed down beside me. With his usual brazen arrogance, he proceeded to besiege my creative moment and of course my precious solitude. Even my coffee break wasn't safe from politicization.

He said, "Give me a cup of coffee Bessie, and put it on the capitalist's bill. Since we're doing that, give me a bagel too, but please hold the schmeckel."

Bessie scowled and returned his impudence by knocking my water glass over and on to his lap. Unaware of Michael's 'origin of bagelry theory', she threw Mel a towel and asked, "Ya want butta instead?"

It was my turn to take aim at the invader, but I chose words over ice water, "Why do you insist that there is a straight-out black-and-white answer when it comes to issues of effort and compensation? It's Capitalism or Communism, a single option of either greedy pigs or people's collectives. Can't you credit our species with having the innate ability to create some range within the extremes? I mean, with the billions of souls that now inhabit the world and the countless others that preceded them, don't you think that we may have gone beyond a choice of two extremes?"

Mel rolled his eyes back and leaned forward. While twisting his Trotsky-like beard he took the issue to the personal level, "What is the difference between what you're doing at a nickel and dime level, and what your Trevor Lasco or any of the pigs on Wall Street or in Zurich do at a multi-national level? You take from the working class and accumulate that which you withdrew from them and then develop the means to exert greater power over them."

Mel was clever enough to try to characterize me as a demon from one of my own poems. I chose plain conversation as my response rather than to play his game, "Mel my Marxist friend, there is a great difference between what motivates me and what dominates those to whom you have referred. Whatever I draw from my efforts is a product of what I have placed back into this tiny enterprise, less the meager maintenance of me, its creator. After vehicle maintenance, I take nothing for myself except for food and room rent. By the way, my rent will be for a room in a commune on Garfield Place that you're going to help me move into one day soon."

His opening mouth shut in deference to my raised finger. I continued, "Which segues me to, the only articles that I call mine, and that we will soon move. They are my trunk that contains my poetry and remnants of September's Child and the cable reels that survived the flood. My journal is the other, but it stays with me in my backpack. Oh yeah, and the large reel that I carved the day that I decided to make my stand and drop out. All that these objects are to me are mere symbols of my personal revolution.

"You see Mel, I lay claim to no property. All that you see other than my form are tools of my expression. I see no difference between the trucks we have and the one that I just drew. One is a vision. The other is a vision that has become realized. Everything is gathered toward the growth of an idea. All that I am is the spirit within this form that powers the idea."

Mel leaned back, preparing to lob a shell at me. He aimed and then fired, "That's well intentioned and maybe true at this point, but the fruits of money spoil and rot in the bellies of the pigs who consume it. The well intentioned soon reflect the assimilated spoils of their efforts and live only for further gain. How can there be an exception?"

Bessie served him the food that I was buying while I responded, "Given the fact that money seen as an end itself is the fruit that you referred to, your point is well taken. Let's look at the idea of tender not as capital, which I have contempt issues with, but as a marker in lieu of material to barter. Let's say that people could purely exchange with one another for goods and services gotten solely by their own initiatives. Meaning this, each sets the course for his own doing. Each created the means for the doing between the parties involved. The terms for the transaction was set and lived up to by each. How then, could any of this be seen as pig behavior? These are fair-minded people only seeking satisfaction for their efforts and an agreeable payment for same, in the form of tender. Mind you now, that same respect must be shown to all of those involved."

"Kenny my friend and exploiter of my abilities, you're describing John Galt's Utopian world within the mountain of an Ayn Rand fantasy. That entire concept of Objectivism excludes the needs of the workers within the rest of the world. The Objectivist and the Capitalist worlds attempt to nullify the power of the collective will of the people. That is why the needs of humanity's groundswell will erase the domain of the power elite."

My turn, "Will any member of this groundswell be able to walk in his own direction and choose a path that might be a little different from that of the masses? Could any speck of sand within this swelling ground set itself apart and decide for itself? What would happen if the ground swelled and every one of the people decided to set themselves apart from the whole? Then there would be no masses, only free thinkers who just might have the free will to carry their own weight or to tell the waitress to put their shit on the pig's bill!"

Bob the Cab leaned into our conversation from the takeout counter and said, "If you want to see fuckin' pigs then spend a day driving their asses downtown to the welfare office like I do. They sit in the back of my cab and then they fuckin' rehearse the bullshit that they'll tell to pump up their food stamp allotment.

"After they have me sit around waiting for them, they come out with a shitload of stamps. Then I drive the pricks to the bodega and they redeem the stamps at half-face value for beer and cigarettes. Oh yeah, either I get half-stiffed for my time or totally stiffed on the tip or both."

Bob looked right into Mel's face and added, "Come to think of it, why the fuck do we refer to low-life people as pigs? The pigs that my folks had on their farm in Georgia were intelligent and looked after their young. Why, I can remember one of our pigs swimming into the river to save her piglet from drowning.

"Every day I drive a bunch of rip-off lowlifes in my cab, back and forth to welfare, while they leave their fuckin' kids home alone in their cribs. It really makes you wonder: Maybe the farm pigs think of their low-life members as humans."

Mel was about to respond. Bob turned away from him and asked me, "Kenny, in all seriousness, I'm dead serious about working for you as either a driver or as a helper. I'm getting a fuckin' pot belly sitting in that cab all day, watching bullshit."

I told Bob that I might call him the next time I need a helper. He saw my drawing and said, "I smell another truck in the works." Bob took his take out order and he split.

Mel suddenly seemed to forget his lines in the character assassination of Kenny when he changed our conversation's direction to, "What are you crazy? How can you think of hiring him to drive? That guy crashed a car into a fucking wall, on purpose! Then he crashed the cab he was driving with a passenger in it."

Was Mel feeling his position as being the only driver, besides me, threatened? If he was just being concerned about the welfare of the business, then I felt that I should put his mind at ease, so I said, "I don't think that there's a problem with Bob the Cab as a driver. He's fine, as long as it isn't his last day with the company. As far as his other crash is concerned, just make sure that no one gives him a blowjob while he's driving."

JE

"How can it be? Such a short time ago, I chose only to implode and shrink to the smallest of confines. Now, I reach outward to the world with such great passion? Will I be able to swim across the river of this world without the weight of possessions sinking me midway? Can I retain what I have learned by keeping in mind, where I end and where the people and tools that I must employ begin? At what point during an enterprise does the entrepreneur lose his identity to that of his objective? In doing so, which prevails? Does he become replicated as a corporation? Is the creator then a slave of his own creation and of those whom he might employ?"

The latest step van couldn't have come at a better time. A large manufacturer of waterbeds and pillow furniture hired me to do its deliveries. Some degree of predictable work had fallen my way. Mel proved to be perfect to handle that part of the business. He did deliveries and assemblies for people who knew nothing of Kenny the Mover so I had little concern about him insulting my moving clientele. If Mel caused complaints from the manufacturer, then I would do the next few deliveries or send Bob in Mel's place.

"Kenny, we have to talk about something important." Somehow there's always something ominous about the words, we've got to talk, especially from one's lover. There I was at Anya's, about to tell her about my important windfall, and she probably had news that would make mine irrelevant. I sat at the table to learn just how right I was.

She got right to the point and said, "A while ago I met this guy. It was before you and I started seeing one another. We dated for a while, and then he went to Europe. Before he left he told me that he'd been planning the trip for years and how he doesn't want to go because he was afraid that it would ruin our budding relationship. He said, 'My luck, you'll fall in love during the three weeks that I'm gone'.

"He hoped I would want to go out with him when he returned. I said, 'Sure'."

She paused momentarily, and then went on, "I told him, 'Don't worry. I haven't fallen in love with anyone in the last three years. I haven't even been serious with anyone in three years. What could possibly happen in three weeks'?"

Her eyes were reddened. She sat very straight in her chair and then said, "I kind of feel like I promised to be here when he got back. Weird how things can change in just a few weeks."

Her next sentence, hit me like it came from a hanging judge, "Well now he's back and he called and I feel I should go out with him."

I felt like "Wylie Coyote" when he finally sees the canyon floor beneath the air he had been running upon. I thought, "The reason this relationship has worked up to this point is we both knew from the beginning that a relationship with one another was impossible. How can I think that a respectable, accomplished person such as this could become as serious about a street creature of the night, turned poster boy with a Minibus, as he has become about her? On the other hand, who knows?"

Hope against hope, I thought, "How will I ever know if she might have changed and she feels about me the way I feel about her, if I stand in the way of her finding out?"

I recalled my father once telling me, "Leave your loved ones to be free. How else will you know that it was by their free will that they chose you?" The single most difficult decision in my life had made itself.

I said, "Anya, if you feel that you should see him, I respect your feelings. So go ahead, I understand."

She looked at me with surprise and relief. She asked me if her doing this upset me. I told her that I had no right to be upset. She even asked if I would be okay that night. I told her that I would probably hang out at the bars with Sally since she was alone on weekends.

She asked why I didn't hang out with my dubious friend, Gordon. I told her that he was off the deep end in a self-imposed isolation behind a locked door. We kissed good night. I told her to have a good time.

Never mind a falling coyote, I thought about how the road he fell upon might feel if it met a steamroller. One could be sure that the road would feel relieved knowing only its pain and not how I felt at that moment. How could I have had the audacity to allow myself to become so delusional?

I opened my clenched fist and thought, "On the other hand, she may have had to wrestle with issues of her own and her decision to tell me took honesty that I have never known in a woman."

Through the wall of smoke and noise of Ryan's, I heard, "This is the fifth weekend in a row that that bastard comes up with an excuse to be somewhere else!"

Sally was on a rant about Paulie, her latest mistake, "Every time I tell myself that he's full of shit, I swallow the next line of crap he feeds me! Net result, I'm here and who the fuck knows where that junkie bastard is?" Sally's pounding fist opened to catch a sliding mug of beer, compliments of the proper aim of Jack the Bartender.

After nearly emptying it in one gulp, she went on, "The funny thing is, next week, we'll fuck all week and for as long as the bags last, we'll be on cloud nine. Net result, he'll get another blowjob and I'll get another snowjob."

Then she sighed and said, "And I'll believe him like I always do. Oh, what the fuck. It's so fuckin' cool to realize your own denial, and then to just ignore it."

Sally hoisted another beer while I nursed my Black Russian. The crowd at Ryan's was intense. It was becoming increasingly difficult for me to sit there and to not tell my buddy Sally, that her lover was an asshole and was fucking someone else as we spoke.

Whenever the lyrics of the song "All by Myself" transitioned to the part where the singer didn't want to be all by himself anymore, nearly every person in the weekend singles crowd would turn to the best-looking ear that would listen and strike up a conversation. They all appeared to be united in a common attempt to drown out the words. Was this a foreshadowing of the end of the free love era and the dawn of relationships, or was I just projecting my own crippled feelings?

Unfortunately for Sally, making love would always be just for fun as far as Paulie was concerned. When he got around to Sally, it was just for laughs. The tear-swelled eyes that entered her handkerchief exited with a sparkle, preceded by a whimper.

She smiled and said to me, "Kenny, enough about me. Like, you look totally different. Short hair–your muscles are popping out of your shirt. Maybe it's true about you being a narc. But I know you would have told me if it were. Incidentally, you've got to hire Paulie so you can keep an eye on him for me and maybe straighten his ass out."

The pit in my stomach was sensing that the question I dreaded was about to be asked. It was right on the money. Sally looked around and then asked me, "By the way, where's your pretty lady, Apples, tonight?"

I took a deep breath and tried to think of how I should answer that seemingly simple question. The truth was too intimate. It was more than I wanted to expose or share right then. Yet a lie would leave me as isolated as Gordon was. I might end up both without Anya and without Sally as a consoling confidante for the rest of the evening. As I was wrestling with the thought of how to answer, I looked beyond Sally's head and saw two smiling blue eyes looking right into my soul.

Anya squeezed her way up to the bar and took a sip of my drink. Then she nearly broke my neck with the force of her hug. I felt every bit of my energy melding with every bit of hers. I looked toward the door, then at the crowd, just to see if there was a new face to be found.

"Kenny, I came here alone. Relax!"

"It isn't even nine o'clock. Didn't you go on your date?"

We sat by a table and she told me straight out, "We parked in front of the restaurant on Montague Street. He opened the door on my side of the car. I got out and told him, "I can't do this! I'm sorry. You were right; I fell in love while you were gone. I have to leave."

Suddenly, I was the "Road Runner", flying through a hand-drawn tunnel toward hope. She said, "I took the train straight to the Slope. I'm so glad that I came here first."

She was trembling. I put both arms around her and at the same time raised my middle finger to the person at the bar who was staring at us.

I looked at Anya and asked, "By the way, who did you fall in love with?"

First she kicked me, then she kissed me, then she said, "You, you fucking idiot! You sneaked into my heart like a thief in the night."

In light of her statement, I stole a kiss. I guess Sally met up with Paulie or someone else, I never noticed her leave.

"Where do we go from here?" Anya asked.

Her place was closest.

Photo by J.K. Savoy

Chapter Sixteen

Phoenix

The great thing about Dylan's song, "The Times They Are A' Changing," is that good old Bob could have written it about any point in time.

I stood at the top of the up escalator, after the subway deposited me in Manhattan, and watched the new Masters of the Universe ascend to lay claim to reality itself. The crowd flowed around me. Each one of them seemed blinded to everyone about them. The anticipation of the opening bell was summoning their bodies from the ground below.

While the Armies of Conscience fought a ten-year battle against the oppressive forces of time that had greed and domination as their goals, who then nurtured this litter of pups that were becoming the wolves of Wall Street? While the soldiers in the fight against social injustice grew weary from their battles, on who's watch did a ship land and deposit these beings? I was sure that this could not be part of the generation that would inherit and further the dream that said, "All We Need Is Love."

"Elvis Is Dead", "Whip Inflation Now", "Is Nixon Making A Comeback?" My choice of self-imposed isolation from the news of the world was reinforced by glances of headlines as I passed the newsstands enroute to the lightpoles and bulletin boards of Greenwich Village.

The Village was the incubator that nurtured the soul and spirit of the creative genius that made New York an art form in and of itself. As the body craves nourishment, then so must the mind. I thought, "If one could select a diet of mind food, then could one determine one's growth patterns and form to come? Who the fuck knows? All I know is, if I'm going to carry peoples' shit up and down stairs, then let it be the shit of the most interesting people in the world. It's best to have the greatest mind food available."

My signs dominated all of bulletin boards and windows for advertising in Park Slope, Brooklyn Heights and other hippie haunts. Both the West and East Villages were the most likely next steps. Armed with a bag of posters and rolls of masking tape, I set out to conquer new lands.

I completed a neat line of tape across the top of my sign then I pulled the next strip from the roll. I looked down and my mind flashed back to my reflection in my shiny shoe at the employment office. The reflection was the same, except for the new beard. Unfortunately, for me, the shoe belonged to a New York City Sanitation cop.

I didn't recall pulling over, but there he stood in the classic foot on the bumper pose, telling me how posting was one of the most heinous crimes against humanity ever. I held back my deepest thoughts while he wrote his. As I waited for him to put the letters in the squares, a question came to mind, "Would a Sanitation cop blot coffee from his mouth with a sanitary napkin?"

I expected a force of New York's Most Sanitary to sweep down and confiscate my signs. A fitting punishment might be to tape me to the light post as a warning to the world. But then they would have to ticket themselves.

Standing at the front window of a train rushing through a tunnel is both visually and mentally stimulating, unfortunately that day it was just annoying. I sat down, returning from my attempt to take Manhattan in defeat.

Then like a gunshot on a still night, it hit me, "I have a big problem! Every poster that I have hung on every public place is a violation. Now who the fuck ever heard of posting? I've been so fuckin' careful to do everything perfectly legal, how did I miss that one?" I consoled myself with a simple thought, "When one sets out to be free, one must remember not to do anything that would land his ass in jail."

I tried to remain positive, even philosophical. I told myself that what I see as a dead end is only a mis-posted detour. This sufficed until I climbed the subway stairs to the street above and looked upward. I had another problem. Half of my sign at the top of the stairs was torn away. I turned the corner to Seventh Avenue only to see the same thing on my next sign. I looked down the street. My relief in seeing the next sign intact was changed to horror as I got closer. The word PIG had been written across the phone number in black marker.

My entire route to Gordon's revealed one sign after another with the same result, until turning the corner revealed Gordon. He turned to me with marker in hand. I ran over to him and kicked his hand. His hand let loose the marker as he let loose a scream.

I grabbed him by the jacket and said, "You motherfucking bastard! I ought to carve pig right across your face, but I can't because you stole my fuckin' knife!"

To grow from adversity is to truly grow to a better form. I took nourishment from my mind food, so I grew into the commune on Garfield Place. I grew to placing ads only in periodicals and newspapers. Was I growing toward respectability?

Let the Gordons of the world go try to find every newspaper in Brooklyn and rip out my phone number or write pig across it. Better yet, let them create an enterprise from their own dreams and place it before the people of the world, who will then determine its future and their survival within it.

"Ah, what the hell, he gave me a place to live when I needed it the most."

"Boy what a group. We must look like the cast of characters in a pirate movie!" I said to my workers as they gathered before me.

Had I conjured up the cast of characters from my contemplation a while back, or was I still dreaming? Could the ship of my dreams that I had drawn recently be on the near horizon? Seeing no parrot on my shoulder, I knew that either Danny ate it or this was reality. I chose the reality option as Bessie scrambled to jot down the breakfast orders of my crew that was piling into the booths at The Economy. We had our first job that required both of my vans and six people.

After a series of failed relationships with Sally and other young girls, my old friend, Mark, was repairing his self-esteem by ending a live-in love affair with a much older woman. Since I once saved his balls, I guess he chose me to rescue his ass by moving him out. The good news was that the job loaded from a garden floor plus a basement. The bad news, it all had to go up four flights to the top floor of his loft building on Union Street.

Mel was well into his daily diatribe. He raised his morning issue like a flag awaiting the bugler saying, "If nobody showed up for work, Kenny couldn't move!"

"Is Mel about to instigate a job action?" I wondered, sitting back while letting him babble on.

The pressure was off me and back on his demons when he said, "If everyone said a resounding, 'Fuck you,' to the pigs in Washington, and burned their draft cards, together with Lana's bras, there wouldn't have been a Viet Nam War."

Lana answered Mel's rant with a dirty look and an upheld middle finger.

Gordon's need for rent money transcended his disdain for pigs so he agreed to work with me day to day. I couldn't figure why he stood silently by our booth for at least ten minutes, listening to Mel until finally he shouted, "How the fuck can a commie bastard like you even have an opinion about something you only saw on TV? I was up to my balls in fuckin' mud in 'Nam because of your commie friends while you were talking bullshit in a lecture hall in Columbia, probably sent there on government subsidies. I wish that they drafted your pinko ass and you spent a few days in my classroom. So just shut your fuckin' Mao-mouth, okay?"

Lana glanced at Gordon, then looked to me and said, "Now my day's complete."

Gordon never said much to me about his two hitches in 'Nam. From what Rico once told me, Gordon was required to stay deep in enemy territory for extended periods of time. While in the jungle, he lived off the land by consuming bugs and snakes. If anyone doubted that he had done this, he would gladly bring a handful of cockroaches from home and eat them while they watched. When it came to 'Nam, you had to be a little careful what you said to him. One can only wash the jungle from his body.

Throughout his time in 'Nam, all that Gordon wanted when he returned was to become a New York City fireman. He must have followed his lazy eye while waiting for the physical because when the time came to take it, he didn't get past pissing in a cup. I could only hope that he might be thinking in that direction again. The physical demands of doing moving jobs might help to clean him up and to strengthen his body for the Department's rigorous tests, if they gave him another shot at it.

Mel went back to something on which he was an authority, eating breakfast on me. Mel took Danny and Freddy to the job in the VW. I felt that keeping Gordon away from

Mel as much as possible would be a good idea. Pairing Gordon with Lana seemed like the lesser of two evils, so I had them ride with me. To my surprise and delight, Gordon was treating her like one of the guys as they rode together. Lana appeared to be open to Gordon's changed behavior.

"Good morning Mark," I said, introducing the customer to the crew, although for the most part, they were no strangers to one another. Mark saw Gordon lurking behind us with his head turned and said nothing. While the crew went about their business of carrying boxes and wrapping furniture, I confirmed the price.

"Just what did you study at Columbia, bro'?" Gordon asked Mel as he picked up his end of the couch.

Not seeing the bear traps set within the very sofa in his hands by Gordon's question, Mel answered nonchalantly, "Mostly Poly-sci, some Government and Social Studies. I threw in a little Economics before I got my B.A." The Gordon end of the sofa came to an abrupt stop as the wind suddenly left Mel.

"Were you one of those fuckin' people who burned their draft cards like you said that everyone should do when you were talkin' shit at The Economy?" asked Gordon.

Mel re-gripped the sofa while looking squarely into Gordon's eye. At some level Mel must have realized that he was in over his head. After all, a theoretical Marxist may very well have been outgunned by a no-nonsense trained warrior.

Mel tried to excuse his actions by saying, "No, but I don't know what I would have done if the SS, you know, the Selective Service, came after my ass. Later, I had a deferment because I was student teaching."

They sounded as if they were engaging one another in peaceful conversation. I relaxed and began directing Danny on the fine points of table disassembly.

Then I heard two opposing points of view, separated by a couch, explode outside as Gordon said, "A fuckin' commie like you gets his chicken ass spared with a deferment, so he can pump his bullshit into kid's heads in a classroom? And you're doing this while I'm trying to finish school and become a fireman or maybe a fuckin' real teacher?

"I had to drop my dreams and lose my chick to some peacenik like you because the SS, as you call it, hauls my ass to 'Nam! How the fuck is that right? How the fuck right is it that a just few years ago, I was stringing a bunch of commie bastards ears to a necklace and now I have to carry a fuckin' couch with one?"

I rushed outside to see Gordon pointing his shaking finger in a gun-like gesture at Mel's eye. I placed my body between them to find the finger in my face say, "This asshole friend of yours probably spit on us when we came to what we hoped would be home. Instead of giving us recognition with a parade for risking our asses while these bastards made winning impossible, commies just like this fuckin' idiot called us baby killers as soon as we walked off the goddamn plane!"

Fortunately the couch was spared of becoming a victim of the conflict. Sensing Gordon's rage, Mel went inside to help Danny with the table. I took Gordon aside and said, "For a guy who threw his fuckin' medals over the White House fence, you're no one to be ragging him about protesting the war. When are you going to fill him in about how you advised kids on draft avoidance after your last hitch?"

While Gordon's lazy eye drifted to the door where Mel hid, his other eye looked squarely at mine and said, "Kenny, being against the war is one thing, but this asshole is against anything that forces him to put himself on the line. He's just a fuckin' coward. He was along for the ride in everything he bullshitted about at The Economy. Look, maybe I'm no one to talk, considering everything, but he's only along for the ride with you."

I was both impressed with how Gordon had humbled himself and had such a read on Mel in so short a time. It had to be foxhole intuition.

Gordon added, "The only reason he's a commie is it allows him to be a lifetime protester of responsibility. Do you think for a minute that he'll ever work at anything that he studied? Not even if he's at it for a hundred years. I know I live off women and all, but I'm up front about it. This shithead's blindsiding everyone along his way. And now it's your turn. Look, bro', I'm sorry but this guy is waking up all kinds of ghosts in my head. Don't worry Kenny, I won't hit him. I just want to break his balls."

Suddenly, a loud shrill voice of reason stepped forth with a different perspective, "Does anyone really believe for a minute, that those people wanted America on their turf? It's all too typical macho bullshit! Every time a small country wants to go off on it's own without permission from the boss of the world, then no way says the U.S.A.! If you're not taking orders from US, then you must be one of THEM.

"It's all about greed! The whole fuckin' thing was from the profit motive of the gangster multi-national corporations with our government providing them with a mercenary force from the get-go.

"War is good fuckin' business. What are a few thousand dead American kids and a couple million dead yellow people against the bottom line of billions in profits from green socks to super-weapons?

"Don't either one of you dignify that whole fuckin' travesty by taking stands in its name. The only good thing about that war is it's over!" Lana seemed as if she was trying to neutralize the hostility, but Gordon waved her off as if he had heard it all before.

Having never seen these sides of either Lana or Gordon, Mark felt compelled to channel the discussion toward a different level by reminding us of the mundane task before us, "Not only is my share of the apartment nearly vacant, my mind feels somehow fulfilled and stimulated. You all managed to both clear everything of mine out and at the same time, broaden my perspective."

I stood in amazement, having never seen this side of Mark. Perhaps in some way his relationship with a full-grown woman did broaden his perspective, allowing his adult to emerge and finally give a shit about something.

He added, "I am thoroughly enjoying this experience, however there is just one little thing I should tell you."

Mark lacked the heart to say it in words. He merely pointed to a behemoth of an antique player piano. The floor had sunk two inches from all the time it had sat there. It appeared so smug with its paint all alligator cracked from the sun that it had basked in since the last century.

Could this beast at rest resist our strength and cunning with only its mass? Had someone struck an ominous bass key as we all looked to one another to see whose jaw had dropped the lowest? If I were the mover, was Mark then the movee?

"Mark, I don't want to go totally negative here and make an issue, but you never said anything about a piano. This does take things to a different level."

My own words rang in my mind as I thought of the stairs before us that would lead to the different level. I knew for sure that Mark was still on track to becoming a righteous dude when he shook his lowered head and said, "Kenny, it seems that everyone wants to cut my balls off for one reason or another. My old lady dumped this thing on me at the last minute. I guess it's her way of saying, "Since you're jumping ship you may as well take the anchor."

He shook his head in disbelief and added, "Just put it on the truck. If you can get up to the fourth floor, then cool. I'll pay what it takes and I'll even help you guys move it. If you can't carry it up to the top, then I'll take a fire ax to it and pretend that it's her face. By the way, is Gordon's ex-old lady, Kathleen, available? I don't want to ask him."

To which I answered, "Then don't ask."

"Is his apartment up there where the building kinda

tapers to a point?" asked Lana pointing upward toward the pigeons circling above Mark's top floor.

Danny said, "Whoopee, another fourth floor on the fifth floor! At least the steps don't have any turns except at the main levels. Should we warm up with the boxes, or go right for the beast?" My breaking out the new piano skid board answered the question. We stripped off the keyboard and everything else that we could.

Then I said to Mark, "It's a good thing that this beast was converted from a regular player piano to a conventional or you'd be kissing your old lady's face with the fire ax right now."

Danny, together with Freddy held one side; Lana and Mark were ready on the other. I was in the front with a burlap sling attached to the board, which was under the beast. Mel and Gordon were chained together in Hell at the bottom.

"When I say go, then go! Okay let's fuckin' go!" The beast could not resist our collective effort. It glided up the concrete steps in total submission to our combined strength. Somehow it knew to give us this one victory. The beast would have its vengeance inside where the stairs narrowed. Only three more flights awaited us.

The inside steps truly were a different story than the stoop. While we had to plot and scheme in order to have our way with this silent mass of wood and brass, it only had to sit there in order to win. Since there was only one sling, I alone could stay in front. The narrow steps allowed room for only Lana to work the side. Every one else had to be the beef at the base.

Gordon said, "Okay, come on. Push this bitch!"

We made progress, one step at a time, then two.

Lana challenged Gordon by asking, "Why does anything difficult for men get called, bitch? Do you guys always have to give a female reference to things if you can't control or understand them? If it's that negative to you, then why don't you call it something masculine or at least something neutral?"

Gordon replied, "We weren't referring to the piano, bitch! Why don't you get off your fuckin' Feminist high horse and stop reading sexist shit into everything you think that you hear? You know something Lana, the perfect woman would have your body and the brains of the inflatable variety."

Lana paused, wiped her brow and then said to Gordon, "Darling, the perfect man might have both your body and brains. But who needs to pay that price for perfection when a ten-dollar appliance and a set of D batteries allow a chance at intelligent conversation too."

Mel pointed to Gordon and laughed while Gordon smiled sheepishly. Then Gordon said, "Okay come on push this terrible thing!"

"Hey bitch, is that more to your liking?" asked Mel. He and Gordon seemed to have finally found a common ground of understanding, but in trying to break Lana's balls, they put themselves at risk of losing their own.

As hot as the banter got, Lana kept her cool. She rose above it by saying, "I find it to be amazing, we have six men involved in a common effort and it seems to be moving in the same direction. This truly makes me proud to be part of history in the making. If you don't mind a woman's perspective, the shorter of you two, squat down and push the bottom while the taller reaches above them and pushes from the top."

A voice from somewhere said, "She's right. Okay, at the count of three, push!"

The count of three saw the beast submit to the first inside flight. High fives were exchanged together with cheers and congratulations.

Was it the sound of one ball breaking when we heard, "Leave it to a man to light up a cigarette before it's over. It might be over for you but the piano has two more flights.

What is this some kind of macho ritual? Do you guys always celebrate the small gains in case you fail at the main effort?"

"Settle down troops! Turn this beast around and let's get lined up for the next flight. Save the bullshit for later," Gordon's sudden assumption of leadership was welcomed by nearly all. The sounds of pigeons cooing and tapping their feet on the skylight above became clearer with every step.

The exception cried out, "Ouch! Son of a bitch! Lower it back down one step. The fuckin' beast is pushing me through the wall. And I'm not one of your fuckin' troops either! Everything has to be in terms of warriors with you guys. Why can't you take on a project without behaving like a wolf pack? Okay, I'm clear. Now let's go for as many steps as we can."

As if the piano's sound board could speak, we heard a voice cry out, "You know, she's got something there. I hated the way we always got pushed into organize this, or organize that as kids. Join the fuckin' Cub Scouts, then the Boy Scouts, then all the sports teams your ass could handle. With all of this organized shit outside of the house, even our own fathers kept cramming some code of ethical warfare behavior down our throats at home. Like, 'Thou shalt not kill, of course unless it's Government sanctioned.' Or, 'We can bypass sin with a simple code of ethics'.

"Face it! We've been molded to become warriors from the day our fathers said, 'Good boy', when we hit the other kid back. No one ever marched off to war with a bayonet up his ass. Face it! Up until this decade, it's what men lived for." A black sleeve emerged from behind the piano as the usually quiet Freddy had spoken out.

Gordon replied, "Freddy my boy, I hope that you don't think you have a chance at Lana's drawers by sucking up to her like that. Someone's got a candle in the window for her already. All I know is that if our guys in 'Nam didn't have a code of behavior, we would have all gotten killed."

Lana was seeing six faces with the same look. She felt she could turn away any challenge. She zeroed in on Mel as the beast's nose was feeling the bridle, “The only reason anyone went to war to begin with was because of blind submission to a code of behavior for boys to follow and the profit motive. Hey, look at Mel all zip lipped and draped in his Marxist Doctrine. You talk about a code of behavior. What do you call it when a committee decides what you eat, when you sleep and even when you shit?”

Mel couldn't hold out any longer. He finally opened his mouth, “I think you call it any branch of the U.S. military. What's the fuckin' difference? If you can't write your own script, then you read someone else's. How many of us can stand alone? There has to be an authority that can underwrite the common good. If we all took a pledge to the welfare of one another, there would be no basis for our conflicts, personal or political.”

“Three more steps! Every one together! Let's go-go-go! I have the corner. Wait till I get under the end then lift it around. Okay, we're there! One more flight!”

When you walk up a flight of stairs, then you turn at the top and go up one more little step, it's no big deal until you try to navigate a six hundred pound piano around it. Our worst fear was realized. The top floor had one of those, just one, but that was more than enough.

“We can do this! Stop sucking on the corporate tit and put that fuckin' cigarette out, Danny. We need a breather, but not with that shit blowing in our faces,” Freddy said, having totally come to life. To show that he meant business he removed his customary black shirt. Of course this revealed a black t-shirt.

Flipping Danny's cigarette down his own stairway, Mark said, “There's a very basic problem with our conditioning as men. We're taught to be totally logical from day one. We ignore our feelings and rely on methodical logic to patch everything. We don't trust our feelings because tradition taught us that we have to be able to think our way through things. Once we make up our minds, there's no backing down. It's somewhere between what Freddy just said and something Danny once pointed out to me, 'In every movie ever made, there's always the hero with his code of honor saying, basically, to make up your mind and stick with it'. You know, we men don't even stop for directions if we're lost."

Lana rested on the piano in silence as she reflected on Mark's words. Gordon snapped, "What's the matter Lana, cat's got your tongue? I'm sorry. Mel, what's that other word for cat?"

Mel laughed with Gordon as they slapped five at Lana's expense. Lana responded to Mark's comments coolly while ignoring Gordon's wisecrack by saying, "You know Mark, that could explain why Moses spent forty years in the desert. He could part the sea, and then jot down a five thousand year code of behavior from God. But he couldn't ask some camel jockey for directions to the doorway of the Promised Land. Never mind ask a camel jockey, the last thing Moses would do would be to ask his wife her opinion."

Then she clapped her hands authoritatively and said, "Okay the break's over! Last flight. Now let's show this piano just who the animate objects are!"

With that call to arms and legs, we were mobilized. The initial few steps had become routine. The new world order awaited us at the top floor.

"Try to back it over on its end. We have to pivot and turn without going through the plaster. When we get it upright, set it on the stairwell, then we straight pick it around. First, everyone hold your position and gather some strength," I said, upon seeing our only way out of our latest lousy situation.

After my call for a rest, Danny said, "That shit that you said before sounds right on Mark. Like I'm one to talk, but maybe it's true. Us men put up our fists every time we feel anything threatening, just to show our shit! So like, maybe the World knows this and plays us. It's like they snap their fuckin' fingers and then use us as a battering ram."

I thought, "Wrong choice of words, Danny!"

Lana lit up like a lamp and blasted, "Phallic symbolism! There you go. Men's ultimate obsession: Fuck the rest of the world!"

"Shut the fuck up Lana; the guys are commiserating. You can't even cut us some slack when we're agreeing with your original point. I guess with chicks it's just all about winning no matter what," answered Gordon. Lana smiled and rolled her eyes back.

We began the last pick to lift the piano around what we saw as the last turn. What we didn't see coming was Gordon's awakened jungle fever suddenly turning on what seemed like his new comrade, Mel, "So tell me faggot! Was it a code of behavior or some other family tradition that your father shoved down your throat during your upbringing? Hey faggot, was that what turned your ass into a fuckin' chicken commie?"

The piano suddenly took on life as Mel exploded. Gordon went four inches into the plaster with the piano on his head and chest after Mel used it as a weapon.

"Get this thing off me!" Gordon screamed, "I can't breathe, help me!"

Emboldened by his rage, the awakened beast within Mel had declared itself, "No you can't breathe you fuckin' bastard, but you can scream like a baby! You don't ever fuckin' ask me about my father! Do you understand that, motherfucker?"

After Gordon nodded to the affirmative, Mel alone lifted the stair end of the piano around the turn with the strength of four. When we cleared the steps and were safely on the landing, Gordon ran toward Mel.

He came to a stop when Lana, with a burning Marlboro planted in her tooth-gap, went between them saying, "Boys, let's not ruin a perfectly beautiful experience by thinking that you have to do what's expected of men when challenged, okay? We all had a good time here today, okay? Look at what we did, the piano is moved. It's over."

She held her hands at each of the combatant's chests. They looked away from one another. Then she turned to the rest of us and said, facetiously we hoped, "Come on guys, let's take it back down the stairs and bring it up the right way!"

Lana smoked away while her breast lay exposed through her torn shirt. We all noticed her tattoo with its fist held high in defiance, but looked away out of respect, choosing only to share in her smile of our earned triumph. After we brought the remainder of Mark's belongings from the vans, he paid me triple what he had promised. I passed Mark's gratitude on proportionately to my stair-warriors.

They were ecstatic, except for one who said, "This is it? This is what I get for all the bullshit I had to put up with?"

Gordon looked at triple-plus of what I told him what he would get from the onset and added, "You can keep your moving gig, Kenny. This shit might be cool for you, but I think there's a better way out there for me, bro'. Later! I gotta check somethin' out." He shoved the money into his pack and headed in the direction of Intelligent John's mansion.

I turned my attention to the trophy that our brief alliance had earned and thought, "How can this beast, whose song is so sweet, seem to hold the cries and screams of movers before us and of those to come within it as it sits saying nothing, yet everything?" The piano began taking root as gravity staked its claim, the floor groaning in submission to its mass, awaiting any who would challenge it at rest.

JE

"What might a jailed, depraved Austrian corporal, when looking upon the blank pages of his unwritten book, envision for the world? In his solitude, was his pen held at the ready about to transcend the vacuum that had absorbed his cries? Did the words that would stain those pages grow from the abyss of the soul of a child long ignored?

"Would the world fulfill his demanding, weeping desperation by accepting his facade of twisted truths as men's new code of honor? Who would know then, that the space between his pen and the page it was about to meet, was the world's last chance? Are the ashes still settling from the scorched bodies of those who would oppose him? Are the embers of his thoughts kindling a code of behavior to come?

"What should we expect from a Universe, which tells of its very own creation as growing from the desperate stroking of a lone man's hand?"

Chapter Seventeen

Inspirations

"Kenny, do you know where Ones is?" The female essence of my universe asked as we met coincidentally on Seventh Avenue.

I answered facetiously, "And you an English teacher. Shouldn't that be where ones are? Her answer to me was preceded by the customary kick to the shins.

She laughed and said, "No you idiot! Ones is a club in the City. It's somewhere in lower Manhattan. Anyway, I'm supposed to meet my friend Sedona and some guy that she's seeing there tonight. Do you want to go?"

If two straight lines had been laid with the tiny black and white tiles on the floor of One Eleven Hudson Street, Sedona would have made a dollar sign of them as she staggered over to me saying, "You must be The Kenny Mover that Ann has told me all about."

"Close, but in Brooklyn it's Kenny the Mover." Her handshake deposited a 'Lude within my palm. Out of courtesy I accepted and I placed it in my pocket. She then reached into the crowd and reeled in her work in progress that was boning up on his frug moves in front of a gigantic speaker.

The all-too-apparent scars of a recently failed marriage traveled from the moist, unsure hand that I grasped, to the trembling voice introducing himself as Alex. His hairline receded back to a spot on his head where perhaps his thoughts of fidelity had been dashed by adolescence getting a second chance. Unfortunately for him, it was his childhood sweetheart who would relive her teens without him. Fate had chosen Sedona to comfort Alex along during his unintended self-rediscovery.

The bass sounds traveled through our ears only to meet at the point within our heads that powered our bodies to seek release on the laser and strobe-filled floor. Slow-to-die old habits caused my stomach to replace my pocket as the holder of the 'Lude. Other stimuli that I thought I had abandoned took refuge in my lungs.

Like marionettes suspended by the single string of a universal driving heartbeat, all became one with the music. Alex's exuberance in becoming one with the collective movement of the crowd perhaps blinded him to Sedona's crotch becoming one with the thrusting leg of a stranger.

The sweat of self-celebration covered Alex's body as he threw his head and hands to the lights above, while Sedona's face fell into a plate of hummus at the stranger's table.

"Sedona, are you all right!" Anya ran over to her friend and lifted her by the hair before she drowned in mashed chickpeas.

Sedona licked her lips clear and said, "Of course I'm okay! I'm okay now and I'll be okay all fuckin' week, Ann! Look at what 'what's his name' here gave me."

She chewed on both her words and the inside of her cheeks. A laugh reminiscent of The Wicked Witch of the West burst from Sedona as she revealed a bottle with a mix of 'Ludes and Tuinals in her fist.

"Sedona, you can hardly walk, never mind dance. Sit

back down!" Anya took charge of her friend as she coaxed her back to her seat. Then she asked her, "Why are you taking so many pills tonight, are you crazy?"

Sedona tried in vain to settle her conflicting eyeballs into the direction of Anya. Failing to do so, she looked at her sleeve and answered, "Ann, I take all these fuckin' pills for a very good reason."

Her eyes fluttered back as her face headed for the food below. The stranger quickly pulled his plate away. Sedona's face surrendered to the power of both barbiturates and gravity, finally hitting the table. She finished her sentence with her head rested on the stranger's fork. It had made four points perfectly clear, in her cheek. Being a trained physician's assistant, Sedona skillfully removed the fork. Leaning her head to the side, she immediately placed her vodka-filled glass over the wounds as an antiseptic.

The semi-inverted glass added some stability to her head while she continued her explanation, "As I was saying before you threw that food at me, I take the fuckin' pills because there's no fuckin' pot on the street! Doesn't everyone?"

She hung on to the stranger's sleeve. As if hailing a cab, she shouted, "Hey, Alex! Go get your fuckin' car. We're all going back to my place to hang out."

Even from my vantage point in the back seat of Alex's car, I couldn't figure out what the attraction in the front seat was of a snoring woman whose head flopped back and forth from Alex's shoulder to that of the stranger's. I could only wonder what extraordinary power a woman with scallions and dried hummus adorning her head could possess to make two suitors feel equally victorious while eating out of her hand, or hair.

The stranger held Sedona's foot and hand in his. She lay slung over his shoulder while the elevator whisked us to her apartment above, her white knuckles hiding the bottle in her other fist.

Alex finally found a parking space. He entered the apartment to find Sedona staggering around while wearing the stranger's leather jacket. Her lit cigarette fell from one hand, but she was not letting go of her pills with the other. The ever-polite and understanding Alex sat by helplessly, watching the show. Learning the unwritten rules of being single can be a rough experience.

In their own world of barbiturate euphoria, Sedona and the stranger stumbled and laughed into her bedroom. As the door was closing we could hear him ask her, "Do you come here often?"

She laughed and answered, "As often as it takes."

The smell of coffee and the sound of Alex struggling with a large bagel and a small toaster woke me. I raised my head from Anya's lap; it fell back down from the weight of the baggage of the traveling Quaalude show within it.

As much as euphoria and relaxation are methaqualone's immediate reward, irritability and fits of rage can be its consequences the morning after, especially if it's the bootleg variety. My next attempt to climb up from the floor was successful. I kissed the air near Anya's face softly, leaving her to sleep.

"Hey, bro', are you okay?" I asked Alex. As surely as his bagel met its fate in Alex's stomach, the cream cheese part found salvation in his mustache. I had to look away from him and wish that these two people would somehow choose more solid food.

"Kenny's your name, isn't it? Will you join me?" Alex grasped my hand with the two of his. His eyes were as bloody red as his mustache was creamy white.

He looked at the closed bedroom door and said meekly, "I can't really complain. I kind of met her the same way he just did. She gets so fucking stoned that she loses any connection with reality. It's only a fuck. I guess I can live with that. I'm sure she's fucked many before me."

He shook his head, smiled and said, "You know, even though I wasn't in the room with her, somehow I still got fucked." His brave-face smile revealed green chives sticking to his teeth.

The door to Sedona's room creaked open, and then creaked closed. The designer-jeans-and-silk-shirt-clad, fifty-dollar-haircut stranger exited that room and entered our conversation. The stranger then had the audacity to hold an unfilled coffee cup up to Alex. How many favors did this dude expect?

Although the stranger's legs were wrapped around the base of the chair, his foot seemed to be placed squarely on Alex's chest. I thought back to the parties at Arlene's. I looked at Anya sleeping peacefully on the living room floor. My fist clenched as I looked back at the stranger.

"Man, I slept like a fuckin' baby. You dudes are up early. I hope everyone slept well," said the stranger while his eye wandered across the room toward Anya.

I locked on to his gaping eyes with my stare. He quickly looked back toward Alex and said, "No hard feelings I hope, brother? It was just one of those things that happens."

How the fuck can someone who just crushes someone else's fragile self-esteem, declare no hard feelings? You're feeling devastated. He's feeling flush from recent orgasms, but he doesn't hold it against you. How generous! Alex smiled, showing his chives while patting his tormentor's shoulder gently, in submission.

"I need a joint! Hurry, someone roll a skinny! Who the fuck are you?" Sedona asked, squinting at the stranger.

After grabbing a pair of her glasses from the table, she said loudly and proudly for all to hear, "Wow, it's the Candy Man!"

She then began singing, "The Candy Man Can!" Alex looked away, realizing how he didn't.

Anya woke up hearing Sedona's outburst. She smiled and stretched, then let out a loud, "Good morning!" I brought coffee for both of us to the living room floor. Sedona joined us, followed by her harem.

We all sat on the floor around the coffee table while watching the remnants of Alex's food solidify to the hairs surrounding his mouth. Sedona looked at him and cried out, "Where's that fuckin' joint? Ain't nobody got no fuckin' ears?"

The stranger in the black jacket, with rolling paper in one hand, dumped a clump of pot from a little Kodak can with the other. Instead of handing the lit finished product across the table to Sedona, he reached behind Anya, leaving his arm on her shoulder as Sedona took the joint from his hand.

Anya shrugged with discomfort. I looked at the stranger and said softly, "Get your fuckin' arm off her."

The stranger looked at me defiantly as if seeking his next victory. I saw Alex sitting like an old tire with a nail in it while Sedona tickled him. I looked dead into the stranger's eye.

As the strychnine from the bootlegged 'Lude coursed through my body, I spoke out even more loudly stating, "I said get your fuckin' arm off of her!"

He tightened his mouth and lowered his brow in defiance to me. His arm moved slowly to constrict its hold on Anya, like a python securing its prey. My intuitive forces together with my post-Quaalude rage met at and by-passed my sense of self-control and they thus prevailed.

I could hear my own words, as if in the distance, "Get your motherf - - - - - -"

Before the " . . . ucking" part of the word could escape my mouth, my left hand snatched his throat and hoisted him up the wall. My right fist was chambered to my side awaiting the next impulse that would dispatch him through the plaster where he hung.

I stood there, with his neck in my hand. The throbbing of his jugular let me know that although this stranger was a lowlife, he was still a life after all.

My knees began to shake. I heard faint voices becoming increasingly louder, “Let him down! He's turning blue! Let go, Kenny! Let go of him, please! His tongue is popping out of his mouth!”

I dropped him. He began wheezing and coughing. I stood over him ready for his retaliation, but none came.

Sedona ran over and asked him, “Are you okay, Harvey? Can you breathe?”

I looked at the pitiful asshole and asked Sedona, “His name is Harvey? No shit? You did say Harvey, didn't you?” I began laughing almost uncontrollably.

Anya asked, “How can you be laughing after what you just did?”

I caught my breath enough to say, “Harvey Wall-banger! Get it? I just made a Harvey Wallbanger!” Alex immediately began laughing. Sedona tried to hold it back, but couldn't.

As the normal color of yellow returned to his being, Harvey Wallbanger turned to me enroute to the bathroom saying with the greatest conviction that an empty threat might evoke, “One phone call and you're dead!”

I replied by asking, “How can you dial a phone with a broken hand?”

Sedona was still hysterical with laughter. She grabbed the bottle of pills from the mantle and showed Wallbanger to the exit door. He left with a cream cheese bagel, with chives, stuck to his ass.

Anya whispered something to Sedona as I felt my jacket land on my chest. Sedona whispered back while shaking the pill bottle, “Ain't no big deal! I got these and a number to call for a refill.”

The sound of the floor sensors was the only break there would be to the silence during our elevator ride after leaving Sedona's. Soon, the streetlights haloed Anya's face. Her eyes swelled and reddened as she looked at me and then she looked away.

After we descended the subway stairs, at last she spoke, "Who are you to play God? If I felt that I was being assaulted, I would retaliate or ask you for help if I couldn't handle it! I don't need you or anyone to make my decisions for me. I appreciate your concern. But your response was inappropriate and brutal."

The sound of a train rushing through the tunnel, fortunately for me, muffled the first part of my answer, having to do with a code of chivalry and shit like that. Somewhere between guilt, embarrassment and a hangover from bad downers, stood I.

Between the trainman's indiscernible chatter over the broken loudspeaker I said, "Anya, it wasn't so much that some lowlife was touching you as it was the thought of him seeing you at his level. I'm really sorry that you're upset. Honestly, I wish that I could un-hit him, for your sake."

The train doors blasted open. Anya shouted into my ear, "That's not good enough, Kenny! How about if you control yourself and think before you rip someone's head off in my friend's apartment? Maybe you should control yourself for your own sake, okay?"

As passengers walked around us, entering and leaving the train, I said, "Anya, I truly love you. I never felt like this about anyone in my life. I accept full responsibility for my actions. There is no one else to blame but myself. I have to tell you something. Maybe you won't like it, but I just hope that you'll at least understand."

We landed on a seat as the train lurched ahead. I took a deep breath and said, "I was involved with someone quite a while ago. She and I would go to what amounted to Quaalude communion parties where couples dropped 'Ludes, then their drawers and then climbed around and ultimately into one another's bodies.

"I could never participate. The whole thing turned me off. When Wallbanger grabbed you, then looked at me like he did, I flashed back to those people and I just snapped.

I'm really sorry. I guess being in a relationship worth fighting for is a new experience for me."

Anya began to gently poke her fingers at my ribs. I began laughing. She pressed me against the train window and said, "Kenny, you're supposed to get flashbacks from acid, not Quaaludes. Our relationship isn't like that of those people. No one stands a chance with me, except you. I love you too and with love comes trust. If you love me, then you have to trust in me to take care of myself. Remember who I am to you. So hang up your loincloth and put away your club. Please don't ever do anything like that again."

The sound of the train's wheels, the sound of footsteps, the sound of opening and closing doors, melded with the passing tunnel lights and intermittent blackouts. All that remained constant was the kiss that lasted from upper Manhattan to The Bowery.

I promised to never attack anyone again. Beyond that, no other promises were needed between us. We each knew what the other felt and that was enough.

If a room has a door on either end, and if the door at the far end has the only bathroom in the entire apartment, then is this truly a room or is it yet another hallway? Whichever it was, it was not the hallway at Gordon's. Although Gordon and I had a workable day-to-day friendship, having a space at the commune kept it so.

I learned to live with the toilet-bound traffic at the commune that had become both my official residence and sanctuary. It became a necessary perch above the noises of distraction.

My space was in the rear of the apartment; the treetops touched the window. I could watch the aerial antics of the squirrels and smell the flowers from the gardens below. I acquired a mattress from a moving job. I surrounded it with my basics. The large cable reel served as a partitioning shield against intrusion and my trunk was a backrest. It was there that I could ponder my aggressive behavior in needed solitude, until of course someone had to use the bathroom.

I sat with my journal in hand thinking of the words that were spoken to me in Jersey City, by Avi. It seemed like an eternity ago when he said, "The warrior in us doesn't always need a war in order for him to surface. Sometimes a just cause will do."

I reflected upon my impulsive actions at Sedona's. On one hand, my perception and persona did behave within the moment as one. On the other hand, the timing was totally inappropriate. A warrior can act on a situation, but a defender should be asked.

JE

"Can a war rage within our selves? Is the enemy the part of ourselves that the World that would enslave us convinces us that we are? Does the warrior within see just cause when devastating any force that would challenge its sovereign? Does the sword finally fall when they see themselves as one?

"How far can I go in my accumulation of materials until I might see them and myself as indistinguishable? Is that which separates us, the one footstep that must stand ready to walk a new path should the present one be blocked by possessions? Is the hand that draws the dream to come, by way of the paper signs, prepared to erase it all should that step become necessary?"

"Louie sent me!" I said, feeling like I was reading a line in a Cagney movie to the guard at the Golem Van Lines lot in New Jersey. He held his hand up in a stop position. Louie, in fact, did send me to see his large moving van that was stuck in his friend's parking lot with a blown engine. The price was right, only five hundred bucks.

A video camera above turned, directing its attention toward me. There was a long moment of silence. The guard picked up a ringing phone. He nodded, and then said to me, "The Boss says go in. After you leave the lobby, walk down the long hall, the one with all the pictures. His office is at the end. Remember, don't touch nuthin'!"

Before I could open the door to the lobby, it buzzed and opened for me. The guard was right; I didn't have to touch nuthin'! I raised my finger to the inner door, it followed suit. Before me was a hall as long as a bowling alley. Where the hall began and the lobby ended, there was a large gold leaf frame surrounding a nearly life-size picture of a twenty-something boy wearing a cap and gown, seated behind the wheel of a new Ferrari.

The massive doors to the Boss's office grew closer while I slowly walked, marveling at the gallery at this moving company. I stopped at another portrait. The face was similar to the one near the lobby. The time period was further in the past, the arrogance less obvious. The car, a Continental.

As I walked along, the frames became less elegant and the portraits smaller. Two of the last three portraits were of men in overalls. One was holding the open door of a vintage tractor-trailer. The next picture revealed a small flatbed truck with three steamer trunks as its cargo. A large gray-haired man stood next to the driver, revealing only the words, . . . And Son, as his body blocked the surname.

I froze in my tracks upon seeing the very last photo. I imagined myself under a black velvet hood, pulling the lens cap and not having to say smile. The passion from the large young immigrant with his arm around his horse's head would have been diminished by that instruction. The open-backed wagon read: Professional Carter for Hire. Was the intense pride that beamed from him brought on by the vision of those to follow in his line? If it was, then lucky for him he couldn't look down the hall.

The scrutinizing eye of yet another camera nodded at me. The enormous doors opened. The Ferrari from the first portrait had evolved into a hand-carved, horseshoe-shaped desk revealing – The Boss. If he was twenty-eight, he was a day. Before him there was a control panel reminiscent of a scene from *Doctor No.* Above him was a bank of television sets showing every possible view of offices, warehouses and his surrounding property.

"So, you want to buy Louie's truck, huh?" he asked, leaning back into his command chair while placing his shiny alligator shoes on his desk. Do people think that by rolling a large cigar around their mouths at those before them, that all will sense their great power? Had they read their Freud, they might choose a toothpick.

He fiddled with his camera controls. While various parts of his empire flashed on and off the screens he said, "Louie came over here from Brooklyn last year to do a job for me. After he loaded up, POW! The fuckin' thing blew a piston. Louie always cries poverty over everything. He said he had no bread to fix it, so he walked away from the truck. The truck ain't that old. I own the title to it, so you can talk to me. All I want for the truck is what he owes me for storing it here. Here kid, check it out on the TV."

A full-size moving truck with a full-length picture of a greyhound came into view as he zoomed a camera along the parking lot. A Harry Chapin song came into my mind, "Take a Greyhound, It's a Dog of a Way to Get Around."

The side panels of this behemoth appeared to have been shot away by artillery fire. Where there wasn't a patch, there was a hole, where there wasn't either, one could soon appear. The outside didn't have any problems that some putty and paint could fix. That which lay beneath the hood however, needed a heart transplant.

What I had there was a potential traveling billboard where I would replicate my paper signs twenty feet long on its sides. All it had to do was travel up and down the streets of Park Slope while picking up and delivering furniture. Its message will create more solid chariots in the passage of time.

"Kenny, you seem like a smart boy. Listen to my idea for you."

Don't you just love it when a spoiled rich brat calls you, boy?

"You gotta fix the engine. This'll cost you maybe a grand. You gotta do the bodywork and paint, maybe letter it. That's another fifteen hundred, easy.

"Tell you what. I deliver the truck to you all painted and running. You drive it outta here and you're in business. All I do is hold back the title and a note for the costs." Somehow I anticipated his next words and pictured them on a sliding board to Hell called, All You Gotta Do Is . . .

He filled in the blanks and said, "All you gotta do is, work off the bill. In the meantime you build up your business out there in Brooklyn and make some bread from me, after expenses of course. How can you go wrong with a great offer like this?"

Visions of Lasco and Roger danced before me. I knew that the only way I could go wrong with this deal was to take it. The wagon in the old picture may be long gone. I saw the specter of the horse's severed head obscuring the horizon, its blood nourishing the barbed vines ensnaring me. My warrior within, forever bound.

While the jowls on the left side of his face accepted his cigar from the right I said, "Antny, tell you what. I'll pay you for it now, as is. You sign over the title to me while I'm here. I'll have the truck towed out in an hour to my engine guy in Brooklyn. I really look forward to having a personal hand in restoring it. Your offer about working for you is something I'd like to think over. Thank you for your confidence in my abilities."

As I shook his hand I could only think, "At what point during his life will Antny's name get the missing h and o? I'm sure the old man in the picture had calluses and a dream as I do. Would his nightmare be the false smile, bloated body and the very hand that I am now shaking?" Could there be no consolation to the founder, knowing that one can awaken from a nightmare?

"Hey buddy! You know there are plenty of junkyards within a mile of here. Why do you want to bury this piece of shit in Brooklyn? You got a family plot over there or somethin'?" asked the tow-truck driver.

I gave him the address of the repair facility. He answered, "Okay, now I get it. You gather up a bunch of truck parts, patch them into this corpse, haul it to the top of the hill and then pray for a lightning bolt to bring it to life. Hey kid, it does me good to finally meet someone who believes in miracles."

The tow truck drove off with my prize attached, leaving behind an oil puddle, a thing with bolts and three old furniture pads. I put the pads into my van and left.

My vision differed greatly from that of the driver's, as did my choice of allegory. The albatross that I envisioned above the derelict brought me some degree of affinity toward it. The same burning passion that drove me to choose starvation above the illusion of security compelled me to put every last dollar into that beached whale.

JE

"How is it possible that I have not advertised significantly more, yet the World's demand for my services has increased dramatically? Could it have anything to do with the fact that most of my new customers keep saying to me things like, 'You moved a few of my friends and they said you guys are the best.' Or, 'Everyone in the neighborhood uses you. Your name is everywhere!' Is the word of the paper signs echoing through the World and becoming a life force unto itself?

"If one views the Death Card as an end, it becomes just that. When it is viewed as the card of change, then the World lies before you. The Universe knows only change. So must I, being of the Universe. Essentially, change is all that will be left in my pocket after I pay for the resurrection of this sleeping chariot, but that's a good thing.

"Holding on to anything, especially money, will only weigh me down and my vision might move beyond me. Whatever brings me to my power position of holding nothing at all is that which gives me the power to be within the dream. I once felt, when backed into a corner, that I should feel grateful for the support. Now being in the corner is a place where I can kick down the walls to see the opportunities ahead."

"Captain Ahab be damned. Let's all go swim with the whale!"

The work on the beached whale, soon to be flagship, progressed unknown to my cohort of fellow mover-vagabonds of the street. The demand for services from my little enterprise not only exceeded my expectations but the ability of the VW and step-van to perform them.

Whether it was Bob Steele, Hoot Gibson or any of my other childhood cowboy heroes, when the old horse couldn't make the hills of the trails any more, it was time for the talk and the walk, through the pasture, toward the setting Sun.

Bob or Hoot would say, "Well, Old Paint!" I guess Paint's a better name than Old Wallpaper for a horse, "It's time to say adiós, my friend."

The next scene might roll up to a view of the clouds then a lone gunshot would be heard. If there weren't a broken leg or anything, we would just see Paint run slowly to a mare in waiting at the end of the field.

If only my arm could girdle the neck of the exhausted VW, I might have made a similar speech. Instead, I handed over the keys and title to the buyer. Keeping with my pledge to never liquidate what my father left me, the money would be recycled for growth toward the next vehicle. I pushed the little van down the street for the last time. It made its usual lurch as it started. I was sure its lurch was to bid, "Adiós, caballero."

As Fate would have it, from under the seat of the VW, I retrieved my Dad's jumper cables and his umbrella. Holding them, I thought back to when I stood on Seventh Avenue one rainy night so long ago as Dad drove off. I asked myself if I truly could ever walk away from the creation of people and machines his Chevy extended itself to. Was I alone in this, or would my ever-present silent partner forever have a say?

Cash in hand, it was onward to the Hertz lot. My next truck wasn't the size of the behemoth that was in the engine shop, but it was a truck nonetheless. In fact, it was a Corvette of trucks, small, fast and able to attack then slip away in wait of its next prey. It could also move three rooms of furniture and start without a push.

The truck would be the first vehicle to bear the name, Kenny the Mover, although only by way of a cardboard sign that was taped to each door. It declared itself as substance to the form that I could once only imagine.

At the same moment that the door to the dispatch office locked behind me, relieving his vision of the setting Sun, Zach said, "I figured you'd have that raggedy-ass hair hangin' down below your shoes judgin' by the last time I saw you here in Jersey City. How the fuck you been, Joe? Damn, you look like you been workin' out! I ain't never figured you to get so full of muscles fuckin' around on the streets like you been doin'."

Zach and I had a lot of high fives to slap. I walked into his private office and saw a seasoned man in charge with a new look of assuredness added to his already ominous presence. No one would dare to argue against his authority. As he had once managed to charge through a gang of militants, he continued his advance through the ranks of management and staked claim to his dignity. I was truly proud of Zach.

"Is that your little movin' van I see pulled up in Roger's driveway?" I nodded to the affirmative. "You really did change your name like you said. Damn, did Roger and Kevin get a look at you? Don't tell me you came to see me first."

"Zach, you're not giving me time to say shit. You're running your mouth so long you better stop to refill it with air before you implode. Yeah, I came to Jersey City to see you. I have nothing to say to those pigs upstairs.

"So tell me Zach, how are they treating you? Your office looks like it's the center of things around here."

Zach signaled silently for me to join him outside. His mouth had a grin that lacked only canary feathers. As soon as we were away from the building, he burst out laughing and said, "Man, you had them dumb ass motherfuckers figured out down to a peg. Every time they ask me about anything, I tell them everything. I give them every little detail like I'm reading it from a book. I let myself look like I'm giving them a story, but all my shit is true to the last word.

"Since the motherfuckers always got an angle, they assume I got one too. But they can't never figure mine 'cause they don't know truth even when it's bitin' their greedy asses. Joe, it's like you once said, they're so full of bullshit that they don't know truth when they hear it.

"They wind up leaving me alone to my shit. Whatever they think I know, I let them think that they know all of it. They know it's better to have me on their side, than against them because I got all the men under my control. I'm also in charge of all of the supplies and all the sub-contractors have to report to me."

Zach was beaming with pride over his rise to power and the consolidation of it. One thing was certain, knowing Zach; he would never have to look back at an ill-gotten dollar. As much as his employers didn't deserve it, they were getting total honesty from Zach. Since his secrets of power were disclosed, we headed back to the building. We were walking through the supply room when I saw a large padlock on my old office door.

I turned to Zach and asked, "What's the big deal now that they keep my old office locked like Fort Knox? The last time I saw it there were only mop heads and buffing pads in there."

Quickly, we turned our heads upon hearing banging, rattling and clicking sounds interspersed with cursing and pounding. As suddenly as the noises began, they stopped. Zach pointed to the light peeking through the half-open door to the parking lot. The force of an oversize shoe swung the door fully open. The light from the setting Sun overwhelmed that of the single bulb in the hall. A large form standing in the doorway cast a shadow reminiscent of the infamous zoot suit, Panama hat, keychain and all.

As if on cue, Isaac Hayes' theme from the movie, "Shaft", played on Zach's radio. The ominous figure in the doorway spoke, "Motherfuckin' key! Spray some shit in that lock, Zach. It's all fucked up again."

Zach shook his head back and forth in what seemed like routine disbelief while saying, "The hardest part of my job is the damn fool making all that fuckin' noise. He can figure a way to put his fat ass in a big chair and fuck up jobs right and left, but he can never figure how to get his key outta the door. I oughta spray this shit in his motherfuckin' head, maybe it can loosen up some common sense!"

In answer to the astonishment pouring from my open mouth, Zach explained, "Mister Kevin made some new companies after you split and put some people, that you just might know, in as the so-called owners. Now they think that they're King Shit, 'specially this prize package comin' in now."

The door closed. A silk-suited Superfly strutted his bloated form into what was once my office. He pitched his sweat-stained Panama to the waiting hat rack while putting the phone to his ear and asking for his messages. Sinking into his executive chair and looking down the barrel of his cigar, he wondered who the white boy might be sitting across from him with folded arms.

I smiled as he tried to place me. He asked, "May I help you? Hey, ya'll work down at the Federal Building for me, don't you?"

I slowly shook my head, no.

Again, he asked, "Man, you look familiar! Where I seen you before, boy?"

The more I sat there shaking my head no, the more he began to resemble the little puffing engine from upstairs. I asked him, "Don't tell me you're in charge of riot control in that building, wherever it is. Because if you do, then I'll have to ask which side of the riot your ass is on."

I maintained my posture, waiting for him to distinguish me from my changes, and then I said, "Maybe if you break that Chivas Regal bottle on your desk and hold a shard of glass to my neck, the face might become recognizable."

He leaned back in his leather lounger and said, "Motherfucker! Joe! What the fuck you doing here? I heard you been flying them little airplanes again somewhere in the Caribbean. Okay, fill me in, motherfucker. What's new and excitin'?"

A black, red and green banner hung over Jamal's head. It was the very same place my poster of winged horses and mythical warriors upon their backs served as my gateway to my own revolution.

Like a parade balloon, decked out for show, sat the once-proud voice of liberation. I sat and asked myself, "Where was the inspired militant that once wanted nothing but to sever the hands that choked his people? Did he lead his army in revolt that November night to show the way, or just to get his way?"

I held no malice toward him for wanting to begin the festivities of his revolution that night with my decapitation, since he had sparked my own in the process. As I looked at him, I could only wonder, "Did the fires of righteous rage and indignation that he had threatened us with find their kindling from his forsaken principles?"

There was no longer a reason to keep our chance meeting in Brooklyn a secret, as if there were in the first place. I knew it would serve as the perfect segue to learn why all the changes.

I said, "Jamal, what's new with me is nothing. What's new with you is truly revolutionary. The last time I saw you, you were running down a flight of stairs in Crown Heights not wanting to be mixed up in some bullshit. Now it looks like you stepped in it."

His overfed cheeks hosted a surprised smile. He slapped his desk and said, "I thought that the dude with Kanika looked like you! Shit, 'cause it was you, finally gettin' some brown sugar. Why didn't you tell me it was you, motherfucker? We coulda' hung out, man. You were a skinny-ass, hairy little white boy. Look at you now."

"I'm still a white boy, maybe my ass got a little bigger. But you have to tell me why you're sitting in your own office, calling upstairs for messages. Don't tell me that Roger became a Muslim and made you king."

By the changed look in his eyes, Jamal saw truth in my jest. He said, "I guess I owe you thanks in two different ways. First, after you began putting Brothers in charge of some stores, the pigs upstairs must have realized that the Brothers could also run businesses. The Berias been losing on bids for jobs to minority companies because of black preference for too long. The idea came to them to join what they couldn't beat. Kevin and me put a company together. Now we got two contracts. I got thirty of my people in that Federal building downtown alone."

I looked through his shiny black-and-white saddle shoes lying across my old desk as he continued blowing his horn, "Hey, man, like I'm not stupid. I know he's gettin' around the whole Affirmative Action thing with us frontin' the company. But who really gives a shit? He gets fat! We gets fat! And I gets me that funky new hat!"

He was right. He was getting fat. I never agreed much with Jamal, but as I looked into the eyes of the person who set my life's change in motion, I saw nothing but Roger masked in blackface. I wondered who sold the pigs upstairs on the idea that made them realize that the Brothers could make them boldly go where no other white man had gone before.

"I see you smoke the same smuggled Cubans that Roger did," Jamal just laughed and straightened the picture of his kids.

He re-lit his cigar and said through a cloud of smoke, "Brooklyn gave you the eyes that you must have overlooked while you were trying to set the slaves free here. You know it ain't too late, they miss you. You could jump back in and make a ton of money."

"I'd rather hear about the other way that you said I helped you," I answered.

"Joe, y'all ain't gonna believe this!" Jamal pointed to his banner and continued, "You left a poster right here on this wall. Every time I passed your old office, I stopped and looked at the picture. It made me wonder about what was going on in your crazy-ass head when you started goin' through your changes.

"I asked myself, what the fuck made a dude hang a picture of soldiers riding flying horses, and what the fuck made him keep staring at it? Then it hit me . . . "

He put his feet on the floor, leaned toward me and said, " . . . After they set you up to make the Brothers hate you with the Eddie thing at unemployment, you musta' seen yourself as tied up like the horse while the others ran off free with the loot. Roger took all the credit for the changes that you made, and all you got was fired! Then you figured you could split and get your own shit together and put it all in your own pocket."

I kept nodding my head, as if to say, go on. He needed no encouragement, "You saw it your way right here from this chair. But I was seeing it different from the hallway. I saw the one guy that stayed back, sitting on the horse, as not seeing the fuckin' opportunities that were growing beneath his feet and reaching out for him. The dude's head was in the clouds and not on his shoulders. All he been seein' was a bunch of silly-ass heroics resulting in nuthin' 'cept ashes and jail time.

"I figured, instead of crying about not being able to get shit with the radicals and without a nickel to feed my kids after all the bullshit, I would make my own Heaven right here on Earth."

He peeked into the parking lot and added, "Judging by that moving truck I see outside, I kinda did like you did, right? Oh yeah, now I get it, Kenny! You said that Kenny was your name back at the commune. The name on the truck is Kenny. Y'all ain't called Joe no more. Alright, so now you're Kenny."

He rubbed my head congratulations and pointed his thumb in the direction of Brooklyn. Then he said, "I left the poster with Kanika back at the commune. She sees it a lot different than we did. To her, it's about all men trying to leave the world with the big old mess they made of it. Like she said, 'Mother Earth is reaching out and strangling them with the barbed tentacles from the seeds that they have sewn with their brutal domination and deceptions.' How can that commie bitch read shit like that into a picture with the real story bein' so fuckin' obvious?"

"Tell me, Jamal, did Kevin and Roger think that the poster was a page from a floor wax supplier's calendar?"

Jamal once kindled a flame within me when he said, "You're going to know what it is to be black! 'Cause you're going to burn!" I will never truly know what it is to be black. I cannot change the pigment of my skin. But I truly know what it is to be marginalized by the pre-opinionation of those who may never know anything at all.

I had lived to see the torch grow cold in Jamal's hand. Yet the words that he both threatened and inspired me with set the fire of my passion to create the ashes from which my phoenix would rise.

I wondered, "Will he climb the rotted rungs up the ladder of his own ignorance, only to take it on the chin over and over during his inevitable descent? Will the flames of his abandoned rhetoric return to consume him? Will he, one day, see his reflection in the glass before it finds his throat?"

One fool couldn't pull a key from a door while another dumb-ass fool couldn't keep his hand from his horn. After moving my truck from blocking the driveway, I saw my two reflections grow larger in Kevin's mirrored glasses while I leaned on his latest Caddy's roof and asked him if all he had to say to an old friend was beep.

After recognizing me, Kevin's answers melded indistinguishably with the roar of a passing jet. When he spoke, I felt his sales pitch reaching for an opening to find a place where he imagined my vulnerabilities might be. He might have saved his breath if he knew that my mind had closed itself to his words of manipulation. He may not have reached out to shake if he knew that I visualized him and Jamal on a little puppet stage with their tangled strings reaching skyward to Roger's hand.

Turning away from Kevin's perfunctory smile and outstretched arm, I thought, "A handshake away from enslavement; a footstep away from freedom."

The three of them had acted out their all-too-comic tragedy for all of us assembled before them. I saw the curtain of this play close before me. I guess one doesn't always have to see a show for a second time to realize why one walked out from the first.

I wondered, "Here I am, thinking that I'm turning a page on the book of my own life only to see the back of the cover.

Who might I have become to realize, the book may have been another's?"

Jamal never opened my throat as he once threatened to. His righteous rage of the past inadvertently opened the door to my own and the emergence of a soul locked in a cage of ignorance and unchallenged values. I must be forever beholden to him for the wayside upon which I had fallen and toward which I drove.

'Soldiers & Sailor's Arch' at the Grand Army Plaza

Photo by J.K. Savoy

Chapter Eighteen

Resolutions

When your canvas is New York, when your brush strokes are tire tracks, when the seal of your name is stamped about for all to see, there comes a time to step back from the picture for some much-needed perspective. When viewing a picture from the crowd's perspective, the voice of a critic might be heard. I interviewed Bob the Cab for a driver's job. Of course, just by showing up at The Economy, he passed the interview.

While the neighborhood cheered my masterpiece, Bob would be far more candid in his commentary, "There are two people that I know of in this neighborhood who had the fuckin' balls to hold their middle fingers up to the establishment and walk away with less than shit. Both of us are sitting at this booth. So don't bullshit me, Kenny. How the fuck do you expect to hang on to the ass end of this rocket that you launched and not get carried away with it?"

I found myself allowing his reactions to my words lending support to my own thoughts. Maybe like in Alcoholics Anonymous, where only a drunk can truly understand and give counsel to another drunk, only one corporate dropout is qualified to provide perspective to another.

I brought both of us up to speed by saying, "Just as strongly as I once needed to taste desperation, Bob, now I have to move in the opposite direction. It's as if my reality is following a rhythm of first tightening and then expansion. Resistance to these forces is futile. I can only go along and grow from the experience."

Bob nursed his coffee while listening intently as I went on, "When I wore my slave-suit and then chose to shed it, I was driven into a cocoon where I transformed. Now I feel an explosion of energy from within. Ideas overwhelm my senses and I find myself totally involved in their manifestation. When I complete any of them, I find that they are only a step toward the next one. Bob, I feel totally possessed but not by anything other than my burgeoning true self.

"If you look at me you see probably the same jeans that I wore when I lived on the street. Even these days, I sleep in a hallway at the Garfield Place commune. Any money that I spend on myself is purely for life support. I see myself only as a conduit through which ideas come and things develop."

"Kenny, do you mean to tell me that you can sit on this pressure cooker and contain it before it explodes or absorbs you?"

I knew he understood. My own words lifted any obscuration of my perspective when I added,"You must realize, Bob, the only property that I admit to is my journal where I maintain a daily record of my own transformation, my trunk where what clothes and little junk I can't shed are kept. Oh yeah, and that large cable reel that I call my birthday cake. That was the wood sculpture that I told you I created the day I broke out.

"Every day I go back to visit them as if they are the remaining shells of the egg from which I emerged. I know that what I've become draws from the experiences that I lived through that they now represent. Bob, the world might recognize what I'm doing as a business, but I can't say that I share that perception."

Bob stopped in half-slurp of his coffee and he asked, "Kenny, if you can't think of your business as a business, then what the fuck is it to you?"

While he gathered the remains of the slurp, I explained, "To me this whole thing is a journey of passion. Whatever I do is done not with a dollars-and-cents purpose, but from a romantic motivation. I never in my life saw myself as being capable of making a rational business decision. My entire vision of this creation is emotionally driven.

"In order for me to avoid spread sheets and other details, my every move must be an expression of my pure instinct. At that level I know that what I do will succeed, since success is measured by elevating my perception to the next level. I must overwhelm the public with all advertising possibilities available to me with my message in order to overwhelm my expenses with revenue. If I don't succeed in this creativity, I will be placed in a position of having to make mundane business decisions. Then I'll fail.

"Business and particularly seeing myself as a business person is a fundamental conflict within my character. If I were reduced to becoming what I despise, that being a corporatist, it might cause me to abandon everything again."

Bob held his cup up to me. It might have contained coffee, but I knew it was as a toast when he said, "Only the bearer of a similar wound can truly know your pain. Tell me, maybe you see the whole citywide experience of Kenny the Mover as performance art, since you don't really see it as a business?"

"Yeah Bob, that sounds like a nice name for it. You know the whole thing began with an inspiration from "Looney Toons". Every time I draw the next truck that I need, I think of how when a cartoon character was trapped he would draw a getaway car. When I'm successful at that level, then comes my release for sculpting. In this case I carve the trucks from scrap."

"Kenny, is there a downside to this?"

"Perhaps, Bob. I do believe that my creative writing has ceased, unless I consider works such as, Undertaker for the Living or, Moving You into the Twenty-First Century and the many variations of, Moving? Call Kenny! such as, Moving, call Kenny! or Moving-Call Kenny.

"Seriously, above all, there is the constant challenge to my understanding of things being merely tools for me to grow from in order to acquire additional tools. If I feel any of the objects that I gather taking on more importance than those personal things that I mentioned, then at an impulse, I have to walk away and never look back. Otherwise I might become a slave to my own creation."

Bob interlocked his fingers and slowly cracked his knuckles while saying, "You are one fucked-up dude. But Kenny, I mean it in a good way. What you're doing makes me think of a blindfolded high-wire cyclist, juggling flaming knives without a net. Just one thing dude, don't stop and take a bow mid-act to please the crowd."

I knew that Bob understood my motivation enough for me to read a little of his own self in his next question, "You mean to tell me that every penny that comes across your hand goes right back toward future growth? It's difficult to imagine how any human can resist the pure seduction of power."

He pointed to a car across the street and said, "There's got to come a time when you're going to feel all full of yourself and you'll go out and buy a big-ass Caddy like that one. Then you'll put your diamond-ringed middle finger up to the world that you knew or you'll become a pig and wallow in the profit process. If you become immersed in your own process of expression, how will you be able to know whether or not it's consuming you?"

"Tell you what, Bob. If I ever buy a Caddy, take it and me for a safety check."

I walked away from the restaurant feeling as if I had just had an attitude alignment. I thought, "Success was measured at September's by its very failure. My perception was elevated by that enterprise's descent to rubble and a much-needed participation in what could only be remembered as pure Theater of The Absurd.

"How would I, back then, perceive that which I do now? Are they so different from one another, except for the fact that September's Child's end was the sole purpose right from its beginning? Am I setting in motion another project when at a time of my choosing, I will detonate my masterpiece in public view, laugh and then walk away?"

As I looked down the hill from Seventh Avenue, I saw a group of people walking with posters saying, Save the Union Street Firehouse! The Budget Cuts Will Kill Us! Looking through the ever-moving circle of protest signs, I finally saw the step van that I waited for coming up the hill. When it stopped in front of me, I saw that every inch of the truck had been covered with graffiti.

Mel jumped from the van and handed me his week's revenue. He shrieked at me with the greatest of indignation, "Those motherfucking pigs! The goddamn bastards! How can they do this to me?"

I looked the truck over and said, "If you parked in the fuckin' lot that we're paying for on Third Avenue, maybe the guard would have stopped them."

He looked puzzled for one moment, pensive for another and then declared dismissively, "Oh that! Don't you think that it looks like the 'Peoples Truck'? It has the pure expression of the Proletariat. The tags and pictures are speaking to the masses saying, 'Let our voices be seen and our message heard'!"

Descending from his romp of lightheartedness, he added, "But that's not our problem. This is."

He held three tickets for storing a commercial vehicle on city streets overnight. After I took the revenue and receipts from his pillow couch deliveries, we went into The Economy and sat at a booth. Mel had the innocent expression of a child who had just broken his toy and handed the pieces over to Daddy for repair or replacement.

With the unwanted scepter of authority showing itself in my unwilling hand, justice was meted out, "Why didn't you park at the lot on Third Avenue as we agreed?"

Mel looked confused. He answered with his usual loud self-righteousness, "After I hump people's shit upstairs all day and night, I'm fucking tired, so I parked on the street! What's the big deal? It's a long walk up the hill."

I hate being placed in the Solomon position for fear of halving the baby sideways instead of down the middle, leaving someone with the ass end of the issue. Solomon the King had the luxury of forcing others to choose by the mere suggestion of the act.

Kenny the Mover's only choice was acting with force, "Here's your sixty percent of the money, less the cost of the tickets. Since my step van is now a 'People's Truck' then let the people clean it. And in this task, you shall lead them."

Mel's faced reddened with rage, he slammed his fist on the counter and screamed, "Kenny, you've become a goddamn capitalistic pig! How can you take what I earned and shove it in your own pocket while you force me to accept less? You've changed! As soon as you have a taste of power, you cut the worker's heads off and post them as a threat to others." Mel put his face in his hands. For a moment his hands parted so he could peek out to see our reactions.

While he trembled and panted like a dog, Danny pulled Mel's hands away and said, "Cut the shit, Mel! Kenny rented a space in the lot for you and you're too fuckin' lazy to use it. And stop that communism for convenience bullshit. It's bad enough that I have to hear your ranting about social injustice and the exploitation of the working class, then you have the fuckin' balls to cop the whole tip and short me for a half-hour every day. Bro', just because I'm always stoned or drunk doesn't make me stupid."

Until then Mel had thought Danny to be brilliant, possibly because he would only talk about great scenes from great movies or just sit silently in the truck and never disagree with Mel's unending tirades.

Mel looked at me and said, "Give me my schedule, I'm out of here!"

Then he looked to Danny saying, "Finish your coffee, traitor. I'll be in the truck."

Mel left Danny to shoving a crumb bun into his beard while Bessie put his coffee into a container. Danny grabbed my arm and said, "Fuck him and the horseshit he rode in on! This is the same attitude and gratitude that made his old man cut him off last week. He can hardly maintain his tuition, never mind his apartment. It's about time he grows up. Kenny, don't let him get to you because you've only been fair to him. Okay, let me go and join Mel on his daily pillow fight with the pigs of Manhattan. Good-bye."

How can fate deal me a double detriment then in the next instance lay out the red carpet to my hopes and dreams? The phone company called me to tell me that a local number became available with four sevens. I could call forward it over to my answering service's number that I had been using. The only catch was that I must have a residence in which to place it.

As much as I loved the Garfield commune, my writing had much too many subliminal references to toilet flushing. First, I would hear the door creak open followed by, "Excuse me if I step over you." Whether I excused them or not, they would then drag their feet across my ear as I tried to sleep. There had to be an alternative to wearing a football helmet to bed. Who knows where the vacancies are better than a mover?

A small garden apartment had become available to me at the same amount as the cost-share for the hallway at the Garfield commune. I would ordinarily reject the notion of exposing myself to such decadent luxury. The usual justification as a tool toward growth and the need for privacy were overshadowed by an odd sensation that allowed no room for argument, like the feeling I got from the First Street store, I belonged there. I complied with the latter.

The smaller area adjoining the small living area was once the pantry for the Luden Brothers. The less small space had been their kitchen. The mansion was their town house where they and their families lived while the brothers would attend to the coughing needs of America. The entire structure had been chopped up into half-floor studios and one-bedroom apartments over the years.

This food preparation room and adjoining pantry were my austere living space and the world headquarters for Kenny the Mover. My basics quickly settled into their new locations surrounding my mattress in the pantry area. I kept only the business phone and my schedule book in the larger space. Although the entire apartment was at my disposal, I could not extend my personal boundary beyond the pantry line.

The beeper sounds, and I call the answering service. They then announce how either a great opportunity has happened my way or a great load of shit has fallen upon my head, the details all unknown to me until I began the calling process.

The great opportunity was for me to replace my driver, Barfin' Billy, who was puking all over the truck and the customer's hallway. Of course, I was the replacement. I had to meet Anya at eight o'clock that night. I thought that the job would be a snap. I still had most of the day to get the goods unloaded and return on time. The great load of shit was the monster piano resting on the landing. The ninety-nine-degree temperature was the impetus for the unforeseeable adventure ahead for Fireman George and me.

I, being the place where the buck stopped, learned to quickly change from one task to another, accomplishing one then reverting to the previous while always prepared to accept the unexpected.

The thick hot air rushed across our sweat-drenched clothing as we exited the truck at the destination apartment house on upper Broadway, near One Hundred Eighth Street.

"Yo, that thermometer over there says one hundred and three. Must be a mistake, it feels like a hundred and ten!" said George who was accustomed to rushing into buildings under far hotter conditions than that of mere outside air temperature. We were to have the luxury of a cool basement and our own chauffeur-driven elevator, which would rise to the intense blazing heat above.

Boxes of books, chair legs, folded carpets, and a mattress that bore the scars of years of missed bathroom opportunities formed the mosaic that girdled our contorted bodies. We seemed locked in a freeze frame within the cage that was the elevator.

"If I can only move my fuckin' arm, I'd push the button an' git us to the fourth floor!" said Al, the elevator operator who was also the building's super. He laughed loudly while he methodically closed the cage door to the elevator with his knee.

As soon as he succeeded, the cage flew back open to the sound of, "Hey, man, I need a roll of tape! You got none down by the supply cabinet."

The super looked at his young assistant and said, "You be on your stupid-ass way! Can't you see that I got a shit load of shit layin' all over my motherfuckin' face? The last thing I need is your sorry ass fuckin' with the elevator door."

As quickly as Al could close the door, it reopened from the assistant's persevering hand. The kid reiterated, "Man, you don't fuckin' understand! The 'lectric be fluttering and I need the tape when I go fix them bare wires in the hall that you said looked bad."

The argument went back and forth with the door's position determining who the speaker was. Having had enough, I reached for the assistant's hand. Just as I grabbed it and prepared my "get the fuck outta here speech", the entire basement went pitch-black, including the elevator.

Al shined a flashlight into the kid's eyes and said, "You see what did, you stupid motherfucker? You done shorted out the elevator and the lights with all your bullshittin' with the door!"

We walked down the hall toward the light of day. The kid opened the door to the street and said with a humble resolve, "Shiiit, man, I done fucked up all the traffic lights and big 'lectric clock next door too! I told you to fix them fucked-up wires, Al. Now you can blame your own sorry ass."

The neighborhood was filled with people running in every direction. A car raced along the street. As if aimed, it crashed through the gates of an appliance store. A crowd assembled like pieces of mercury forming a mass and followed the Buick battering ram inside. As quickly as one person went in, another ran out. They were carrying air conditioners, televisions, washing machines and everything that wasn't nailed down. If it was nailed down, it was soon ripped from the walls and floors.

We secured the rest of the load into the basement hallway. Al was slapping his assistant up and down while yelling, "You see what your dumb-ass did?"

Our customer shed a little light, at least on the situation by saying, "The whole city has gone dead." Both Al and his helper froze in their blank stares at one another upon hearing the extent of the power failure.

The customer told us, "You can't even get radio stations on the portable. I have the emergency frequency on. You guys better get back to Brooklyn as best you can, right now." Then he showed some real class, "Here, Kenny, take this money for what you guys did today. Call me tomorrow, if there is one, or as soon as you can and we'll worry about the rest of the job then."

My first thoughts were of Anya who would be waiting for me at eight o'clock. I thought, “Where is she now? Did she take the subway? Is she stranded in a worse condition than that which Fate's hand, in the form of Al's assistant, had just saved us from? I have no idea what lies ahead of us as we try to get home. Shit! If the rest of the city is anything like this, there's no telling when I might get back to Brooklyn where I'll at least know where she is or isn't.”

I tried calling her from at least five different phones. Every phone played the same message, “I'm sorry, all of the circuits are busy. Please try your call again.”

“Cool guy!” said George as he stuffed a big tip in his pocket.

We headed toward the truck, dancing our way through the mass of humanity that was accumulating on the street from the walls of buildings surrounding us. They followed the lead of others, picking up debris from the ground, throwing it at windows, creating more in the process. Then, like ants in search of sugar piles, the people poured into the breached storefronts, carrying loot from the shops along Broadway and back to their lightless apartments.

The city became an incessant roar of human voices interspersed by a distorted symphony of car horns as massive gridlock choked the streets. The already budget-thinned ranks of New York's Finest tried in vain to control the pandemonium of traffic, never mind the anarchy that had become New York. The denial of electricity to The Big Apple was tantamount to the absence of gravity to the Earth itself.

Was the bankrupt Gotham without postage never mind payment for its utilities? Chaos would be the order of the day as it would power the World's Capitol in its self-consumption.

“I'm sorry; all of the circuits are busy. Please try your call again.” So I did try again and again only to get the same recording. I jumped back into my oven of a truck and noticed that the radiator gauge showed that it was beginning to overheat. I knew there was no leaving the truck anywhere in the mayhem. We had to go on.

While I agonized over the absence of a phone system, and tried to remain positive regarding Anya's safety, George was as laid back as anyone could be. He knew that this anarchic insanity was a once-in-a-lifetime event in New York, and he was taking it all in.

The next few phones that I tried were stone dead. The temperature indicator on the dashboard was creeping upward. Signs for The Manhattan Bridge began to appear.

"Kenny, we gotta hire that dude! He can run like a halfback at the same time he can carry a sofa. Put that brother on a set of stairs and he can empty the whole truck while we sip lemonade," said George as we watched a couch with legs turn the corner.

While riot conditions and looting prevailed in upper Manhattan, the streets of Greenwich Village filled with its inhabitants and became one massive carnival. The throngs of people slowly separated before us, allowing passage.

As we crawled along, George reflected to me, "You know if that kid didn't need that tape, we might be between floors in that elevator right now with your truck visiting every store on the block." How quickly an obstacle becomes a path in a momentary change of perception.

The normally loud banging within my engine's walls was drowned out by the ever-growing din of human voices and sirens that echoed from the canyons of New York. We made our way through the madness of a city unplugged. The ghostly towers of Manhattan, framed by the bridge's steel skeleton, faded in my rear-view mirrors while Flatbush Avenue lay in our path. The gentle slope of First Street challenged my steaming truck as the banging of the engine became more ominous.

The cars in front of us came to a stop. George jumped from the truck and ran to his crib two buildings down from the renovated store that was formerly September's Child. I

Empire State Building and Manhattan Bridge

Photo by J.K. Savoy

sat on the little step in front of the store and lit a cigarette while I waited for George to bring me some engine coolant from his basement.

"I'm sorry; all of the circuits are busy. Please try your call again." was heard on the street phone at the corner.

After pouring the precious coolant into the thirsty radiator, I jumped back into the truck, hoping to make my way to Anya's. The traffic along First Street had become one enormous gridlock with that of Seventh Avenue. If it weren't for the fact that my truck was in the middle of the street, I would have run there. Since I couldn't go anywhere, I walked back to the tiny store. Once more I sat at its doorway, looking to the sky.

What was once the store that drew me to it like a magnet seemed somehow void of its mysterious aura. I listened to the sounds of the streets and tried to focus on better things. The Moon had risen and broken through the clouds above the buildings in the direction of Anya's apartment. Although worried, deep down, I felt that all was well with her. The more subdued low roar of humanity of Brooklyn seemed almost soothing, in comparison to the thunderous turmoil of Manhattan's darkest day turned night.

The commotion of Park Slope, albeit low-key, was interrupted by the shrill chirping of a shopping cart's wheel, the wind blowing it into the school's fence across the street from where I sat.

"Could it be 'Lung's home on wheels?" I thought. No sooner than this registered in my mind, I saw a heap of blankets and rags ten feet from the cart. Atop the heap were 'Lung's trademarked, urine-soaked plaid pants. Looking closer at the heap, almost indistinguishable from the rags, I saw his steel-gray bearded face. His eyes held an eternally fixed stare at the store's hatch. I waited for him to blink, he didn't.

The street darkened as its only light, the Moon, became covered by the passing clouds. It was soon supplanted by numerous, red rotating lights from the patrol cars, the reason for the gridlock. Before I could get up to see if 'Lung was really dead, the two police officers that once visited September's arrived at his side.

An officer's voice echoed from the school wall as he reported over his radio, "It's just a dead vagrant." In the pulsating red glow from the patrol car's lights I saw the other cop lower 'Lung's eyelids and then place one of the raggedy blankets over the mysterious derelict's body.

An ambulance soon arrived driving along the sidewalk without a siren. The para-medics rolled out a wheeled stretcher and lifted 'Lung from his sepulcher of rags. The cops and the young ambulance driver talked casually with one another, not noticing that 'Lung's right arm fell from his chest. The red flashing lights reflected on 'Lung's ghostly white hand. A dead finger pointed to the dead issue of September's Child's door.

I ground out my cigarette on the street that we had shared and looked at the trap door that 'Lung pointed to for the last time. Whatever held him to this place, even in death, had lost its hold on me in life. The compelling force, from what I always thought of as Brooklynite, seemed to have led me there to an open door where I found my questions. Those questions had evoked but one answer. Finding Anya was all that ever mattered. I looked up the hill toward her apartment. I jumped into the truck and drove as the traffic jam became as clear as my intentions.

The flickering flame of a lone candle from Anya's apartment window shined like a guiding light, telling me that she was safe at home. I left my truck in the middle of her street as I charged through her building's door and ran up the stairs to her apartment.

Her face glowed from the radiance of a Moonbeam, shining through her window. The flame of the candle that was her study light reflected in her deep blue eyes. At that moment I knew that all that I had been drawn to since I abandoned my other life was meant to take me there, to her, forever.

We answered one another's hours of hopes and fears as we met and embraced. I felt as if I had run the gauntlet or lived the Journey of Ulysses, my only objective being to hold her and to be held. We looked deeply into one another's eyes and I thought, "Home was never The Brooklynite. It was anywhere a moment like this might be."

Could the words of a political system that I despised create a stronger bond between us than what we truly felt from within? Could the Universe's own harmony through a woman and man, united by a mutual realization of eternal dedication, be of a greater sanction if by a magistrate's order? Might it only be demeaned by the same set of laws that conversely endorse separation? Our love would stand the test of time. But unless there was something in writing, it would not survive the test of Anya's parents.

The city returned from the darkness of its turmoil to the light of newly found power, thanks to Canada. The rubble was being cleared from the streets of The Big Apple. The Sun was rising on us as we rode off in search of a happy beginning.

The temperature was over one hundred again. Anya's Chevy Vega was without air conditioning. We were heading south to the land of instant marriages only to discover that they were preceded by three-day waiting periods. Maryland said, "Check out North Carolina."

North Carolina said, "Go back to Virginia." Emporia, Virginia said, "We close in one hour, come back tomorrow." We said, "But you just told us that we had an hour."

Our blood was drawn. We sat among the others awaiting the process that would sanction what we already knew. Our turn came and we stepped forward.

"I think that we are being married by a typewriter!" said Anya, as our information was united on the certificate that we would share.

I answered the clerk's questions while she sat behind her Remington and clicked away. She turned to Anya and asked routinely, "And what is your national ancestry, Dearie?"

Anya smiled and responded by saying, "Jewish."

The clerk's eyes became vacant. Her hand paused before setting the letters in her official stamp. She tightened her lips and drew closer to us and asked, "You said, Jewish. Is that correct? "

The sound of the word, Jewish, echoed as if from the walls of an antique German train station, melding with the screeching whistle of an outbound escape to salvation. The rising steam from its engine engulfed the black leather-clad official while she stamped the passport with the ominous red J.

The scene of this Berlin nightmare of 1937 was juxtaposed by a Southern Man of 1977 whose mindset had not grown beyond 1877, saying, "Y'all please step into this here chamber."

We complied and the door shut behind us. Our fears were put at ease since he joined us in the room. The ceiling was reassuring. It hid no showerheads. He gave the smile, required of a man in his position, and opened a black book that rested on a podium. The three of us stood alone in the tiny space.

He introduced himself saying, "Evenin' folks, I'm The Marriage Celebrant."

Reading the words from the black book, he asked, "If anyone present knows of any reason why these two should not be joined in matrimony, please speak now or forever hold your peace."

I wondered about the spelling of that word. Since we were the only others in the room, and saw no reason to not be joined, we rested on our right to remain silent. The ceremony proceeded. He said, "Do you uh, On-yer, er uh . . . Onion?"

To which I added, "An-ya. Her name is Anya."

He answered, "Okay An-yaa". He went on to his next obstacle, "Do you Anyan Appleyan . . . uh, Apple-inn . . . " Then he shook his head and grunted, "Hey I'm sorry, y'all know we don't get too many of your kind down here! How do y'all say this name?"

After much practice he uttered Anya's last name, Appleman. We repeated the words that he offered, so we could earn our degree in the form of a legal decree that said far less than we already felt. Hence, he pronounced us Man and Wife.

The Celebrant must have been embarrassed after his wrestling match with Anya's name. Perhaps that's why he restored his Southern dignity by bestowing upon us a small package of Procter and Gamble cleaning samples to launch us into eternal wedded bliss.

Upon closing the doors to the nineteenth century, we stepped into the sunlight of the twentieth and the howls and whistles of a carload of black teenagers, admiring my new bride.

The wedding procession consisted of a sole Chevy Vega on a hot drive north to escape The Real America and on to swimming in a cold stream, behind a guesthouse, in Woodstock, New York. Right near Beth-el.

"Mom, Dad, I want you to meet Kenny, my husband." I always wondered how Anya could maintain an eternal smile while the world might be collapsing around her. Seated before us at the table in their deli in Sheepshead Bay was the answer. Her mother and father remained in the upright position after hearing the news via my introduction. Their eyes glanced slowly toward one another, and then back to Anya, then over to me. The broad smiles of Ruth and Sam remained intact as they beckoned me to sit.

Sam asked me, "So, do your parents speak Yiddish?"

Anya interrupted him with, "Kenny's parents are both dead. While they were alive, they never spoke Yiddish to the children."

The smiles continued, so did the questions, "So, while your parents were alive, did they speak Yiddish to one another?"

Anya saw that the wagon was surrounded and said, "Maybe you should make that call Kenny. There's a phone on the corner."

I finally met two of the five weary, saddened, yet smiling faces in the picture that stood on Anya's mantle. One month after their arrival from the D.P. camps of Europe to the HIAS, an immigrant D.P. camp in Manhattan's lower East Side; Anya would be born to them.

At the time the picture was taken, the promise of a new life in The South Bronx was their American dream. Hitler's ministers of The Final Solution caused the few survivors of their families to flee the Nazis, from what were once their family's homes in Poland, to the sanctuary of Russia. It was there where they would live as refugees and at times as captives.

After the defeat of the Germans, again they would have to escape. This time it would be from the tyranny and oppression of Polish anti-Semitism. The Nazis had handed seized Jewish properties over to their Polish accomplices. When the few surviving Jews returned at war's end to reclaim what was stolen from them, they were turned away if not killed. The new owners of the Jew's lands were reluctant to return what the Germans never had the right to give them. As irony would have it, protection from their pursuers would be in the very place that the terror began, Germany.

Security would be found at the Displaced Persons Camps established by the victorious Allies. During their separate escapes, Ruth and Sam met and married. Their honeymoon would last for three years in the D.P. camps. This would be the lesser of the evils since the majority of their family member's eternities had begun in Hitler's death camps. Anya had always described us as being from two different worlds. I had entered hers and we set forth to create the one that might be ours.

While we rode back to Park Slope, I could see relief on Anya's face. There was a difficult road ahead of us, but it was to be an open one. The silhouette of brownstones became a solid wall of doors and windows, resulting in a question, "Which one of our apartments will we share?"

When you fail to plan, only then may you truly be in touch with life's plan for you. Since pre-opinionation and prejudicial thinking are luxuries that have been overlooked, circumstances may point the way.

"I don't know how this could have happened! Someone must have fallen asleep upstairs with the water running, it must have been on all day," said Doctor Renfield as she tried in vain to both hold back the deluge that was breaking through the tin ceiling of Anya's apartment as well as assign culpability for it. Her attempt to point the finger of blame was as futile as her trying to hold back the water with her broom handle.

The apartment above Anya's had been long vacant except for the Doctor's frequent visits. We gathered Anya's clothes, stereo and books. They alone had miraculously survived the flood.

The ceremony was complete. My truck rolled up to my little place on Eighth Avenue where I kept those few things that were the fuel for my very being. My trunk, cable reel and journal would forever share space with those things of Anya's.

Anya's black-and-white Zenith, which would sit on our windowsill, would entice us with Star Trek reruns. The ancient set had an operating duration of fifty minutes after which the picture and sound would be beamed from our reality. We would choose to either watch the beginning of an episode, only to imagine and debate the ending, or to do the reverse. While the Zenith held back information, it also held a plant.

The name that I had created, from the rubble that once was my life, had grown to reach beyond its own needs to share those of another.

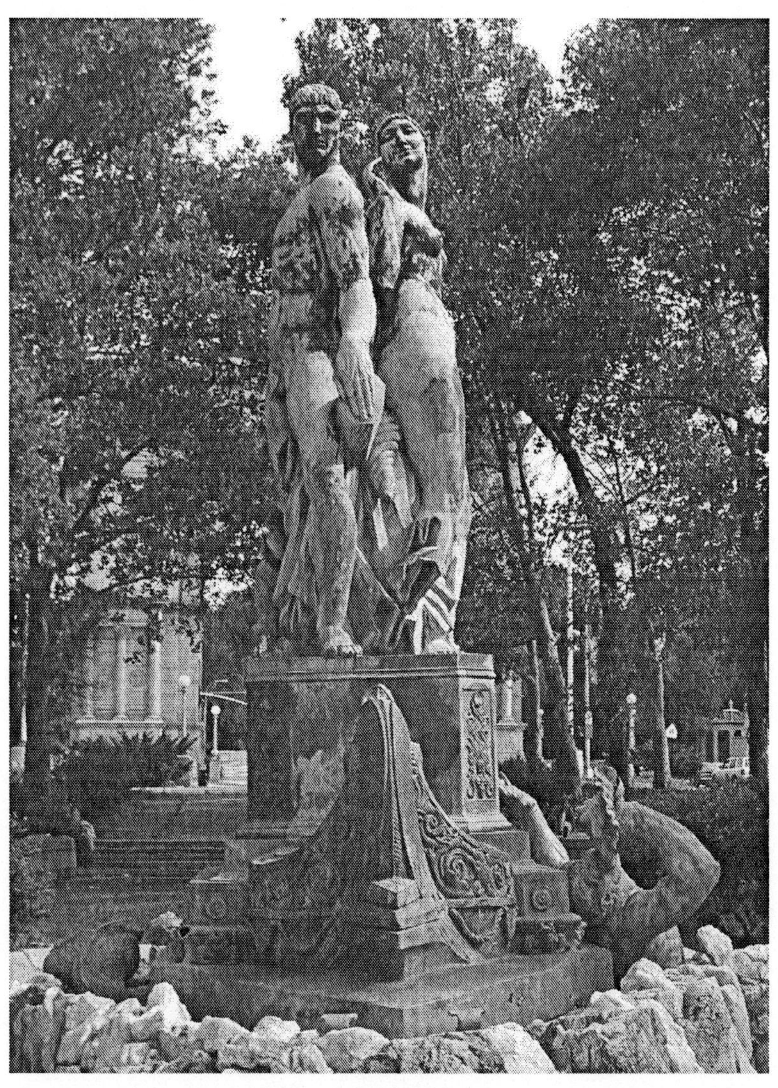

Fountain at Grand Army Plaza

Photo by J.K. Savoy

Chapter Nineteen

Synthesis

Ivan, a concert pianist, was having it tough making in roads in his profession. Shelly was a writer who couldn't get read. Jimmy always had to answer cattle calls for acting jobs just as the piano was getting readied for the stairs.

Andy was a mover. That's it, a mover. Those who worked with him were but his serfs on his dominion that was my moving truck. He made no claims to moving as a means toward some other end. All that he was was a mover. He also happened to be a practicing occultist. His ability to pierce one's soul with an immediate characterization of their inner self was almost as eerie as was his sect of followers, most of whom became movers in my enterprise.

These additions to my already solid group would each make brushstrokes with every box and sofa that they might lift, as the living expression that was Kenny the Mover spread through the streets of New York. With gains come losses. Mel found a scholarship and a woman to commune with. They became practicing Californians.

If you sat at the first booth and squinted just right, then the little paper sign that I hung over a year before on the bulletin board at The Economy appeared to be at the lead of the line of golden and black chariots parked outside awaiting their warriors. I squinted again to capture the vision. It was pure magic. Just draw a picture and contemplate the result, work endlessly and the substance fills the form.

Like a cry in the distance, I heard Anya say, "You need a rest. I don't think anyone can continue their focus being as immersed as you are without breaking. If you get some distance, you will see from the outside what you only think you're missing from the inside. Bob said that he can look after things if we want to get away. Half of the city leaves over the Christmas break. There are only a few jobs on your schedule during that time. Justify it as overdue prime engine maintenance. Also, Florida is cheap now."

Anya squeezed my hands as she spoke. I was listening but somehow her words blended with those of Bob's. He was assigning the jobs to the men. My thoughts were beyond it all. There was a much-needed office to open. I had just taken a second-floor space on Seventh Avenue. I was planning to surprise my workers with the opening. There was to be a full-size sign framing the picture window, made to appear as a large version of my original paper ones.

Anya must have sensed my inner distractions. She pulled my arms abruptly and said with loving patience and reminiscence, "Think back to the way you felt when you drove the beached whale up and down the streets of the Slope after you resurrected it from its grave. I sat alongside of the happiest kid on the block who had just brought a thirty-five-foot trophy home for all to see. You told me that it would reproduce itself six-fold and it did, even faster than even you imagined.

"After nearly two years of creating your own advertising, then creating your chariots and still doing a moving job every day yourself while returning phone calls and scheduling work, let me ask you a question."

My eyes opened wide as I heard her ask, "Is holding the tail of your creation, as it grows beyond your comprehension, the only thing that keeps you from the whirlpool of fatigue into which you're spiraling? Okay, I don't know if the fact that you didn't even blink is because you didn't understand me or that you're dead. Let me ask you another question. If your sovereignty requires you to be able to keep yourself from becoming a slave to your own creation, can you truly say that you can distinguish yourself from the creation from your present point of view?"

The loudest, ugliest jet in the sky by far has got to be the Boeing 727. The worst passenger in the world has got to be a pilot. Those two entities met on a rainy morning flight from LaGuardia Airport bound for Miami. I couldn't stop thinking about how irony might have placed one of my worst flight students seated in the sealed compartment before us.

Could a clod with two left feet that took forever to buy his commercial pilot's license have jumped ahead of high-time pilots only because he worked for this airline as a ticket agent? Perhaps this is one reason the pilot's compartment is sealed.

Why would I have to walk away never to look back, when I can fly away and perhaps see everything clearly? I grasped Anya's hand. We sat as close to the three loudest engines in the sky that any holder of the short straw could. Between my feet was my entire wardrobe in my backpack, between my knees was my journal. To my side was the person who was the lifeline that pulled me ashore to myself.

Somehow there was a familiar sensation as the plane banked right and my balls flew to the left. After the magic blue liquid dispatched my urine to the clouds, I looked at the names on the pilot's compartment. I took comfort in seeing no name that I knew.

Anya had fallen asleep. I looked beyond the wing tip at the all-too-familiar sight of towering cumulus clouds rising from below and the altostratus hanging above and beyond. The world outside became an indistinguishable blur. My eyelids flickered as my mind gave in to the overpowering force of the flashback!

"Trevor Lasco will prove to be the greatest genius in world finance. If his balloon keeps soaring, as it is now, he very well may soon become one of the greatest men in America," Woody said as he taxied the Grand Commander twin turboprop toward the engine run-up area.

I had never flown in that type of craft before that day. I was to be Woody's co-pilot on the flight. My duties were to work the radios, find the required maps and charts, and basically be his second pair of hands. Woody had me hold the airplane's manual out for him. He had referred to it too many times. I began to feel uncomfortable with him.

"You know Joe, when you have the opportunity to work in the shadow of greatness as we do with Lasco, I must say, let him forever see the light."

"Woody, I can't get all knocked out by how you think this hustler is the greatest man alive. One of my students, an emergency room doctor, once described the greatest person in the world as the one who sponge bathes and changes the bedpans of the terminal cancer patients in his hospital."

Woody looked at me with an unbelieving smirk and replied, "That's ridiculous. How can you compare one with the other?"

"Well, Woody, I guess we'd have to ask the cancer patients, now wouldn't we?"

His smirk changed to a look of consternation as he fumbled with the controls during run-up. I began the task of consuming every page of the aircraft's manual while watching the sweat stains growing under his arms.

"Woody, you are aware that the air traffic controllers are

staging a strike or at least some kind of work slow-down beginning today, aren't you?" Woody's hands reached one way, and then changed direction as he searched the panel while trying to convince me that he knew his way around. I was not convinced.

He circumnavigated my question and answered inappropriately, "I checked the weather between here and Boston. It's just calling for some high overcast by the time we touch down there and only light showers when we return here. We won't be needing them or their help."

I had to call off the speed sequences as we rolled down the runway. It began to seem to me that Lasco's aircraft salesman might not know his product as well as he or I originally thought. My stomach met my asshole as he lurched the craft from the runway. It was then that I immediately placed the airplane's manual on my lap, studying with my right eye while keeping my left on my new Captain.

"Woody, do you know that you still have about fifteen degrees of flaps hanging out there? I might have bled them off after our initial climb myself, but I'm just here to build up hours. What do I know?"

Quickly, he dumped the flaps. The airplane's nose reacted to his choice and he reacted to the subsequent pitch change by abruptly over-controlling. I settled the argument between man and machine by holding the yoke on my side perfectly still.

I had to keep telling myself that the difficulties that I saw within this cockpit were, by far, overshadowed by the importance of our mission. Lasco's accountant's son had to be picked up at Boston Logan International, following his dental appointment.

Woody turned right and then he looked right. The sweat stains from his armpits were enroute to meeting at his tie. I set the radio to Newark Departure Control. There was an eerie silence from where there was normally constant chatter. The story was the same on all frequencies.

The contents of the manual and I were becoming as one. It was enough to see that Woody knew half of it at best. I settled in to my instructor's mode. Each of my suggestions was being accepted by him, followed by, "Yeah! Of course, I knew that!"

"Eastern five eleven out of three thousand for six. Heading two seven zero, over."

"Roger, five eleven," answered Departure Control.

That was the first communication I had heard since take-off. At least the radio was okay. I looked ahead as we flew northeast. We were on top of a cloud deck that was increasing in both density and upward slope.

"Woody, I'm going to try to contact departure for an instrument clearance to Boston. Okay, boss?"

His hands were frozen to the yoke. We were at seven thousand feet, still heading northeast at nearly two hundred miles per hour. I said into the mike, "Newark departure, one Papa Charlie, I say again, one Papa Charlie is requesting instrument clearance to Logan International. Do you copy?"

The hissing sound of dead air was all we would hear in response to our predicament. Where were the voices of our salvation? We knew that they lay silenced by their need to protest the government's refusal to hear their plight as they ignored ours.

"One Papa Charlie, you're loud and clear. They're not talking."

I recognized the familiar voice of the Eastern pilot. It wasn't general aviation's day, I guessed. I picked my head up from the Boston approach chart that had become irrelevant. The gauges before me differed with what the seat of my pants felt. As an instrument pilot and instructor, I told myself what I always taught my students, "Trust the gauges, because your ass is full of shit."

My attitude indicator said descending left turn. We were shedding nearly a thousand feet per minute. Woody had dropped flaps and the motors for the landing gear were announcing their actuation. I'm sure that it was my voice that disrupted this symphony of malpractice. I shouted, "What the fuck are you doing?"

The airspeed indicator was advancing beyond the white arc of acceptable flap operation. I felt my asshole tense up in direct proportion to the tightening spiral. My wits must have been about me because I tried to determine which wing would blow off first and if there would be any sense for me to attempt to control this bird afterward.

I thought about a pilot, who a year before, had an engine failure on takeoff from Teterboro Airport. After misidentifying the live engine as the troubled one, he shut it down. The good engine then blew. Having neither engine running, in a final act of heroism, he placed the Cessna 310 into a knife-edge between two buildings. He killed only himself.

Crashing that day was not an acceptable option for me. I had a date that night. I thrust my elbow into Woody's ribs, pulled his seat handle thus launching him rearward. I then secured the controls and leveled the wings. The only thing thicker than the clouds that surrounded us was the sweat that filled Woody's shirt in its entirety.

I returned the craft to a normal flight configuration. After hearing the barometric pressure from a stray radio transmission, I reset my altimeter and saw that we were only at twelve hundred feet. I tuned my navigation radio to the Sparta New Jersey beacon and flew to it after broadcasting, "Mystery aircraft inbound Sparta, heading two four zero, squawking ident out of two thousand for six and I do hope you hear me!" There were clicks over the speaker. I knew that I was loud and clear. My mutiny headed west.

Woody's eyes stared forward. His fists remained clenched as if they were still at the controls. His knees wobbled uncontrollably as did the blubber hanging off his belt. Tears flowed past his quivering mouth that grasped for words. None would come forth as it felt the back of my hand. This salesman was not buying the farm with my ass on board.

"You have to be the most stupid motherfucker to ever fall out of the puking mouth of creation! What was on your mind, throwing us into a graveyard spiral over some little town in Connecticut, probably filled with kids? Could anybody walking down a street below imagine that some moron would drop a fucking plane on them?"

He slid his seat forward and then complied with my signal for him to sit on his hands. His voice choked out the worst justification for stupidity that I'd ever heard, "I figured that there would be an airport somewhere down there! I just wanted to pop out of the clouds and sneak a peek."

"You tell me right to my face, Woody! At what altitude were the bases of those clouds back there?"

His blank stare and silence were met with another sobering backhand from me. My knees ceased their trembling. The clouds below us broke intermittently, revealing the familiar terrain of northern New Jersey.

I passed the Sparta Beacon and made a descending left turn, heading toward highway Twenty-Three which would lead us toward a straight-in approach under the clouds to Runway Nine at the closest facility, Caldwell-Wright. The ceiling over the highway was less than five hundred feet. Fortunately, I knew every hill and power line along that road on a first-name basis. There was an eerie, never-ending static hiss from the Newark Approach frequency. I was on my own.

I looked over to the human wreckage sitting in the captain's chair and asked, "Have you ever flown this airplane under instrument conditions before?"

The cabin filled with the smell of shit. Apparently, Woody was searching his mind for an answer. It blended with his body odor that was permeating the fabric of the airplane's interior and of our clothes. I asked myself, "If I weren't hanging around the airport today, would he have taken off alone?'

His explanation itself made him worthy of a beating, "I'm

supposed to be able to fly what I sell. If I can't, the Lasco people will chew me up and spit me out on the street. This job is my only way to become a real part of Lasco's corporation, and then I can work my way up the ladder. Most of my sales commissions are in stock options. I want to join the regular flight crew in order to get salaried."

My answer to his pleas was stone silence and a stare. Then he said, "Okay Joe, to answer your question, neither! I never flew this airplane before. I never flew anything in actual instrument conditions. Please don't hit me again."

Did I know that the usual Lasco pilot, whose qualifications were only surpassed by their arrogance, would have a sniveling incompetent salesman as their stand-in? The real pilots were away on the Boeing 727 with Lasco as he carpetbagged the world.

The welcome sight of Caldwell Airport appeared. I announced our arrival over the Unicom frequency. With help neither offered nor needed from Woody, I landed.

While walking to the pilot's lounge, I said, "If I ever see your ass behind the yoke of anything bigger than a single-engine Cessna, or during any condition other than unlimited ceiling and visibility, I will tell everyone who will listen, what you did today. This will be followed by a public ass kicking from me of biblical proportions!"

"Kenny. Kenny, wake up. They just turned on the fasten your seat belts sign. We're on approach to Miami. Are you alright?"

I turned to Anya. She was returning me from my reverie by shaking my body. I assured her that all was cool by saying to her while I gave her a big hug, "Yeah, I'm okay, I was just trying to keep my mind off the flight."

An endless procession of airplanes descends, another rises. The tropical promise of rejuvenation in four days and three nights awaits the labor weary. Those who lay upon the lounges are those who paid with days of toil for their moments in the Sun. The smell of coconut-scented cooking oil from their bodies challenges that of the sea as it permeates the sand.

"Could the sand, soon to be beneath me, be an accumulation of the emptied hourglasses that signaled the final moments in Paradise of those who passed before me?"

My body joins the heap. My hourglass' grains, one by one, become the beach. An application of cooking oil and the rotisserie that is the Miami Sun will have its chance to soothe my weary body where it has landed as it awaits the arrival of my mind.

With the eternal sound of waves crashing on the shore before me, my eyes close. Images of the beach become visions of boxes flying through stairwells, crashing open below! Tables and chairs gouged and scratched! Jobs end with the customers claiming,

"Your mover stole the carton that had all of my money! Now I can't pay you!"

"No one showed up for work today, no one in Brooklyn will ever call Kenny."

"The entire fleet was burned last night!"

"You have been in a straightjacket for over two years, following your last acid trip and hallucinated everything since."

My mind meets my body. I leap from my blanket and ask myself, "Has all that I have created washed away in distant surf? Did I save the airplane in my flashback, while my business was lost in a flash?"

I look to the sea and I think, "Why does a wave rise to its pinnacle, then crash and dissolve upon the beach? Can't it see the fate of those before it? What of all of the waves that follow in this endless procession? Are their efforts worth the all-too-predictable conclusion? Will eternity itself be remembered by that which might perceive it and its futility?"

Tobacco pouch and paper in hand I wonder, "What if the allure of the Brooklynite returns? What if I find Kenny the Mover in ashes, shambles or in the form of floating debris? Would I then be as the undertow, to rise and crash again until I am but vapor dreaming of the sea? Or is the experience of the attempt a prize unto itself?"

Looking down I realize, "Every time I replace the tobacco from the rolling paper that I coughed out, I cough it back out. Then I salvage the debris, mixed with some sand or dirt, depending upon the location, and repeat the process. Does managing to place the cigarette in my mouth and finally light it mark success? This causes me to repeat the whole coughing, salvaging and smoking progression until my lungs beg for another."

Then, melded with the din of the surf, I hear, "Why don't you just quit?"

I tried to look Anya squarely in the eye as the waves crashed behind her silhouette. I had to give her an honest answer. I couldn't find any. I looked to the sand. I breathed in the vapor from the sea's eternally triumphant messenger. I looked at Anya's questioning eyes.

After a long moment of reflection, three words emerged confirming the end of a fifteen-year habit, "Okay, I quit!" I shoved the cigarette into the sand and formed a mound above it in memoriam, denying it the chance to one day do the same to me.

All anticipate their long-awaited provider. Pelicans perch on its crest. Surfers assemble below. All will ride the eternal moment that is to be the wave. The watery mountain gathers mass. The journey begins.

The twenty-foot wide sign read, "Moving? Call Kenny." It hung above a window of equal size above The Carvel ice cream store on Seventh Avenue. Our new office's window contained the new phone number, 555-7777, as would all of the trucks and every bit of advertising. The Economy Restaurant had served its last day as our dispatch office. Six large billboards of trucks assembled downstairs, their crews standing in awe of this presence.

My slogan, "Moving You into the Twenty-First Century," was just as quickly removed as it was installed. After reading it, potential customers objected to paying us by the hour.

New dramatic artwork adorned the golden tee shirts that were given for all of the drivers and crewmembers to wear. Each family that was moved would also receive shirts. Special sizes were made for the kids. There was even a baby's size because everyone looks into strollers and carriages. Gone were the hand-drawn ads in the newspapers; enter the look from professional print shops.

A bouncing ball in a nineteen-forties cartoon, a little Minibus, a roll of tape, paper signs and endless advertising had given birth to people saying things like:

"Kenny the Mover, hasn't it always been around?"

"Kenny the Mover has been the neighborhood's official mover for years, right?"

"I think my parents used him when I was a kid."

"Isn't it horribly commercial for a neighborhood poet to advertise his name on those big, yellow, moving trucks?"

"Didn't Kenny move 'The Dodgers' to LA?"

Somehow my overwhelming the present with media had spilled into the past. I had bridged the gap between my starvation and myself. In the process, somehow I bridged the public's perception of time itself.

A somewhat grownup and still outspoken Steven, from First Street, had reluctantly become one of my drivers. He stood alongside of his truck holding his bag of t-shirts that he was to give the customers and their kids.

He waved a shirt at me in protest and said, "This is really great! You give out free tee shirts for all of the rich bitch's kids while the two little league teams you sponsor run around in whatever's on top of the hamper. By the way, shouldn't a league have more than two teams?"

He added, "The fuckin' city has no dough to keep up the ball fields in the park and the kids get lost in the shovel."

I looked at him wondering at what point, since he first walked into September's, he lost control of the English language and asked, "Lost in the what?"

Steven looked back at me as if I were from Mars and said, "The fuckin' kids get bounced around and mixed up. You know, for a smart guy, sometimes you don't understand the easy stuff. There seems to be times that you don't see nothin' unless it hits you like a ton of pricks!"

Steven and Willie, who long ago helped me knock plaster from September's Child's walls, were the coaches of the two teams that I sponsored. These were the two teams of the local little league, in its entirety. Steven would coach one team, while Willie would coach the other. Steven began working for me one day after I had given up calling one dead end after another from the pay phone at The Economy.

I was ready to call it quits and jump on the truck and leave when I heard Evita, Steven's new wife, say, "If you need a helper for today, take Steven. All he does all day is sit around watchin' soaps and bothering the shit out of me. He ain't much, but he's all I got. I know you can't make a sow's purse from a silk ear, but he'll give you a good day's work. Take my husband, please!"

If this were an auction, mine would be the only hand held up. Besides warning me about phantoms that were never realized, Steven never said much and he never appeared to do much either. My only recollection of Steven actually doing any work was during the Sanitation Worker's strike when the usually lazy Steven showed uncanny ingenuity.

The trash piled eight feet high in front of his mother's building, right next to September's. The garbage men would not remove it. Steven drenched the trash with gasoline. One well-placed match by Steven and the Fire Department was forced to remove the burned debris.

"Come on, Steven! You can work with me, let's go!"

He looked at his wife, and then he shrugged and said, "What? What the fuck? You think I got nuthin' to do? You gotta open your big fuckin' mouth and volunteer my ass on a moving truck? If I ain't home in time for The Gong Show, you an' me will be like two shits you pass in the night! Big fuckin' deal, so I get to work with the boss. Okay Kenny, let's go."

Steven slammed the remains of his burger down on his plate in anger as he stood up. Evita immediately ate it. Steven walked toward the truck as if it were an awaiting gallows.

Evita held her hands out in a helpless gesture and spoke through the half-chewed burger saying, "Hey, Sweetheart, one day all good ends must come to a thing."

Steven may have been a nice little kid himself who grew into someone who would do anything for the neighborhood kids, but somewhere along the line he developed an incorrigible personality and syntax. Being with Steven was like being with vinegar. When he opened his mouth to speak, it was like meeting garlic. Above all, in this case he was right, the little league deserved better.

I reflected on my earliest perception of Steven, Willie and the other kids of the Slope when I sat on the stoop next to what would become September's. When they raced along the tops of the parked cars, I marveled at their innate sense of brotherhood though overshadowed by their disregard for property. Perhaps it was time for me to pay them back for the inspiration that they brought to me.

I slapped Steven across the back and said, "Steven, I'll tell you what. My office is, as of now, the headquarters for the little league. You don't have to use your apartment any more. I'll have at least five other merchants from Seventh Avenue commit to sponsoring teams for this spring."

I said to myself, "I already agreed to allowing The Park Slope Chamber of Commerce to use the space as The Seventh Heaven Street Festival's headquarters, so what's one more thing?"

"Steven, you talk to all of the kids' parents that are in the league and get some of them to agree to become coaches and get their friends involved, too. The kids will finally have a real league. Dammit, why not have a parade too? We can have the Union Street firehouses' truck leading it along Seventh Avenue. This way two stories can be told?"

The stairs of the office buckled beneath the feet of my army of golden-shirted warriors as they descended to their chariots. We had truly become the undertakers for the living. "One goes on to their reward and we bring unto them all of their worldly goods. Yes, you can take it with you, and we in the golden hearse shall bring it forth!"

Our wave of influence swelled, as did the multitude upon and within it. The mounting fame of Kenny the Mover spread throughout Brooklyn. I saw the shoreline before me withdraw to the horizon, in anticipation of the approaching wave.

Chapter Twenty

Crossroads

Intelligent John made his way between two trees after casually dumping a bunch of soda bottles and sandwich wrappers into a trash can. Whistling the theme from Happy Days, he wiped his hands on some paper towels from the trunk of his Mercedes. His driver was about to open the back door for him when John saw me wave and walked over.

My fifth container of Economy coffee barely allowed my mind to catch up to my mouth. John leaned back with me on the bench near the Prospect Park wall. He became the sounding board that would absorb the litany of functions that I envisioned for the little office space within my gigantic sign above Seventh Avenue as I tried to simply answer his question, "So what's new, Kenny?"

He went on to ask, "If you took the space as a base of operations, then why are you here with your beeper and pad? It would seem that nothing has changed except that your answering service has grown into your hiring my ex-old lady to man your own phone on Seventh Avenue."

He was right. Like every other piece that I placed within the puzzle, I also withdrew from the office in order to create the next step elsewhere.

Driven by the force of caffeine, the words flew from my tongue, "I can't seem to draw myself into the picture. I mean, if I were to allow my body to take form at a desk, I might lose the overview of the work in progress. I have to be peripheral to all of this in order to sketch and shape the entity and not allow it to engulf me.

"John, this bench or the booths at The Economy have always been to me like multi- colored, paint-stained stools that an artist can't seem to discard. It's where my ass goes when I have to allow my mind its space.

A bench at Prospect Park
Photo by J.K. Savoy

"Enough about me," I answered. I had to go next to the obvious, if for no other reason but to clear the air, so I said, "Look, this is awkward, John, Cindy just does her job. She doesn't talk about anything between the two of you and I never ask. As far as I'm concerned, whatever happened is yours and her business. She runs the office for me and that's it. So I hope you and I are still cool."

I refused a hit from the Maui-Wowie joint that John lit. He made up for my share. After three long hits, he laughed dismissively saying, "Whatever, bro'. She's living with her choices, I'm living with mine. Kenny, just in case she ever does rap to you about me, I want to tell you how it really happened."

"John, she doesn't talk. Don't worry."

"Kenny, I ain't worried, I'm just stoned and quite accustomed to people listening when I feel like talking. So like listen up, bro'!"

When he saw me back away, he said, "Sorry, Kenny, I do get a little pushy sometimes. Just indulge me for old time's sake."

John began his story, "We were upstate camping. There's always been something special about magic mushrooms.

Whenever I start eating them, I don't think that I've had enough until, well this time a hawk seemed to seek me out.

"I was sitting on top of a large rock waiting for the Sun to break the horizon. He saw me and began circling. I never knew the power of their stare until then. Then he screeched to me. It wasn't the noise of an animal that I heard, but it was like he screeched my name in a way that was somehow deeply familiar. Every time I heard it, I felt summoned to join its presence within the brightening sky, until I did and became him.

"From high above, I saw my own pathetic human form sitting as if dead upon the rock below. As much as I called it, there was no response. The most radiant Sun ever broke the horizon. All that remained within the vacuous eyes that once were mine were the reflections of the brilliance of the rising Sun.

"The sound of my form in flight filled my ears. It pierced the air before me, announcing itself as the zenith of all aspiration. The awakening of the pitiful being below me was all that prevented me from eternal rapture. I circled and swept down to smash into the back of what was once me. I felt my life force as the hawk's screech itself and from that moment all that I was had but one purpose, to cause John to fall to his end and to fly free.

"Instead, I felt our forms collide! I fell and saw the hawk fly off toward the Sun. I tumbled forward, grasping on to some roots. After hanging over the ravine, I began pulling myself back to the top of the rock. Finally, I returned to the campsite."

John's eyes began scanning the inside of the park as if involved in yet another search. I wondered where Cindy Burp was during his journey to the center of the strychnine.

So I asked, "Was Cindy with you during all of this?"

John's eyes returned from the search of the park and rolled back into his head as if to seek the hawk. He replied, "Yeah she was in the tent crying and clutching my sleeping bag. I asked her what was wrong. She blamed her fear on me because I was tripping and that I left her alone. I looked at her and saw her as if she were a baby sucking on the corner of her blanket.

"When I told her of my out of body and that I could not be free to explore my true self, living with her and her total dependence upon me, she threw a lit kerosene lantern at my head.

After showing me the scar, he said, "The cunt even had the fucking balls to say, and I can still hear her words, 'John, you've drowned so long ago in your own imagined fountain of wisdom that you think everyone bathes in your every thought and word.'"

It appeared that John was reflecting on Cindy's words, instead he was noticing the Sun reflecting on his Mercedes. When his thoughts returned to the bench he said, "Then she told me, 'When I couldn't find you, you fucking asshole, I was worried that you might be lost or dead! Finally, I see that lost or dead describes your love for me. John, let me be the one who finally shows you the light'!"

I asked, "Then came the lantern?"

Without hesitation, he answered, "Yeah, she grabbed it right off the table. I turned around to answer her and she got me directly in the temple. The tent caught fire from the burning kerosene and all my camping shit burned. She took my Land Rover and threw it in gear. The fucking spinning wheels sprayed my face with rocks. She disappeared down the dirt road and I haven't seen her since. Then I realized that the rest of my mushrooms were in the cooler in the back seat."

John looked up, took a deep breath, then sighed. He looked at me and said, "God, I miss those mushrooms so much! Even I can't find any around."

I thought back to Cindy's painting of the gallows at their mansion and I envisioned a snipped jock strap dangling in the wind. I wondered, "Did the forest, if the forest could care to listen, hear the fading echoes of one girl burping that soon become the sound of one woman driving?"

John looked back at me while shaking his head, "Wow, man! I can't believe I just laid all that shit on you. I felt like we were lying back on the pillows at September's Child. Speaking of old times, every time I see you grow with this moving thing, I can only wish Rico was here to see it all."

"John, if Rico were here, he would be sharing it all with me. I know that somehow he would have become a big part of this. Too bad he got stupid or plain sloppy in the end and got caught."

John looked at me as if I had no idea of the difference between up and down. Then he said, "Rico never got stupid with his business, Kenny. Rico got stupid with his dick, as usual. Don't you know what happened?"

I merely shrugged, not wanting to break the flow of information to come forth. John assumed the pose of a sage on the bench as he prepared to reveal how life really was through the portals of two well-placed smoke rings.

At that moment, the chauffeur leaned back into the Mercedes front seat while John leaned back on the bench saying, "Jeff, you know him, Terry's old man. Well Jeffy was having a live-in thing at the mansion with one of his ex-hookers, Celia. One night, the two of them were celebrating at Minsky's Pub. Jeff bought Celia a diamond because she did this special thing for him. She kept telling him over and over, 'I did it for you, and you alone, Baby!'

"They were on their second bottle of champagne and Celia insisted that she pick up the tab. She laid a fifty down on the table. When Jeff looked at the fifty, he saw a bunch of handwriting in Spanish. He translated it and suddenly whacked her across the face, yelling, 'You bitch, you just fucked with the wrong sucker! '

"The handwriting on the fifty was familiar to him. It read, 'This is for shaving your pubic hairs for me', it was signed, Rico. The boys from Jeff's limo grabbed Celia. She was seen back at the whorehouse a week later with her head shaved and Jeff's name tattooed backwards across her forehead."

I had only thoughts of pity for Celia, the once-aspiring writer, who will forever see another's by-line covering a mind that may never see its own.

John continued, "Two days later, Rico is diving out of his old lady's bedroom window with the Feds on his ass. The next thing he knows is that his ass is back in some Caribbean country that he only knew when he was a little kid. He never even had a chance to put it all together."

The silence that I heard was the numbness within all that was me. Had I been so naïve all along, or was I as self-absorbed as all of those around me?

"I haven't seen Jeff around either since Rico disappeared, come to think of it."

John slapped my leg, laughing and said, "Sure you have, Kenny. He's a lot skinnier and hairier now. He lives right here in the park where his ongoing agony of begging for food and getting hassled by the cops can be watched and enjoyed right from this very bench. It's a real breath of fresh air to see him scurry for crumbs and scraps like a fucking squirrel.

"Jeff's sentence to Hell is to live as Rico must be living, wherever the fuck that is. Jeff can't leave the boundary line of Prospect Park. By the way, Terry, and your old roomie Gordon, took over Jeff's whorehouse and porn shops. Jeff was told that his mother is an unknowing hostage in his own mansion right down the street from the bench where he sleeps. She probably thinks that he's on one of his business trips. Jeff is a dumb-ass, but he's smart enough not to cross the line.

"You know, Jeff was once my favorite earner of all. He had a certain panache about the way he carried on with his businesses. Too bad he fucked with a kid that everyone liked, especially by bringing in the Feds to do his dirty work. It's amazing how power like his can unravel with a single gesture from the hand that feeds him."

John's 'Benz pulled away to reveal a sign across the street from the park saying, "Another Cinderella Project, sponsored by Brooklyn Union Gas." Like a claim-stake in my eye, this harbinger of corporate intent spelled itself on plywood window boards of the limestone mansion on Prospect Park West. A chained door seconded the motion.

"Cinderella Genocide", was the orange spray-painted response overlaying the corporate message. The hippies who shared their lives in that space had been displaced to less fashionable surroundings. Another property awaited the ever-tightening tentacles of Wall Street to grasp it as its prize.

I finished the last drop of my Economy brew. Memories of loudspeakers announcing a party for all, blasting from that limestone's windows, danced through my mind. The chains upon the door fell from sight as my eyes blinked. I thought back to the times when that very door stood open and people would say as you entered, "Just walk right in and dance all night! Who gives a rat's ass what your name is or who you're with?"

From the park bench where I sat, I looked at the finished Cinderella Project beside the newly conquered commune. My mind was filled with the sound of Waterford Crystal tinkling in a toast. Perhaps it might be to the tycoons of another century who built Park Slope and displaced the working class victims of that age. Where once there were commune parties, cellists played to select groups of guests as denim surrendered to silk.

The writing on a piece of scrap wallboard lying in the dumpster read: "We the Unwilling Are Led by All the Unhip, To Do the Unnecessary for All the Ungrateful." Flower Power slogans that once rallied a generation in search of social justice joined it in unrelated fragments. Could they spell the end? The power of revolutionary statements, which once echoed from those walls, were being replaced by the force of financial statements that would see to their dismantling.

It was less than a year before that I had sat on that same park bench. Then, the random sight of dumpsters signaled sporadic renovations. They would place themselves in front of the buildings like pods from "The Invasion of the Body Snatchers". As much as the occupants resisted, they would drift off to sleep and be substituted by successors who would then summon others to join them.

I watched how the leaves became caught in the wind swirls near my feet. Waves of flashback presented themselves to my fluttering eyes. It was as if I returned to a time when I was sitting right near that very bench, one year before.

A case of writer's block is one hell of a thing for a writer to flash back to! Yeah, I was trying to write but the pen stalled halfway down the page of my journal. Thick black circles resulted, like eyes staring back at me.

I recalled how I had stared into those circles and jumped up when suddenly Danny the Flick skidded his bike to a stop in front of the bench after running over my foot. His dilated pupils peered at the circles on my notepad as he said, "Hey, man, I'm sorry!" Then he squinted, looked at me and said, "Kenny, my man, it's you! Qué pasa?

Danny was working off some righteous shit by peddling three hours of loops of the park to burn off the speed-laced acid that he had dropped the night before.

He sat on the park wall with me and we heard, "Far fuckin' out, man! I can't believe my eyes; it's Kenny and Danny! I hope you dudes don't mind that we're all out of food. We had a real bad case of the munchies and finished everything in the basket."

Danny lurched back and focused his eyes on the new arrivals and shouted, "Sally! Paulie! Oh wow! This calls for a joint. You got anything, man?"

Like the ghosts in Our Town, sitting upon their headstones, we all sat upon the stone wall that surrounds Prospect Park, reminiscing about all of the other spirits from September's Child, long departed from Park Slope. The warm sense of being with old friends in that magic moment was overshadowed by a feeling that our paths were crossing for a last time, while enroute to our separate ways.

Through the clarity of Purple Haze, Danny confided in us that besides movie watching, his main ambition in life was to have his name changed to Ellis Dee. He began rolling skinnies as fast as Paulie could lay the pot on him and he could lick the joints. Sally took her guitar from its case, sat on the wall and sang.

Paulie sat on the bench and pointed to the dumpster across the street saying, "I just got a notice that my landlord wants us to buy our apartment. How the fuck do you buy an apartment, man? Like, you can buy a house that sits on the ground, but you can't buy a fuckin' apartment that's stuck inside a fuckin' building, man!"

Paulie's eyes nearly crossed as he sucked in the pot smoke. Like a master of his craft, he managed to contain the smoke in his lungs and ask, "Is he goin' to rip the fuckin' apartments out and spread them out or something? What if I want to move someday? If I want to leave, do you think anybody else besides me would be stupid or stoned enough to buy an apartment, man? Even if this shit's possible, I got no fuckin' bread to live on, never mind buying something stupid like an apartment."

Sally stopped singing "Both Sides Now" to sing, "If we can't afford to buy it, he will pay us to leave it. And we'll just move on down the line."

Paulie took another much-needed hit and disclosed his survival strategy, "I gave the fuckin' papers to my brother. He's in law school, man. These people don't know who they're fuckin' with! Maybe he can figure out a way to make the dude stop hasslin' us. If we're supposed to be rent controlled, doesn't that mean that we can just sit there and the owner can't do shit to us?"

He exhaled saying, "My brother said that if the dude wants us out, he would have to lay some serious bread on us, man. But if we take it, we got no way back. Two people in the building took the buy out from the dude already and your trucks moved them out, Kenny. I mean, like you didn't do it or anything, like nobody's blaming you. Ah shit, you'll probably be seeing it happen all the time."

He interrupted himself to yell, "Hey, Tank! Get your fat ass over here. Danny, roll a skinny for the fatty."

Smelling the lit joint, Tank headed over to join us, "What's happening, everybody? If we've become flies, then this is shit-heaven."

Tank grabbed the joint and passed it around. I passed it up.

"What the fuck happened to your hair, Kenny? You look like a new recruit. You didn't go and join the fuckin' Army did you?"

"No Tank, my hair got caught in the door when I got thrown out of the coffee house, so I cut myself free."

Tank examined the joint as if looking for booby traps, finding none he took a hit.

"Shit Tank, you left a fuckin' one-inch flame!" said Paulie, burning his finger as he grabbed the roach. Sally threw him a clip so he could tame the burning beast.

Then she strummed her guitar and sang to Tank, "We're helpless and hopeless; soon to be homeless 'cause we ain't got a dime.

"Someone find us an answer, or you'll find us in a shelter a-wastin' our time."

Sally put her guitar down and said to Tank, with tears in her eyes, "They're trying to throw us out of our crib, Tank. Do you know anybody that can do anything? If they get their fucking way, then they'll have to haul mine and my kid's asses out of my home with a rope!"

Leaning her guitar on the wall, she stood before us and said, "Let Paulie talk to his idiot brother about making a deal all he wants. I don't give a rat's ass how much they offer Paulie, it'll go up his nose and in his arm in less than a month.

"This fucking neighborhood is getting to be all about money! It used to be about people helping people, now it's about helping rich people walk over our bodies."

Since Sally's daughter, Tammany, was born, the needles' trips into Sally's veins became a little less frequent. Her latest old man, Paulie, took up any slack.

"Right on Sally, right fuckin'on!" yelled Tank. He took a long hit and passed his freshly rolled double E-Z Wider joint that was capable of handling his mass to Danny. Tank's face reddened. When it neared crimson, he exhaled.

Tank took his turn standing before us and shouted for the world to hear, "You say to me that people are going to put up with this bullshit without a fight? Man, we got the fuckin' Movement behind us and it stopped a fuckin' war! These fuckin' realtors can't stop the people who stopped Washington's fuckin' guns.

"So we sure as shit can stop speculators from dropping eviction notices in our mailboxes if we could stop Nixon from dropping bombs on Cambodia!"

Tank took another long toke, looked into his heart and to the sky for inspiration and predicted, "The people of this neighborhood are going to stand tall and look the realtors and speculators right between the eyes and tell them to shove their blood money right between the two cheeks of their fuckin' asses with the rest of their bullshit!

"Money can't buy off the will of the people if the people will stand their ground! I'll give this block bustin' shit until 'seventy-nine, and that's a stretch. Those realtor pigs will pack it in and split, looking elsewhere for bodies to bleed.

"Like the talon of an eagle, the hand of the people will swoop down and strike to free our homes from greed's grip. Then, word of our resistance will spread on the wings of doves! No offense, Kenny but, we will not be moved! We will not be moved!"

Tank's chorus of three joined him in shouting, "We will not be moved! We will not be moved!"

Tank reached down deeply to his Weather Underground roots and predicted, "The Peace and Love Movement is in hiatus right now. The greed thing that's going on here, and all over the city, will cause us only to regroup and fight again! This time it will be heard all over America! Songs of protest will again sound. We will march for our liberty and for our homes against the Wall Street-real estate conspiracy! The will of the masses will consume the wasted abundance of the gluttonous and wealthy!"

Tank's voice then shouted loudly, but solely, "Eat the rich! Eat the rich!"

The chorus was busy smoking and missed their turn to join in shouting out their support. Many a worthy cause is lost while an inhale fills the ears as well as the mind.

Tank went on, "The next twenty years will be again about society nurturing itself. This money thing is an aberration that will serve to remind us of our true goal, people!

"Power to the fuckin' people! Right on, brothers and sisters! Right on!"

Danny was so inspired by Tank's words that he stood up on the bench and said, "You watch these Yuppies, or whatever they fuckin' call themselves. They're goin' to look down the block at the Methadone Clinic and see the dudes with the tracks on their arms and they'll shit bricks!

"Every morning the dudes line up to get their shit. After they're hooked up, they look for a stoop to hang out on and just chill. These money people ain't goin' to like it one fuckin' bit seeing a bunch of heroin addicts slapping their kid's asses as they go off to their private schools. They'll split sure as shit!

"Let the yuppies put up their fancy-ass gaslights. We'll climb them and light up a joint the size of a horse's cock with the flame! Let them knock my friends from their storefront homes to make another Ristorante and we'll knock over their dumpster in the middle of the floor in the middle of supper hour and make them eat the garbage while we sit and watch, sipping their fuckin' wine! Our come has time. Power to the people!"

Danny turned to Paulie and asked, "Hey, man, you got any more of that shit we been smokin'? It was fuckin' gooood!"

Paulie shrugged and showed his empty hands. Danny slapped one of them. Tank slapped the other. Having blown all of the pot smoke up one another's asses, they all split. Power to the people.

Sally sang, "Turn-Turn-Turn," while they walked toward Seventh Avenue. As Paulie held his fist high to the air, his fading voice reverberated from the canyon walls of the buildings around him, "Yuppie pigs! Fuck you and your money!"

The echoes of their singing and shouting are accompanied by the sounds of clashing symbolisms still rumbling in my memory. Would the generation that set out to change the world be forced to change with the world? Will they become servants and attendants to the lords of the land that they once saw as their own? Will the flames of the torch that was the Revolution evolve to embers-becoming ashes-becoming dust?

Will the delirious lead the oblivious toward further ambiguity? Has the Movement turned to stillness, dissolving in its own inertia? A song of desperation whistles through the branches of ideas that grew from the trees of truth that hang leafless from the winds of change.

The sound of the leaves of the past swirling around my feet was mixed with that of the present as the loud hiss of airbrakes interrupted my daydream of days gone by. A large, yellow moving truck had parked in front of me. My fragmented reverie joined the swirls of leaves, dissipating skyward as my consciousness looked ahead.

Bob jumped out from the cab, followed by an enormously muscular black kid. He must have been the new helper that he found the other day who claimed that he knew me from way back.

I heard, "Kenny, if you keep staring at that building you're not going to make it rise, although its selling price probably doubled since you started looking at it. Hey, Boss, remember me?"

I recovered slightly from my memory lane stupor. The kid's face and voice were somehow familiar, but his body was almost out of science fiction. I shrugged and said, "I give up. Who the hell are you, Kid?"

"I'm Demetrius. You don't remember the dude that helped you knock down the plaster in your coffee house a few years back? You gave me the weights from the basement one day when you were giving everything to anyone who would take it."

"And I see that you used them. Holy shit! Your biceps have to be eighteen inches. I guess you must be putting all of the weights on the bar at the same time now."

"Well actually I go to a gym. They give me a free membership just to show myself around the floor because I won a bunch of contests. By the way my biceps are twenty-and-a-half inches. Kenny, you gotta get some bigger T-shirts. I'm breaking outta this one. See you around, Boss! Hey, and thanks for hiring my brother, Willie."

Demetrius walked down First Street toward his apartment. I turned to Bob, who was counting the money from the moving job that he had just finished, and said, "I wonder how long he'll be able to call First Street home before his building becomes a breeding nest for yuppie puppies.

"You know, Bob, I was sitting here thinking about how quickly the neighborhood changed from hippies in bell-bottoms and sandals to three-piece suits stuffed with lawyers and bankers. It's like someone turned the lights on and everyone yelled: "Surprise, The Movement didn't happen at all, it's still the 'fifties! It's just better at it."

Bob finished counting. He gave me the money together

with his perspective, "Do you think for one minute that the Movement, for the most part, was anything but a fashion statement? Most of those suits that are marching through town right now marched to Washington five years ago in torn bell-bottoms flying a freak flag while quoting Bobby Kennedy and Doctor King.

"They talked the talk and wore the look that they thought would get them high or get them laid. Whatever it took, they did. All along they were picking up the pieces of the walls that the movement broke down only to reconstruct the same establishment that inspired their parents whom they supposedly rejected. It was their true destiny after all.

"Fuckin' irony, man, it's all smoke and mirrors. Yesterday they passed a smoke around and talked about peace and love. Today it's a mirror that they pass with a thousand dollars worth of lines on it and all they talk about are mergers and acquisitions.

"The true idealists never changed throughout the entire time. These were, and still are, the real people who first inspired the so-called Movement. They had, and still have, a sincere desire to change America from the Pig's Pen to a Utopia of peace and equality. Now they play to nearly empty houses at community colleges while the rest of what once was the crowd is gobbling up all the chips and dips at the next party.

"You watch, within two years, most of the long hairs that work for you on the trucks right now will become realtors, investment bankers or go right back to what they said that they rejected originally to follow the Pied Piper of that day."

I could feel that Bob had something else to tell me, I put it plainly to him, "Where do you think you'll be in two years, Bob?"

He knew that I was reading him and seemed relieved saying, "Kenny, I'm going to split for California in two weeks to hang out with Mel for a while. That might determine where I will be in two years. I guess you knew that I wouldn't be driving cabs nor moving trucks as a career choice for long. After I get my shit together, a friend of mine who also quit the company that I worked for is going to teach me about software."

"Bob, what the hell is soft wear? Let me guess, is it a rubber for a flaccid cock?"

He looked at me like I was supposed to know what the hell he was talking about and answered, "No! Software is the programming for the hardware of computers. My friend thinks that there will be a future in making these programs because as computers get smaller, more people will use them. It seems like a gamble, but if I'm making a stupid choice, at least there's a year round beach to fall back on if I crash.

"Kenny, I'll be around to help you until I split. I've got to tell you, man, you inspired me to do this when you said, 'Every day I put everything that I have done on the line for tomorrow, if there is one.' I thought that you were full of shit then, but you still haven't gone one dollar in debt and everything you have was paid for in cash.

"Kenny, when the fuck are you going to get a car and stop driving around in a moving van? Why the hell did I even ask you that? Hah, you're going to tell me that a car is decadent and you justify the use of the truck by advertising as you drive. What should I expect from a guy who still lives out of a backpack and a journal?"

All I could do to answer Bob was to nod, yes.

"Kenny, if I can do the same for me in California that you did for yourself here, then I'll never have to look back the same as you don't. It's really crazy. A while ago, I lost myself in a career. Then I spent an eternity drifting with the wind. Recently, it seems like I found myself in a single moment. Now I'm living in it, and looking forward to a future of hanging on to what I found.

"Remember, Kenny, you'll always have your ideas and ideals, if you keep them in mind and your spirit keeps you.

One more thing, people make statues of those who stand alone so they can get shit-on forever."

While squinting at her reflection in an antique plate, my silver-haired customer said, "Please take extra care when you pack these dishes, they belonged to my grandmother, and I'm ninety-one years old. You can only imagine the age of this set."

Steven reassured the woman by showing her the care he placed in his packing. She was being relocated from the Hotel Margaret in Brooklyn Heights, where she lived for fifty-one years, to the neighborhood in Flatbush where she spent her early days.

Placing the plate into Steven's hand, she said, "It's certainly much louder in Flatbush than I remember it to have been when I was young. I couldn't read any of the lettering, but it seems that people write all kinds of names and draw pictures on their houses now instead of painting them."

After she left the room, Steven said to me quietly, "This poor old broad is burning her britches behind her."

I asked, "Burning her what?"

"You know, Boss, sometimes you don't talk English too good. Now don't tell me you can't understand it neither. She ain't got no way back after she takes the buy-out!

"These fuckin' real estate gangsters have a real devil-make-hair attitude about everything. They always got enough dough to lay out for squeezing old ladies and cripples from their homes. But if you ask them for a nickel to help kids or baseball and they'll all cry, broke."

I wondered if one person's reference to money as dough meant that it wasn't ready, since another next person might refer to it as bread. Oddly enough, this ignited an epiphany, "Since I can't single-handedly stem the tide of change that's sweeping not only Brooklyn, but time itself, then maybe I can hold my hand up to it and by doing so encourage others, by example, to do the same." A little arm-twisting won't hurt either, if it makes people look in a better direction.

Regardless of who dominates Park Slope, the more traditional families of old or the yuppies and their puppies, the little league can give them a popular cause in common to work toward, at least for the sake of all of their kids.

I felt the inner sensation of a plan in motion. The puzzle's pieces declared themselves and awaited formation. Perhaps the only fight left for the soon to be vanquished is to open the eyes of the victors to their humanity.

My attention returned to the task at hand. Although all of the moving expenses were paid by the lord of the land, this grand lady of The Hotel Margaret shared what she saw as her windfall as a generous tip to the movers.

I wondered, "Were there coins under her tongue for Charon, in the guise of a truck driver? Was the weight of the pennies covering her eyes blinding her to the river that she is being sold down?"

She was only one of the many residents that were to be scattered throughout the city by the salivating opportunists whose grand design for this relic of a building did not include the people whose lives gave The Margaret its own for so many years.

Again, we were chosen as the undertakers for the living. My chariot was to be the lanterned craft that would float down the River Styx, albeit Flatbush Avenue, and bring yet another soul to her reward.

The landmark hotel that overlooked New York harbor and sheltered those who only sought to spend their remaining years waking to glorious sunrises, framed by the towers of Manhattan, had its own time of infamous spectacle. People driving along the F.D.R. Drive would look across the East River and pause to witness massive Roman-candle-like explosions of flame rising from the Margaret as its emptied shell disintegrated under a smoky cloud of mystery.

Leaning across the beer spills on the bar I said, "Henry, you, me and as many merchants as I can convince, will each have a team wearing a uniform with our business name and colors on it. Participation this year will guarantee you with a team next year and every year thereafter as this thing grows. All you have to do is pay for your sponsorship and show up for your plaque at the awards banquet at the end of the season. The kids, the coaches and the interest of the community will reward your patronage of the little league with their patronage of your tavern."

I told him that every merchant that I talked to was interested and that a limited number would be chosen that year. Since he and I were the first I talked to, and he was interested, then it was true. Henry's answer was, "Anything for the kids. Sign me up."

Of the next four merchants that I visited, each and every one of them signed on to and loved the idea of an opening day parade with a marching band leading the kids along Seventh Avenue enroute to the games at Prospect Park. A space on their walls awaited a plaque of recognition.

I wandered through a land of complacency with promises of recognition for all. What else would I have to include in addition to awards for valor, hearts for courage and degrees for merit? Might it be that one day they would all return to the heartland that they had abandoned in their quest for their castles in the sky?

The Union Street firehouse would also support our cause, and state its own, by virtue of their truck's presence at the lead of the parade, barring of course any greater burning issue. Steven and Willie did their parts by accumulating as many interested parents to serve as coaches and volunteers as possible.

A teacher, from a local high school, promised us a marching band. This would serve to awaken the neighborhood to our triumph as the people's kids reclaim the "peoples' park".

After hearing us state our case that, "A city is comprised of its various communities and that each is a stone in the overall structure," City Hall would stretch its already depleted budget and have the ball fields in playing condition. They also promised police presence and street closings for the parade. Enough kids signed up to point the way for additional teams for the year after, as all awaited the spring.

"Anya, this is fuckin' bizarre!" I said. I would say the same thing again as I turned the corner to Saint Mark's Place. I would say it again as I ascended the steps and again as I looked upon the massive new mahogany door with solid brass hardware where once a sheet of plywood covered the entry to the commune, where I once lived.

Pointing down I said, "We entered through the iron gates at the garden floor level. There was never enough money to replace the rotted hinges on the stoop door. This is the commune where I used to sleep when I was starting to set up September's Child."

The thundering echoes from the large brass doorknocker summoned yet a greater surprise, "Howie? How ironic, two people from the old commune get invited to a party to celebrate the completion of the renovation by the new owners."

Brylcream answered, "Kenny, it's even further ironic that we're also celebrating my engagement to your wife's friend, Lois, in addition to my renovating our old commune. Come in, I don't have to say make yourself at home, since it was once just that. Except, I don't think that you could sleep in your old room, it's now part of my law library. You've got to see it."

I held my hand up to Howie's, expecting him to grasp mine in our old familiar shake as commune brothers. He extended his outwardly. I patted his shoulder in response and accepted his permission to look around on our own.

After placing my bottle of Mateus Rose next to the vessels of Dom Perignon, we took him up on the house tour and ascended the inside stairs that once held a half-century's worth of white paint. Like Brylcream for buildings, they glistened in polyurethane that covered their restored hardwoods.

My old closet-sized room had been joined with Howie's to form his massive law library. Where a bed sheet once hung in vain to protect my privacy, there were sliding solid hardwood pocket doors. Where posters of Jimi and Janice had hung, there were shelves containing The New York Commercial Codes.

I was surprised to see a familiar small potter's bowl that I had used as an ashtray. It was on the windowsill where Howie and I would smoke and talk about the military-industrial complex that was consuming the world at the expense of humanity.

There was a V-shaped crack in the bowl where we would snuff the roaches to save them for the next day. I wondered, "Is the roach that rests there a means of passage to a happier then, or a device to escape from a frightening now?"

The radical law student, who set out to become a public advocate that would take the people's causes to highest court, brings the establishment's cases to the highest bidder instead. How did he get past the other commune members and obtain the insider's price from the widow in Florida who owned the building without everyone taking it over as a group. Was the eagle that flew among the doves merely a vulture in disguise waiting for his time to kill off his prey after stealing their nest?

I was sure that the blood of Cesar Chavez was cleansed from the Iceberg Lettuce that dropped as randomly from salad plates, as the boastful chatter did from the mouths of Howie's friends,

"I have a brownstone, even bigger than this on Lincoln Place. We're going to use the top floor as both a nursery and living space for the Au Pair."

"We're going to use ours for Oliver's daughter from the other marriage. This way we'll keep out of one another's way."

"I run up my BankAmericard balance and pay it with my Master-Charge. The next thing you know someone else sends me an offer for a card and I pay the last one with the new one. This can go on forever."

"I've seen the future and it's Ivan Boesky! Wherever he puts his money, you'll find mine."

"I bought on President Street. Then I renovated the wreck of a brownstone and flipped it in one year. We made sixty thousand bucks! Now we're doing the same thing on Carroll Street. If the market keeps going like it is, my houses will pay me more than my job does. I just have to figure a way to get rid of the tenants on rent control."

"I can bill almost double per hour for my practice by showing a Park Slope address. God, I love this neighborhood!"

If only The Movement could have somehow foretold of this wave of Young Urban Professionals. In anticipation of the yuppies' arrival, might they have renamed their neighborhoods, Squalor? Imagine a yuppie bragging about living in Squalor.

I sought the echoes of the once-annoying memories of the fights over the odd penny on the phone bill to escape the sounds of decadence that filled those halls. Neither recall nor silence could be found.

Enroute to rescue Anya from Lois's constant bragging about having landed a lawyer, a large painted face placed itself in my way and said, "Hi, my name is Amy, I'm in investment banking. What do you do?"

Instead of saying, "I keep what I work my ass off for away from people like you," I answered, "It would depend upon what had to be done at the time I had to do it, Amy." Her contorted face rewarded me as a sign of more confusion than I had set out to cause.

Amy was saved by Lois, who came over to join us with her friend, Anya, in hand. Lois said, "Amy, don't let Kenny fuck with your head. He has a whole bunch of people working for him." Amy's eyes bulged with anticipation.

Anya freed her hand from Lois' and took mine. We walked toward the gourmet chips and dips. Amy followed us and asked, "And what do your people do, Denny?"

I paused and gathered as profound a look on my face as I could muster. I looked deeply into the eyes of my accounts-challenged harasser and replied, "Whatever I tell them to do, Janey!"

The inside of the large mahogany door kept generating my interest in seeing its other side again. We feared that it might close behind us before the Mad Hatter's ears might blindside us again.

When the door handle seemed to be within my grasp I heard, "Kenny, I see your trucks and advertising all over the place. Tell me, how big is this Kenny-the-Mover thing going to become? I think that I would like to come on board."

His name was Andre. Howie smiled and nodded to him upon seeing Andre engaging me in conversation. There was something familiar about him, but I couldn't quite place it. Maybe it was somebody I read about.

I asked Anya, "Wasn't there a British officer named Major Andre who helped to guide Benedict Arnold into his place in history?"

Sipping her Mateus, Anya said, "That was also probably the result of ambush."

I thought that I responded quite fittingly to his question by asking, "So, you would like to become a mover, would you?" I couldn't stop thinking of him as a Red Coat officer out to curtail any movement toward independence.

Andre saw our mental swords crossing and stepped back as if to say, touché. But instead he said to me, "Get serious, Kenny. I have investors, not to exclude myself, who would like to get behind you and this moving thing with some big money. With the right people involved, together with the proper business plan, the sky could be the limit for Kenny the Mover."

Thinking back to when I would look down to the ground from the limits of my career in the sky, I said, "Okay, Andre. Maybe I'm thinking a little slowly from all the polyurethane vapors in here. Just what do you mean by getting behind me? Let me get this straight, they would give me the money and just stay behind me and that's it. Right?"

Andre rolled his eyes back as if to consult with the others that he had in mind. Upon their return he said to me, "There would be a major part for you to play as the name behind the corporate structure. You must understand how corporations work. Everyone has a function to serve within the overall body. Your place would be very important. You would be the living symbol that inspires the others through your original vision."

If heaven could fart, it may have been my father's message to me to pass on to Andre. I thought of the magical day that I rode through Prospect Park and missed the exit only to find the Minibus and my future.

Andre appeared uneasy as I stared at him while still trying to place him. Perhaps he seemed uncomfortable because he was doing the same to me. Failing to recognize him, I pondered my answer while visions of horns rose from his forehead.

While Anya eyed the door and our escape, I replied, "Would the first official change to Kenny the Mover be to rename it, Mephistopheles' Movers?"

He seemed to put himself in every direction that I chose to flee. Having nowhere left to turn, I answered, "Andre, I do know very well how corporations are. But you have absolutely no idea how I am. If I were to agree to accept your financing, you would have to accept my placing every penny of it on the line toward equipment and advertising as I see fit, without compromise or consultation with others.

"The investors must remain virtually invisible without any say at all in decisions, policy or planning. As far as directions and goals are concerned, they will have no say at all. Are you still interested?" Anya and I nodded in total agreement and smiled politely.

He grumbled in response, "You are being absolutely arbitrary and ridiculous, Kenny! Why would anyone want to place great sums of money into a venture that's ruled by one who is so capricious? The corporate structure that could take your business to the next level requires disciplined, selfless professionals who would dedicate themselves to devising the overall formula through collaborative planning and acquiescence of self-interest in deference to the greater good."

"Andre, keep in mind, you're the one who brought this whole thing up. By the way, ever notice how the words, corporation and corpse, have a lot of the same letters?" I asked, while picturing the hand that he had set upon my shoulder dubbing me, Sir Idiot.

I remembered the promise that I made to Anya, not to hit anyone. So I gently removed his hand from my shoulder. However, I allowed myself some inner satisfaction by imagining how his wrist might snap if I twisted his arm behind his back.

Again, I smiled quite politely while he continued, "Your concept for a community-service-minded moving company could be cloned into a larger spectrum. But with your present attitude toward corporate behavior, we would have to take over running the operations completely. Kenny, let's cut to it. What's your price?"

Suddenly, like a frying pan from the past whacking me across the back of my head, it hit me. I recalled how long ago, I was cutting my deepest feelings into a cable reel in front of September's Child when two people tried to impose their values on them.

While their bodies blocked the soft November sunlight, I remembered Andre's girlfriend voice it like it was yesterday saying, "Buy it for me, Andre."

Then I recalled my stoned-out response as I said through my curtain of hair, "You would put money in my hand and walk away with this creation of mine?" Then I looked across the room and realized another thing: Amy the banker was the girlfriend.

I thought, "Wow, first they want to buy my cable reel, now they want to buy my ass. No way then, no way now!"

He had no idea who I was. I only wished that I could throw this guy's car keys to Bob. Bob could break his vehicular components outside while I broke his balls inside.

Not being one to rely on wishes or dwell on the past, I twisted his head instead of his wrist and said, "Andre, I am truly flattered by your offer and interest, but I really don't give a flying fuck about money and what or whom it can buy."

I recalled how much fun I had at his expense years before. That memory inspired me to say, "Consider this price, you just give me a shit-load of money and I'll spread the name Kenny the Mover far and wide, but I'll stay in charge of all day-to-day activities. You guys can tag along and hang with me, having a shit-load of fun while we're at it.

"For instance, if I feel like being Kenny the Mover tomorrow, as I did today, then I will. If I feel like creating plans for a hundred kids to march down Seventh Avenue, following a fire truck, then I will do that or both. If I decide, since I now run five miles a day, that maybe I would like to create a Brooklyn Marathon, just to be able to run in it myself, then I will. I may have to settle for a half-marathon, but that's still cool!"

I placed my hand on his shoulder. He rolled his eyes down, looking at it while grinning politely. I went on to ask, "Seriously, bro', how can your money help me have the kind of fun that my whimsical attitude can? I chose to live on the streets where I dreamed myself into the position that I now enjoy and that you seek to enjoin. My free will sustains my power over my destiny. If I surrender control to you, true, I still will have attained my destiny, but as your slave."

I shouted over his attempts to speak, saying, "I will never settle for having my individuality relegated to that of a subatomic particle within a group of others behaving like hairs pulled along in a comb until we part one another down the middle of our identities.

"Your entire corporate idea is to mold humanity into a living extension of the blind will of your lifeless charter. How does that concept take into account the importance of applauding a sunset while screaming, encore?"

I jammed my index finger first into his chest then mine while shouting into his face, "You want to absorb me as food into the body of your corporate being? My question is, following assimilation, what does food become? I really think that your corporate people should re-evaluate their priorities and jump into the sandbox and play.

"You know, if I ever took even a single partner when I started this business, all I might have left is half of a good idea, or by now just the memory of it."

While Andre walked away, he nearly fell face first in the punch bowl when I said, "You know, we would really like to hear more of your ideas, but Anya and I have to plan our trip to, The Netherlands!"

Then I turned to our hosts and said, "Lois, Howie, congratulations on finding one another. Good luck with your new home. May the memories of all the great thoughts and song that happened here, when we lived as commune brothers, fill your dreams with their messages."

Lois answered, "Did you notice the footnote on your invitation, Anya?"

Lois placed herself between the door and us and pointed to a small line on the invitation that read, "Twenty-five dollars per couple."

I looked at her smug lover-host of this event, who was chewing on a pickle and said, "Howie, why are you telling everyone how much the party cost you? You shouldn't brag. And by the way, you could have had it catered for even less than that. You know, if you didn't have those trays of little dead critters soaking in hot sauce, then even less."

We did get their message at the door. Unfortunately the footnote was on the back of the invitation.

As if the entire crowd sang in unison we heard, "No, Kenny, each couple pays twenty-five dollars as their contribution. This is how our group finances these events."

Anya waved at them in disgust. She snapped out a check and slapped it into Lois's waiting paw. I reached for the door handle and our long-awaited exit and asked in parting, "Tell me something, Howie. If it were thirty dollars a couple, would you still use plastic champagne glasses?"

I heard the cries of our Mateus bottle pleading for rescue from the Dom Perignon bullies who were nestled among the more fashionable ice cubes in the cooler. I snatched it from the cradle of condescension and we left.

I thought, "Was it within those very walls that I sat and smoked with Howie and our friends and talked of dreams and feelings rather than acquisitions and manipulations? Was it there where we dropped Windowpane acid as a group and listened together while the definition of personified life was explained to us as, "Energy describing itself, unto itself by way of form, ad infinitum?" Could those life forms within those walls that night perhaps be characterized best as something that exists between food and shit?'

It's been said that "Treasure might be trash that somehow everybody wants. Much like after a plant cycles shit into flowers, people get in line to buy the arrangement."

Before that night, some of the folks who ambushed me at the party may have treasured absorbing the hippie that sprang from the trash and became a neighborhood institution into their realm. I believe that I either quelled any such design or encouraged even greater curiosity by my intransigence. Time will tell those who can tell time.

The important lesson from that night's experience was, "If I were going to survive in an ever-changing stage, I must remain consciously detached from the character that I had apparently created. It must be done, if for no other reason than to defend the integrity of its creator."

I couldn't help but reflect upon my friends who had recently and involuntarily left the Slope. How would those hippies adjust to the yuppies' circumstances if they were suddenly thrust within them? Conversely, how would the yuppie deal with only the basic necessities in the place of their lifestyle of excess?

Beneath all of the outward differences, are they one and the same as I discovered while living on these streets? The hippie once championed defiance to the Establishment as enthusiastically as the yuppie champions status, for the sake of status, within it.

JE

"Do all of those in a herd just blindly follow the asses of the cattle ahead? Do all in the herd just inhale the exhaust of their predecessor and thus pass it on to those behind them, and so on? If there is a herd, who if anyone leads it? Might the fate of humans be the same as that of lemmings who blindly follow those before them over the cliff, after their unseen leaders are dead on the rocks below? Is that what is meant by a movement?"

Found in September's Child's guest sketch book

Chapter Twenty-One

The World

The crowds along Seventh Avenue, which scurried so purposefully during the day in search of mortgage rates and restaurants, were in stark contrast to those who wandered slowly and aimlessly so many nights before in search of love, self or both. My perch above it all from the window of my office afforded me a vantage point to observe and reflect upon the world below in its constant quest for fulfillment.

Seated on the windowsill, beneath the plants, I waved to Andy and his crew as their truck passed the office enroute to that day's drop-off. I thought of the call I received the week before from their customer during pick-up, "This is Doctor Corian. Please come to where your driver, Andy, is loading my goods on Carroll Street, immediately!"

Not wanting to end my treasured time of recreational street observation, I asked her, "Is there any way we can discuss your concern on the phone?"

My attention was diverted from the street below to the frantic voice on the phone that had begun speaking so deliberately, when she said, "If there were, then we would be doing just that. I need you here now! This is an emergency."

Doctor Corian was a very prominent psychiatrist. She specialized in treating the mental disorders of the incredibly wealthy. We were moving her to her new digs on Grammercy Park, Manhattan. Apparently I neglected to add on the paperwork, "This is the most important person in the world, please bow accordingly." I was sure that she wanted this missing detail addressed.

Even more intense than Andy's expression, when I passed him carrying boxes to the truck, were the Doctor's words as I walked into her apartment, "Your driver is mind fucking me! From the very beginning of this job, he has been trying to demonstrate that he's in charge of the situation and that I only have to learn from him as far as this entire experience is concerned. His attitude is that women must be directed by a man in matters such as moving. He has made it clear that not only is he in charge of his crew, but also of me. I want you to remain here until he either changes his attitude or you change drivers."

Surely, Andy underestimated his prey in this case. As a practicing warlock, he could reach to the depths of one's soul and drive them to submit to his will. As a practicing psychiatrist, she was trained to break the strongest of wills into total submission to hers, and then later to her billing department's.

Upon hearing that his customer felt threatened by his demeanor, Andy immediately shifted gears and apologized. The move went smoothly, as did their date that evening. Andy had his charm.

My thoughts turned to the clock: last truck in by eight; pick up Anya; head for Minsky's; have dinner; join the evening procession along Seventh Avenue. Just a routine day. If ever there is a kiss of death thought, then that's it.

"Kenny, Ernesto from the pizzeria says it's important. You

better take this," said Cindy while transferring the call to my desk. I wondered if maybe I left my journal or something at the pizzeria. If only it was that simple.

Phone in hand I said, "Hell . . . ," an apt description of what would follow.

Before I could say anything else, I heard, "Kenny, Kenny! We have a big problem! You have to come over here right away. I can't discuss this on the phone."

I ran down the block to meet Ernesto where he worked. He was pacing up and down in front of the pizzeria. When he saw me coming down the block he ran over and hugged me.

He cried and said, "They won't burn your trucks or hurt you or your business! They know that you had nothing to do with any of this. Your driver, you know which one, the big fellow with the deep, loud voice; the one who was wearing the black t-shirt with the skull. Well, he did the worst thing that he could do."

Ernesto bit down on the base of his index finger. At first I imagined that perhaps Andy raped or killed someone. Did he lose control of the truck and crash into a crowd? If that were it, wouldn't the police be calling me rather than a waiter?

"What did Andy do, Ernesto? What is the worst thing that a mover could do in the hour that passed since I saw him drive by my office?"

Ernesto brought his shoulders to his ears and frowned as his head leaned to the side. He pointed across the street to a Cadillac in a parking space. Then he unraveled the events from earlier that day, "Andy, your driver, he come along the street like he own it. Ralphie, he open up the Caddy door maybe a little too sudden. Andy hit the truck's brakes real hard. He jump from the truck and call Ralphie a fuckin' asshole. Ralphie say to Andy, he a fuckin' asshole and he's so fuckin' stupid that he don't know that he's a fuckin' moron! Your other two movers, one black fella, the other one a white boy, they jump from the truck. Ralphie's son, you know the football player, he stand behind his father."

Ernesto became increasingly animated. His head began bobbing back and forth, changing from one character to the other as he said, "They start with the fuck you, fuck you, talk back and forth, then Ralphie throw a punch. Andy ducks, leans back and kicks Ralphie in the stomach. Then Andy jumps on Ralphie and beat the daylights out of him while the two movers held the son back from helping his father."

Ernesto folded his hands and looked skyward while saying, "It's a good thing that Andy spit the other way when he finish and not on Ralphie. I know Ralphie would have killed him right there on the street."

I had to glance at my reflection in the store window just to be certain that it was I standing on that spot, having that conversation. I had to ask myself, "How did my reality extend itself into the fists and jaws of people that I never would have even known had I not made silly little signs?"

Quickly, I accepted my responsibility and role as diplomat and hopefully, as a mediator and said, "So, you called me to tell me that they're going to kill Andy somewhere else, but not with a Viking funeral in my truck? Ernesto, I have a feeling that maybe something can be done to make this go away. Do you have the same feeling?"

If there were daisies in Andy's immediate future, the delivery might have been arranged already. I only hoped that this was a way to see if I was willing to intercede on the behalf of Ralphie's self-respect and maybe save them the cost of a bullet.

Ernesto pointed to a storefront behind him with his thumb while rolling his eyes in that direction. Then he said, "Maybe if you want to talk to someone, maybe he might want to talk to you. I can't promise nothin', but it's worth a try, right? I see if he want to see you." Ernesto crossed his lips with his finger. He wiped his brow with his apron and walked back into the pizzeria.

The nearly empty cargo area of Andy's truck added resonance to my message, "You dumb macho motherfucker! Do you think that this world has been waiting all of this time for you to come along and set it straight? Because you can flip a Tarot card and convince someone that you hold their fate in the next turn, it doesn't make you God!

"You mind-fuck my customers as foreplay to handcuffing them to your bedposts, then issue membership cards in your harem to them! You even have my movers thinking that Andy's the Messiah hanging on a piano board! You're fuckin' king of the world, right, bro'?"

Andy's eyelids fluttered. His head lowered as he let out a sigh and heard me say, "Now since you're so fuckin' smart and powerful, go convince the dude with the gun why he shouldn't shove it up your ass and blow your brains out. You are in over your head and mine. Your fuckin' mouth has finally caught up to your fuckin' ego and now they're both spinning down the fuckin' toilet."

The Hierophant had suddenly transformed into the Fool card in the hand of an unknown force. Andy's customary black attire contrasted his ghostly pale face. The usual booming voice of confidence meekly explained his actions, "Kenny, I got the message when the guy showed the gun handle in his belt to me and blew me a kiss. What the fuck can we do? I know I should have kept my mouth shut, but one thing led to another and the next thing I know, we're duking it out on the street."

Andy backed into a pile of furniture pads when I went into his face saying, "You were duking it out while my name is on the truck that you jumped from? As far as the neighborhood was concerned, I was duking it out with the brother of anybody in their right mind's worst fuckin' nightmare and not you! You get your rocks off and I can wind up in a fuckin' pine box. How fair is that?"

Andy's legs were shaking. He was sweating profusely and his lips trembled. He spoke in a halting manner. This was completely unlike him. Good! Andy was mortal just like the rest of us. But it had become incumbent upon me to keep his ass alive.

When you employ others to represent you to the world, you truly understand the posture of Atlas.

I felt that my entire life was but a training experience toward that single moment. The sign above the door of the unmarked storefront read, "Members Only," much like the label on the jacket of the person guarding it.

I heard the sound of a peephole cover reveal my face to the observer within. A loud grumbling voice yelled indistinguishable words to an unknown presence that answered him with a single undistinguishable sound.

The door opened slowly. I felt the air from within grasp me from behind like cold damp fingers and usher me in. I heard the thud of the closing door. The small neon beer signs and the jukebox that played "Earth Angel" repeatedly, served as the room's only light. What little illumination they provided was obscured by the cloud of cigar smoke that overwhelmed what once was a tavern.

The grumbling voice that greeted me was housed in a form that was as tall as it was wide. His tree-sized arm pointed to the end of the bar. He uttered some words that were just as indistinguishable as those that I heard from him while I stood outside. If there were light, I may have been able to read his lips. It didn't matter; he never moved them when he spoke. Instead, I followed his finger past the row of shadowy figures that turned on their stools and followed my every move as I walked past them.

The bar ended at a wall where an old nineteen-fifties beer poster was half-covered by the last of the shadowy figures. An old wrinkled fedora with a turned down brim covered his face. He removed an onion from his drink and threw it to the floor.

He must have noticed me because he lifted his fedora back to reveal a small face that was wrinkled even more than the hat. He raised his hand. I slowly raised mine and we shook. He pointed to the stool next to him. I complied with his gesture to sit. The bartender complied with his gesture to pour.

I never drink beer. But that day, the instant one found my hand, I drank it. He never gave his name. I never asked for it. Somehow absolute power over life and death needs no name. But it is remembered just the same.

A voice, a level above a whisper, with the certainty of a zipper being pulled along a body bag said, “So you're the kid who's making all the noise on the street these days. Relax, I mean it in a good way. I see some people who've been on their fat asses forever, coming into the delis wearing your t-shirts. They order sangwiches and soders then run like there's no tomorrow to your trucks and head for work. This is a good thing you did with these bums! Maybe now they can pay the people that they owe.”

I wanted to thank him for acknowledging my efforts. Everyone in the bar became immediately quiet as he held his palm up to stop me from speaking. My mouth hung barely open while my words, frozen over in terror, hung from my tongue.

He shouted, “Wait a minute! I ain't done yet! Kenny, I really like what you been doing for the kids with the little league. Maybe these snobs that you been moving into the neighborhood can start mixing with the people who made it a safe place all these years and do some good for all of the kids around here. Okay, now you can tell me about your fuckin' bum who beat up my brother.”

As dimly lit as the room was, I felt as though a spotlight had found me. The living mountain of the usher that showed me in leaned on the jukebox across from me, blocking the light. The men from the bar formed a semi-circle around the little man and me.

The little man leaned back on his stool. His fedora cushioned his head from the wall. I found it easier to look beyond him and address the eyes of Miss Reingold, 1954, on the poster, since they were directly behind his. The smell of beer mixed with stomach acid breath, from the surrounding crowd, engulfed us. My heart was pounding like a gavel at the base of my brain as if to say, "Speak from me if you want to live!"

I began to form my words. The little man interrupted me with, "Hey, turn off that fuckin' nigger music and play my Frankie Valle! Who the fuck can concentrate with all that fuckin' howlin' and whining?"

Then he said, "Yeah, go ahead Kenny. Tell me about the guy you wanna help."

The interruption served me with the moment that I needed to gather my composure. My mouth remained in the ready to speak position. I needed only to find the words. There was nothing at all to say in defense of Andy or his actions. There was only my acknowledgement of his stupidity. Our only hope rested in this judge's–and his jury, built like piers–understanding.

I allowed the intuition that kept me alive from the street to that moment to guide my every word as my mind yielded to my heart, "How can anyone apologize for the actions of a grown man who acts worse than all of his five kids put together? I wouldn't be here talking to you on his behalf if this were the way the man always was, rather than the stupid way that he reacted in that, uh you know, situation."

The little man's eyes pierced me. He sat quietly, listening to my every word. He placed his hand on my forearm, smiled and said in a very paternal, consoling voice, "It must be tough moving people's shit up and down stairs all day. I'll bet these yuppies are all over your ass for the stupidest little thing, huh?"

His soothing tone lowered my guard. My jaw lowered as my mouth began to form the answer to his question. He raised his hand to stop me. Where one moment there was consolation, in the next there was blinding rage.

The hairs from my forearm ripped away in his grip as it became an upheld fist, shaking in my face. I cringed as he screamed, "Still ain't no fuckin' reason to jump outta the truck and pound on a guy for swingin' his fuckin' door open! When you put your hands up in this world, you put your life up for grabs. And you better be careful, 'cause you don't know who might grab it.

"I've pissed blood that grew into somethin' better than your boy! Ya know, he sounds like the type of schmuck who pushes people around who got small balls. If it ain't too late, he might need a lesson."

He held his hands out and turned his lower lip down as if to demand an answer. One of the faceless figures in his crew offered one, "No fuckin' way this moron had the right to do what he did. Maybe Kenny should split now and we should let life go on."

I heard a slap followed by an, "Ow!" Another voice in the group said, "Shut the fuck up! Ain't nobody asked you nothin'! Just fuckin' listen, asshole!"

Black overcoats covered my view. The crew had formed a huddle around the little man. I could only hope that they would choose to pass Andy's fate to my hands. I was about to go into my, what's done is done, speech. Followed by the, where do we go from here, follow-up question when I heard mumbling and whispering. The words gradually elevated to the nearly distinguishable as their dilemma unraveled. The crew slowly wandered back to their positions at the jukebox and the bar.

Then I heard, "Yeah-yeah-yeah! But he's my fuckin' brother and it's my fuckin' decision. So shut the fuck up!"

The little man in the big hat removed himself from the huddle and said, "My fuckin' brother's no fuckin' better than Kenny's boy. Imagine actin' like a fuckin' teenager right in front of his own kid!

"He got no respect for the neighborhood or anyone in it neither. Fuckin' hot head idiot! He meets his idiot match and cries like a fuckin' baby 'cause he gets his stupid ass kicked."

I felt the pressure of the large overcoats that had created a backdrop around me. I sat motionless, except for my pounding heart crashing into my powder-dry throat. The little man drew a twisted black stogie from the bartender's shirt pocket. A lit Zippo emerged immediately from the crowd.

With a cloud of smoke above his head covering Miss Reingold's face, I looked toward where his eyes might be and heard, "Kenny, I got no control over what Ralphie might do. I can talk to him and maybe hope for a solution. Your gorilla made a monkey outta my gorilla in front of his kid, and now all of his friends know about it. It seems to be a question of face. You know what I mean by face? Do you see a solution to this problem? Tell me if you do."

I felt like a contestant on a quiz show with the big hand sweeping around, marking off the seconds that he had to come up with an answer to win his prize. I had to come up with an answer to save Andy's and perhaps his crew's lives. My mouth opened as the sweep hand stopped short of the buzzer.

It was as though I was a witness to my own heart issuing words to the ears of all around me when I said, "Andy is going to have to make an apology to your brother in front of his kid and his friends. I will tell Andy that this is the first and last time that I will put my self on the line for his actions. Instead of swinging his fists at strangers, he should be at little league with his son, teaching him to swing a bat and catch a ball.

"I will guarantee his presence wherever you want him, whenever you want him there. He will have to bring whatever he has to in order to settle this problem."

The slightest upturn took place from the corner of the little man's mouth. The smoke seemed to rise within the room, although slightly. Frankie Valle sang about his rag doll with her pretty face while I hoped only to save face for another.

"Tell you what, Kenny. I'll talk to my brother. Maybe he had time to cool down a little. You tell your driver to stick around. He shouldn't run from his problems. You remind him that no one wants to help a coward. You should hear something in a couple of days. You got that straight?"

All of the heads had become visible. I extended my hand. As we shook I said, "I got it straight and Andy will get it straight too. You can count on that."

I began walking past the bar stools. When I neared the jukebox, the giant usher grabbed my arm and turned me toward him. He moved his cigar to the side of his mouth.

Then in a nearly clear voice, I thought I heard him ask me, "Do you go to Queens?" If he weren't referring to the boro, this could truly become the worst day of my life.

I deliberated my answer, and then I said, "Yeah, we move people to Queens."

He took a long puff on his cigar. Again, he rolled it back to the side of his mouth. The light from the jukebox showed the whites of his eyes alternating from top to bottom as he checked me out.

With exhaled cigar smoke carrying every word to me he said, "My mother is moving to Queens. I'm going to tell her to call youse. She better get a good job! You know, no bullshit or nothin'. If she's happy with your work, then youse will get all my friends' business."

I slowly strolled toward the front of the bar and my much-anticipated exit. The fading notes from The Four Seasons accompanied me as if I were a graduating class of one, about to bring the message of all that I had learned, to the ears of just one other. The door swung open to the daylight and the task before me.

"I feel like the next thing you're going to do is to put a hood over my head and ask me if I have any last requests," said Andy.

He walked into my office with a bottle of wine in hand

and wearing a new white shirt. The word had come to me through Ernesto that Andy was to stand before the brother, the brother's son and all of his friends. Andy was to offer a heartfelt apology and the willingness to accept any consequences.

Andy would tell them that he wanted his helpers to be thought of as bystanders to the incident. Any blame for their actions would be all his. There were no guarantees offered, nor requested. He was on his own.

I asked the brave fool, "Would your last request be that I take your place today? Andy, I'll go to the club with you just to introduce you at the door. I don't know if I'm to join you or if this is going to be a solo flight on your part. I do have to tell you that I respect the fact that you stuck around and that you are going in there to try to make things right. Just show them that you're a man whose apology is worthy of acceptance. I'm sure that you, of all people, know what's in the cards for today."

"Just the driver!" said the giant usher as he stood between Andy and me.

He signaled that I should wait on the stoop across the street. When the door swung back into view, Andy was nowhere to be seen. During the next two hours I counted six of my trucks roll by. Andy's truck sat in front of my office like a loyal stallion awaiting its mount.

"What's going on? Where's Andy? Don't tell me that he split on us because of the bullshit we got into the other day!" asked Shelly.

He and Hammer, Andy's other helper, had spotted me on the stoop. They were waiting patiently for their guru. I pointed to the storefront and signaled for them to split and wait at the office. As much as they doubted their spiritual mentor at that moment, I couldn't tell them that he was prepared to take it on the chin for them as well."

Andy's expression was matched equally by the rain-filled, darkening sky. He stumbled out of the door followed by the emergence of the usher's tree like arm. Yesterday's peacock walked across the street toward me looking like today's mud hen.

The laughing faces of the once shadowy figures, gathered at the front of the store as they filed out one by one. Had the cigars that burned in the mouths of the father and son, who stood arm in arm, been lighted with the dignity of the vanquished visitor?

"Just walk with me to my truck, Kenny. Please look straight ahead. If Satan takes on many forms, I think that I've just been with all of them. As far as anybody else in the company is concerned, today never happened. I would appreciate it if the subject of the meeting in that gateway to Hell ends here and now. I'll pick up my paperwork and my helpers and get to my job."

Months passed since the incident at the club. I had given it no more thought. Our objective had been met and life did go on. Andy worked as hard coaching his son and his team at the little league as he did bringing pianos to new heights within the mundane world of brownstones.

Every job that moved to Queens would always have my best crew and newest truck. Those drivers were instructed to repair any damage before it found its place in the new residence. I envisioned a scar that might be left on a coffee table somehow replicating itself on someone's body part if it remained as a conversation piece.

I opened the office one morning to find a large picture frame wrapped in brown paper leaning in front of my desk. There was a small "To Kenny" written across it. I opened the wrapper to discover a multi-colored, hand-drawn reproduction of a Tarot Card of a unique design. In some of its detail, the elemental references were unlike those of the Waite deck that I had used in my readings, but the message was still the same.

The Chariot held its driver as he sat cross-legged, holding a sphere. Four untethered beasts gave the impetus to thrust the driver's will as he set the course, even though blinded by his helmet.

It was captioned; "Movement is the spirit of the Universe. Remember yourself always and everywhere." It was signed, Andy.

"The only sponsor that gets yellow or gold uniforms is Kenny! It don't matter if they're your favorite or if they're the colors of your store, pick something else," said Steven while defending his flag. The phone went crashing to its cradle, denying another to wear our colors on the battlefield of baseball.

Steven paced around the desk mumbling, "Big deal. What the fuck's the difference? You know, it's like, half of one or six dozen of the other. They never had a team before, never mind a color, now why do they all of a sudden want the same thing? So pick blue or red before someone else gets it 'cause gold and black is ours! If they wanna play fuckin' games and wait 'til the last minute to choose, then they get shafted. You know, it's like the old saying, 'You made your bed, now you gotta pay the fiddler'."

The demand for participation as players in that season's schedule of our six teams was exceeded only by that of the merchants who wanted sponsorship in the next. The newcomers and the old guard worked hand in hand toward their goal of giving back to the neighborhood, through the kids.

It was really a nice time and place. Every truck that roamed the street was paid for in cash. Every bit of my advertising was paid for on the spot. The only envelopes that arrived in my mailbox were filled with words of congratulations from happy customers.

My road ahead was paved with payments in advance. There was an ironclad rule in place at my office: "Never order anything unless the cash was in hand." As a result of this premise, I never had to look back. The only footsteps that I would hear behind me were those who sought to follow my success by following my example.

My journal sat in my trunk. My trunk sat beneath my shield. My shield was carved by the bloodied hand of a slave's last day as a slave. Each day I sat among them and looked back and then thought ahead, sometimes only to look back. Those elements remained through all of the experiences that I had tumbled through, as the only materials that I accepted as an extension of self. I ended there. It would be the world's perception of me that might make extensions. I remained vigilant of where my line was drawn.

If the next step that I was to take would bring me from all that I had beyond those three things, then so be it. It would then be a step that I would take hand in hand with Anya. If the little world that I had woven from the thread of my life that survived the street were to burst into flames around me, it could only serve to kindle the thoughts for what was next. After all, where would the world be if Isaac Newton waited for the apple to return to the tree?

"You can go to the firehouse and ring the bell on your own time, if they let you!"

"Stay away from the truck and remain with your teams!"

"Don't go on the street until the police signal that it's closed to traffic!"

"Then and only then are you to assemble with your group for the march to the park!"

A small man with a large bullhorn walked up and down past the army of kids and the shiny red Union Street fire truck shouting the orders of our big day.

"You know, Kenny, I remember when you sat at that booth with that mob of derelicts and barely had enough to pay for the privilege of remaining. Now you put together a mob scene, under police protection no less, to march along Seventh Avenue," said Spiro, the owner of The Economy.

Neither he nor I could believe the chaos outside was slowly organizing itself into a parade of kids about to get the attention that they deserved. I enjoyed an exhilarating inhale of fresh air; it was to be deflated by the news that our marching band had won the right to compete in a contest in another state at that very time.

I ran to the other organizers and shouted, "Don't these fuckin' people keep fuckin' schedules? I'm very happy for their success, but I guess it leaves me with just one question. What fuckin' music do all of these kids standing in the middle of Seventh fuckin' Avenue march to?

"Maybe the coaches could count cadence like drill instructors! Or, if we leave the mike in the fire truck keyed, someone could whistle 'The March of the Wooden Soldiers' and blast it through the siren speaker! Better yet, I could just keep singing, 'Those motherfucking assholes', at the top of my lungs and the parents and kids could provide the rhythm with their pounding feet!"

I looked at Anya with perhaps a look that might define the word incredulous itself. She looked back at me with a wry smile and a raised finger to make a point, "How about I run to the apartment and get my cassette deck. I have a tape with the theme from "Rocky" that I used for a school project. If you go and get your new Kenny truck, we can hook up that guy's bullhorn to the tape deck and play it from the truck."

Everyone scurried to gather the elements. It wouldn't be the loudest music, but it was better than walking in front of the kids and banging two metal garbage can lids together. By the way, that was plan B.

From the power of four D batteries to the cassette player and the cigarette lighter socket to the bullhorn on the Kenny truck, the little procession-to be gathered behind the music that would lead them. The shrill sounds of "Rocky" blasted from the truck. I drove it along Seventh Avenue and sounded the advance.

The long march to Prospect Park began. The Union Street fire truck would blast its air-horn and siren periodically to help awaken the neighborhood to our presence and welcome them to join us in our journey to opening day at Prospect Park. The Pied Piper may have led the children from Hamlin, but our children were to lead all of those who chose to awaken from their complacency that Sunday morning. Visions of kids running atop parked cars filled my mind as we passed First Street. I looked around me and saw those same kids marching and ready to coach.

Another neighborhood's little league would share in the glorious march of the kids from Park Slope's league. They joined us as we turned toward Prospect Park.

The throng of followers and the curious swelled as the mob overwhelmed the police protection. The traffic was held back by the shear volume of people who paraded behind the parade as it marched to the dying sounds of "Rocky". The batteries had seen their end. The kid's voices in the chorus of joyous anticipation would relegate music in any form at that point, to understatement.

The president of the undeniably visible little league announced from the podium at the parks entrance that the games were about to begin. The fading notes of the music of triumphal procession had given way to that of my beeper as it had sounded my retreat to the nearest phone booth.

As the president began his speech, I said to Anya, "Andy is at one of the jobs. He needs an extra pair of hands just to get an old player piano up the ramp and on to the truck. He has tried calling everyone in our book and it's come down to me. I'm going to run down to Third Avenue to help him. I'll be back long before the third inning."

Every level of one's evolution and every moment of celebration within it are subject to calls of obligation. I guess these are meant to either remind or to awaken an entrepreneur to the nature of the things that have created the event from which he may be torn. Failure to address these issues could foreshadow the end of what he has created.

There was a strange gnawing feeling in the pit of my stomach. A large nine, my number of detriment, flashed before my eyes.

Steven's words flashed across my mind, "It's bad luck to be superstitious."

I thought beyond myself and recalled a literary lesson. Knowing that he was soon to die, El Cid ordered that his body be mounted by ropes to his saddle. His horse then led his troops to victory under the leadership of his corpse. In fulfilling his final wish, he both won a battle in death and lived on in the form of the cliché, "Duty above passion."

I thought, "With such a grand symbolism in mind, is it so difficult for me to lend a simple hand to send my movers on their way to the victory of a piano moved?"

"Sorry to take you from the parade, Kenny. I tried everything I could do and everyone I could call," said Andy as he and Demetrius were struggling to push the six-hundred-pound piano up the truck's walkboard.

The walkboard would bend in the middle and show signs of slipping from the edge of the truck's flooring. Ordinarily, I would focus on the job at hand and consider each possibility to arrive at a workable miracle. That day, I felt the pressure of events elsewhere. Good judgment gave way to expediency.

The movers yielded to my authority when I said, "Demetrius, you pull with the straps from the top. Andy, you push from behind me. I'll prop this dolly under the walk board. It'll keep it from sagging. Lucky for you it gets delivered on a level loading dock; otherwise we would have the same problem at the other end."

I placed the wooden dolly on its edge midway down the ramp and then joined Andy at the base of the piano. The piano, on its wheeled dolly, yielded and moved up the ramp, powered by the three of us pushing and pulling. It was nearly at the top when I heard and felt a loud cracking from the bottom of the ramp. My authority, and the ramp I stood upon, instantly surrendered to gravity.

My heart and senses remained three feet above my body as I plunged together with the ramp to the street. The ramp had slipped from the edge of the truck's flooring under the piano's weight and mine. I saw the piano grow larger as it began its journey toward my face. I had fallen into such a precarious position that I could only reach my arms out and prepare to protect myself in vain as I was about to get crushed. Would the stenciled words on bottom of the piano, "Steinway and Sons", be my last thought and message to the Eternity I was about to address?

Suddenly, the piano stopped its descent and began to slowly rise away from my helpless body that quickly rolled off to the side. My panic was replaced by an immediate calm as I watched two massive arms, like ebony tree trunks descending from above, slowly pull the behemoth on to the truck.

Andy recovered from his fall and shouted, "Alright, Demetrius!"

I managed to stand up while panting with my hands leaning on my kneecaps, a helpless victim of my own carelessness.

I said, "Whatever doesn't kill you makes you stronger."

On the other hand, surviving the whatever can also encourage one toward later and greater heights of stupidity. I was very happy to see the piano, which would otherwise become my headstone, being secured to the wall of the truck as part of the cargo.

Demetrius' holding the Steinway back was no less heroic than if he grasped the reapers scythe in mid-flight to my head. I recalled the day, just a few years before, when a skinny little kid found treasure among the last of my worldly possessions from a life that I abhorred. Little did we know that he was rescuing more than barbells from the trash pile that day at September's Child. You never know when you are nurturing the arms that may one day reach out to save you.

I heard, “Hey, Boss! Are you okay? I don't think I ever saw you do anything as dumb as that. You ought to get your ass back to the place that your mind is, 'cause it sure ain't here,” said a smiling Demetrius, taunting me from the truck.

I reached up toward the sunlight and shook the hand of my salvation. He assured me that he and Andy would be better off without me, and my lousy ideas. I assured them that they were right and that I would remain in the park.

Contrary to the days when gravity or Danny's strong back would bring the VW to life, the diesel engine of my latest moving monster started on a single click. As quickly as a whoosh of air entered the engine, a black cloud bellowed from beneath, belching the gaseous remains of the noble reptiles that preceded our coming.

As the cloud rose above the truck I wondered, “Would our distilled collective mass of human bodies one day fuel the vehicles of a new species of polluters in the distant future? Will they choke on our infectious dust as another lesson goes unlearned? Will the solution escape those who are offered it then, as they too will be absorbed into the problem, as we are today?”

The drive in my big yellow truck back to the park along First Street should have been anticlimactic to the parade that it had just led, but every moment of that ride seemed to have an extra pinch of flavor. Perhaps it was because I had, moments before, literally walked the plank. In that single step, when the board gave way, I felt that I had finally caught up to myself.

Enroute to the park, every traffic light turned green just as I approached it. People walking to and from the park all looked strangely familiar. They paused and shouted words of praise and encouragement to me as I drove by.

If old 'Lung had a look-alike son, it would have to have been the police officer that pointed to the park's access-way where he told me to leave my truck. He said, "Have a great day, Kenny the Mover!" I complied with both of his instructions.

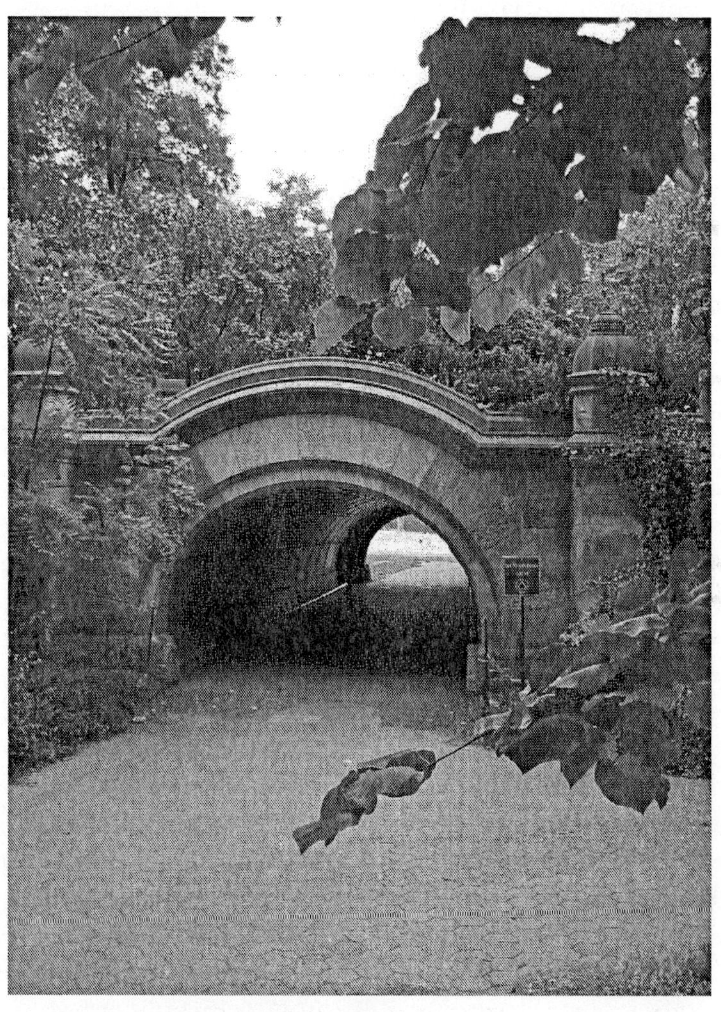

Meadowland Park
Photo by J.K. Savoy

I stood at the access-way and wondered, "Where would I have been, if this exit were blocked by a truck like mine the day my gasless Chevy rolled through on its way to be traded for the Minibus? If this outlet were not an option at that exact time, how many days and nights might I have spent in homeless desperation in this park? Will my truck deny exit to another who may enter his destiny at a turn further down the road? Was the magic of that moment in Prospect Park Fate's hand throwing me, like a dart, through the portal of my life's beginning?"

Parents filled water pails, yelled at umpires, cleaned bruises and coached their kids on to the day's victories and defeats. Weaving their way through all, a pretzel vendor chased a thief, who bore a strong resemblance to Jeff while a Doberman, who bore a strong resemblance to Terra, pursued them both.

The Sun shined more brightly on Anya's face than ever before. I didn't recall moving through the crowds that were suddenly behind me. She stood before me on the bleachers. Her azure eyes summoned my spirit to gaze where I was so often lost. I felt the warmth of her energy and mine embrace only to feel that another's had begun. My hand melded with hers, feeling the tiny arms and legs of the life forming within her.

I could only hope that one day those arms, probing for a world to touch, would know life's completeness in an embrace such as ours. I could only hope that those legs would grow strong and sure of where they might one day stand. I could only hope that all of its worldly struggles will serve only to challenge and not deter this child from seeking the glorious vision of a ride above a winged steed to living's dream.

It was then that I knew, though I may have been born in another place, I sure as hell came to life somewhere in Brooklyn.